DOGS DON'T EAT DESSERT

Dear Morgan,

    Good luck in your new school! I will miss you!!

        Love,

           Mrs. Lawrence

DOGS DON'T EAT DESSERT

BUT WE LIKE TO BE ASKED

Charles M. Schulz

TOPPER BOOKS

AN IMPRINT OF PHAROS BOOKS · A SCRIPPS HOWARD COMPANY

NEW YORK

First published in 1987

PEANUTS Comic Strips: © 1985
United Feature Syndicate, Inc.

Cover Art: PEANUTS Characters: © 1958, 1965
United Feature Syndicate, Inc.

Library of Congress Catalog Card Number: 86-63046
Pharos ISBN: 0-88687-299-5

Printed in United States of America

Topper Books
An Imprint of Pharos Books
A Scripps Howard Company
200 Park Avenue
New York, NY 10166

10 9 8 7 6 5 4 3

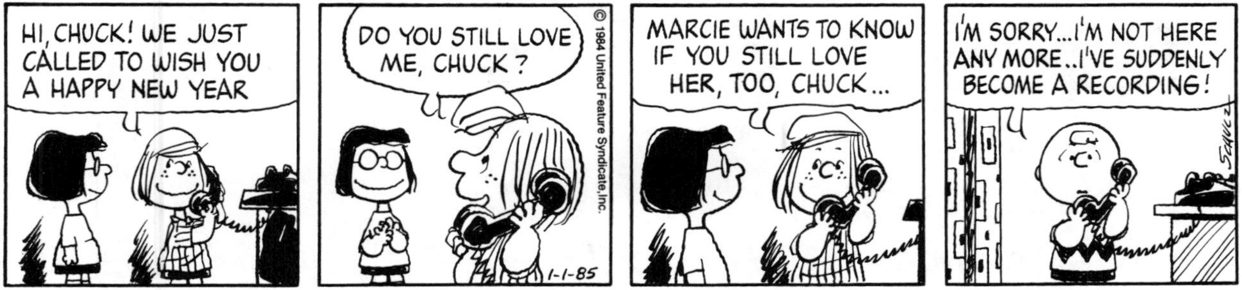
HI, CHUCK! WE JUST CALLED TO WISH YOU A HAPPY NEW YEAR
DO YOU STILL LOVE ME, CHUCK?
© 1984 United Feature Syndicate, Inc.
1-1-85
MARCIE WANTS TO KNOW IF YOU STILL LOVE HER, TOO, CHUCK...
I'M SORRY...I'M NOT HERE ANY MORE..I'VE SUDDENLY BECOME A RECORDING!
SCHULZ

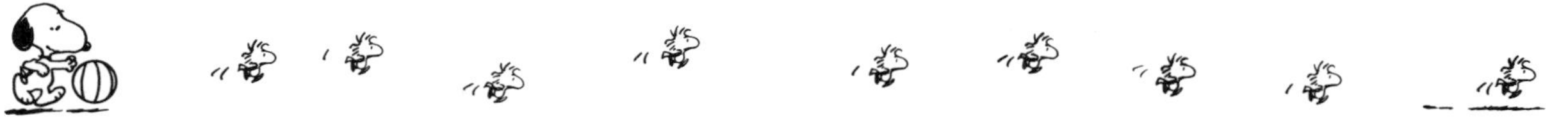

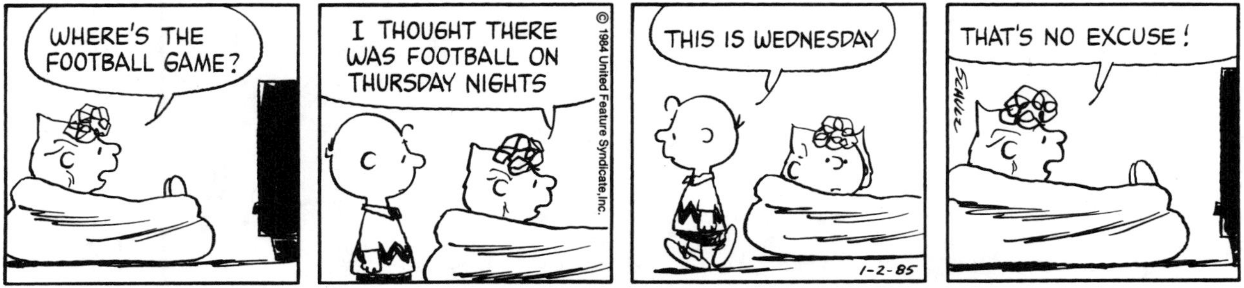
WHERE'S THE FOOTBALL GAME?
I THOUGHT THERE WAS FOOTBALL ON THURSDAY NIGHTS
© 1984 United Feature Syndicate, Inc.
THIS IS WEDNESDAY
1-2-85
THAT'S NO EXCUSE!
SCHULZ

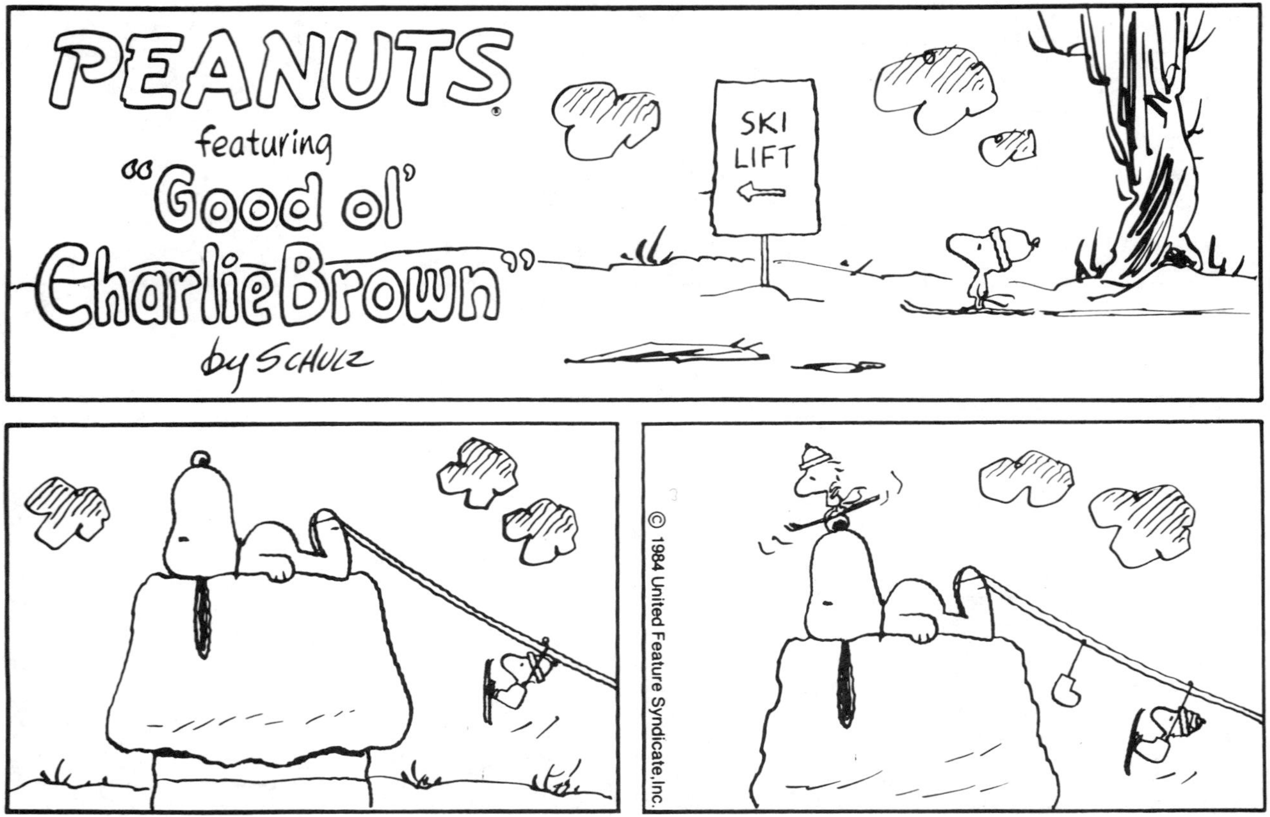
PEANUTS
featuring
"Good ol' Charlie Brown"
by SCHULZ
SKI LIFT
© 1984 United Feature Syndicate, Inc.

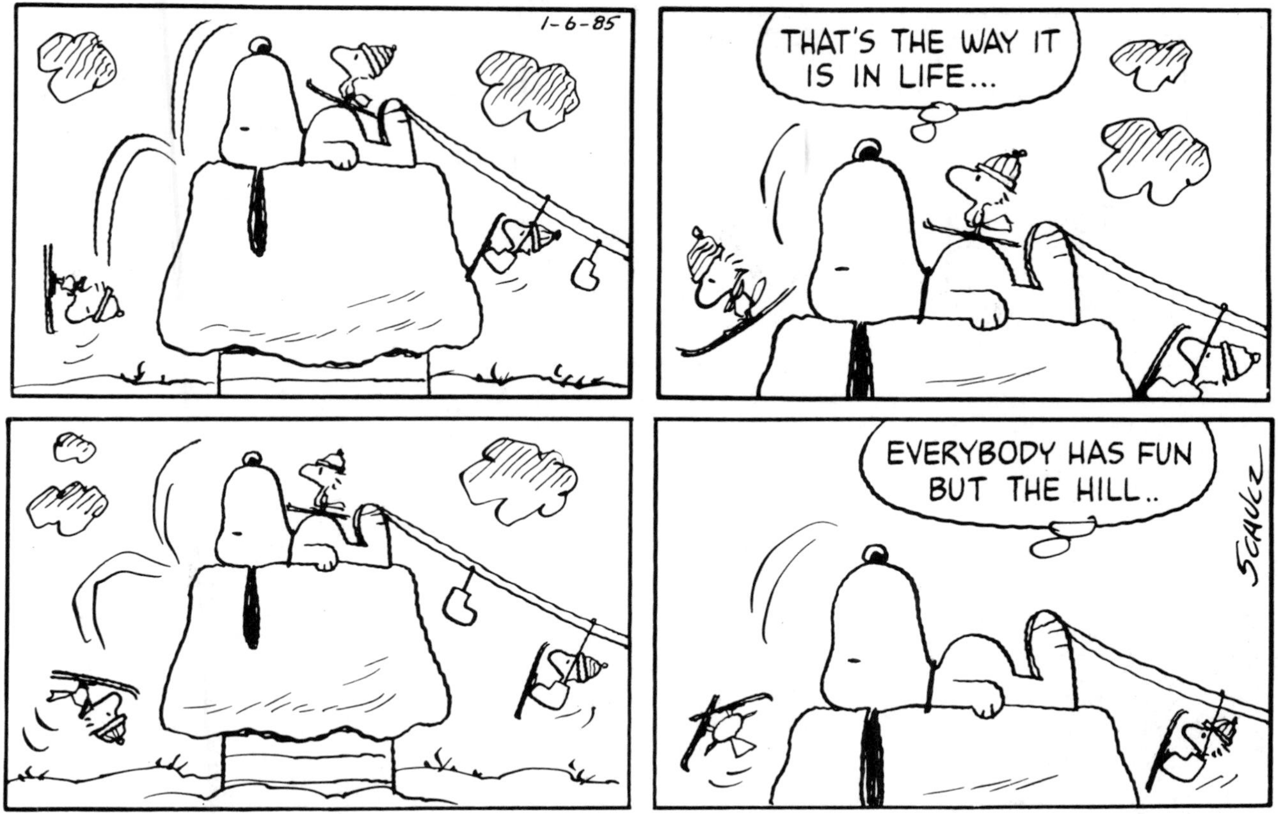
1-6-85
THAT'S THE WAY IT IS IN LIFE...
EVERYBODY HAS FUN BUT THE HILL..
SCHULZ

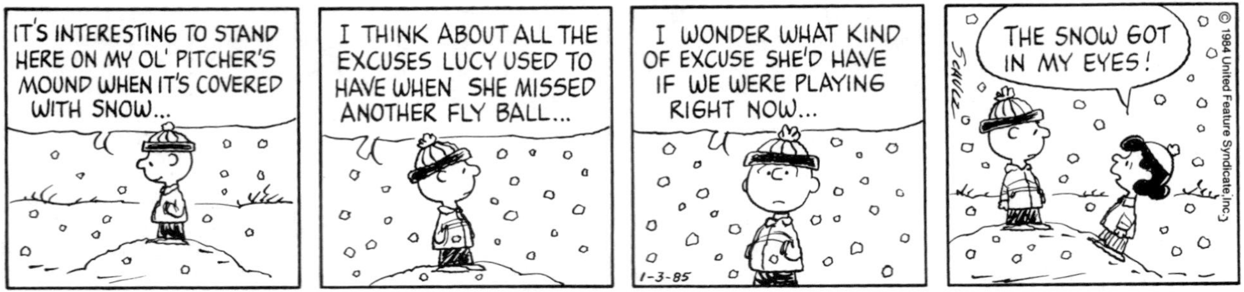
IT'S INTERESTING TO STAND HERE ON MY OL' PITCHER'S MOUND WHEN IT'S COVERED WITH SNOW...
I THINK ABOUT ALL THE EXCUSES LUCY USED TO HAVE WHEN SHE MISSED ANOTHER FLY BALL...
I WONDER WHAT KIND OF EXCUSE SHE'D HAVE IF WE WERE PLAYING RIGHT NOW...
1-3-85
THE SNOW GOT IN MY EYES!
SCHULZ
© 1984 United Feature Syndicate, Inc.

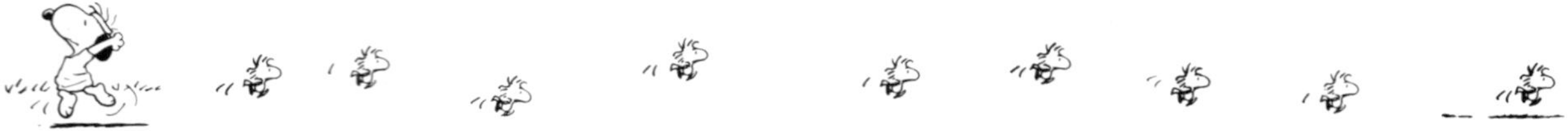

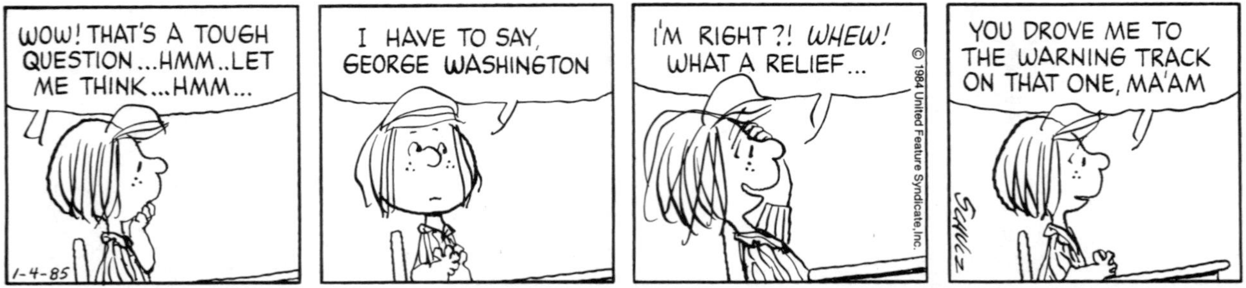
WOW! THAT'S A TOUGH QUESTION...HMM..LET ME THINK...HMM...
1-4-85
I HAVE TO SAY, GEORGE WASHINGTON
I'M RIGHT?! *WHEW!* WHAT A RELIEF...
© 1984 United Feature Syndicate, Inc.
YOU DROVE ME TO THE WARNING TRACK ON THAT ONE, MA'AM
SCHULZ

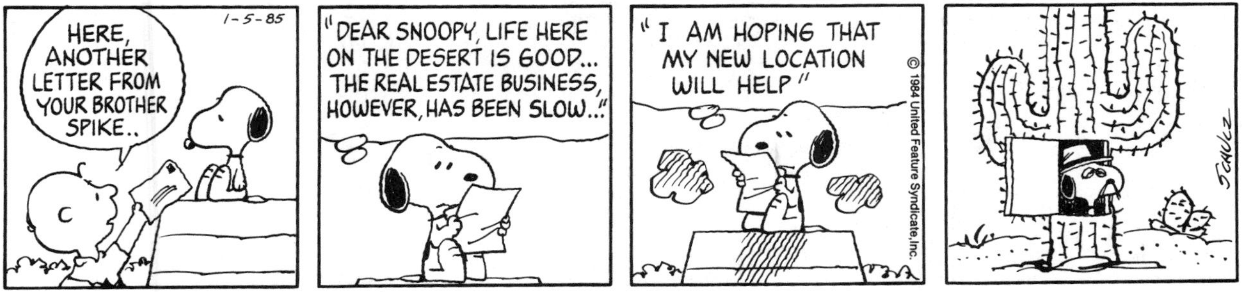
1-5-85
HERE, ANOTHER LETTER FROM YOUR BROTHER SPIKE..
"DEAR SNOOPY, LIFE HERE ON THE DESERT IS GOOD... THE REAL ESTATE BUSINESS, HOWEVER, HAS BEEN SLOW..."
"I AM HOPING THAT MY NEW LOCATION WILL HELP"
© 1984 United Feature Syndicate, Inc.
SCHULZ

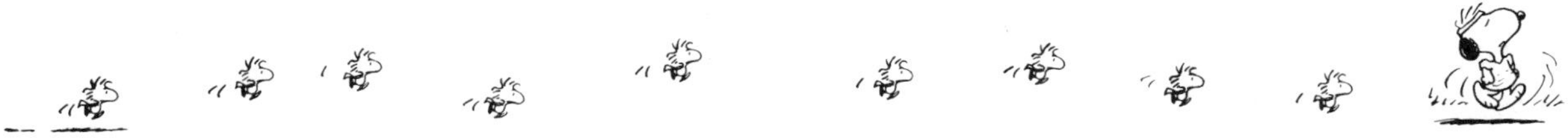

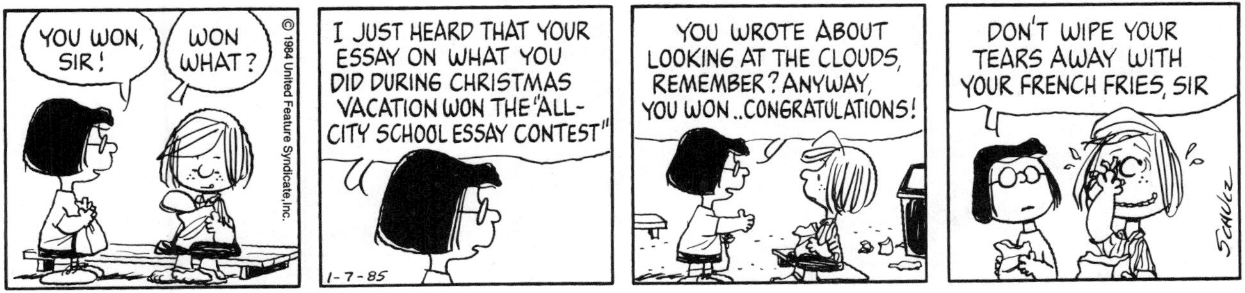
YOU WON, SIR!
WON WHAT?
© 1984 United Feature Syndicate, Inc.
I JUST HEARD THAT YOUR ESSAY ON WHAT YOU DID DURING CHRISTMAS VACATION WON THE "ALL-CITY SCHOOL ESSAY CONTEST"
1-7-85
YOU WROTE ABOUT LOOKING AT THE CLOUDS, REMEMBER? ANYWAY, YOU WON..CONGRATULATIONS!
DON'T WIPE YOUR TEARS AWAY WITH YOUR FRENCH FRIES, SIR
SCHULZ

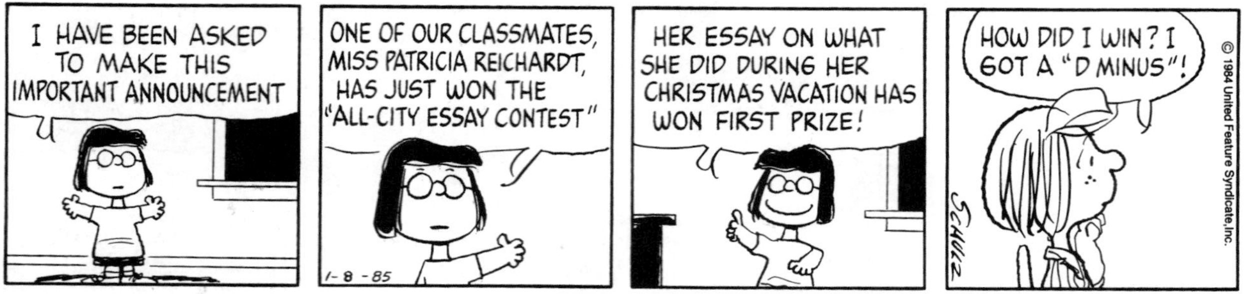
I HAVE BEEN ASKED TO MAKE THIS IMPORTANT ANNOUNCEMENT
ONE OF OUR CLASSMATES, MISS PATRICIA REICHARDT, HAS JUST WON THE "ALL-CITY ESSAY CONTEST"
1-8-85
HER ESSAY ON WHAT SHE DID DURING HER CHRISTMAS VACATION HAS WON FIRST PRIZE!
HOW DID I WIN? I GOT A "D MINUS"!
SCHULZ
© 1984 United Feature Syndicate,Inc.

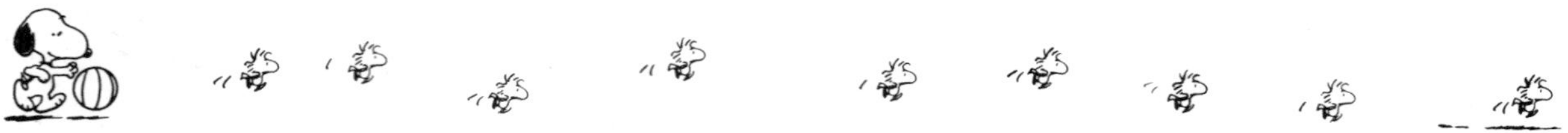

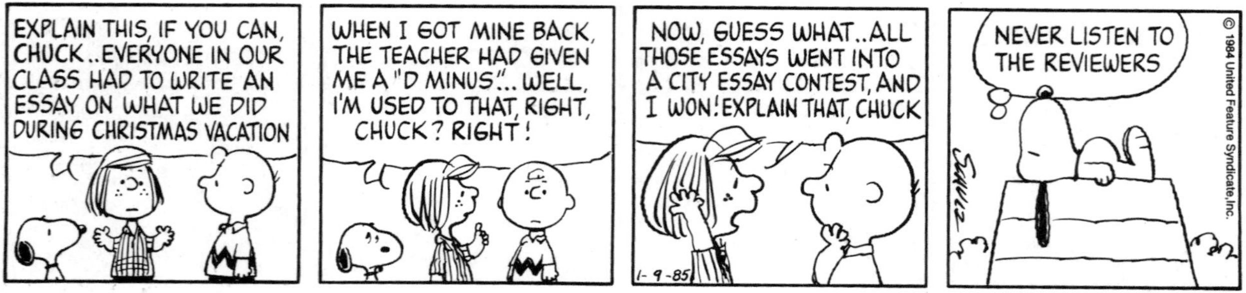
EXPLAIN THIS, IF YOU CAN, CHUCK..EVERYONE IN OUR CLASS HAD TO WRITE AN ESSAY ON WHAT WE DID DURING CHRISTMAS VACATION
WHEN I GOT MINE BACK, THE TEACHER HAD GIVEN ME A "D MINUS"... WELL, I'M USED TO THAT, RIGHT, CHUCK? RIGHT!
NOW, GUESS WHAT..ALL THOSE ESSAYS WENT INTO A CITY ESSAY CONTEST, AND I WON! EXPLAIN THAT, CHUCK
1-9-85
NEVER LISTEN TO THE REVIEWERS
SCHULZ
© 1984 United Feature Syndicate,Inc.

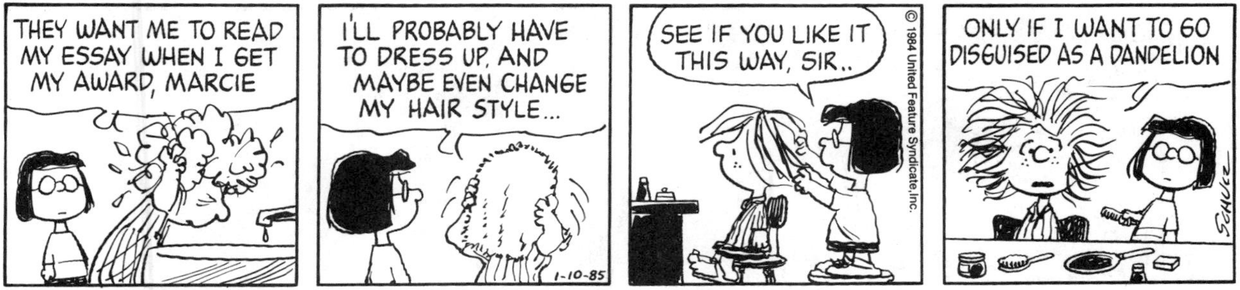
THEY WANT ME TO READ MY ESSAY WHEN I GET MY AWARD, MARCIE
I'LL PROBABLY HAVE TO DRESS UP, AND MAYBE EVEN CHANGE MY HAIR STYLE...
1-10-85
SEE IF YOU LIKE IT THIS WAY, SIR..
© 1984 United Feature Syndicate, Inc.
ONLY IF I WANT TO GO DISGUISED AS A DANDELION
SCHULZ

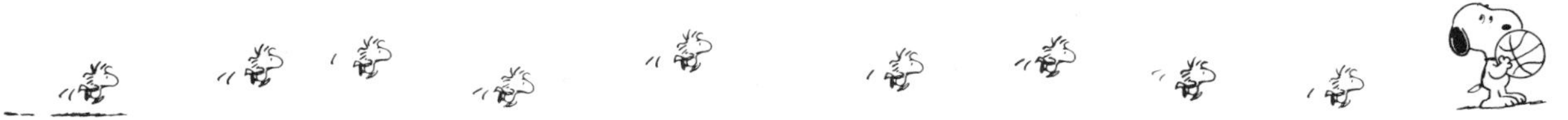

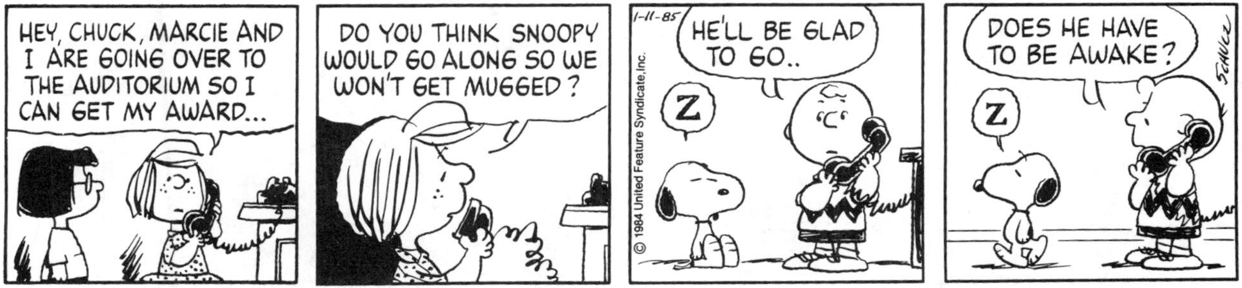
HEY, CHUCK, MARCIE AND I ARE GOING OVER TO THE AUDITORIUM SO I CAN GET MY AWARD...
DO YOU THINK SNOOPY WOULD GO ALONG SO WE WON'T GET MUGGED?
1-11-85
HE'LL BE GLAD TO GO..
Z
© 1984 United Feature Syndicate, Inc.
DOES HE HAVE TO BE AWAKE?
Z
SCHULZ

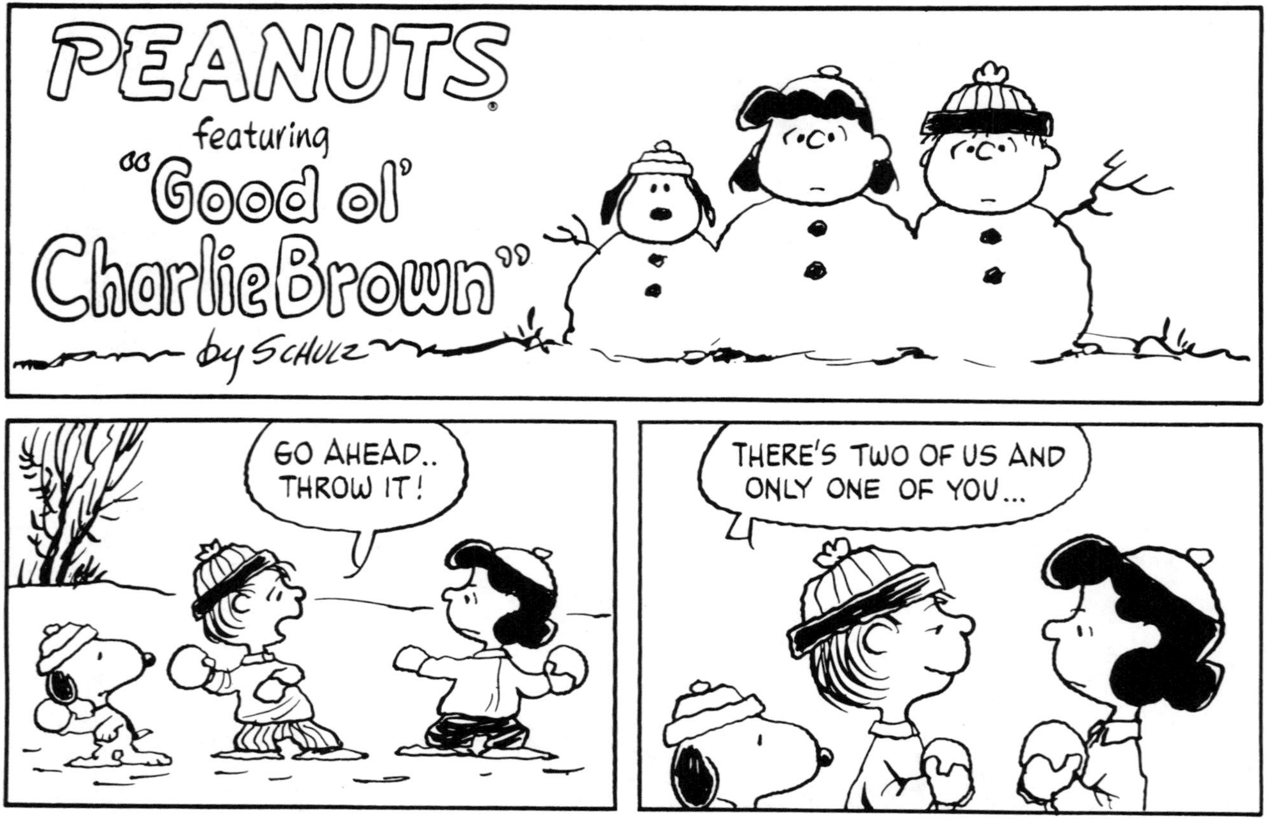
PEANUTS®
featuring
"Good ol' Charlie Brown"
by SCHULZ
GO AHEAD.. THROW IT!
THERE'S TWO OF US AND ONLY ONE OF YOU...

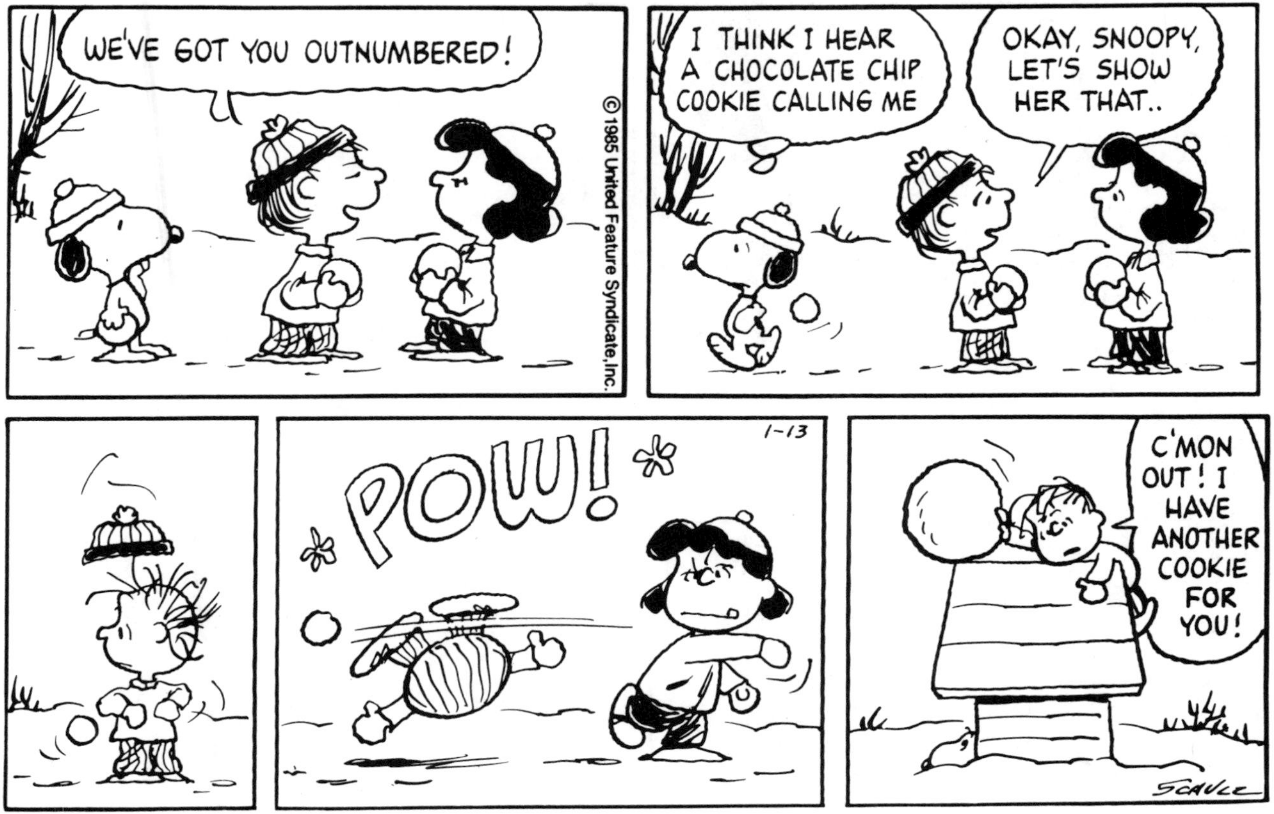

WE'VE GOT YOU OUTNUMBERED!
© 1985 United Feature Syndicate, Inc.
I THINK I HEAR A CHOCOLATE CHIP COOKIE CALLING ME
OKAY, SNOOPY, LET'S SHOW HER THAT..
1-13
POW!
C'MON OUT! I HAVE ANOTHER COOKIE FOR YOU!
SCHULZ

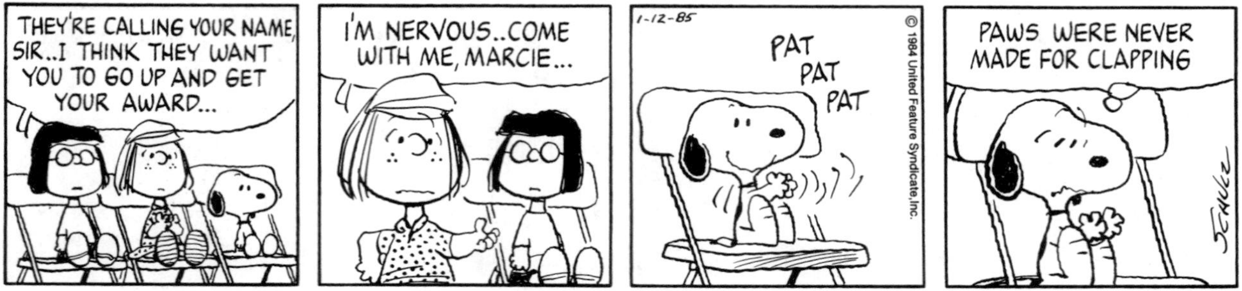
THEY'RE CALLING YOUR NAME, SIR..I THINK THEY WANT YOU TO GO UP AND GET YOUR AWARD...
I'M NERVOUS..COME WITH ME, MARCIE...
1-12-85
PAT PAT PAT
© 1984 United Feature Syndicate,Inc.
PAWS WERE NEVER MADE FOR CLAPPING
SCHULZ

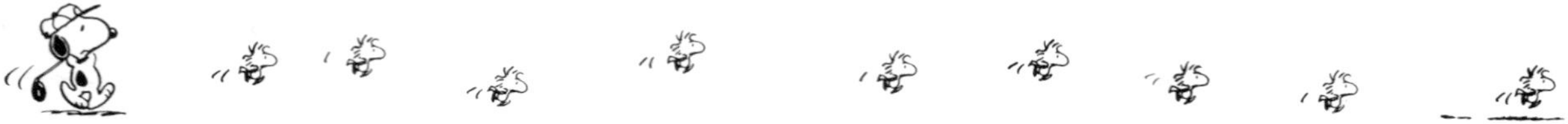

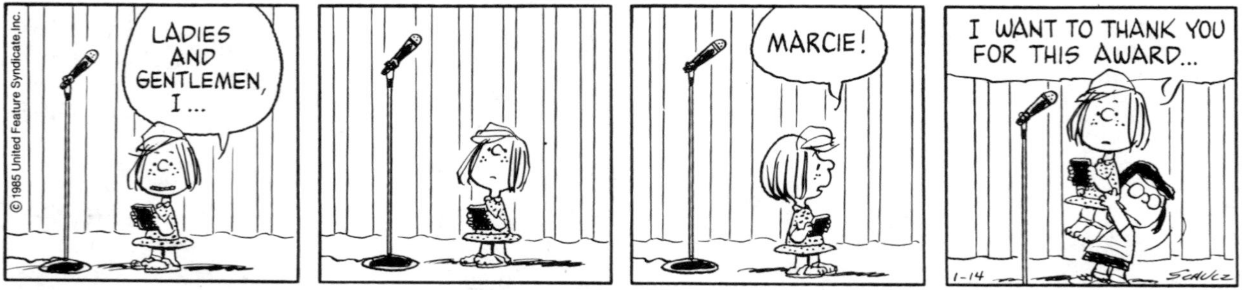
© 1985 United Feature Syndicate,Inc.
LADIES AND GENTLEMEN, I...
MARCIE!
I WANT TO THANK YOU FOR THIS AWARD...
1-14
SCHULZ

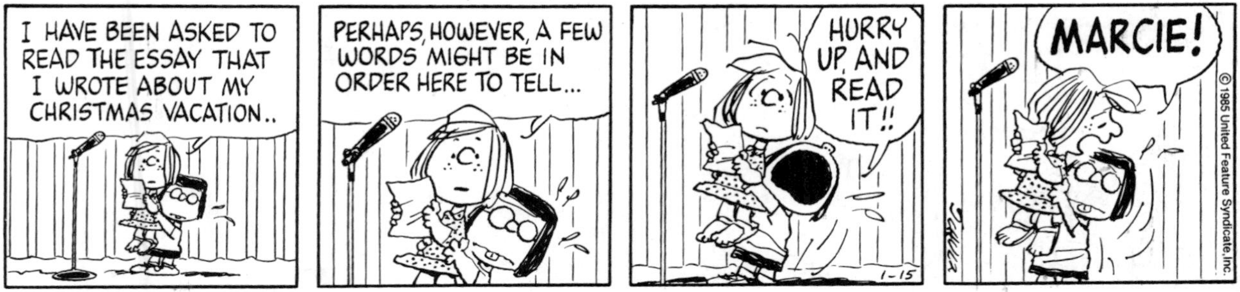
I HAVE BEEN ASKED TO READ THE ESSAY THAT I WROTE ABOUT MY CHRISTMAS VACATION..
PERHAPS, HOWEVER, A FEW WORDS MIGHT BE IN ORDER HERE TO TELL...
HURRY UP, AND READ IT!!
1-15
MARCIE!
SCHULZ
© 1985 United Feature Syndicate, Inc.

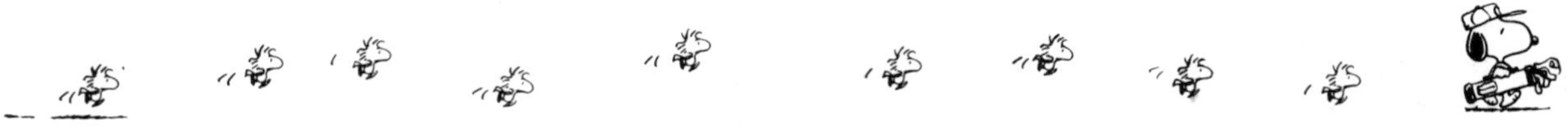

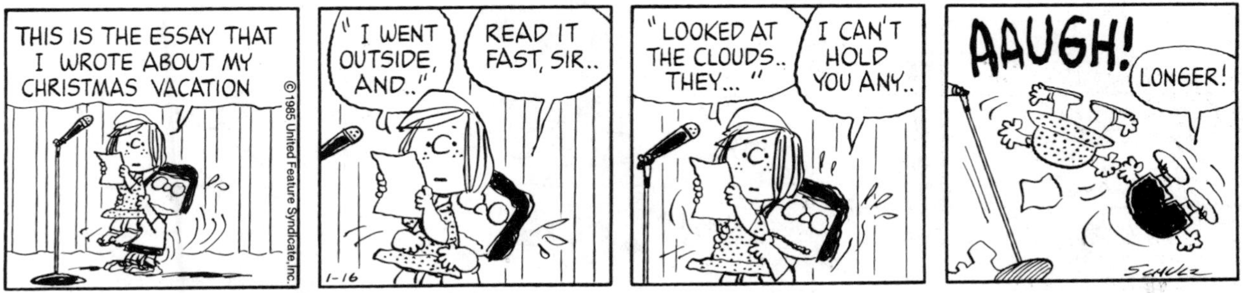
THIS IS THE ESSAY THAT I WROTE ABOUT MY CHRISTMAS VACATION
© 1985 United Feature Syndicate, Inc.
"I WENT OUTSIDE, AND.."
READ IT FAST, SIR..
1-16
"LOOKED AT THE CLOUDS.. THEY..."
I CAN'T HOLD YOU ANY..
AAUGH!
LONGER!
SCHULZ

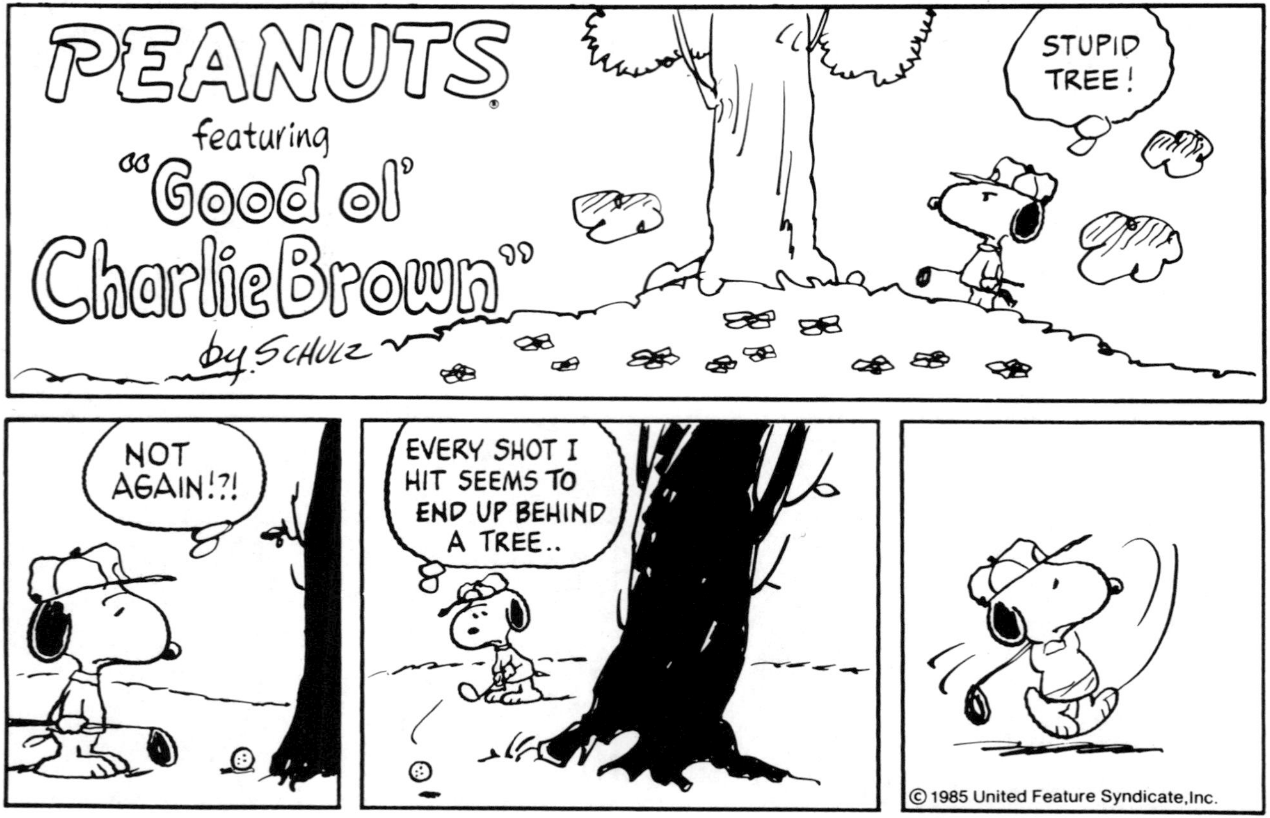
PEANUTS
featuring
"Good ol' Charlie Brown"
by SCHULZ
STUPID TREE!
NOT AGAIN!?!
EVERY SHOT I HIT SEEMS TO END UP BEHIND A TREE..
© 1985 United Feature Syndicate, Inc.

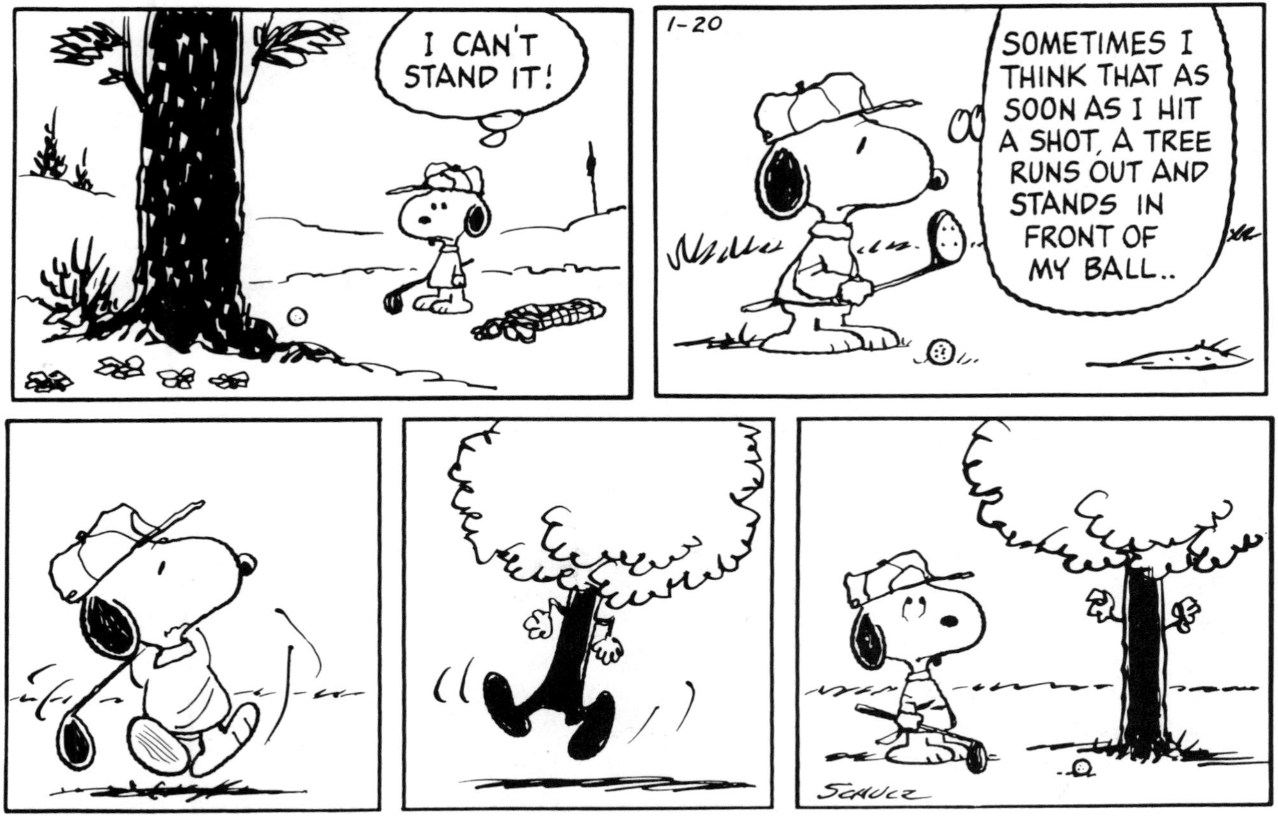
I CAN'T STAND IT!
1-20
SOMETIMES I THINK THAT AS SOON AS I HIT A SHOT, A TREE RUNS OUT AND STANDS IN FRONT OF MY BALL..
SCHULZ

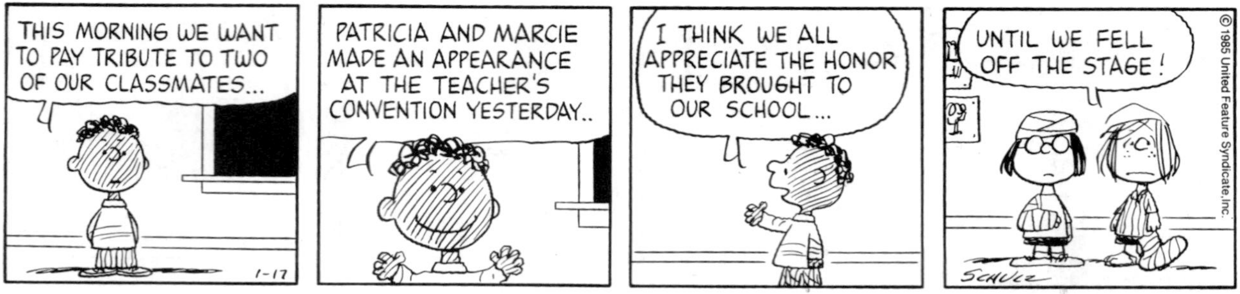
THIS MORNING WE WANT TO PAY TRIBUTE TO TWO OF OUR CLASSMATES...
1-17
PATRICIA AND MARCIE MADE AN APPEARANCE AT THE TEACHER'S CONVENTION YESTERDAY..
I THINK WE ALL APPRECIATE THE HONOR THEY BROUGHT TO OUR SCHOOL...
UNTIL WE FELL OFF THE STAGE!
© 1985 United Feature Syndicate, Inc.
SCHULZ

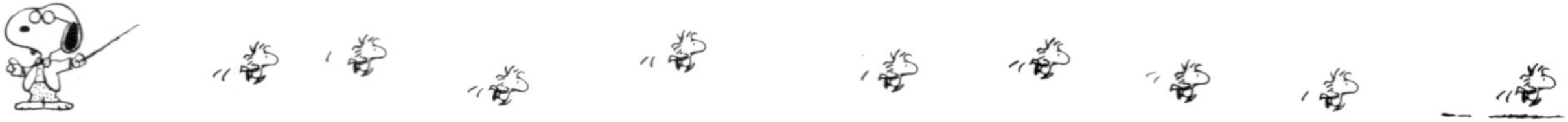

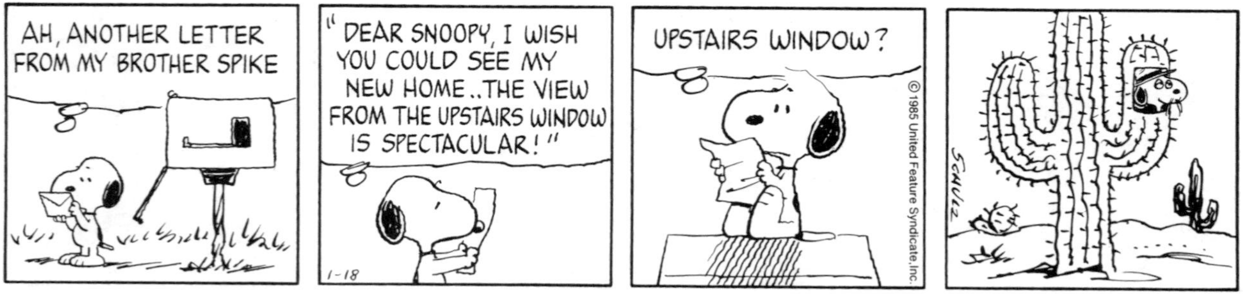
AH, ANOTHER LETTER FROM MY BROTHER SPIKE
"DEAR SNOOPY, I WISH YOU COULD SEE MY NEW HOME..THE VIEW FROM THE UPSTAIRS WINDOW IS SPECTACULAR!"
1-18
UPSTAIRS WINDOW?
© 1985 United Feature Syndicate, Inc.
SCHULZ

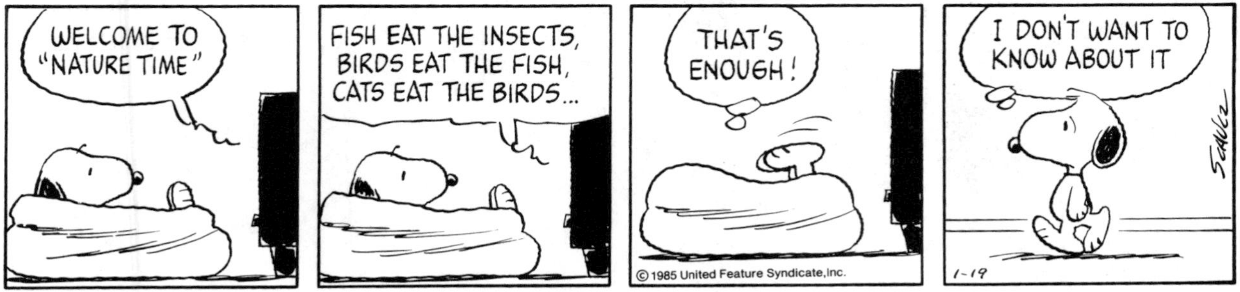
WELCOME TO "NATURE TIME"
FISH EAT THE INSECTS, BIRDS EAT THE FISH, CATS EAT THE BIRDS...
THAT'S ENOUGH!
I DON'T WANT TO KNOW ABOUT IT
© 1985 United Feature Syndicate, Inc.
1-19
SCHULZ

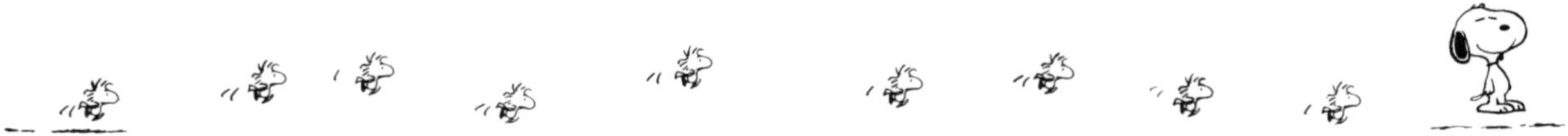

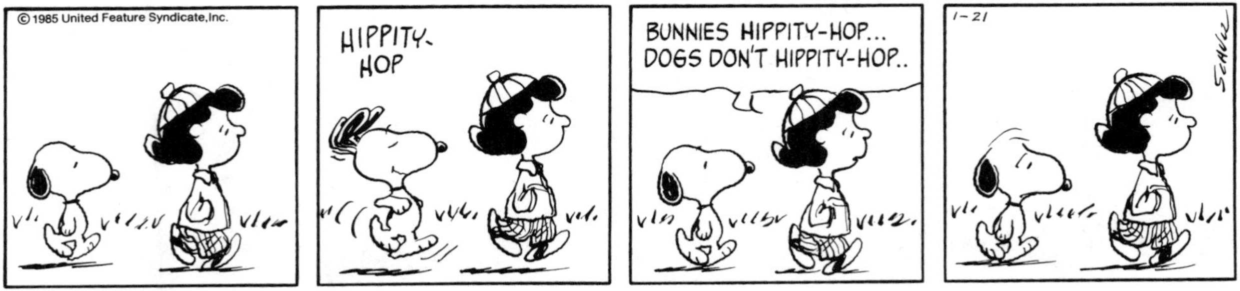
© 1985 United Feature Syndicate, Inc.
HIPPITY-HOP
BUNNIES HIPPITY-HOP... DOGS DON'T HIPPITY-HOP..
1-21
SCHULZ

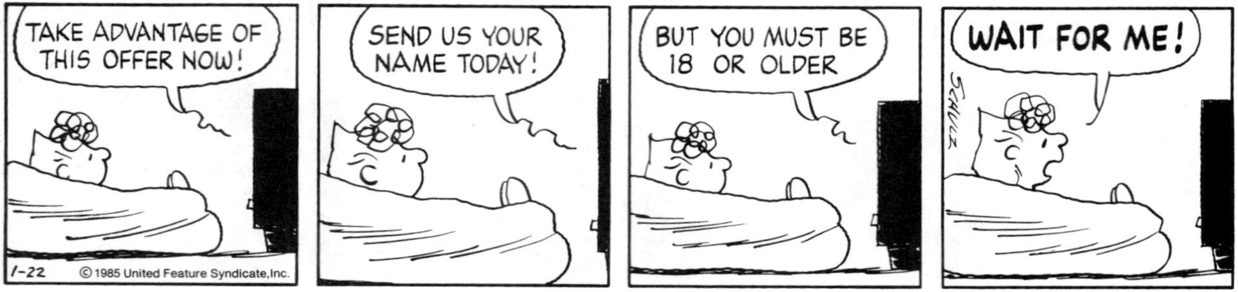
TAKE ADVANTAGE OF THIS OFFER NOW!
SEND US YOUR NAME TODAY!
BUT YOU MUST BE 18 OR OLDER
WAIT FOR ME!
1-22
© 1985 United Feature Syndicate, Inc.
SCHULZ

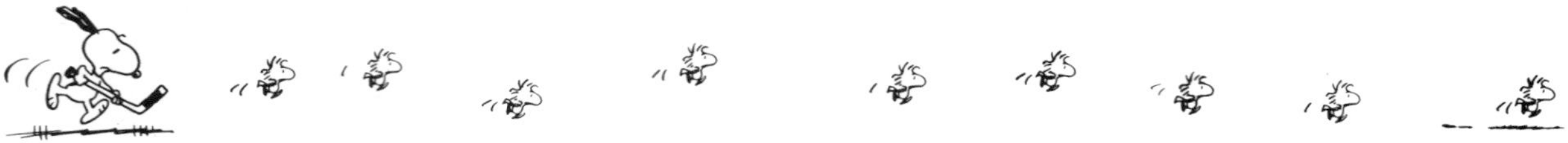

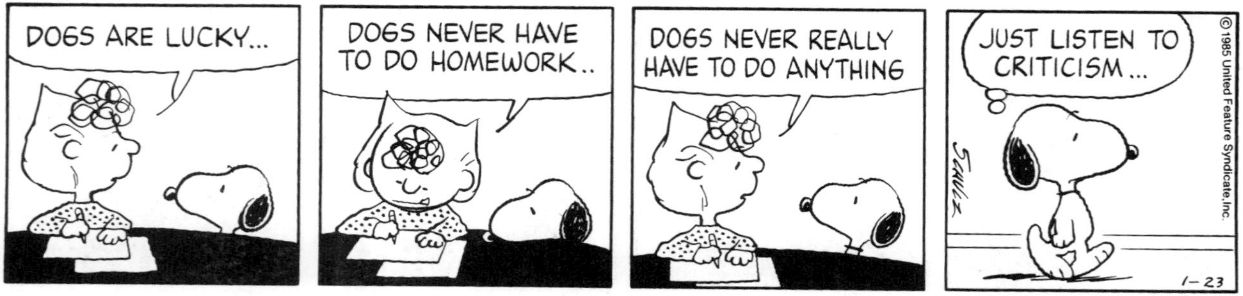
DOGS ARE LUCKY...
DOGS NEVER HAVE TO DO HOMEWORK..
DOGS NEVER REALLY HAVE TO DO ANYTHING
JUST LISTEN TO CRITICISM...
SCHULZ
1-23
© 1985 United Feature Syndicate, Inc.

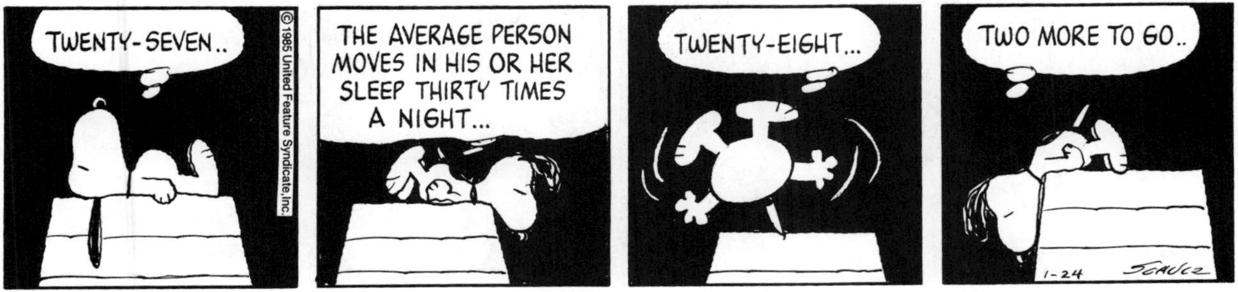
TWENTY-SEVEN..
© 1985 United Feature Syndicate, Inc.
THE AVERAGE PERSON MOVES IN HIS OR HER SLEEP THIRTY TIMES A NIGHT...
TWENTY-EIGHT...
TWO MORE TO GO..
1-24
SCHULZ

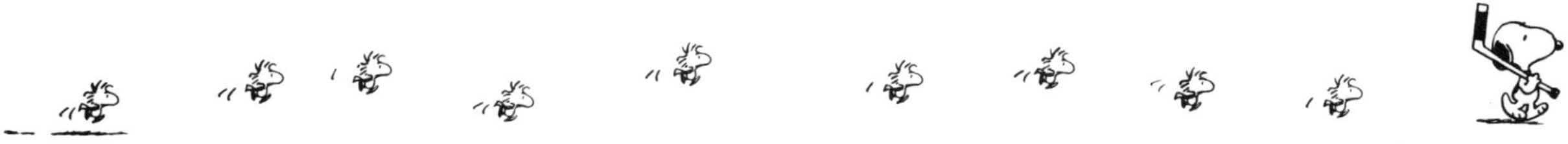

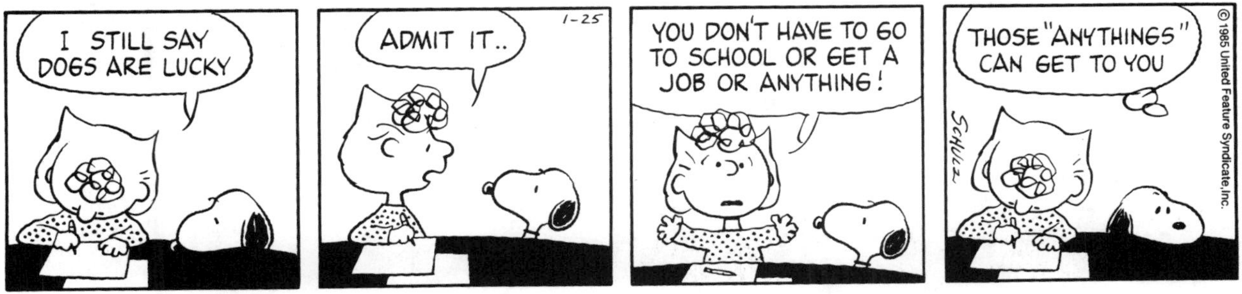
I STILL SAY DOGS ARE LUCKY
ADMIT IT..
1-25
YOU DON'T HAVE TO GO TO SCHOOL OR GET A JOB OR ANYTHING!
SCHULZ
THOSE "ANYTHINGS" CAN GET TO YOU
© 1985 United Feature Syndicate, Inc.

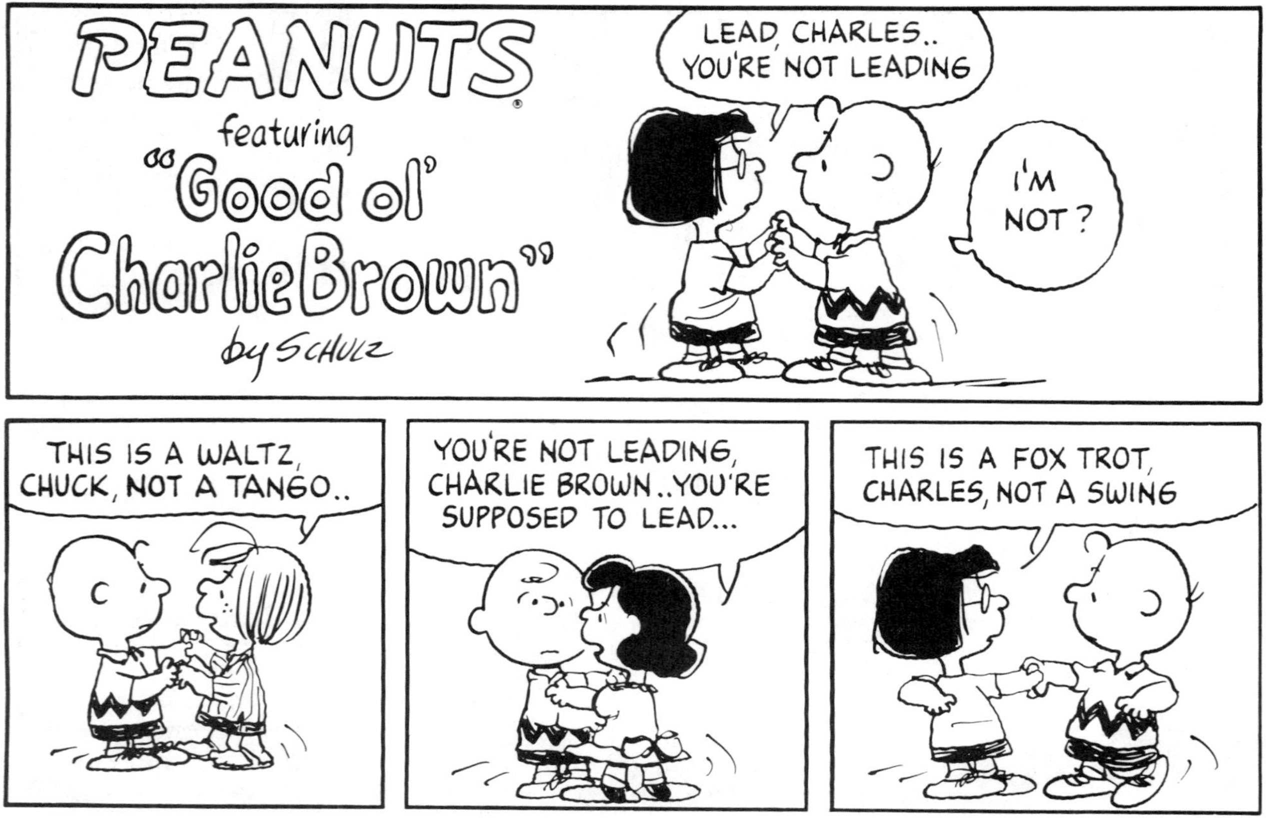
PEANUTS
featuring "Good ol' Charlie Brown" by SCHULZ
LEAD, CHARLES.. YOU'RE NOT LEADING
I'M NOT?
THIS IS A WALTZ, CHUCK, NOT A TANGO..
YOU'RE NOT LEADING, CHARLIE BROWN..YOU'RE SUPPOSED TO LEAD...
THIS IS A FOX TROT, CHARLES, NOT A SWING

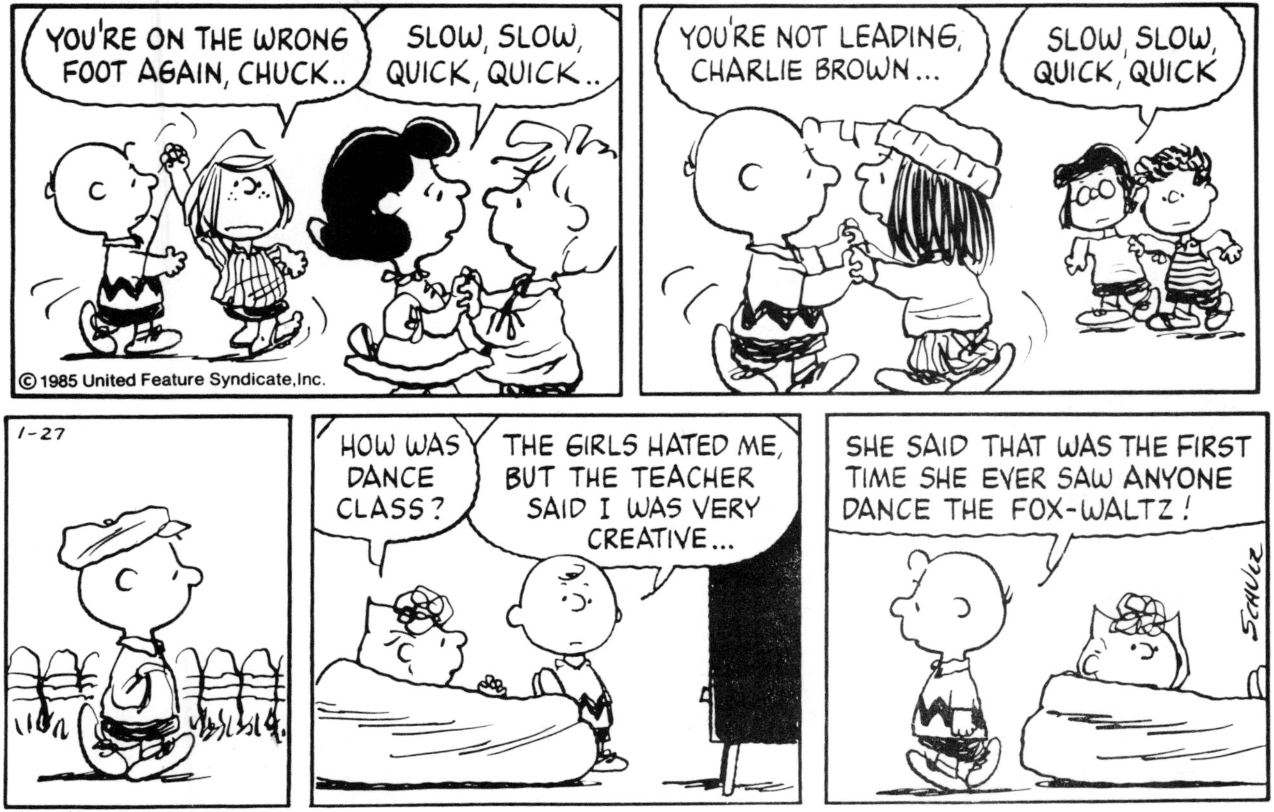
YOU'RE ON THE WRONG FOOT AGAIN, CHUCK..
SLOW, SLOW, QUICK, QUICK..
YOU'RE NOT LEADING, CHARLIE BROWN...
SLOW, SLOW, QUICK, QUICK
1-27
HOW WAS DANCE CLASS?
THE GIRLS HATED ME, BUT THE TEACHER SAID I WAS VERY CREATIVE...
SHE SAID THAT WAS THE FIRST TIME SHE EVER SAW ANYONE DANCE THE FOX-WALTZ!
SCHULZ

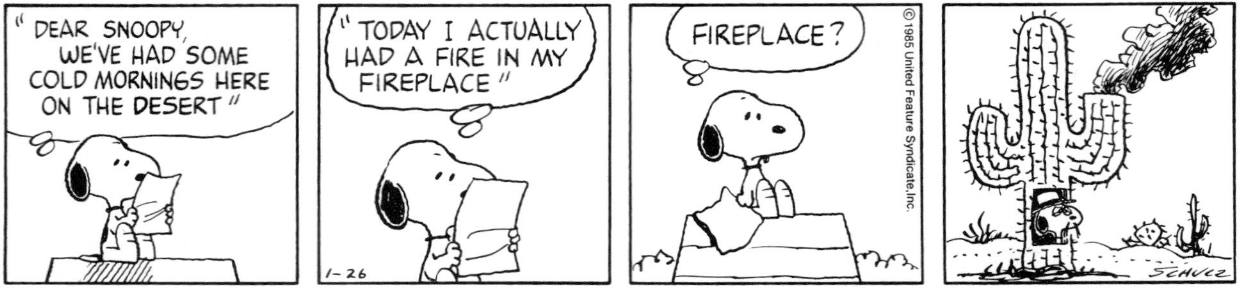
" DEAR SNOOPY,
WE'VE HAD SOME COLD MORNINGS HERE ON THE DESERT "
" TODAY I ACTUALLY HAD A FIRE IN MY FIREPLACE "
1-26
FIREPLACE ?
© 1985 United Feature Syndicate,Inc.
SCHULZ

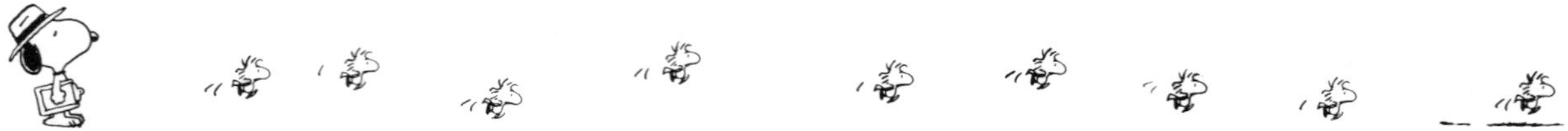

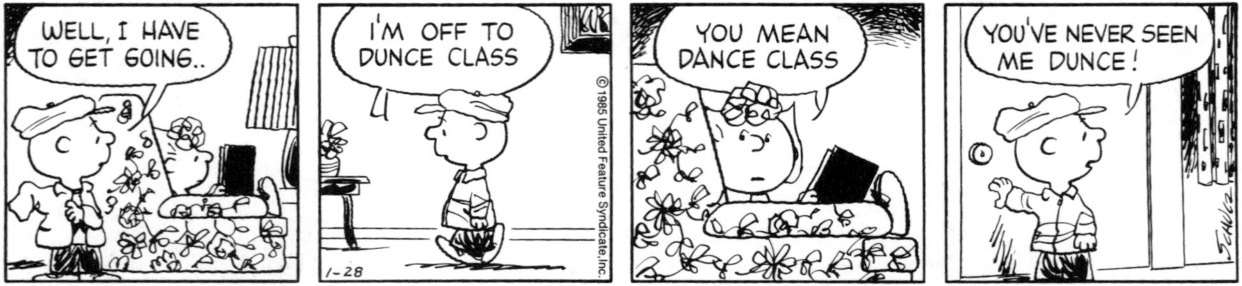
WELL, I HAVE TO GET GOING..
I'M OFF TO DUNCE CLASS
1-28
© 1985 United Feature Syndicate,Inc.
YOU MEAN DANCE CLASS
YOU'VE NEVER SEEN ME DUNCE !
SCHULZ

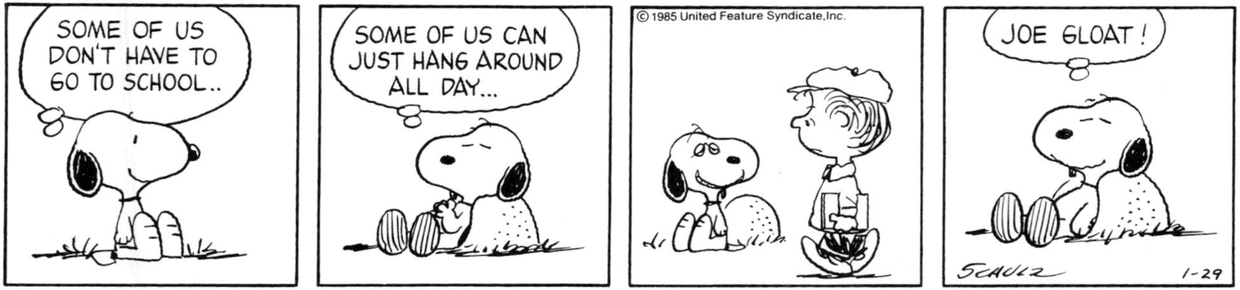
SOME OF US DON'T HAVE TO GO TO SCHOOL..
SOME OF US CAN JUST HANG AROUND ALL DAY...
© 1985 United Feature Syndicate, Inc.
JOE GLOAT!
SCHULZ
1-29

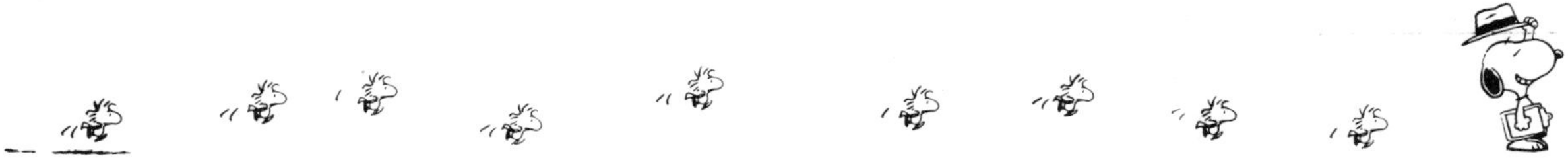

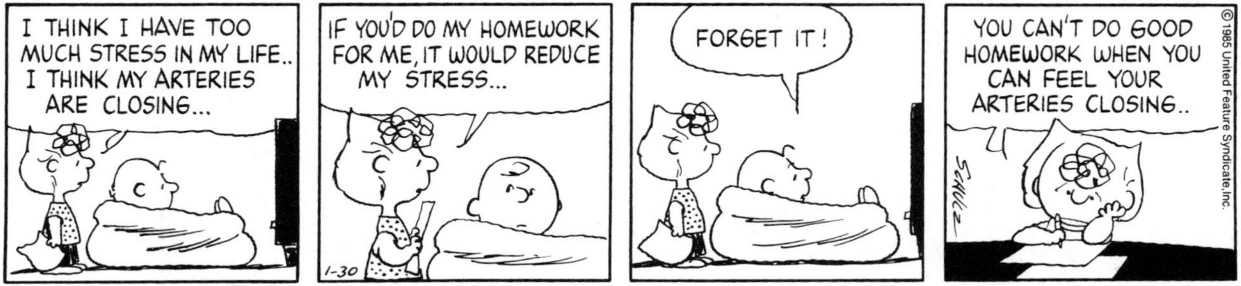
I THINK I HAVE TOO MUCH STRESS IN MY LIFE.. I THINK MY ARTERIES ARE CLOSING...
IF YOU'D DO MY HOMEWORK FOR ME, IT WOULD REDUCE MY STRESS...
1-30
FORGET IT!
YOU CAN'T DO GOOD HOMEWORK WHEN YOU CAN FEEL YOUR ARTERIES CLOSING..
SCHULZ
© 1985 United Feature Syndicate, Inc.

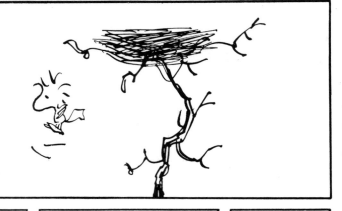

PEANUTS
featuring
"Good ol' CharlieBrown"
by SCHULZ

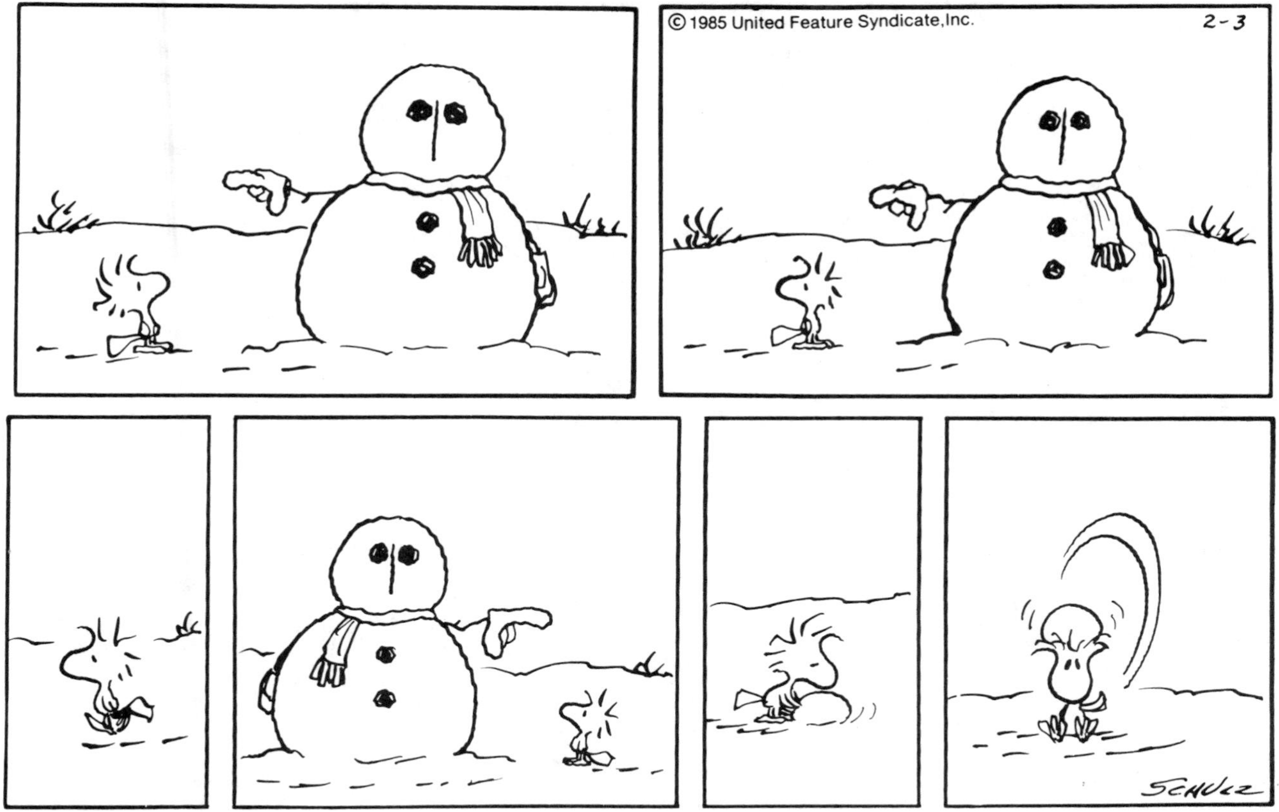
© 1985 United Feature Syndicate, Inc.
2-3
SCHULZ

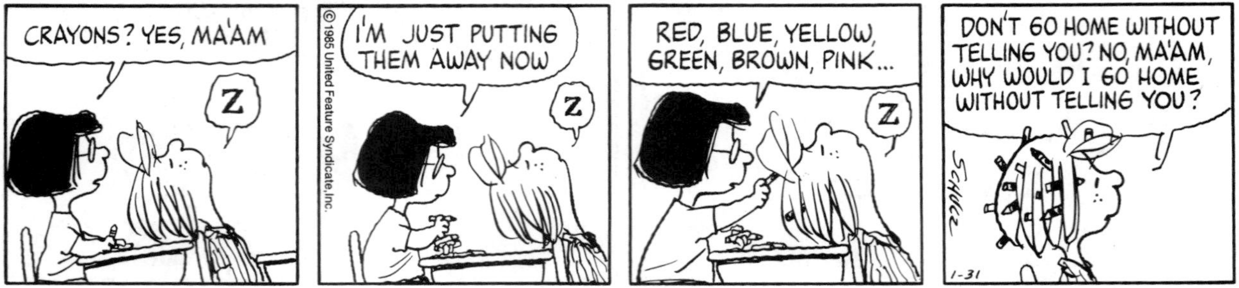
CRAYONS? YES, MA'AM
Z
© 1985 United Feature Syndicate, Inc.
I'M JUST PUTTING THEM AWAY NOW
Z
RED, BLUE, YELLOW, GREEN, BROWN, PINK...
Z
DON'T GO HOME WITHOUT TELLING YOU? NO, MA'AM, WHY WOULD I GO HOME WITHOUT TELLING YOU?
SCHULZ
1-31

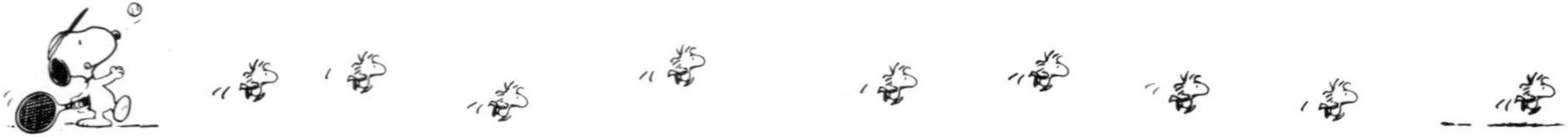

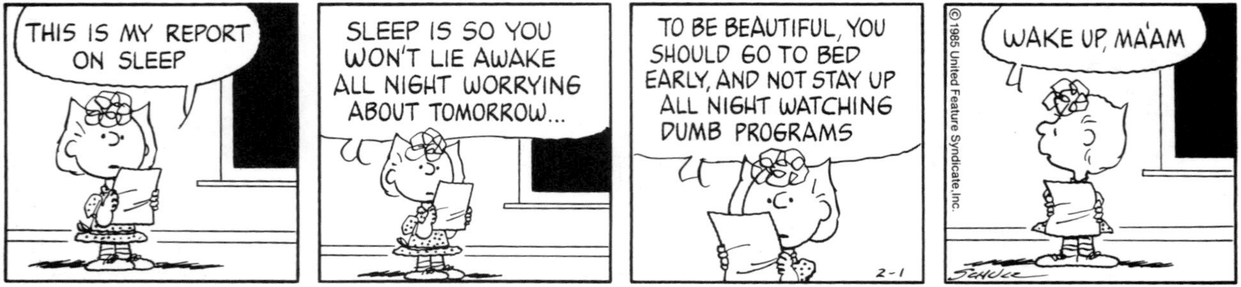
THIS IS MY REPORT ON SLEEP
SLEEP IS SO YOU WON'T LIE AWAKE ALL NIGHT WORRYING ABOUT TOMORROW...
TO BE BEAUTIFUL, YOU SHOULD GO TO BED EARLY, AND NOT STAY UP ALL NIGHT WATCHING DUMB PROGRAMS
2-1
© 1985 United Feature Syndicate, Inc.
WAKE UP, MA'AM
SCHULZ

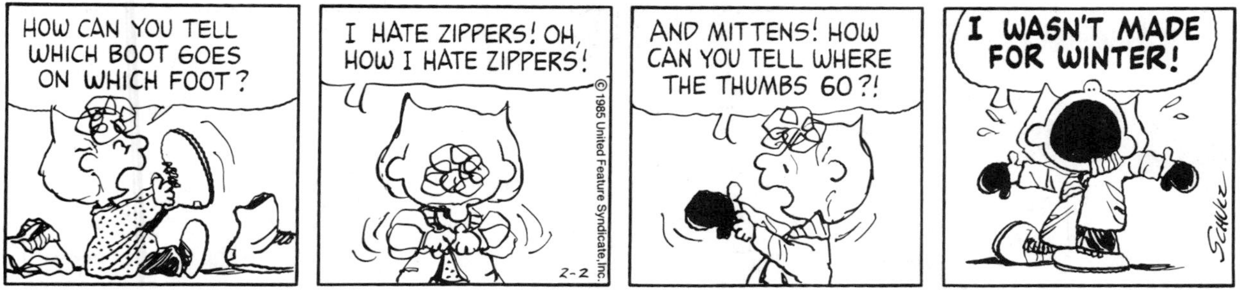
HOW CAN YOU TELL WHICH BOOT GOES ON WHICH FOOT?
I HATE ZIPPERS! OH, HOW I HATE ZIPPERS!
© 1985 United Feature Syndicate, Inc.
2-2
AND MITTENS! HOW CAN YOU TELL WHERE THE THUMBS GO?!
I WASN'T MADE FOR WINTER!
SCHULZ

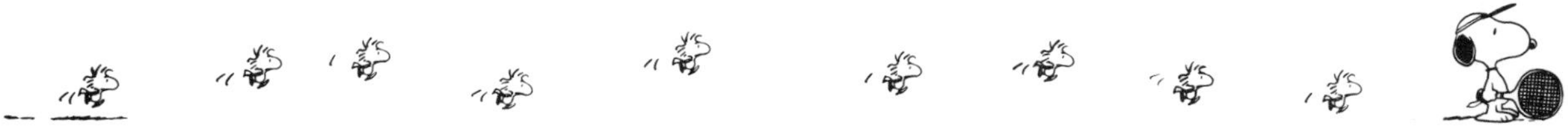

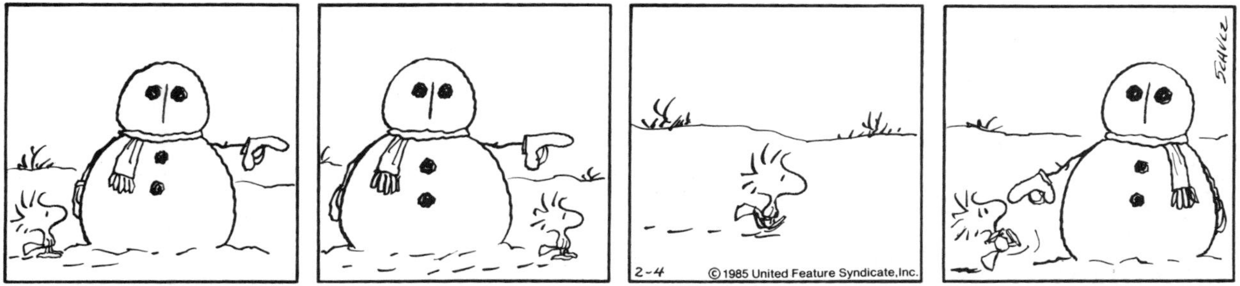
SCHULZ
2-4
© 1985 United Feature Syndicate, Inc.

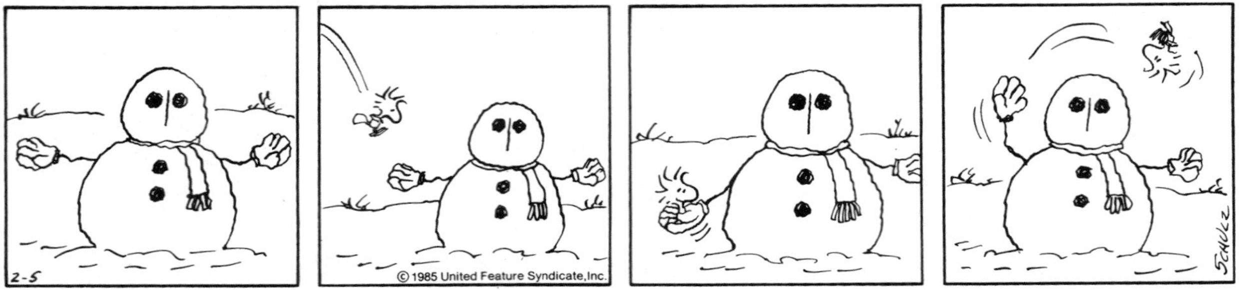
2-5
© 1985 United Feature Syndicate, Inc.
SCHULZ

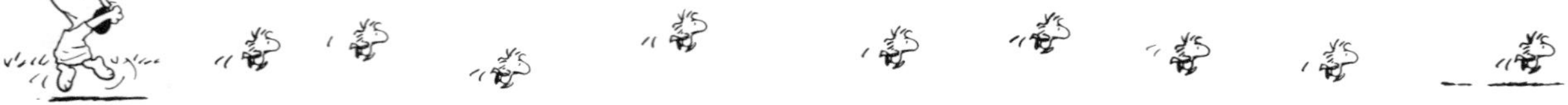

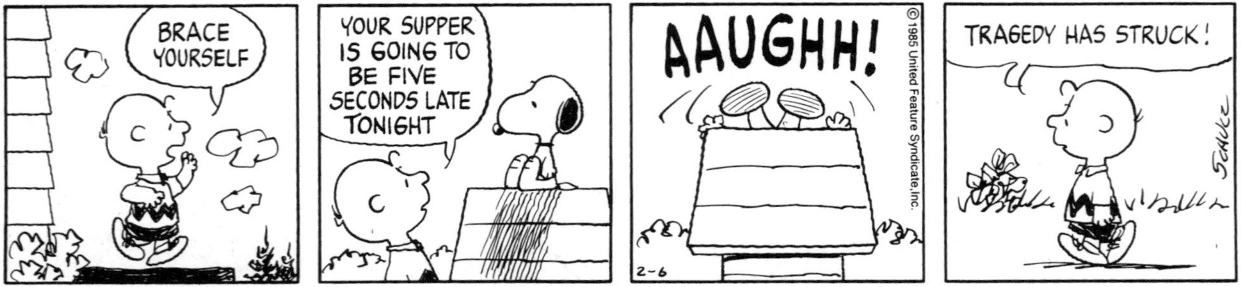
BRACE YOURSELF
YOUR SUPPER IS GOING TO BE FIVE SECONDS LATE TONIGHT
AAUGHH!
© 1985 United Feature Syndicate, Inc.
2-6
TRAGEDY HAS STRUCK!
SCHULZ

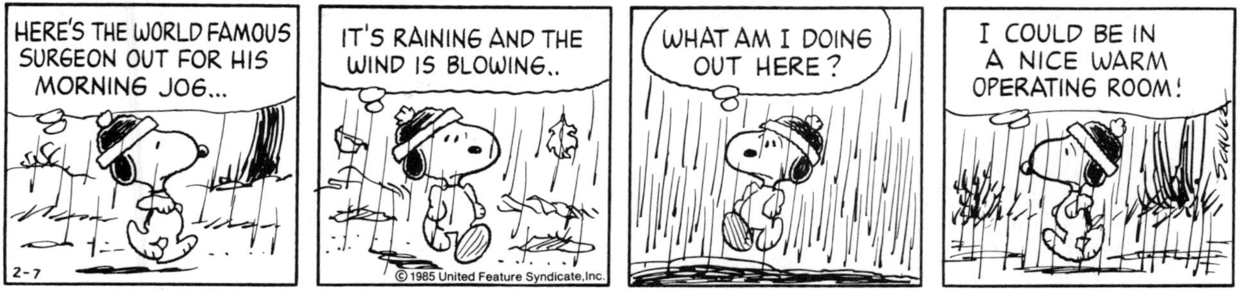
HERE'S THE WORLD FAMOUS SURGEON OUT FOR HIS MORNING JOG...
2-7
IT'S RAINING AND THE WIND IS BLOWING..
© 1985 United Feature Syndicate, Inc.
WHAT AM I DOING OUT HERE?
I COULD BE IN A NICE WARM OPERATING ROOM!
SCHULZ

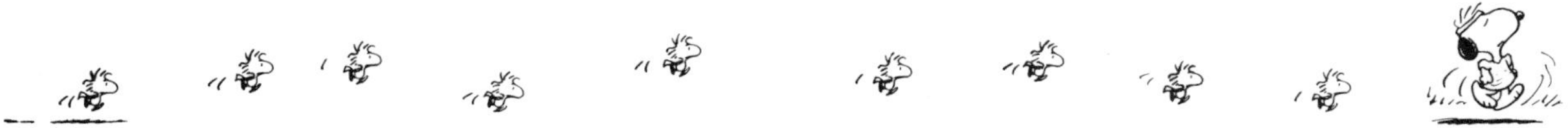

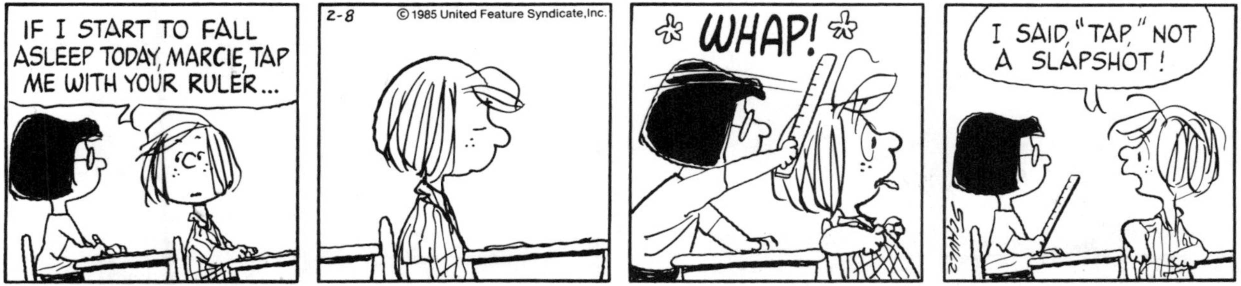
IF I START TO FALL ASLEEP TODAY, MARCIE, TAP ME WITH YOUR RULER...
2-8
© 1985 United Feature Syndicate, Inc.
WHAP!
SCHULZ
I SAID, "TAP," NOT A SLAPSHOT!

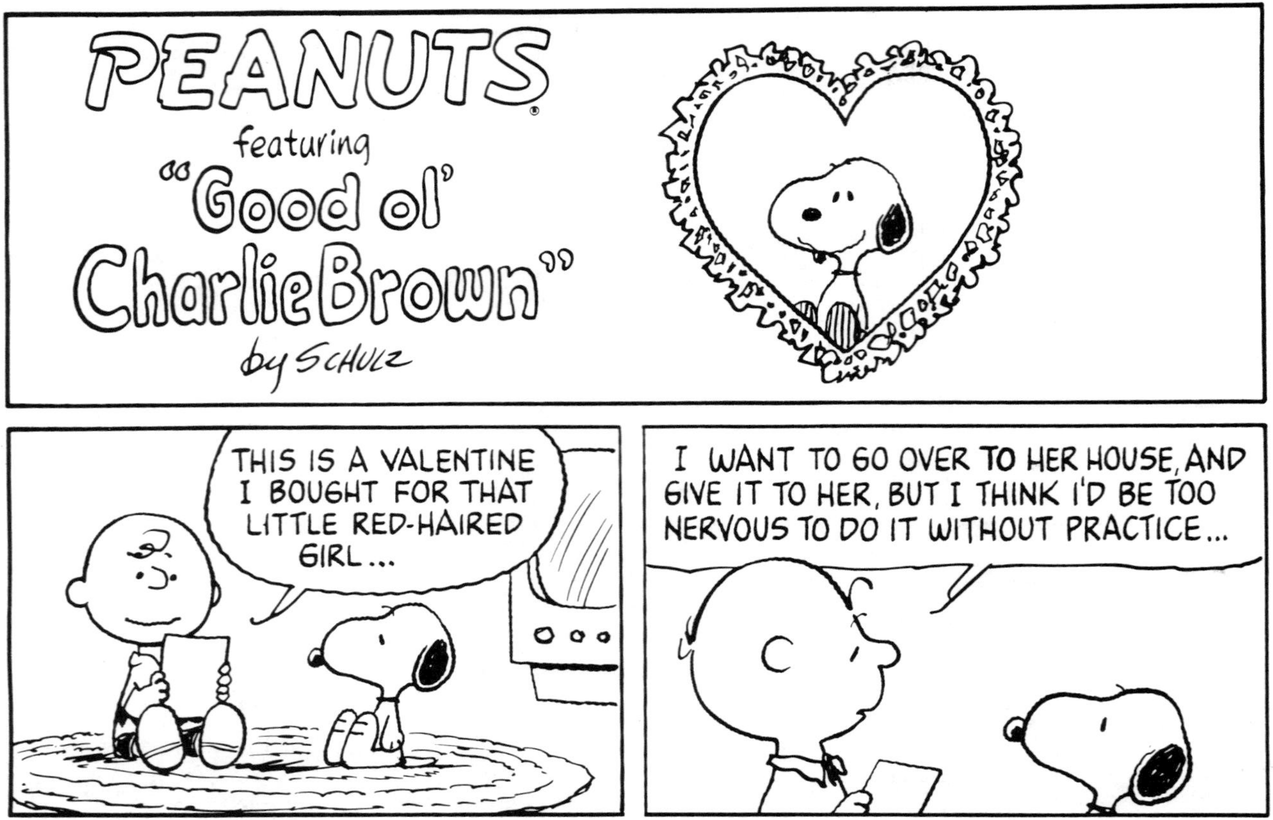
PEANUTS
featuring
"Good ol' Charlie Brown"
by SCHULZ
THIS IS A VALENTINE I BOUGHT FOR THAT LITTLE RED-HAIRED GIRL...
I WANT TO GO OVER TO HER HOUSE, AND GIVE IT TO HER, BUT I THINK I'D BE TOO NERVOUS TO DO IT WITHOUT PRACTICE...

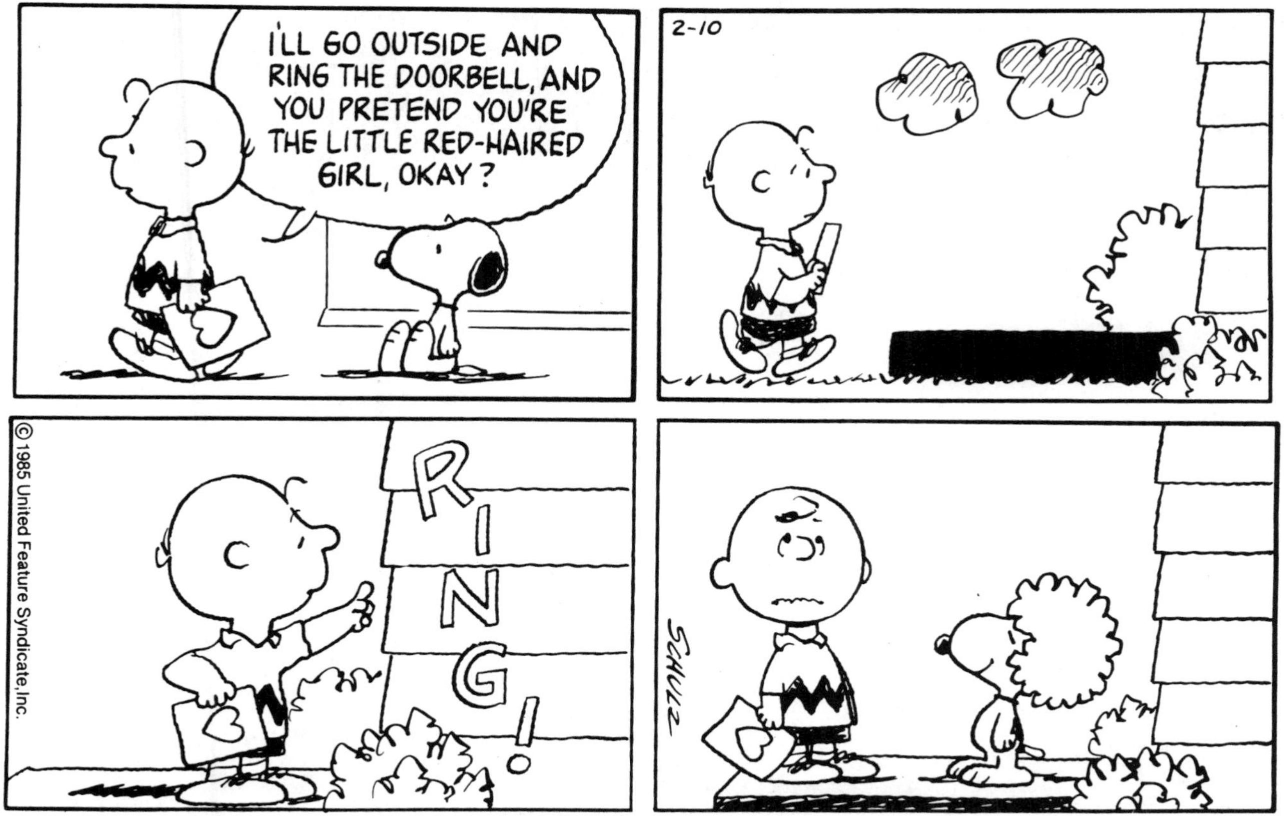
I'LL GO OUTSIDE AND RING THE DOORBELL, AND YOU PRETEND YOU'RE THE LITTLE RED-HAIRED GIRL, OKAY?
2-10
RING!
SCHULZ
© 1985 United Feature Syndicate,Inc.

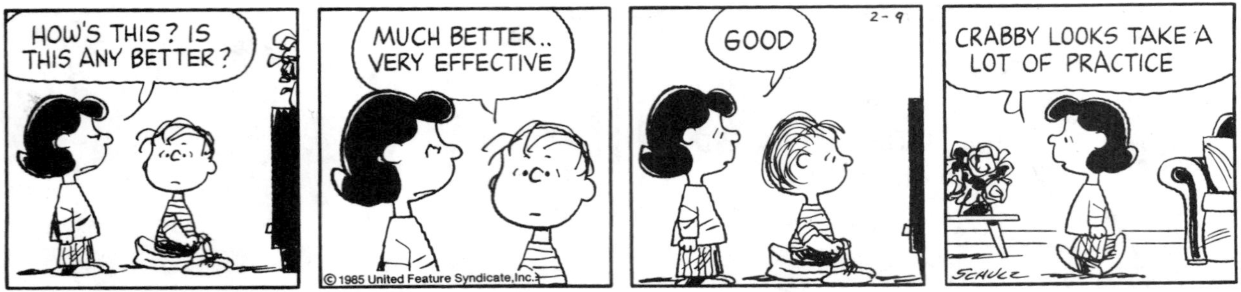
HOW'S THIS? IS THIS ANY BETTER?
MUCH BETTER.. VERY EFFECTIVE
© 1985 United Feature Syndicate, Inc.
2-9
GOOD
CRABBY LOOKS TAKE A LOT OF PRACTICE
SCHULZ

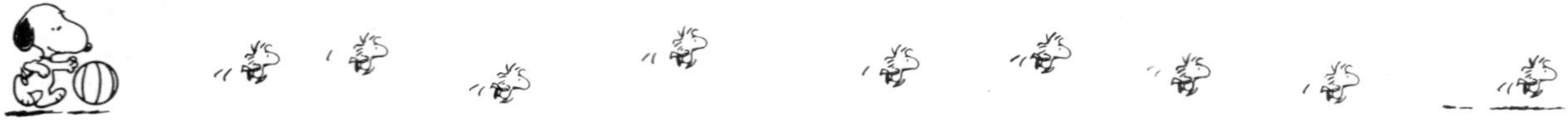

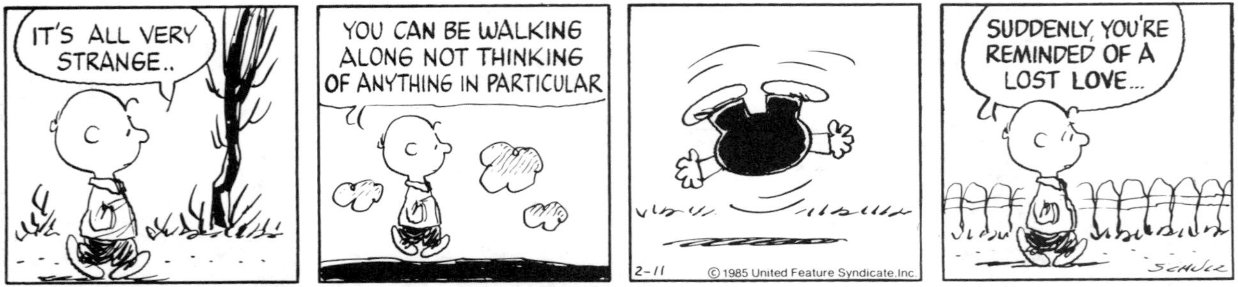
IT'S ALL VERY STRANGE..
YOU CAN BE WALKING ALONG NOT THINKING OF ANYTHING IN PARTICULAR
2-11
© 1985 United Feature Syndicate, Inc.
SUDDENLY, YOU'RE REMINDED OF A LOST LOVE...
SCHULZ

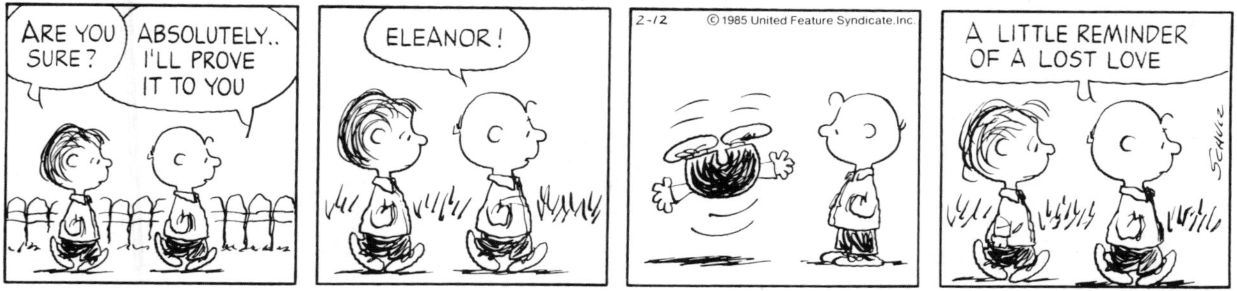
ARE YOU SURE?
ABSOLUTELY.. I'LL PROVE IT TO YOU
ELEANOR!
2-12
© 1985 United Feature Syndicate, Inc.
A LITTLE REMINDER OF A LOST LOVE
SCHULZ

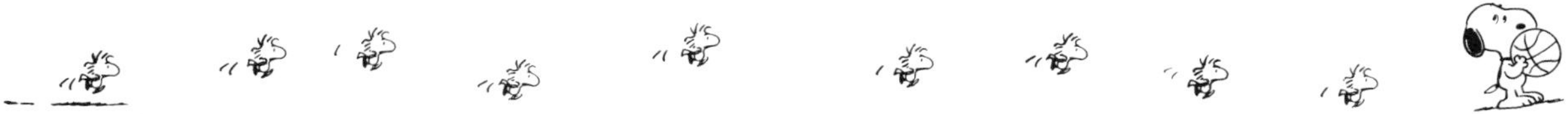

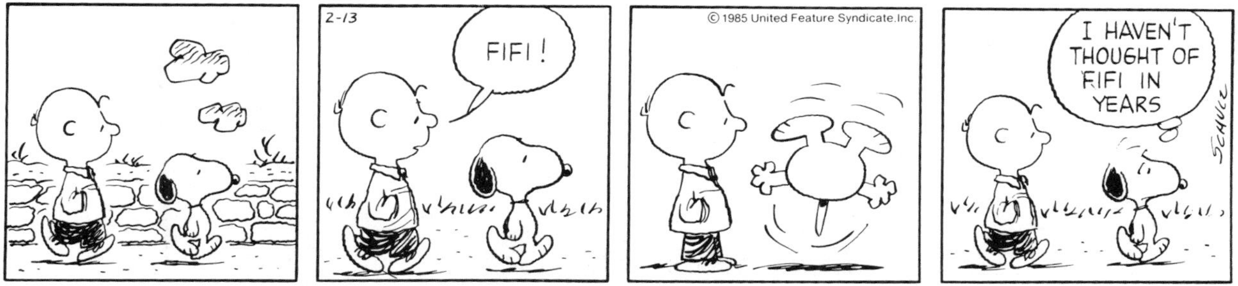
2-13
FIFI!
© 1985 United Feature Syndicate, Inc.
I HAVEN'T THOUGHT OF FIFI IN YEARS
SCHULZ

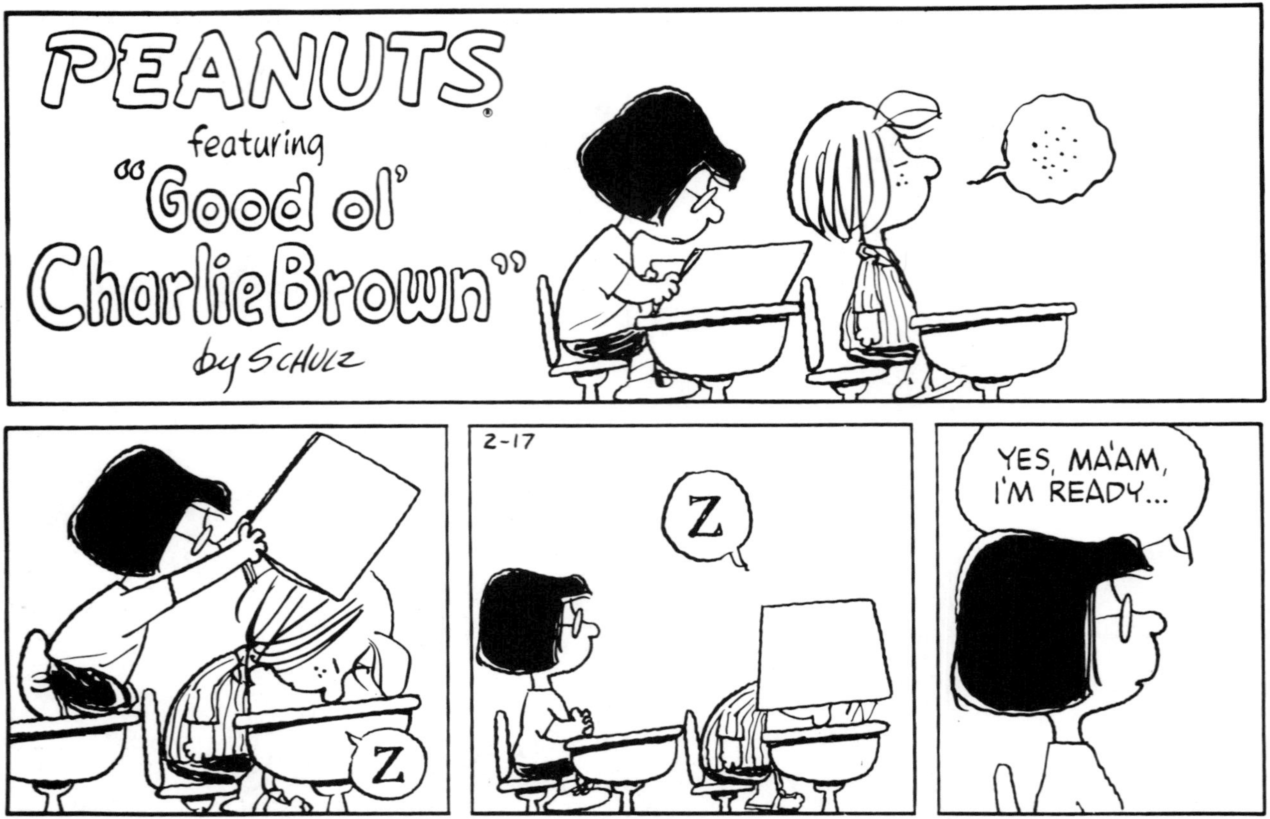
PEANUTS®
featuring
"Good ol' Charlie Brown"
by SCHULZ
Z
2-17
Z
YES, MA'AM, I'M READY...

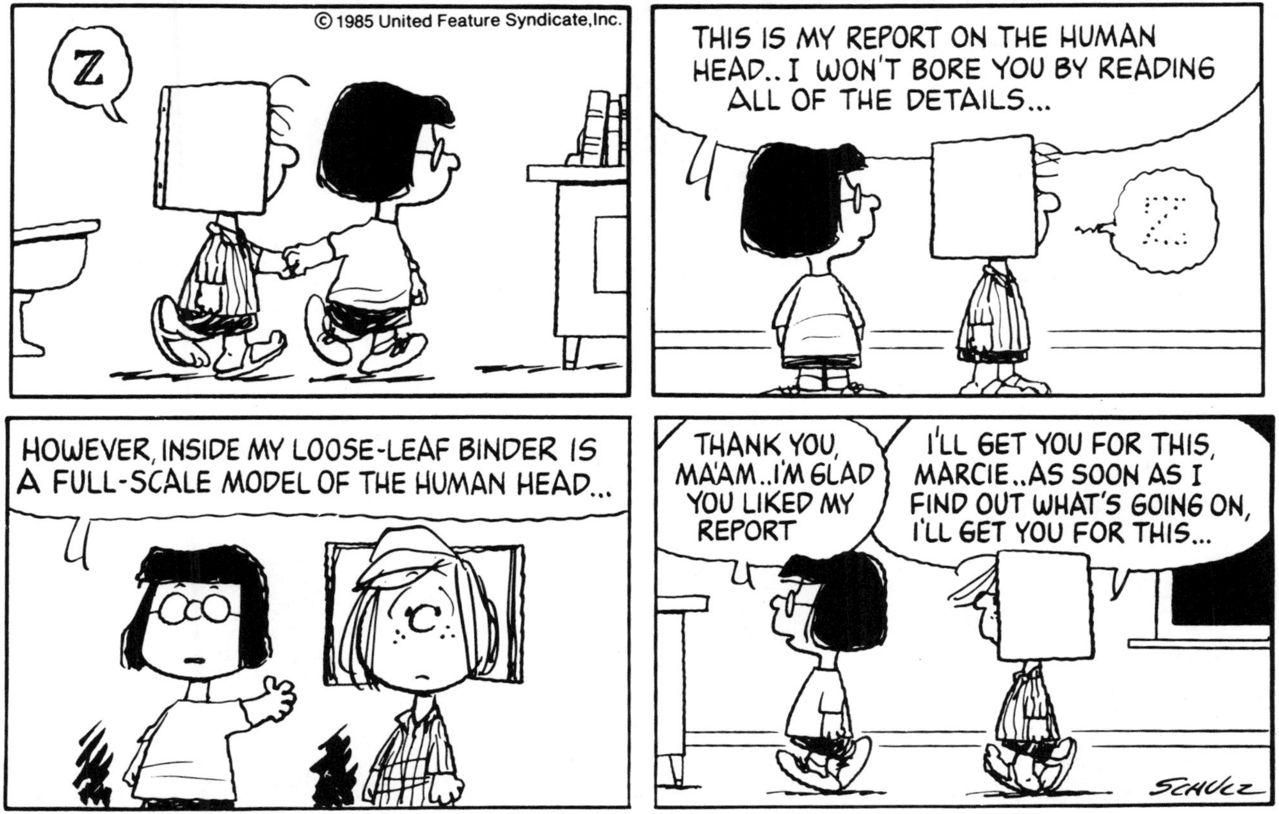
© 1985 United Feature Syndicate, Inc.
Z
THIS IS MY REPORT ON THE HUMAN HEAD.. I WON'T BORE YOU BY READING ALL OF THE DETAILS...
Z
HOWEVER, INSIDE MY LOOSE-LEAF BINDER IS A FULL-SCALE MODEL OF THE HUMAN HEAD...
THANK YOU, MA'AM..I'M GLAD YOU LIKED MY REPORT
I'LL GET YOU FOR THIS, MARCIE..AS SOON AS I FIND OUT WHAT'S GOING ON, I'LL GET YOU FOR THIS...
SCHULZ

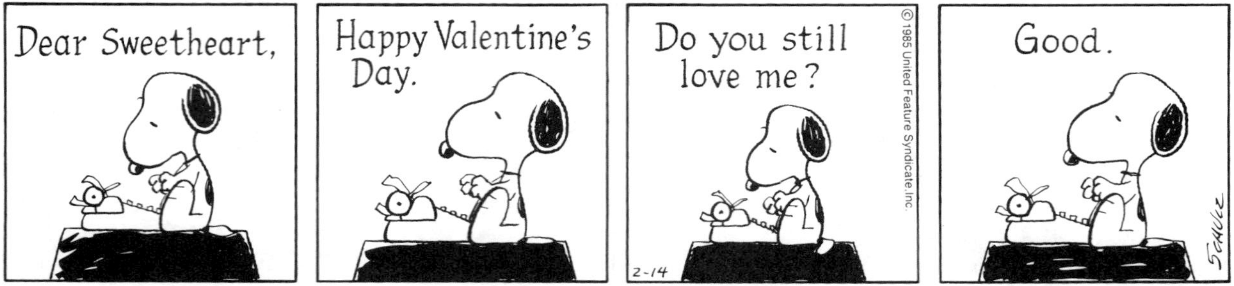
Dear Sweetheart,
Happy Valentine's Day.
Do you still love me?
Good.
2-14
© 1985 United Feature Syndicate, Inc.
SCHULZ

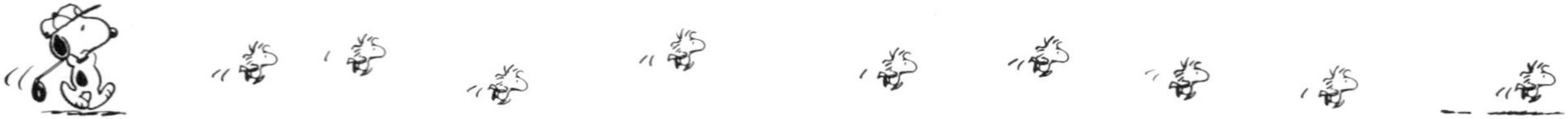

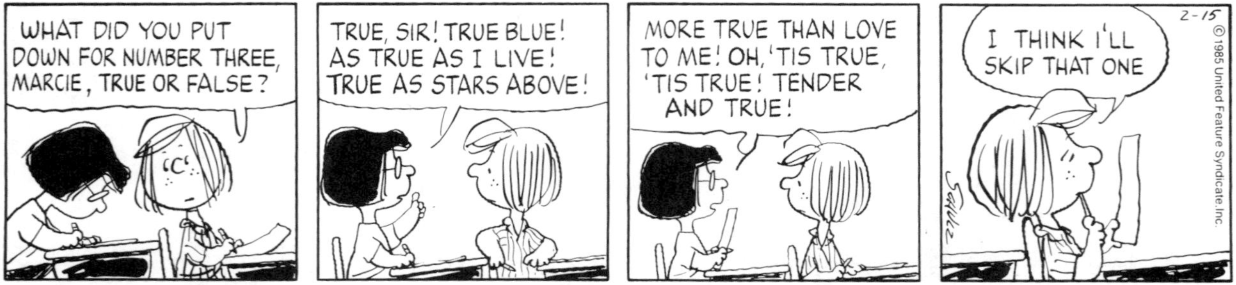
WHAT DID YOU PUT DOWN FOR NUMBER THREE, MARCIE, TRUE OR FALSE?
TRUE, SIR! TRUE BLUE! AS TRUE AS I LIVE! TRUE AS STARS ABOVE!
MORE TRUE THAN LOVE TO ME! OH, 'TIS TRUE, 'TIS TRUE! TENDER AND TRUE!
I THINK I'LL SKIP THAT ONE
2-15
© 1985 United Feature Syndicate, Inc.
SCHULZ

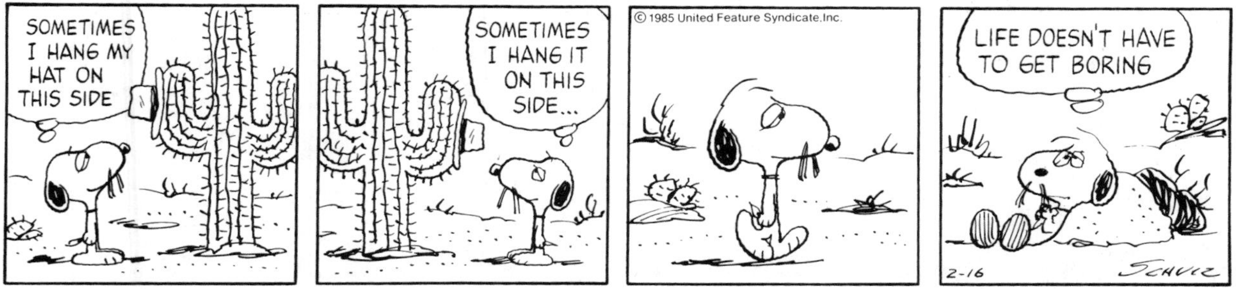
SOMETIMES I HANG MY HAT ON THIS SIDE
SOMETIMES I HANG IT ON THIS SIDE...
© 1985 United Feature Syndicate, Inc.
LIFE DOESN'T HAVE TO GET BORING
2-16

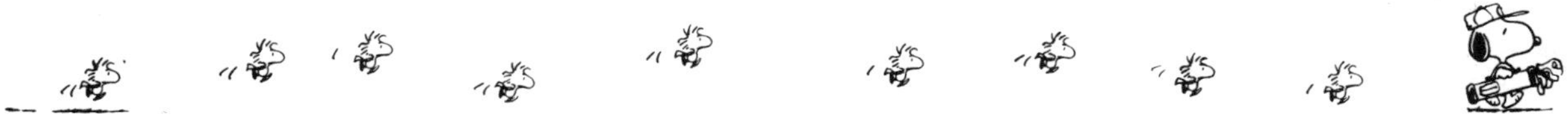

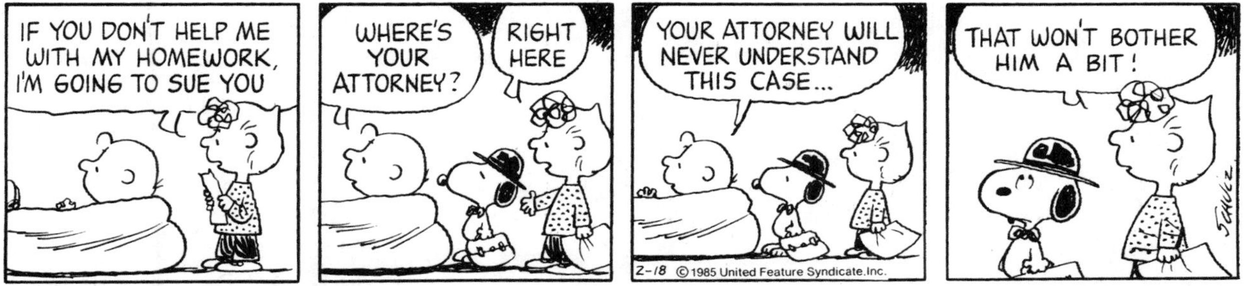
IF YOU DON'T HELP ME WITH MY HOMEWORK, I'M GOING TO SUE YOU
WHERE'S YOUR ATTORNEY?
RIGHT HERE
YOUR ATTORNEY WILL NEVER UNDERSTAND THIS CASE...
2-18 © 1985 United Feature Syndicate, Inc.
THAT WON'T BOTHER HIM A BIT!

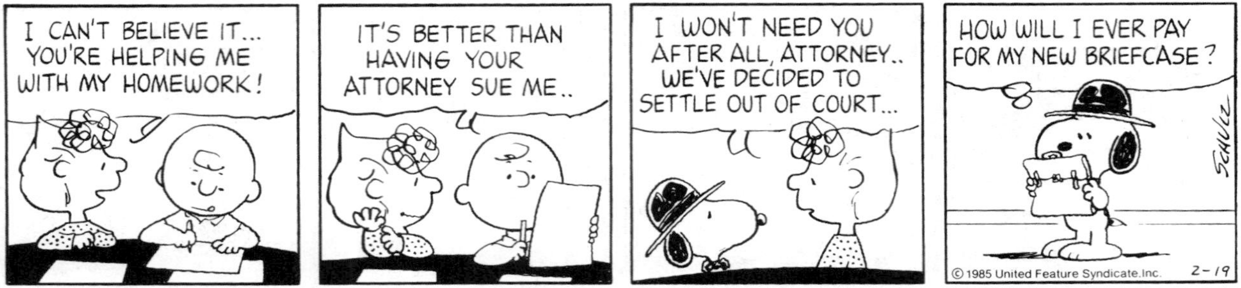
I CAN'T BELIEVE IT... YOU'RE HELPING ME WITH MY HOMEWORK!
IT'S BETTER THAN HAVING YOUR ATTORNEY SUE ME..
I WON'T NEED YOU AFTER ALL, ATTORNEY.. WE'VE DECIDED TO SETTLE OUT OF COURT...
HOW WILL I EVER PAY FOR MY NEW BRIEFCASE?
SCHULZ
© 1985 United Feature Syndicate, Inc.
2-19

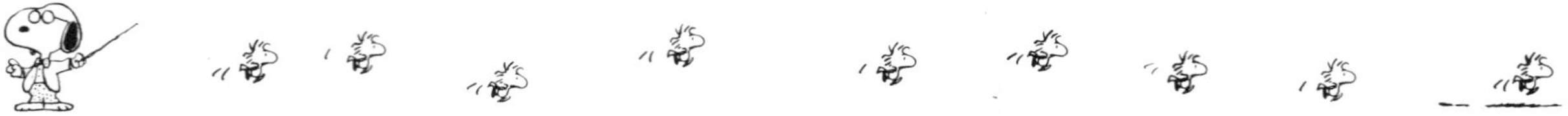

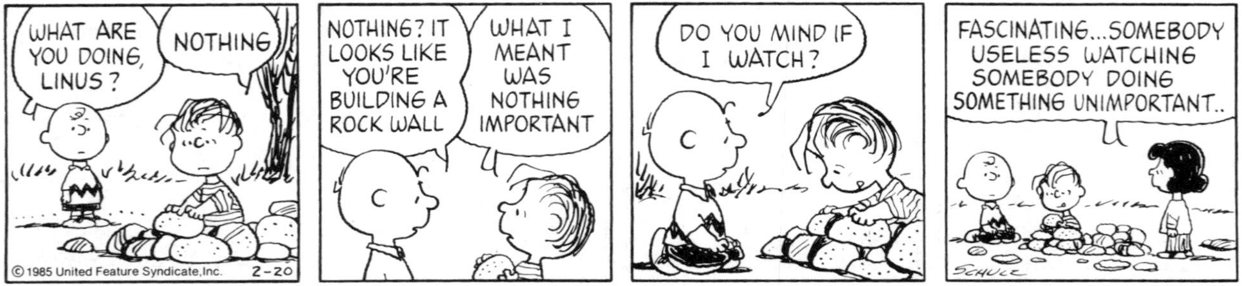
WHAT ARE YOU DOING, LINUS?
NOTHING
NOTHING? IT LOOKS LIKE YOU'RE BUILDING A ROCK WALL
WHAT I MEANT WAS NOTHING IMPORTANT
DO YOU MIND IF I WATCH?
FASCINATING...SOMEBODY USELESS WATCHING SOMEBODY DOING SOMETHING UNIMPORTANT..
SCHULZ
© 1985 United Feature Syndicate, Inc.
2-20

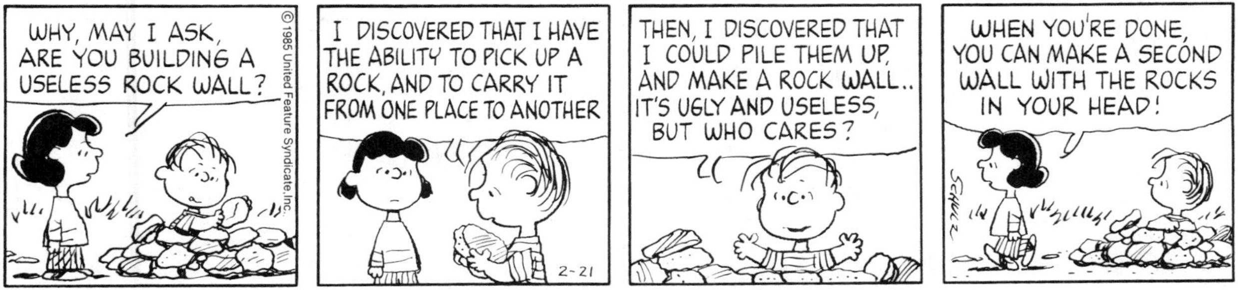
WHY, MAY I ASK, ARE YOU BUILDING A USELESS ROCK WALL?
© 1985 United Feature Syndicate, Inc.
I DISCOVERED THAT I HAVE THE ABILITY TO PICK UP A ROCK, AND TO CARRY IT FROM ONE PLACE TO ANOTHER
2-21
THEN, I DISCOVERED THAT I COULD PILE THEM UP, AND MAKE A ROCK WALL.. IT'S UGLY AND USELESS, BUT WHO CARES?
WHEN YOU'RE DONE, YOU CAN MAKE A SECOND WALL WITH THE ROCKS IN YOUR HEAD!
SCHULZ

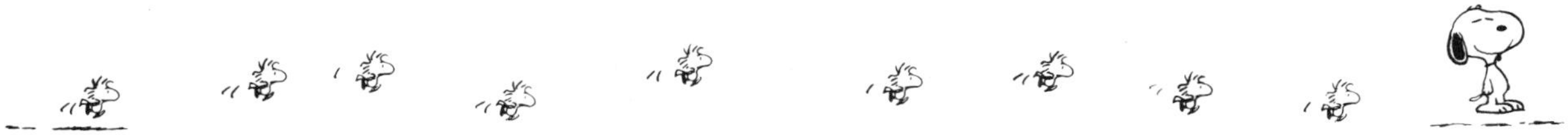

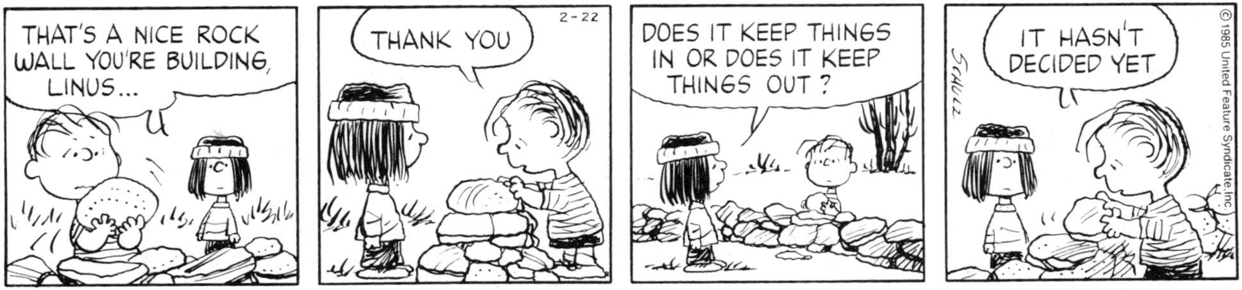
THAT'S A NICE ROCK WALL YOU'RE BUILDING, LINUS...
THANK YOU
2-22
DOES IT KEEP THINGS IN OR DOES IT KEEP THINGS OUT?
SCHULZ
IT HASN'T DECIDED YET
© 1985 United Feature Syndicate, Inc.

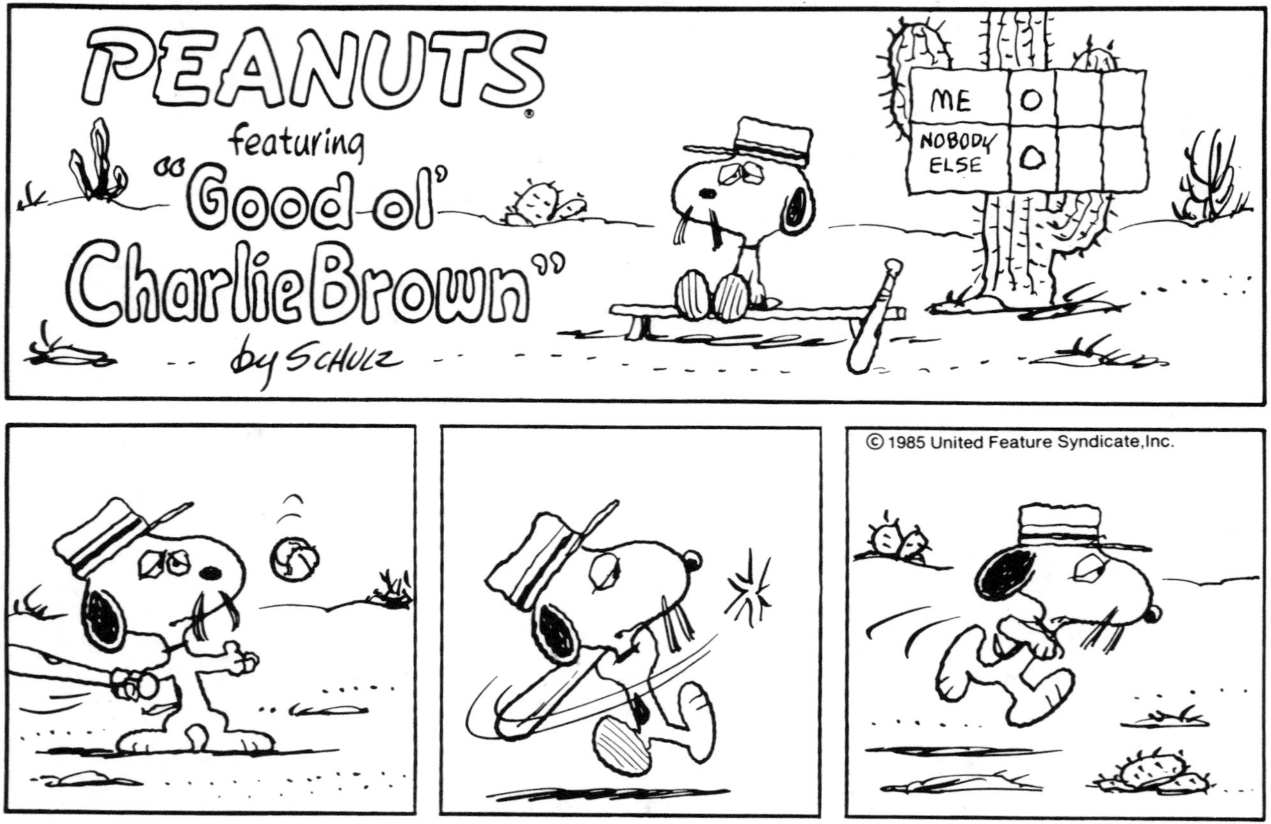
PEANUTS
featuring
"Good ol' Charlie Brown"
by SCHULZ
ME O
NOBODY ELSE O
© 1985 United Feature Syndicate, Inc.

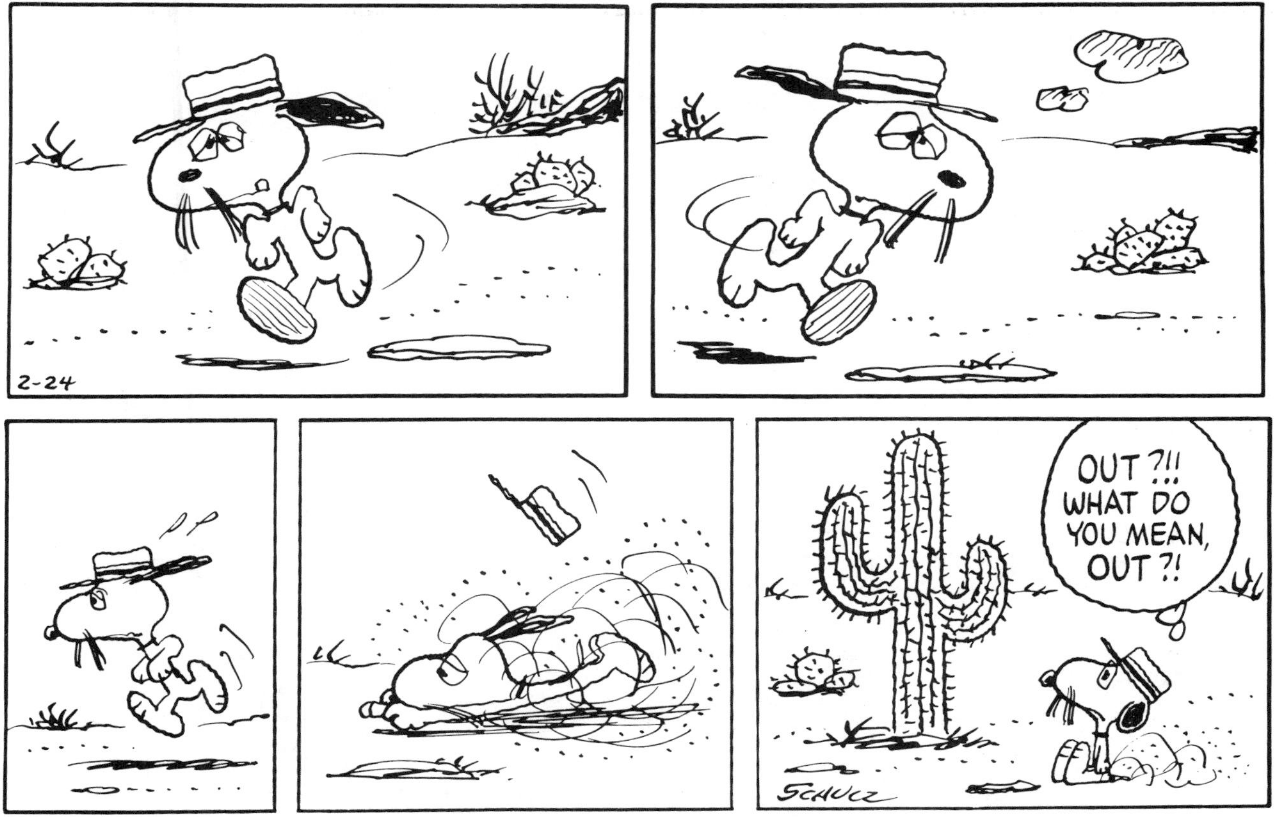
2-24
OUT ?!! WHAT DO YOU MEAN, OUT ?!
SCHULZ

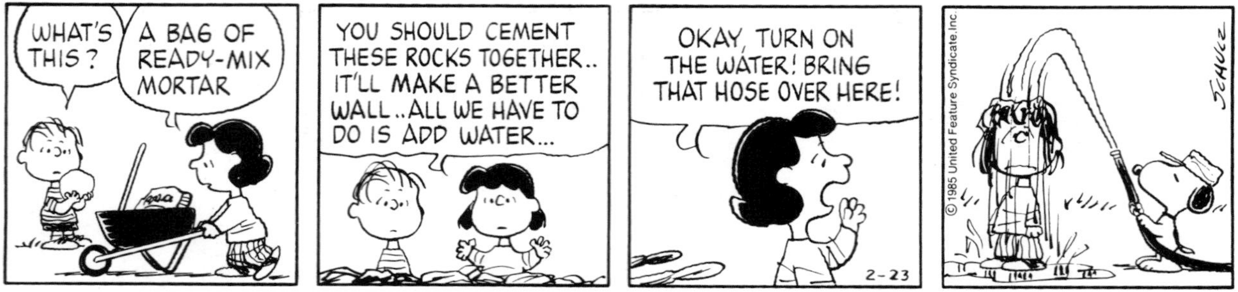
WHAT'S THIS ?
A BAG OF READY-MIX MORTAR
YOU SHOULD CEMENT THESE ROCKS TOGETHER.. IT'LL MAKE A BETTER WALL..ALL WE HAVE TO DO IS ADD WATER...
OKAY, TURN ON THE WATER! BRING THAT HOSE OVER HERE!
2-23
© 1985 United Feature Syndicate, Inc.
SCHULZ

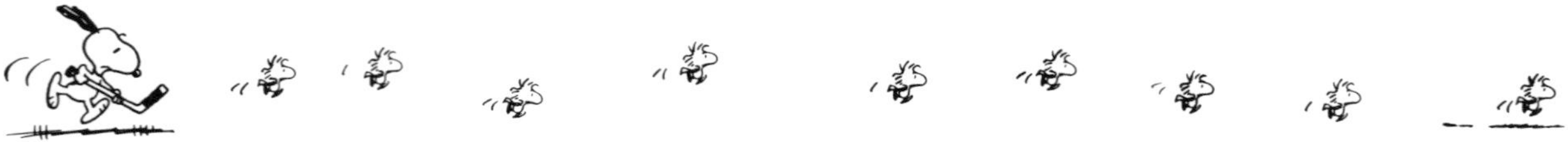

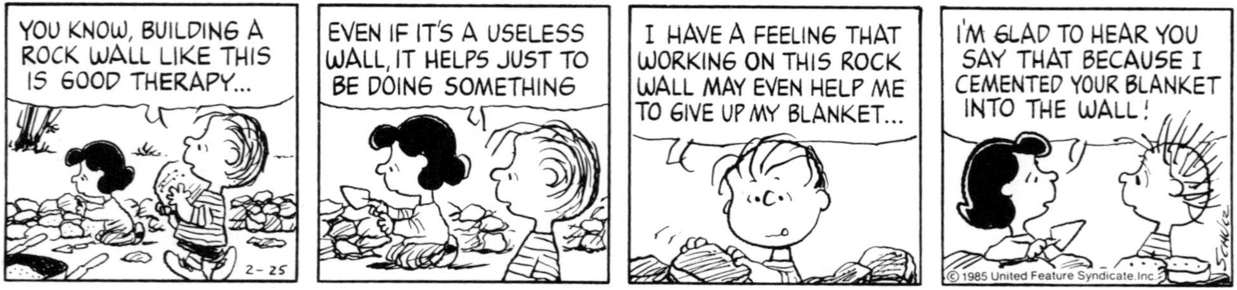
YOU KNOW, BUILDING A ROCK WALL LIKE THIS IS GOOD THERAPY...
2-25
EVEN IF IT'S A USELESS WALL, IT HELPS JUST TO BE DOING SOMETHING
I HAVE A FEELING THAT WORKING ON THIS ROCK WALL MAY EVEN HELP ME TO GIVE UP MY BLANKET...
I'M GLAD TO HEAR YOU SAY THAT BECAUSE I CEMENTED YOUR BLANKET INTO THE WALL!
© 1985 United Feature Syndicate, Inc.
SCHULZ

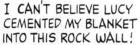 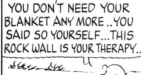 

Panel 1: I CAN'T BELIEVE LUCY CEMENTED MY BLANKET INTO THIS ROCK WALL!

Panel 2: YOU DON'T NEED YOUR BLANKET ANY MORE..YOU SAID SO YOURSELF...THIS ROCK WALL IS YOUR THERAPY..

2-26 © 1985 United Feature Syndicate, Inc.

Panel 3: EVERY TIME YOU HAVE A LITTLE STRESS IN YOUR LIFE, YOU CAN COME OUT HERE AND ADD A FEW ROCKS TO YOUR WALL...

Panel 4: THERE AREN'T THAT MANY ROCKS IN THE WORLD!!

Panel 5: I WAS ONLY KIDDING... I REALLY DIDN'T CEMENT YOUR BLANKET INTO THE ROCK WALL...

Panel 6: I DID GIVE HALF OF IT TO THE KID NEXT DOOR, HOWEVER... HE NEEDED IT..

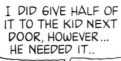 

Panel 7: YOU GAVE HALF OF MY BLANKET TO THE KID NEXT DOOR?!!

© 1985 United Feature Syndicate, Inc.

Panel 8: ONLY THE MIDDLE HALF!

2/27

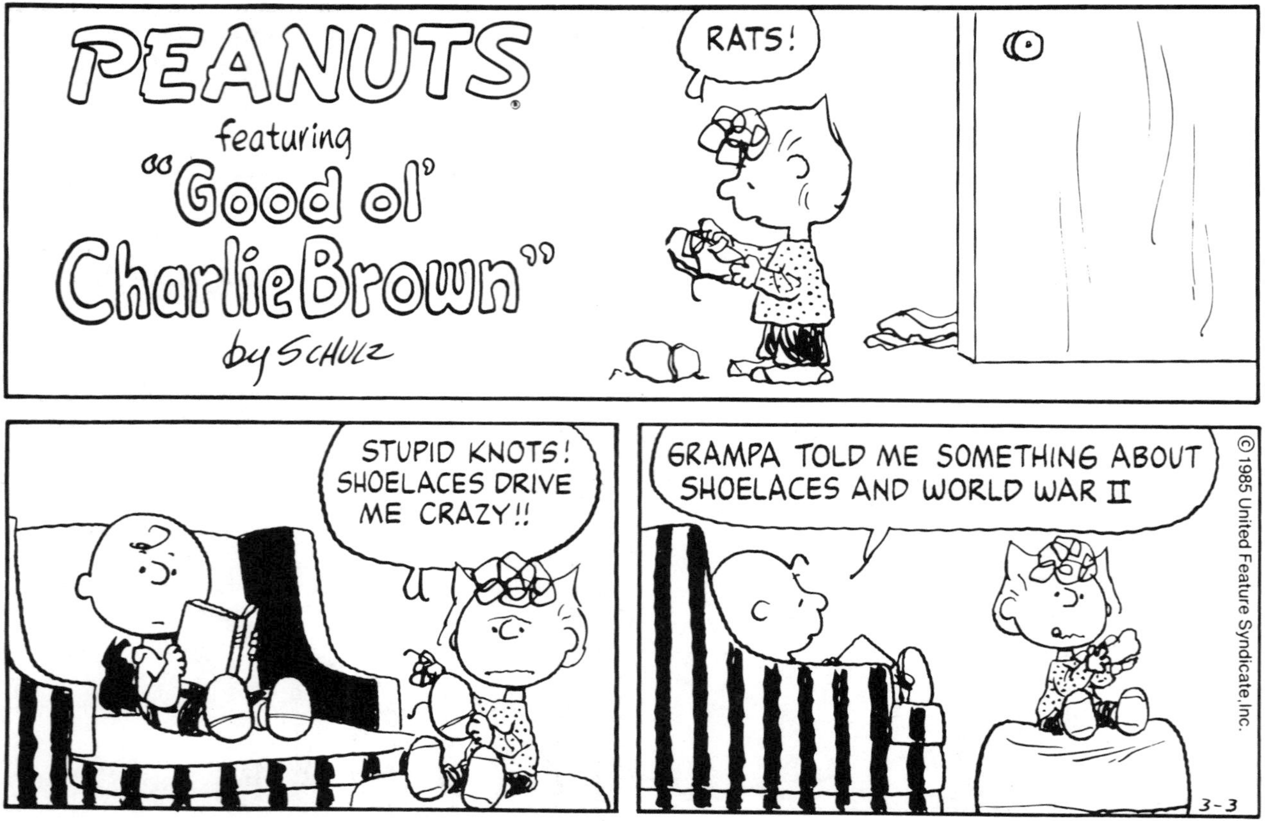
PEANUTS
featuring
"Good ol' Charlie Brown"
by SCHULZ
RATS!
STUPID KNOTS! SHOELACES DRIVE ME CRAZY!!
GRAMPA TOLD ME SOMETHING ABOUT SHOELACES AND WORLD WAR II
© 1985 United Feature Syndicate, Inc.
3-3

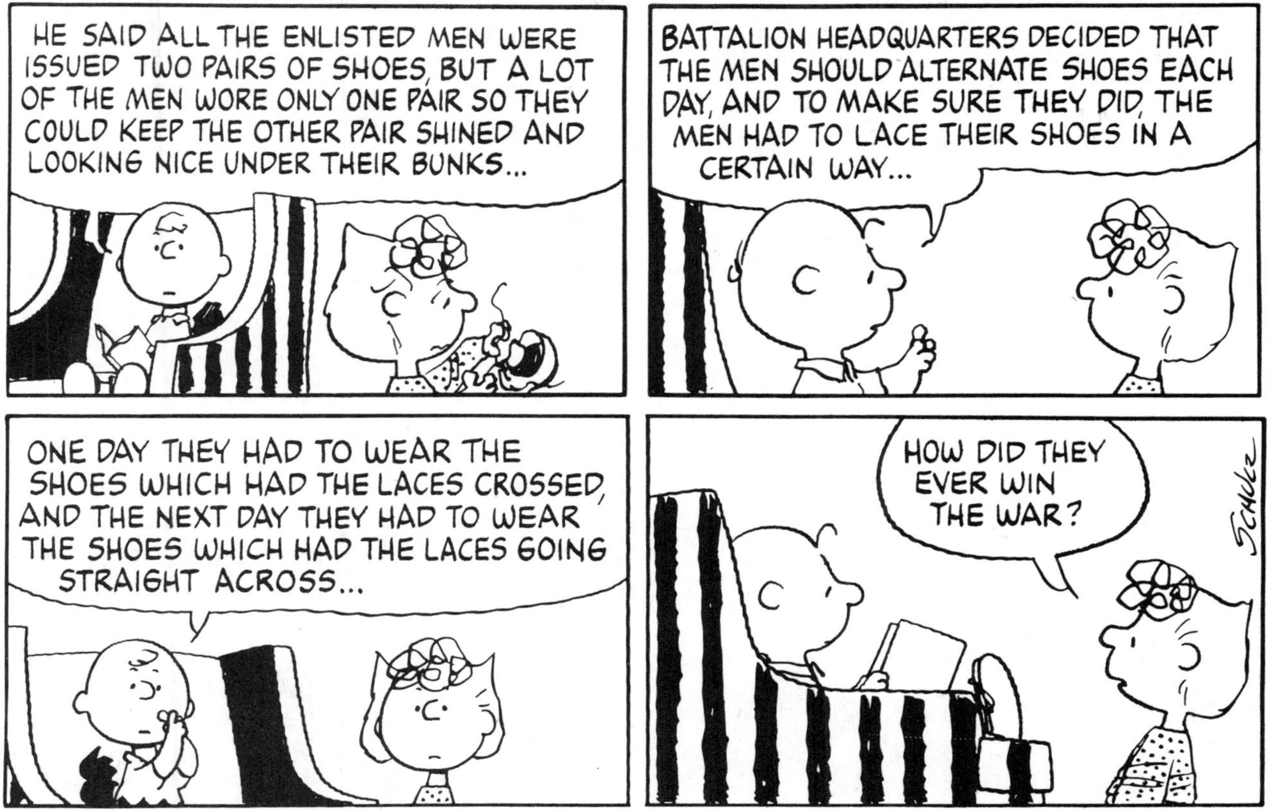
HE SAID ALL THE ENLISTED MEN WERE ISSUED TWO PAIRS OF SHOES, BUT A LOT OF THE MEN WORE ONLY ONE PAIR SO THEY COULD KEEP THE OTHER PAIR SHINED AND LOOKING NICE UNDER THEIR BUNKS...
BATTALION HEADQUARTERS DECIDED THAT THE MEN SHOULD ALTERNATE SHOES EACH DAY, AND TO MAKE SURE THEY DID, THE MEN HAD TO LACE THEIR SHOES IN A CERTAIN WAY...
ONE DAY THEY HAD TO WEAR THE SHOES WHICH HAD THE LACES CROSSED, AND THE NEXT DAY THEY HAD TO WEAR THE SHOES WHICH HAD THE LACES GOING STRAIGHT ACROSS...
HOW DID THEY EVER WIN THE WAR?
SCHULZ

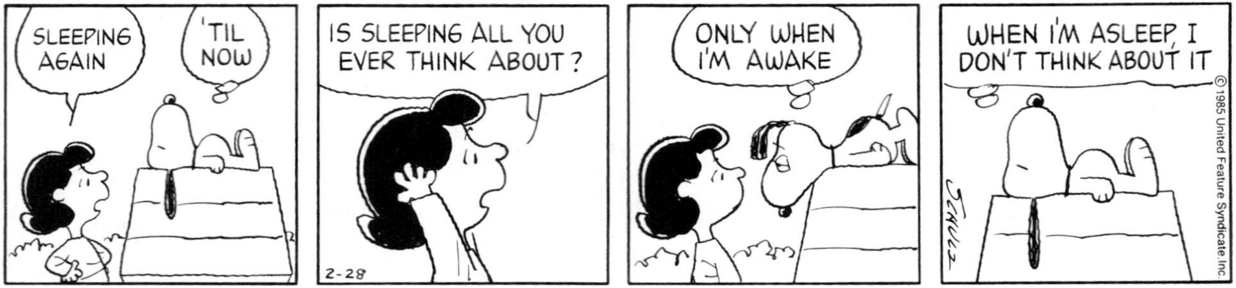
SLEEPING AGAIN
'TIL NOW
IS SLEEPING ALL YOU EVER THINK ABOUT ?
2-28
ONLY WHEN I'M AWAKE
WHEN I'M ASLEEP, I DON'T THINK ABOUT IT
© 1985 United Feature Syndicate, Inc.
SCHULZ

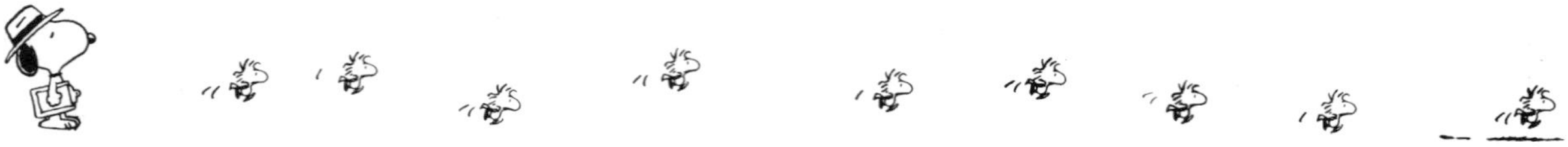

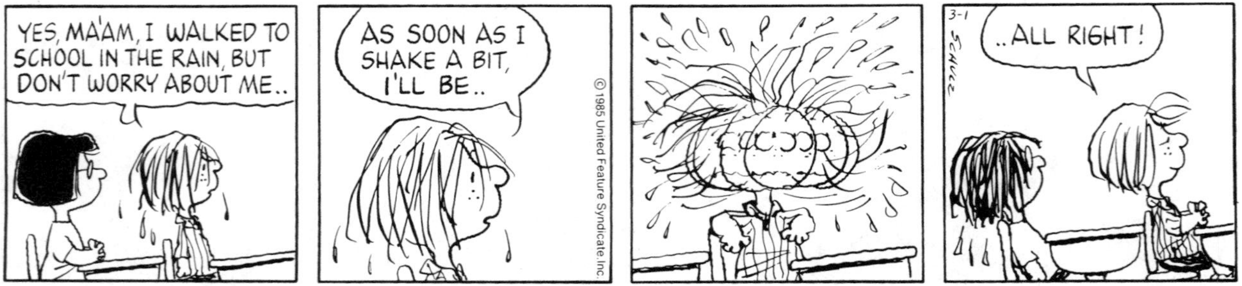
YES, MA'AM, I WALKED TO SCHOOL IN THE RAIN, BUT DON'T WORRY ABOUT ME..
AS SOON AS I SHAKE A BIT, I'LL BE..
© 1985 United Feature Syndicate, Inc.
3-1
SCHULZ
..ALL RIGHT!

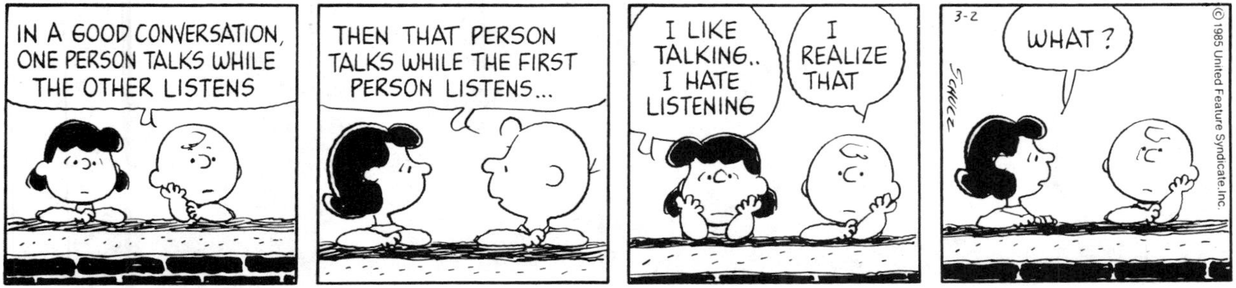
IN A GOOD CONVERSATION, ONE PERSON TALKS WHILE THE OTHER LISTENS
THEN THAT PERSON TALKS WHILE THE FIRST PERSON LISTENS...
I LIKE TALKING.. I HATE LISTENING
I REALIZE THAT
3-2
SCHULZ
WHAT ?
© 1985 United Feature Syndicate, Inc.

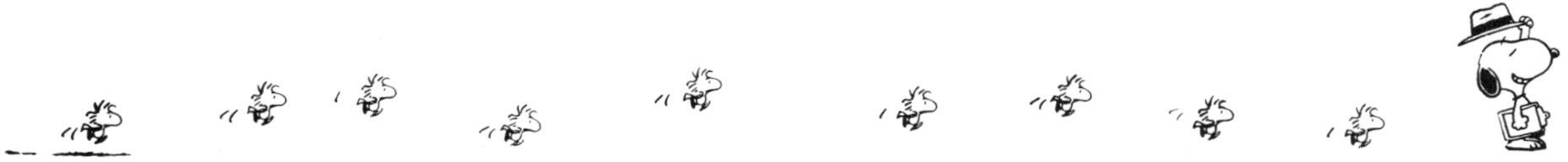

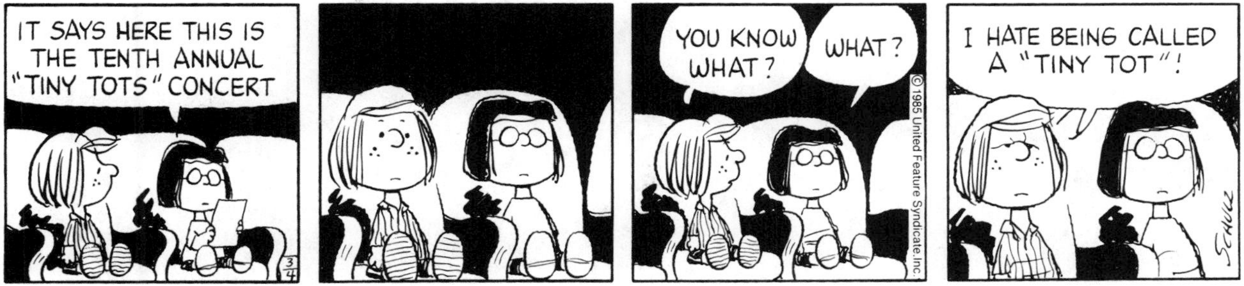
IT SAYS HERE THIS IS THE TENTH ANNUAL "TINY TOTS" CONCERT
3-4
YOU KNOW WHAT ?
WHAT ?
© 1985 United Feature Syndicate, Inc.
I HATE BEING CALLED A "TINY TOT"!
SCHULZ

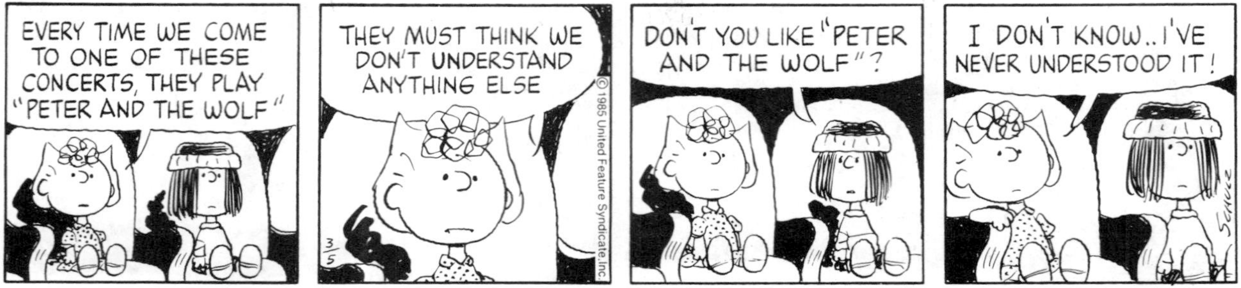
EVERY TIME WE COME TO ONE OF THESE CONCERTS, THEY PLAY "PETER AND THE WOLF"
THEY MUST THINK WE DON'T UNDERSTAND ANYTHING ELSE
3/5
© 1985 United Feature Syndicate, Inc.
DON'T YOU LIKE "PETER AND THE WOLF"?
I DON'T KNOW.. I'VE NEVER UNDERSTOOD IT!
SCHULZ

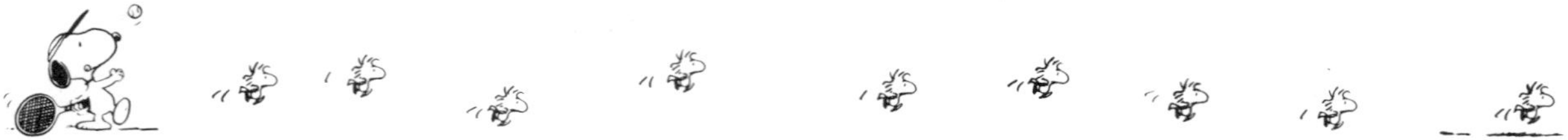

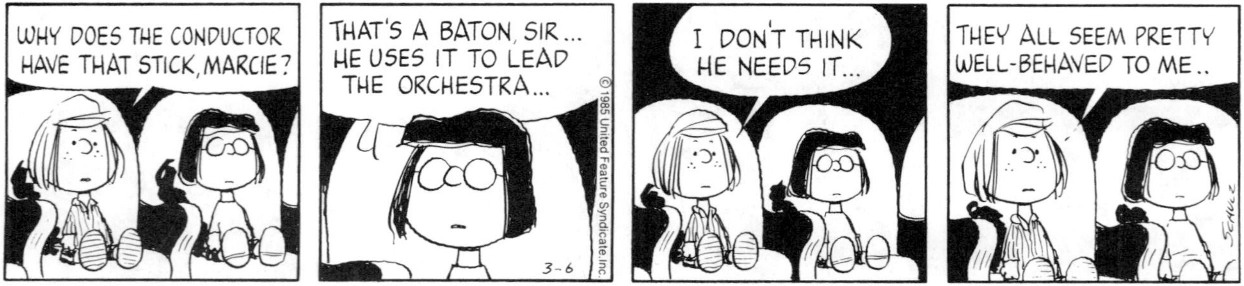
WHY DOES THE CONDUCTOR HAVE THAT STICK, MARCIE?
THAT'S A BATON, SIR... HE USES IT TO LEAD THE ORCHESTRA...
3-6
© 1985 United Feature Syndicate, Inc.
I DON'T THINK HE NEEDS IT...
THEY ALL SEEM PRETTY WELL-BEHAVED TO ME..
SCHULZ

Panel 1:
THAT WAS BEAUTIFUL, WASN'T IT?
IT WAS GREAT, SIR!

Panel 2:
A STANDING OVATION...

Panel 3:
WHOOP!!!

Panel 4:
EVERY PLACE WE GO, MARCIE, YOU EMBARRASS ME!

© 1985 United Feature Syndicate Inc
3-7

Panel 5:
THEY TOOK OUR CLASS TO A "TINY TOTS" CONCERT TODAY..IT WAS IN A BIG AUDITORIUM DOWNTOWN

Panel 6:
THE AUDITORIUM HAD LONG AISLES WITH A RED CARPET...

Panel 7:
WHAT WAS YOUR FAVORITE PART OF THE CONCERT?

Panel 8:
WALKING ON THE RED CARPET!

© 1985 United Feature Syndicate Inc
3-8

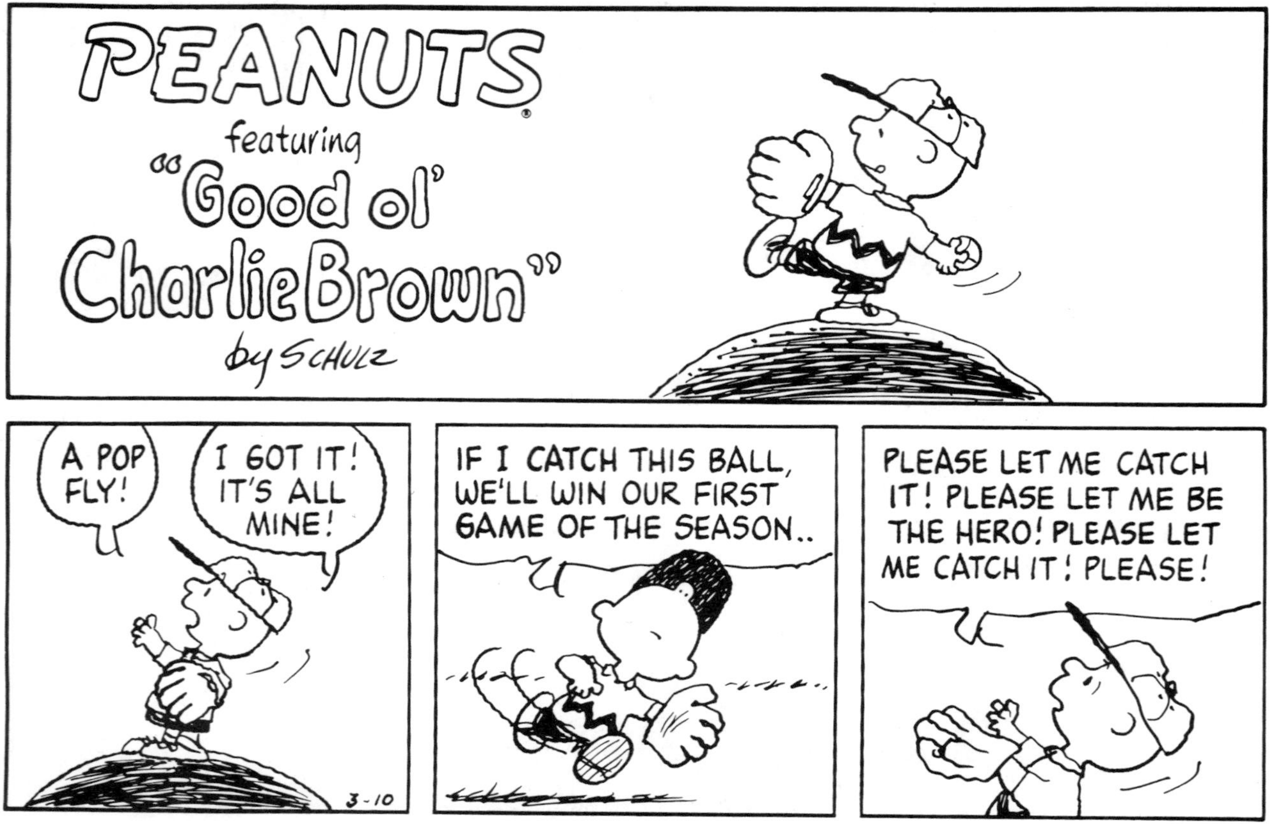
PEANUTS
featuring
"Good ol' Charlie Brown"
by SCHULZ
A POP FLY!
I GOT IT! IT'S ALL MINE!
3-10
IF I CATCH THIS BALL, WE'LL WIN OUR FIRST GAME OF THE SEASON..
PLEASE LET ME CATCH IT! PLEASE LET ME BE THE HERO! PLEASE LET ME CATCH IT! PLEASE!

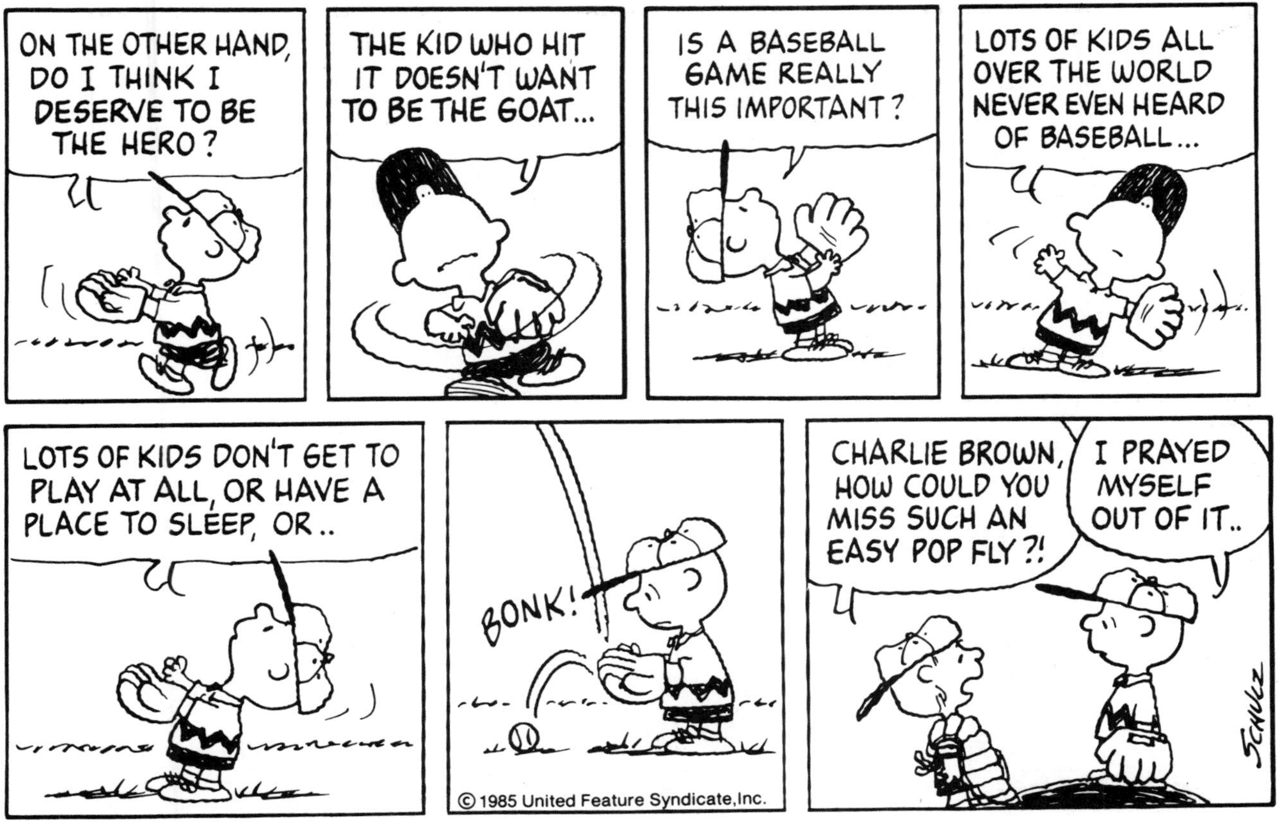
ON THE OTHER HAND, DO I THINK I DESERVE TO BE THE HERO?
THE KID WHO HIT IT DOESN'T WANT TO BE THE GOAT...
IS A BASEBALL GAME REALLY THIS IMPORTANT?
LOTS OF KIDS ALL OVER THE WORLD NEVER EVEN HEARD OF BASEBALL...
LOTS OF KIDS DON'T GET TO PLAY AT ALL, OR HAVE A PLACE TO SLEEP, OR..
BONK!
CHARLIE BROWN, HOW COULD YOU MISS SUCH AN EASY POP FLY?!
I PRAYED MYSELF OUT OF IT..
SCHULZ

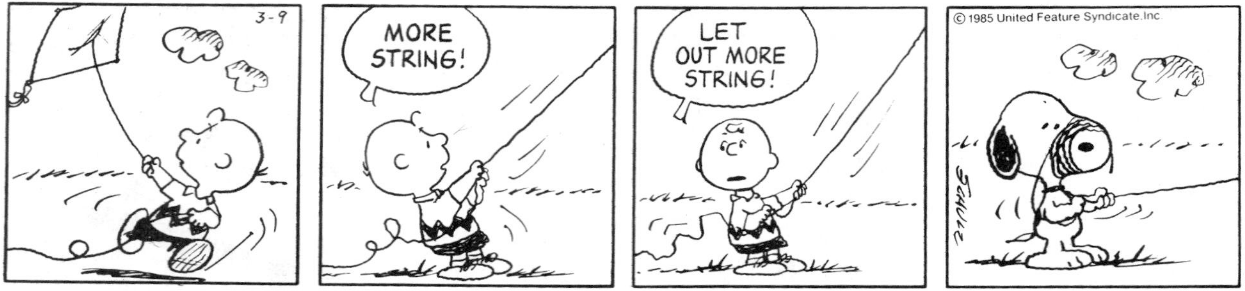
3-9
MORE STRING!
LET OUT MORE STRING!
© 1985 United Feature Syndicate, Inc
SCHULZ

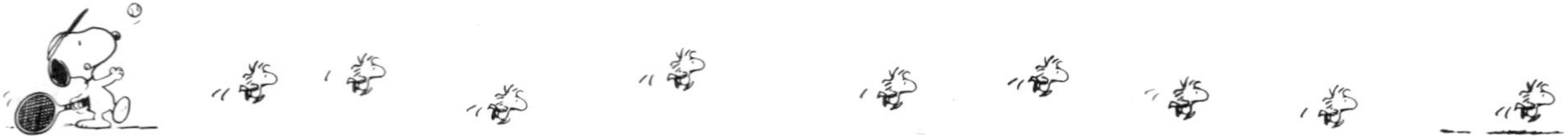

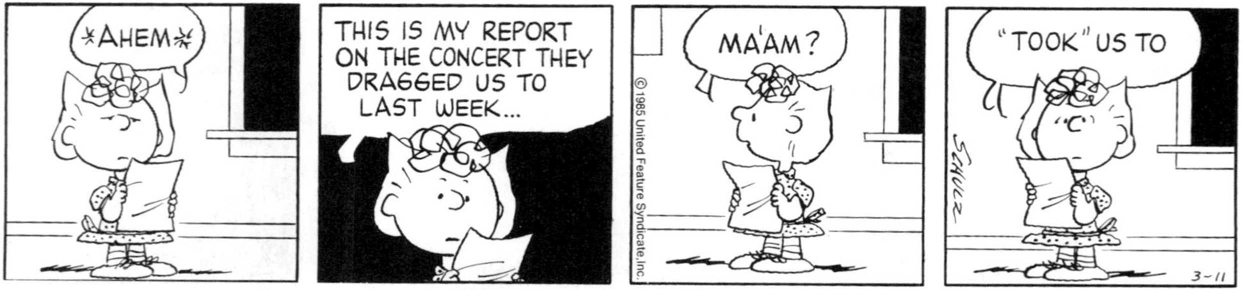
AHEM
THIS IS MY REPORT ON THE CONCERT THEY DRAGGED US TO LAST WEEK...
© 1985 United Feature Syndicate, Inc.
MA'AM?
SCHULZ
"TOOK" US TO
3-11

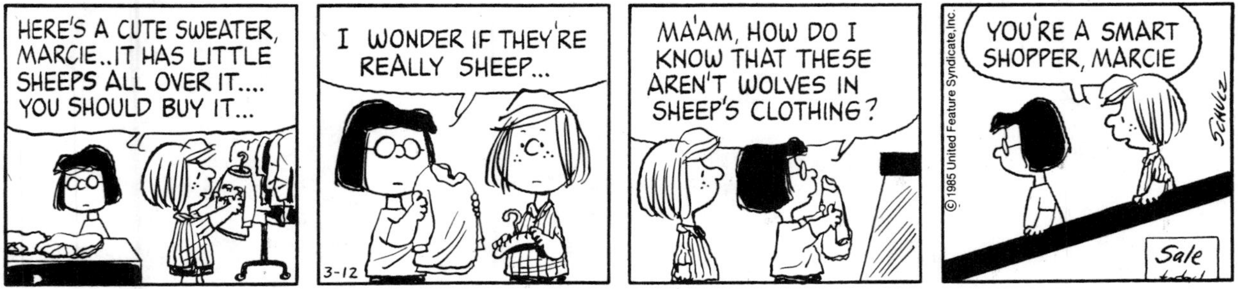
HERE'S A CUTE SWEATER, MARCIE..IT HAS LITTLE SHEEPS ALL OVER IT.... YOU SHOULD BUY IT...
I WONDER IF THEY'RE REALLY SHEEP...
3-12
MA'AM, HOW DO I KNOW THAT THESE AREN'T WOLVES IN SHEEP'S CLOTHING?
YOU'RE A SMART SHOPPER, MARCIE
© 1985 United Feature Syndicate, Inc.
SCHULZ
Sale

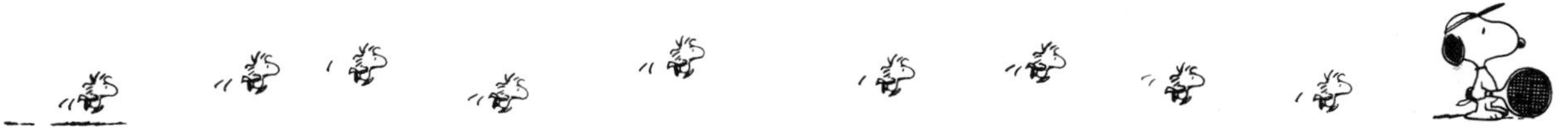

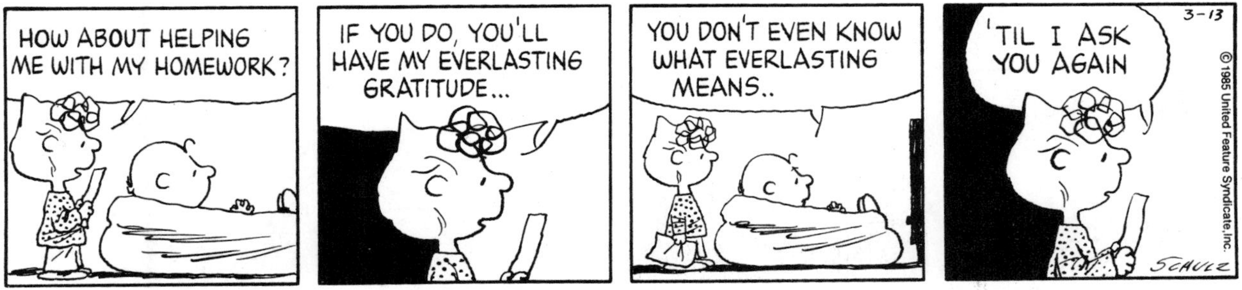
HOW ABOUT HELPING ME WITH MY HOMEWORK?
IF YOU DO, YOU'LL HAVE MY EVERLASTING GRATITUDE...
YOU DON'T EVEN KNOW WHAT EVERLASTING MEANS..
'TIL I ASK YOU AGAIN
3-13
© 1985 United Feature Syndicate, Inc.
SCHULZ

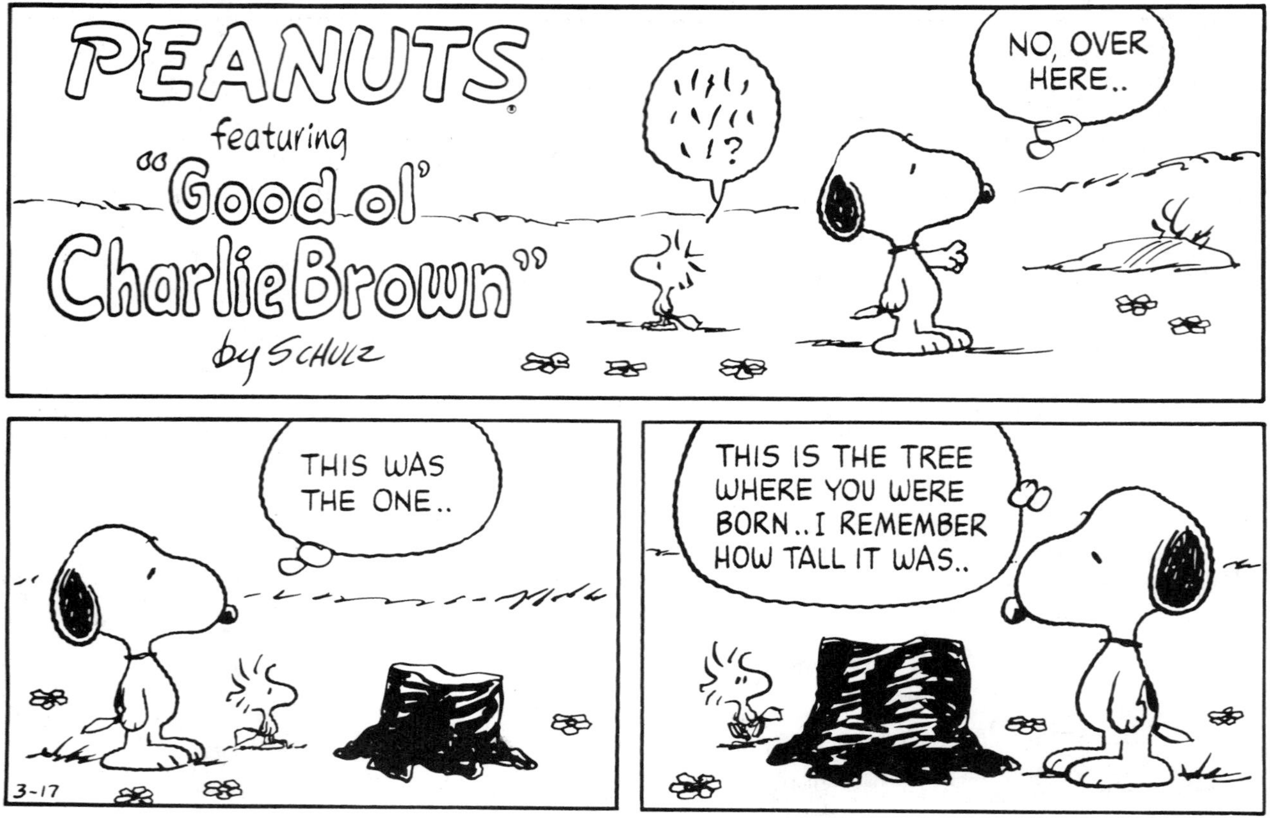
PEANUTS
featuring
"Good ol' Charlie Brown"
by SCHULZ
?
NO, OVER HERE..
THIS WAS THE ONE..
3-17
THIS IS THE TREE WHERE YOU WERE BORN..I REMEMBER HOW TALL IT WAS..

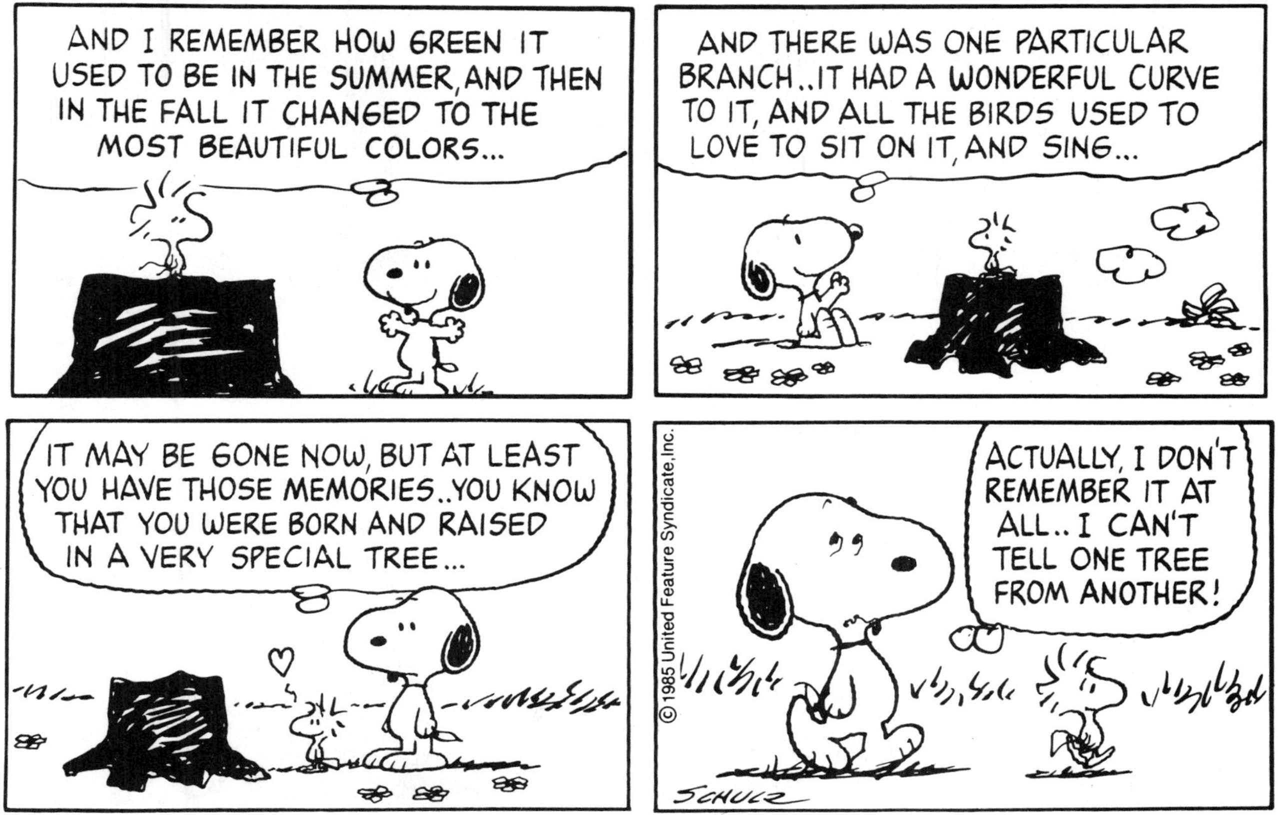
AND I REMEMBER HOW GREEN IT USED TO BE IN THE SUMMER, AND THEN IN THE FALL IT CHANGED TO THE MOST BEAUTIFUL COLORS...
AND THERE WAS ONE PARTICULAR BRANCH..IT HAD A WONDERFUL CURVE TO IT, AND ALL THE BIRDS USED TO LOVE TO SIT ON IT, AND SING...
IT MAY BE GONE NOW, BUT AT LEAST YOU HAVE THOSE MEMORIES..YOU KNOW THAT YOU WERE BORN AND RAISED IN A VERY SPECIAL TREE...
ACTUALLY, I DON'T REMEMBER IT AT ALL.. I CAN'T TELL ONE TREE FROM ANOTHER!
© 1985 United Feature Syndicate, Inc.
SCHULZ

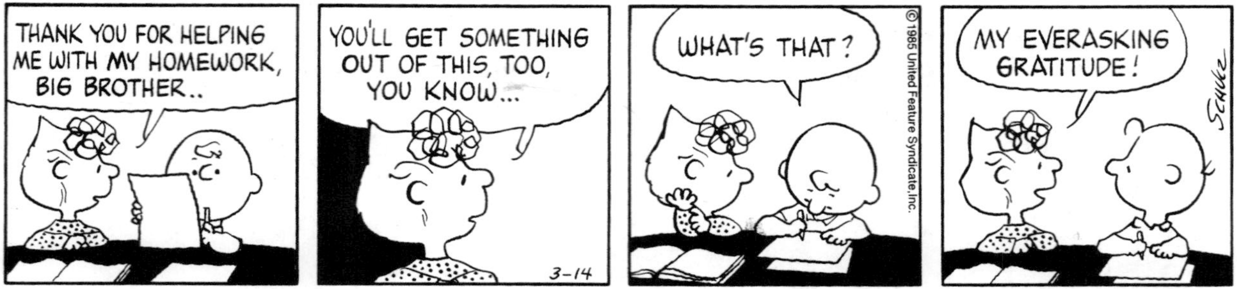
THANK YOU FOR HELPING ME WITH MY HOMEWORK, BIG BROTHER..
YOU'LL GET SOMETHING OUT OF THIS, TOO, YOU KNOW...
3-14
WHAT'S THAT ?
© 1985 United Feature Syndicate, Inc.
MY EVERASKING GRATITUDE !

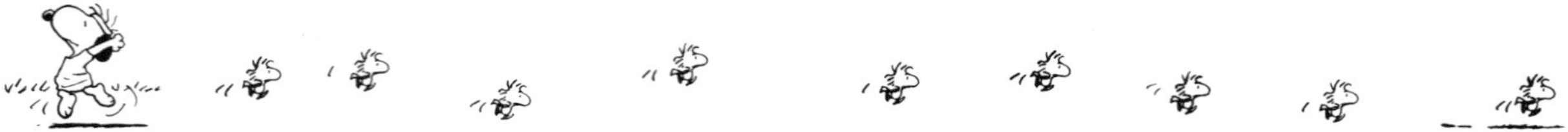

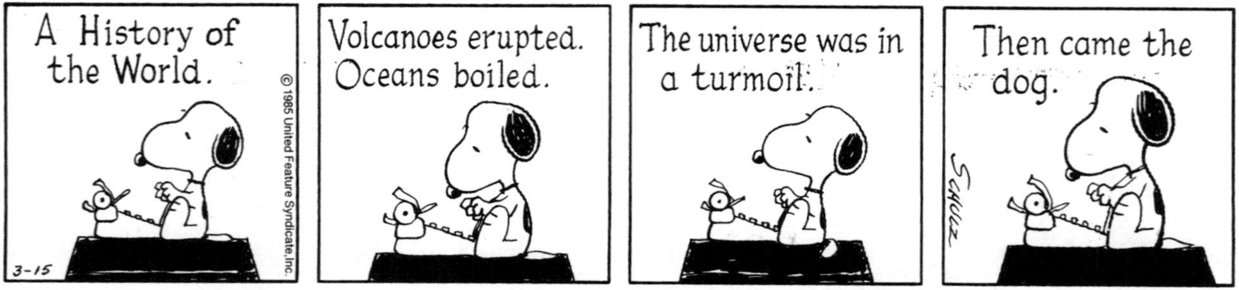
A History of the World.
3-15
© 1985 United Feature Syndicate, Inc.
Volcanoes erupted. Oceans boiled.
The universe was in a turmoil.
Then came the dog.

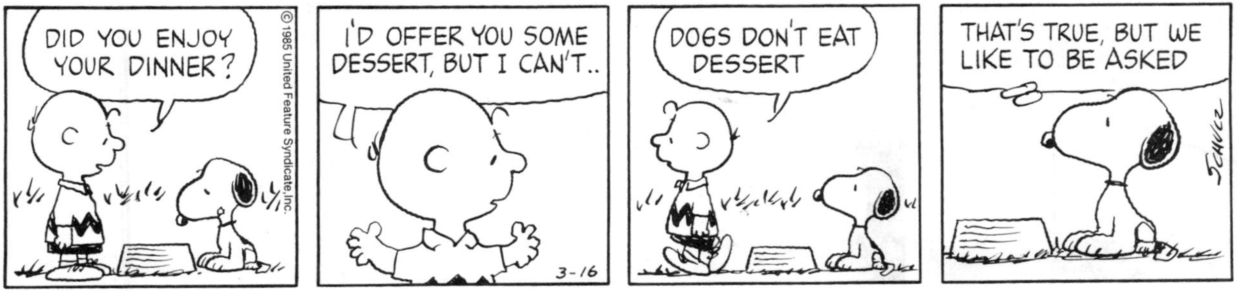
DID YOU ENJOY YOUR DINNER?
I'D OFFER YOU SOME DESSERT, BUT I CAN'T..
3-16
DOGS DON'T EAT DESSERT
THAT'S TRUE, BUT WE LIKE TO BE ASKED
SCHULZ

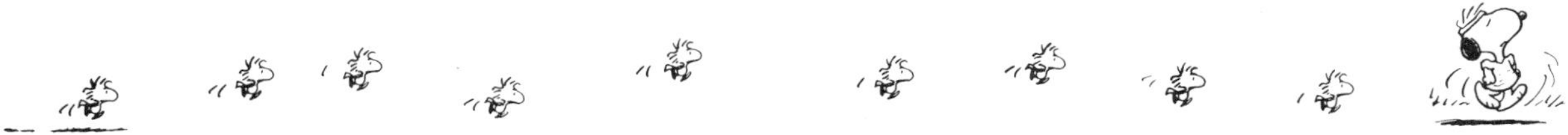

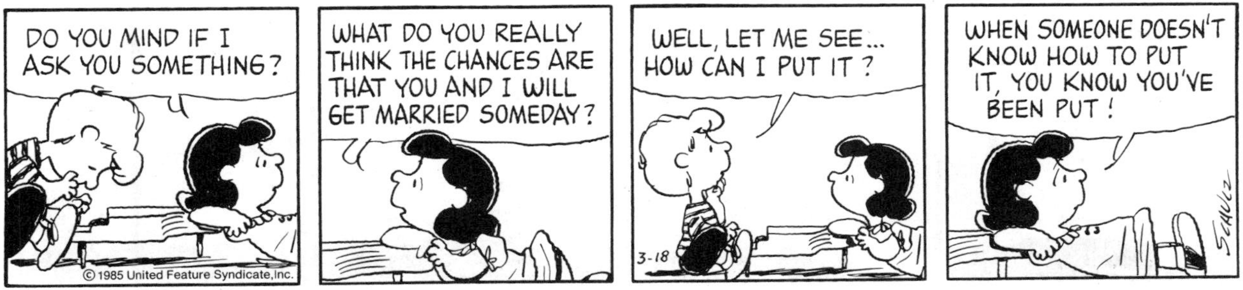
DO YOU MIND IF I ASK YOU SOMETHING?
WHAT DO YOU REALLY THINK THE CHANCES ARE THAT YOU AND I WILL GET MARRIED SOMEDAY?
WELL, LET ME SEE... HOW CAN I PUT IT?
3-18
WHEN SOMEONE DOESN'T KNOW HOW TO PUT IT, YOU KNOW YOU'VE BEEN PUT!
SCHULZ

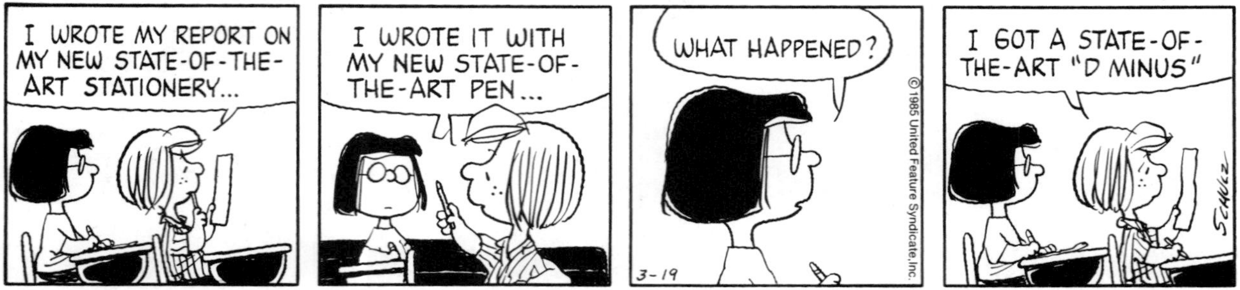
I WROTE MY REPORT ON MY NEW STATE-OF-THE-ART STATIONERY...
I WROTE IT WITH MY NEW STATE-OF-THE-ART PEN...
WHAT HAPPENED?
© 1985 United Feature Syndicate, Inc.
3-19
I GOT A STATE-OF-THE-ART "D MINUS"
SCHULZ

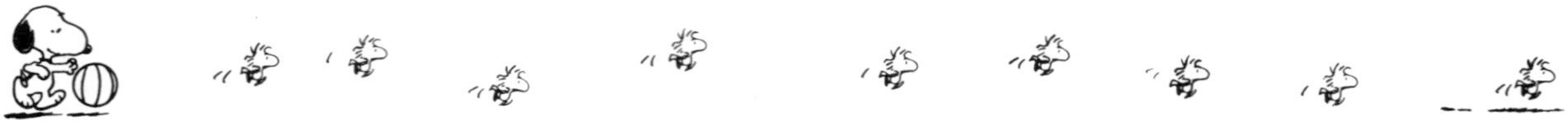

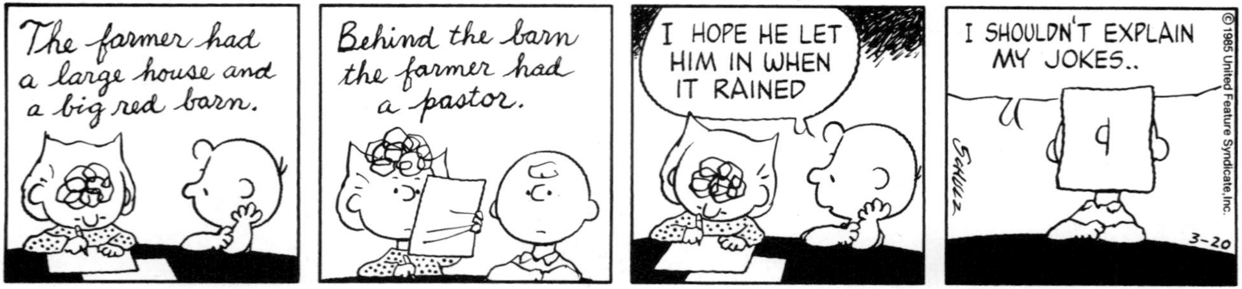
The farmer had a large house and a big red barn.
Behind the barn the farmer had a pastor.
I HOPE HE LET HIM IN WHEN IT RAINED
I SHOULDN'T EXPLAIN MY JOKES..
SCHULZ
© 1985 United Feature Syndicate, Inc.
3-20

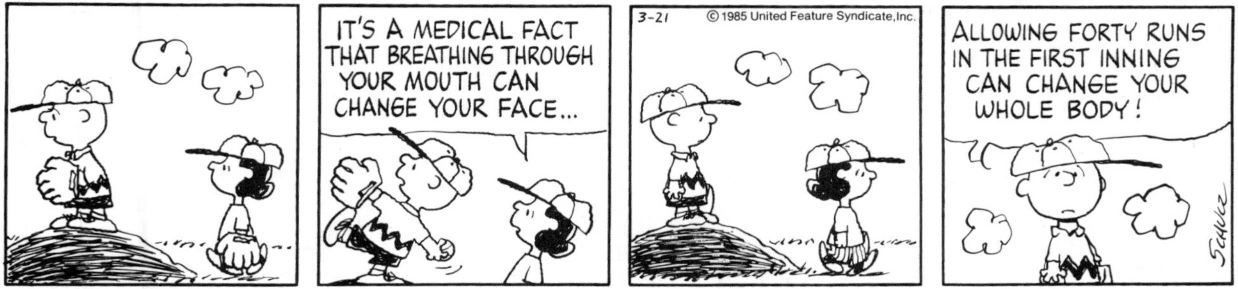
3-21
© 1985 United Feature Syndicate, Inc.
IT'S A MEDICAL FACT THAT BREATHING THROUGH YOUR MOUTH CAN CHANGE YOUR FACE...
ALLOWING FORTY RUNS IN THE FIRST INNING CAN CHANGE YOUR WHOLE BODY!
SCHULZ

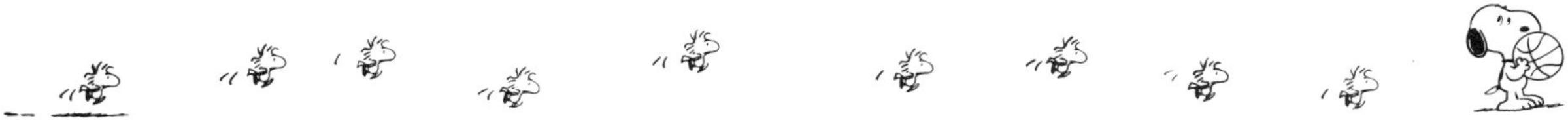

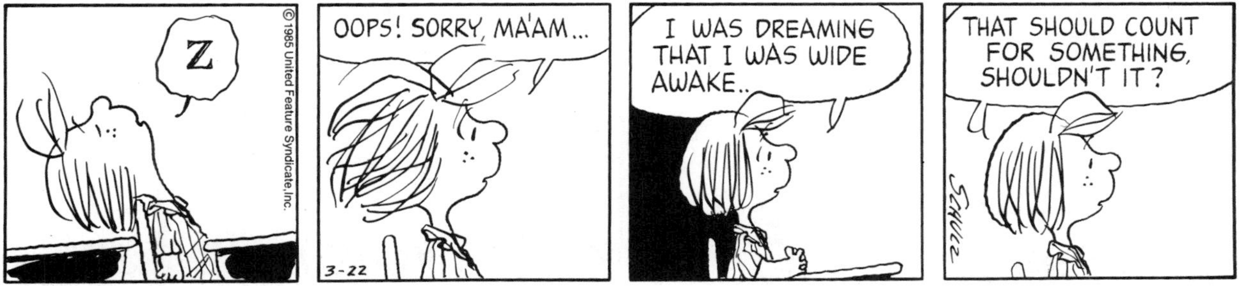
© 1985 United Feature Syndicate, Inc.
Z
OOPS! SORRY, MA'AM...
3-22
I WAS DREAMING THAT I WAS WIDE AWAKE..
THAT SHOULD COUNT FOR SOMETHING, SHOULDN'T IT?
SCHULZ

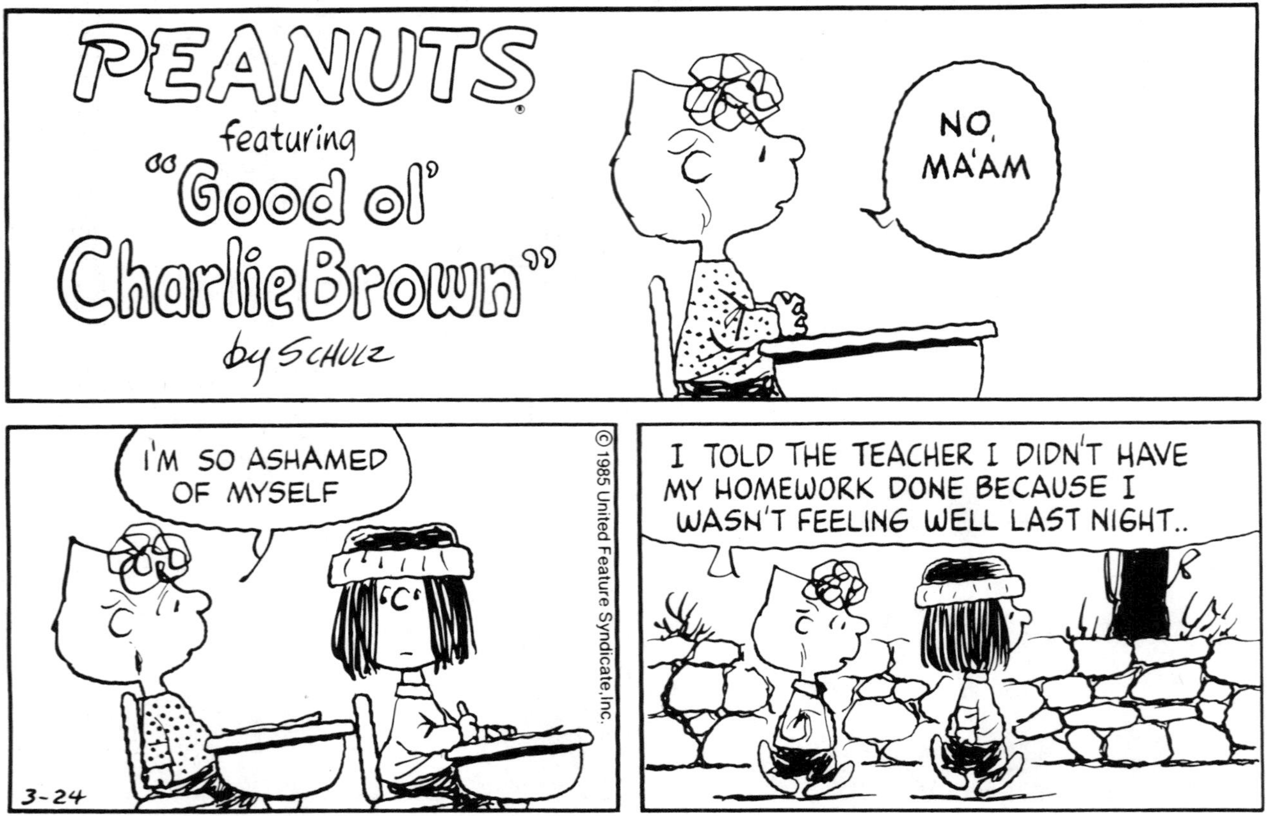
PEANUTS®
featuring
"Good ol' Charlie Brown"
by SCHULZ
NO, MA'AM
I'M SO ASHAMED OF MYSELF
© 1985 United Feature Syndicate, Inc.
3-24
I TOLD THE TEACHER I DIDN'T HAVE MY HOMEWORK DONE BECAUSE I WASN'T FEELING WELL LAST NIGHT..

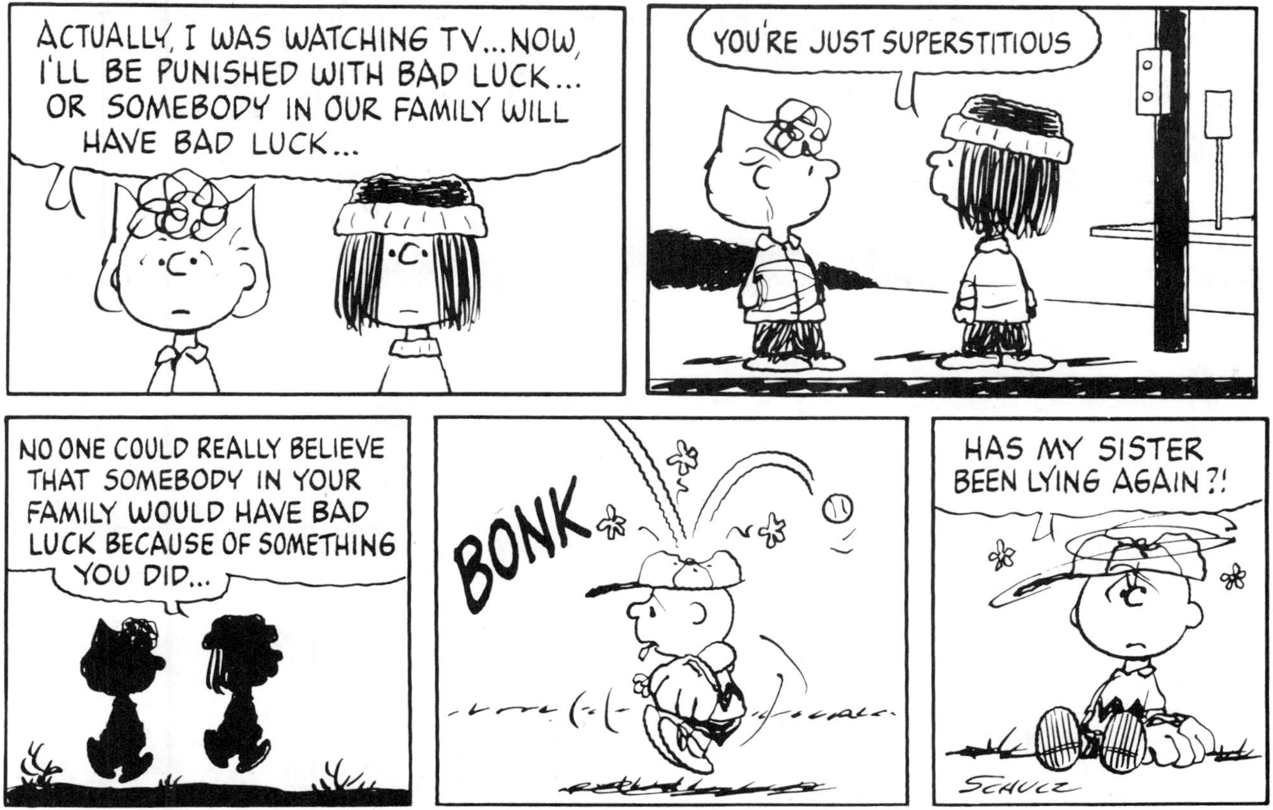
ACTUALLY, I WAS WATCHING TV...NOW, I'LL BE PUNISHED WITH BAD LUCK... OR SOMEBODY IN OUR FAMILY WILL HAVE BAD LUCK...
YOU'RE JUST SUPERSTITIOUS
NO ONE COULD REALLY BELIEVE THAT SOMEBODY IN YOUR FAMILY WOULD HAVE BAD LUCK BECAUSE OF SOMETHING YOU DID...
BONK
HAS MY SISTER BEEN LYING AGAIN?!
SCHULZ

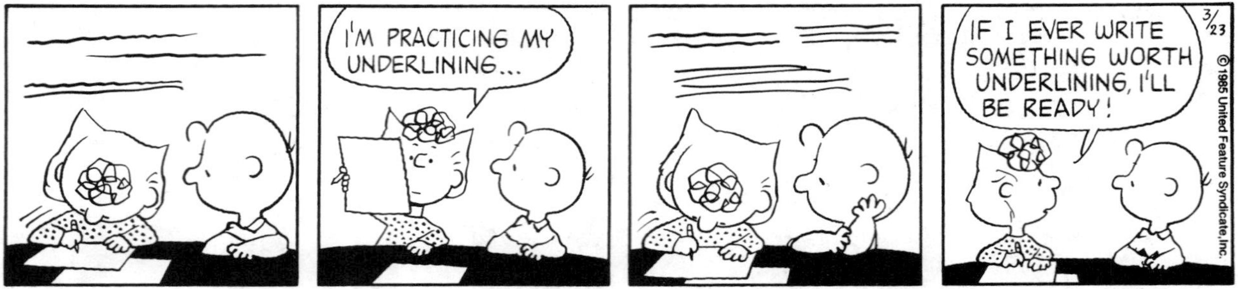
I'M PRACTICING MY UNDERLINING...
IF I EVER WRITE SOMETHING WORTH UNDERLINING, I'LL BE READY!
3/23
© 1985 United Feature Syndicate, Inc.

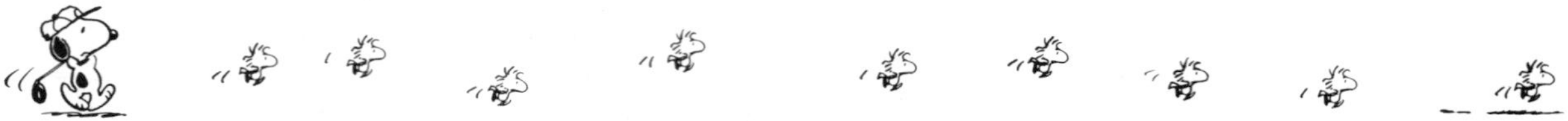

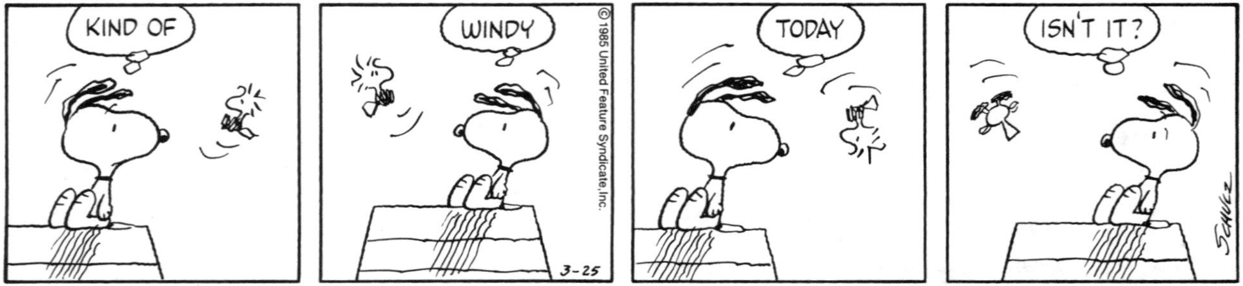
KIND OF
WINDY
TODAY
ISN'T IT?
© 1985 United Feature Syndicate, Inc.
3-25
SCHULZ

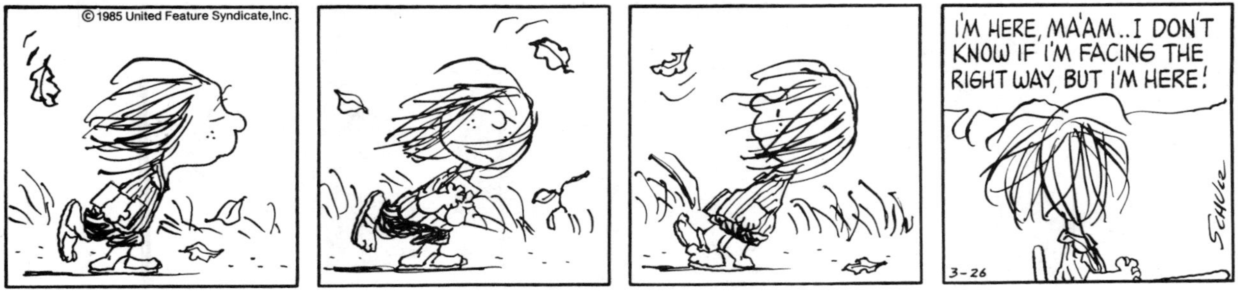
© 1985 United Feature Syndicate, Inc.
I'M HERE, MA'AM.. I DON'T KNOW IF I'M FACING THE RIGHT WAY, BUT I'M HERE!
SCHULZ
3-26

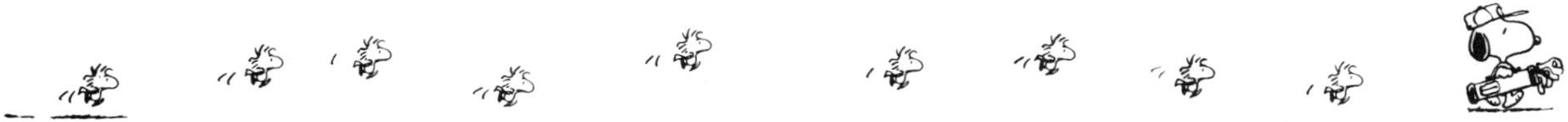

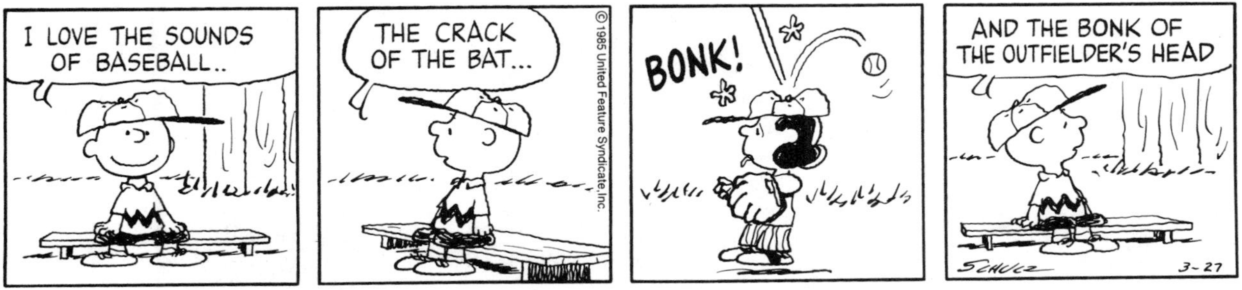
I LOVE THE SOUNDS OF BASEBALL..
THE CRACK OF THE BAT...
© 1985 United Feature Syndicate, Inc.
BONK!
AND THE BONK OF THE OUTFIELDER'S HEAD
SCHULZ
3-27

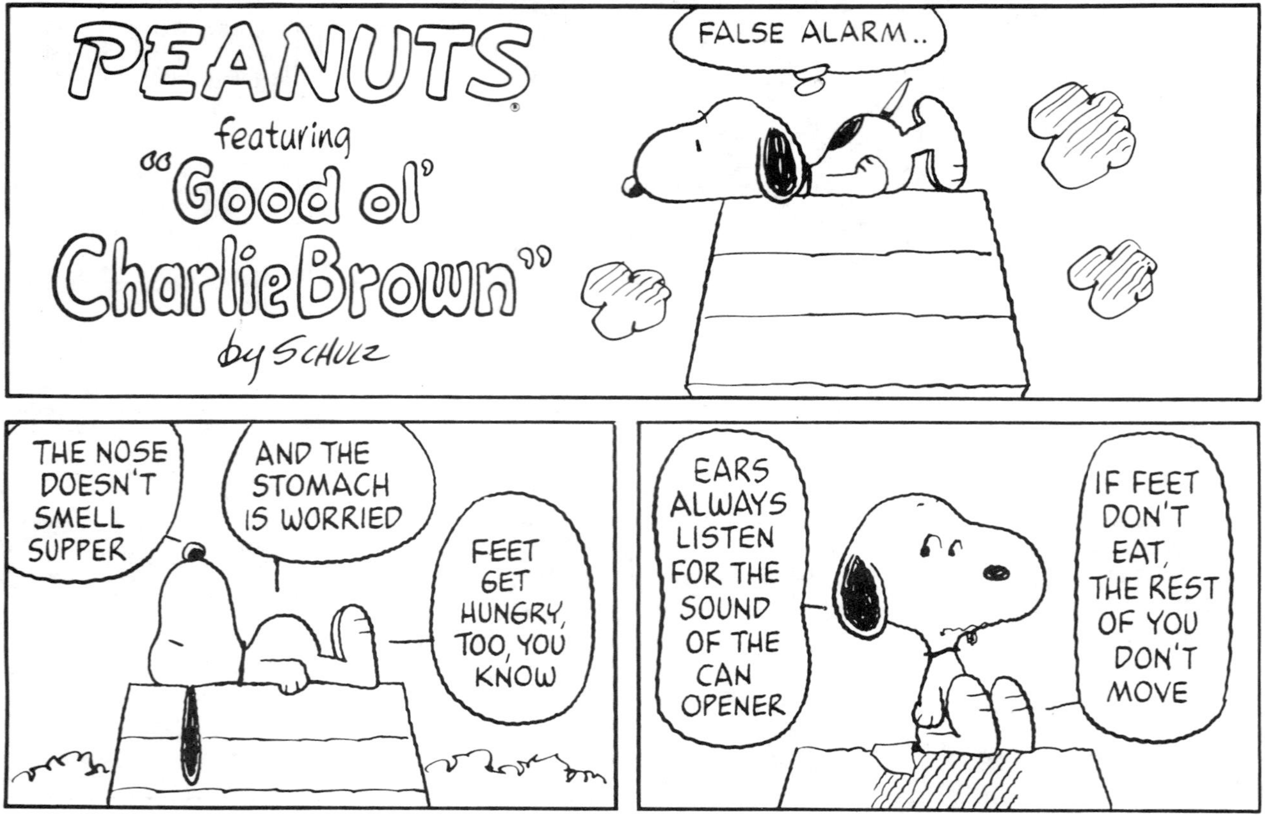

PEANUTS
featuring
"Good ol' Charlie Brown"
by SCHULZ
FALSE ALARM..
THE NOSE DOESN'T SMELL SUPPER
AND THE STOMACH IS WORRIED
FEET GET HUNGRY, TOO, YOU KNOW
EARS ALWAYS LISTEN FOR THE SOUND OF THE CAN OPENER
IF FEET DON'T EAT, THE REST OF YOU DON'T MOVE

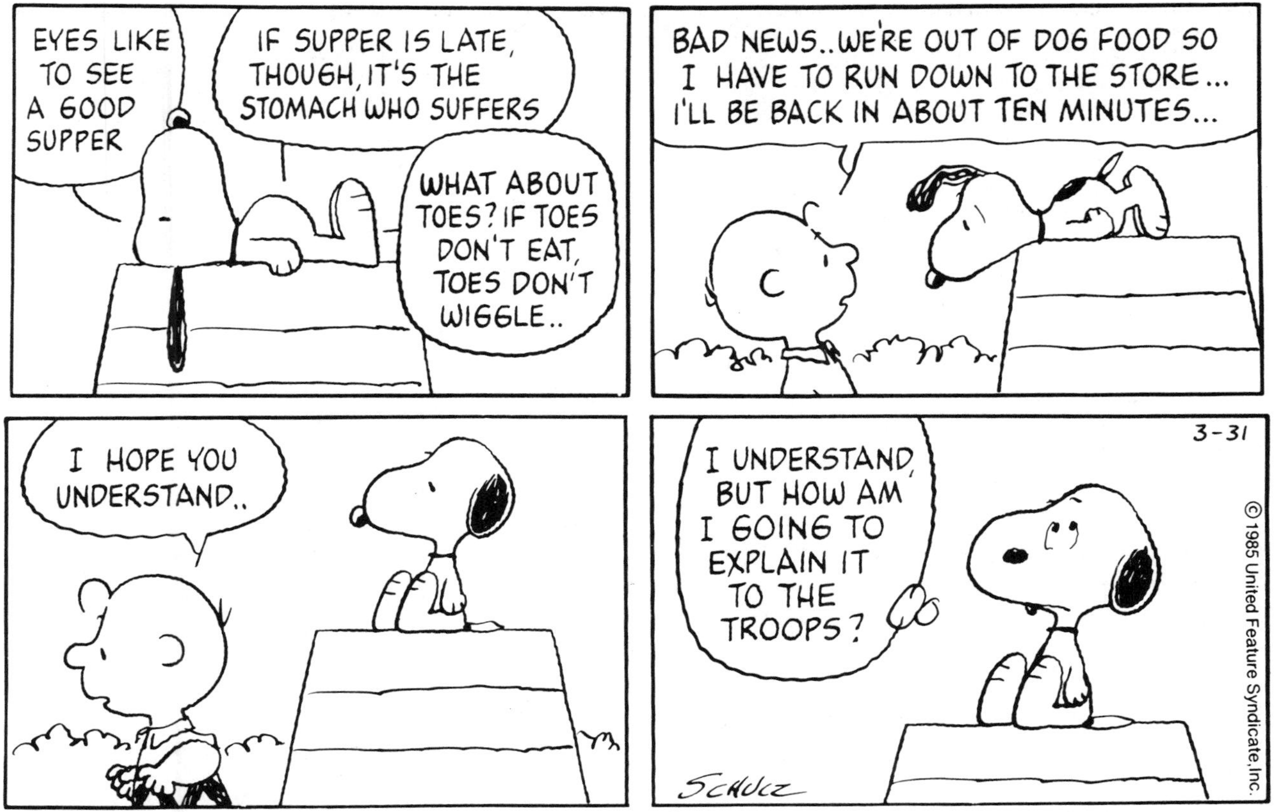
EYES LIKE TO SEE A GOOD SUPPER
IF SUPPER IS LATE, THOUGH, IT'S THE STOMACH WHO SUFFERS
WHAT ABOUT TOES? IF TOES DON'T EAT, TOES DON'T WIGGLE..
BAD NEWS..WE'RE OUT OF DOG FOOD SO I HAVE TO RUN DOWN TO THE STORE... I'LL BE BACK IN ABOUT TEN MINUTES...
I HOPE YOU UNDERSTAND..
3-31
I UNDERSTAND, BUT HOW AM I GOING TO EXPLAIN IT TO THE TROOPS?
SCHULZ
© 1985 United Feature Syndicate, Inc.

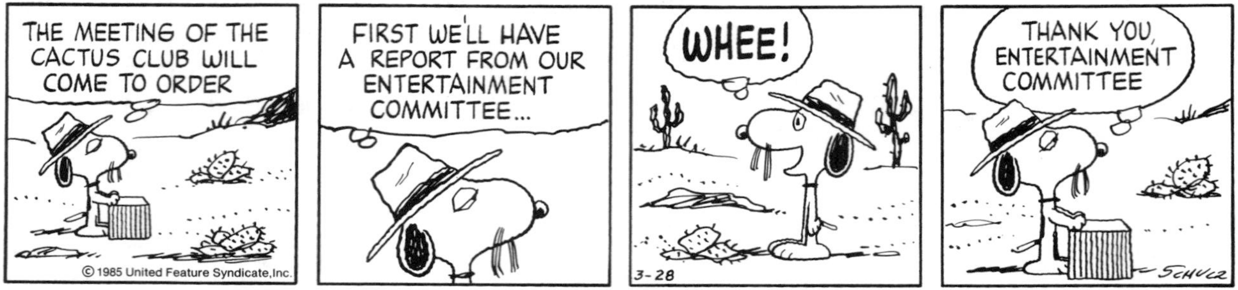
THE MEETING OF THE CACTUS CLUB WILL COME TO ORDER
© 1985 United Feature Syndicate, Inc.
FIRST WE'LL HAVE A REPORT FROM OUR ENTERTAINMENT COMMITTEE...
WHEE!
3-28
THANK YOU, ENTERTAINMENT COMMITTEE
SCHULZ

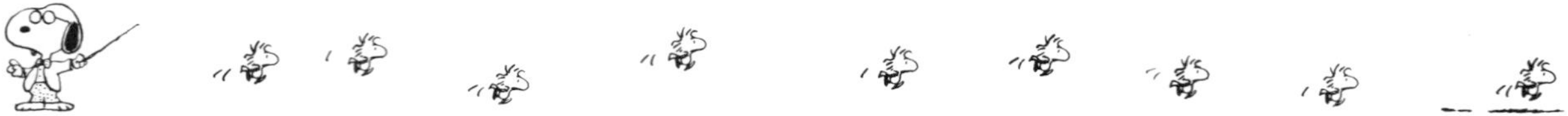

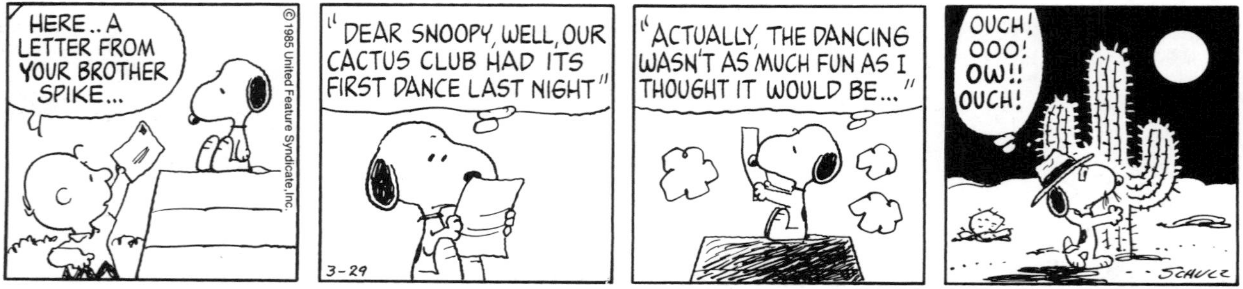
HERE.. A LETTER FROM YOUR BROTHER SPIKE...
© 1985 United Feature Syndicate, Inc.
"DEAR SNOOPY, WELL, OUR CACTUS CLUB HAD ITS FIRST DANCE LAST NIGHT"
3-29
"ACTUALLY, THE DANCING WASN'T AS MUCH FUN AS I THOUGHT IT WOULD BE..."
OUCH! OOO! OW!! OUCH!
SCHULZ

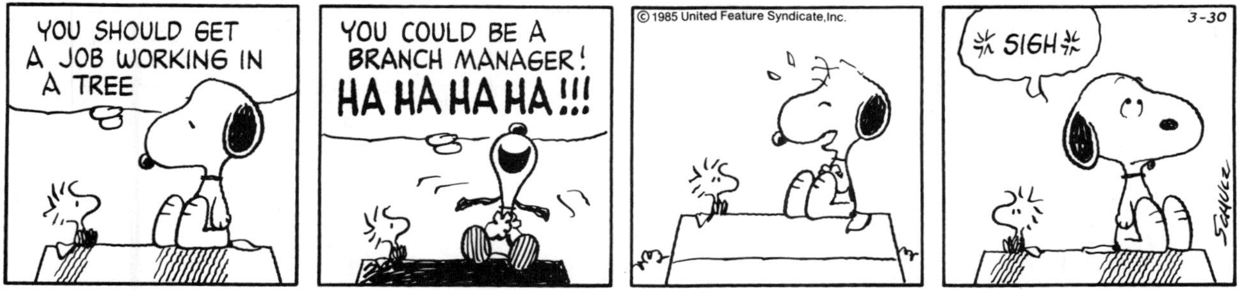
YOU SHOULD GET A JOB WORKING IN A TREE
YOU COULD BE A BRANCH MANAGER!
HA HA HA HA!!!
© 1985 United Feature Syndicate, Inc.
3-30
SIGH
SCHULZ

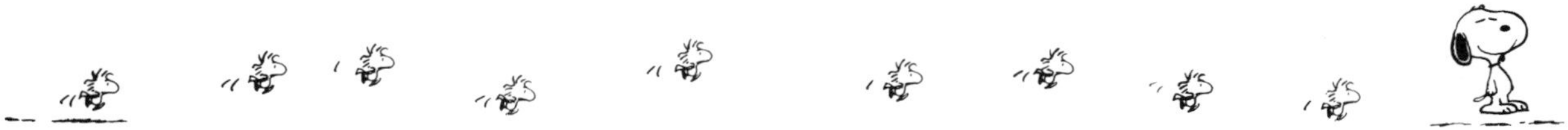

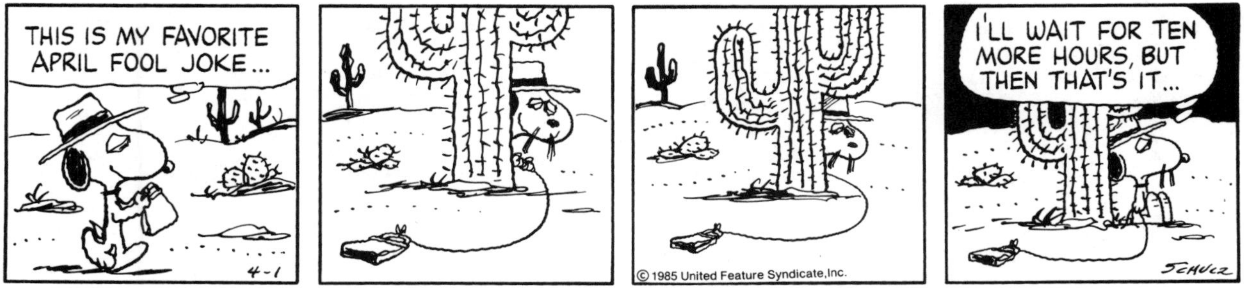
THIS IS MY FAVORITE APRIL FOOL JOKE...
4-1
© 1985 United Feature Syndicate, Inc.
I'LL WAIT FOR TEN MORE HOURS, BUT THEN THAT'S IT...
SCHULZ

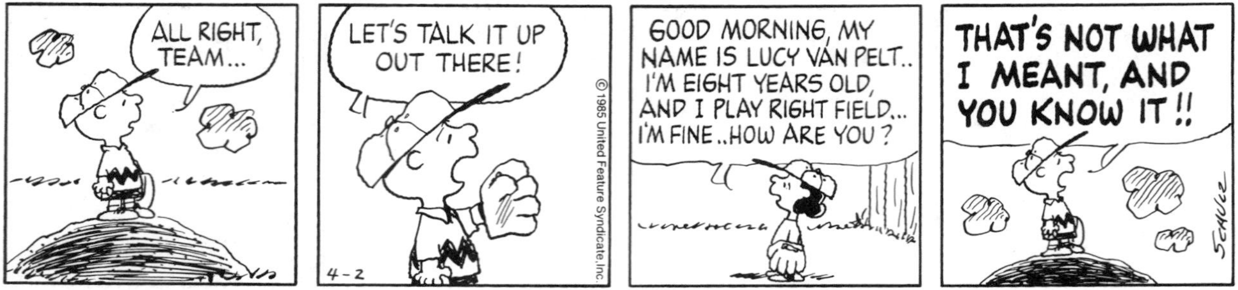
ALL RIGHT, TEAM...
LET'S TALK IT UP OUT THERE!
© 1985 United Feature Syndicate, Inc.
4-2
GOOD MORNING, MY NAME IS LUCY VAN PELT.. I'M EIGHT YEARS OLD, AND I PLAY RIGHT FIELD... I'M FINE..HOW ARE YOU?
THAT'S NOT WHAT I MEANT, AND YOU KNOW IT!!
SCHULZ

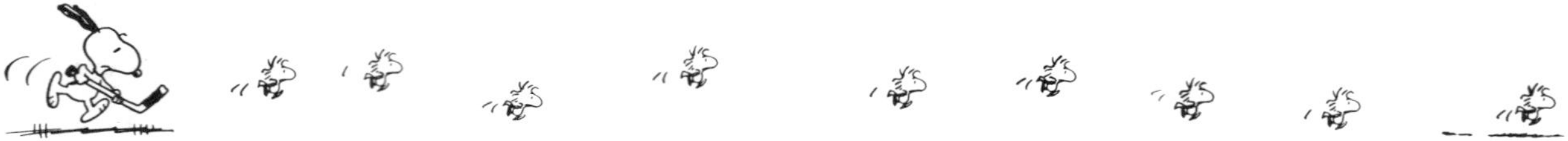

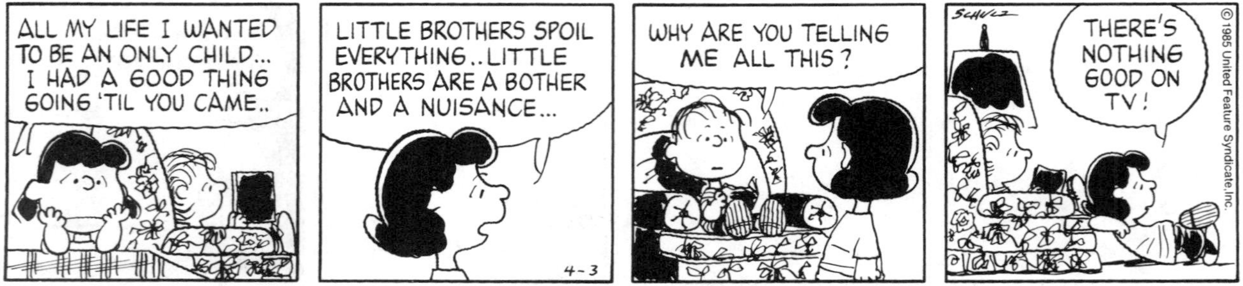
ALL MY LIFE I WANTED TO BE AN ONLY CHILD... I HAD A GOOD THING GOING 'TIL YOU CAME..
LITTLE BROTHERS SPOIL EVERYTHING..LITTLE BROTHERS ARE A BOTHER AND A NUISANCE...
4-3
WHY ARE YOU TELLING ME ALL THIS?
SCHULZ
THERE'S NOTHING GOOD ON TV!
© 1985 United Feature Syndicate, Inc.

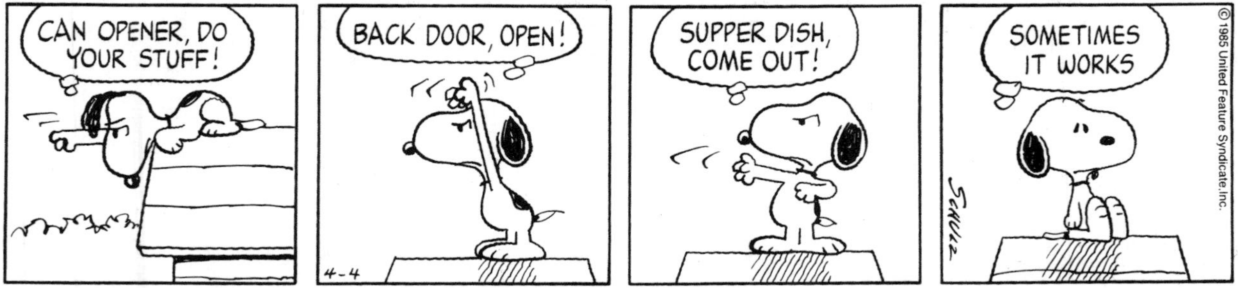
CAN OPENER, DO YOUR STUFF!
BACK DOOR, OPEN!
4-4
SUPPER DISH, COME OUT!
SOMETIMES IT WORKS
SCHULZ
© 1985 United Feature Syndicate, Inc.

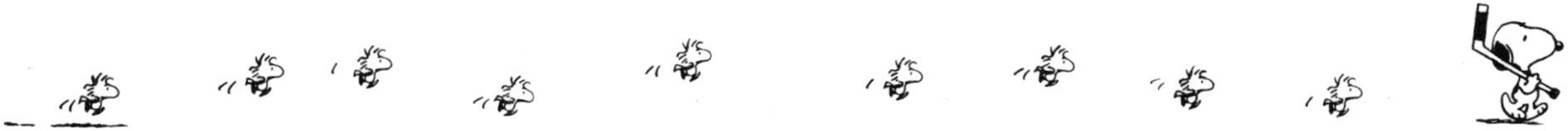

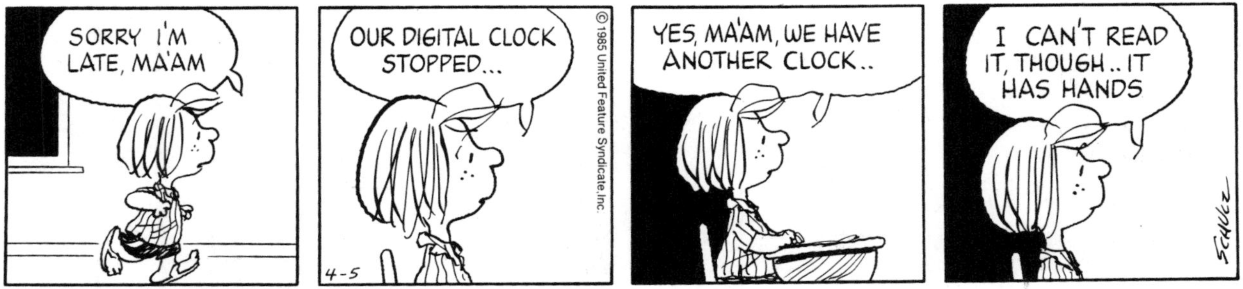
SORRY I'M LATE, MA'AM
OUR DIGITAL CLOCK STOPPED...
4-5
© 1985 United Feature Syndicate, Inc.
YES, MA'AM, WE HAVE ANOTHER CLOCK..
I CAN'T READ IT, THOUGH.. IT HAS HANDS
SCHULZ

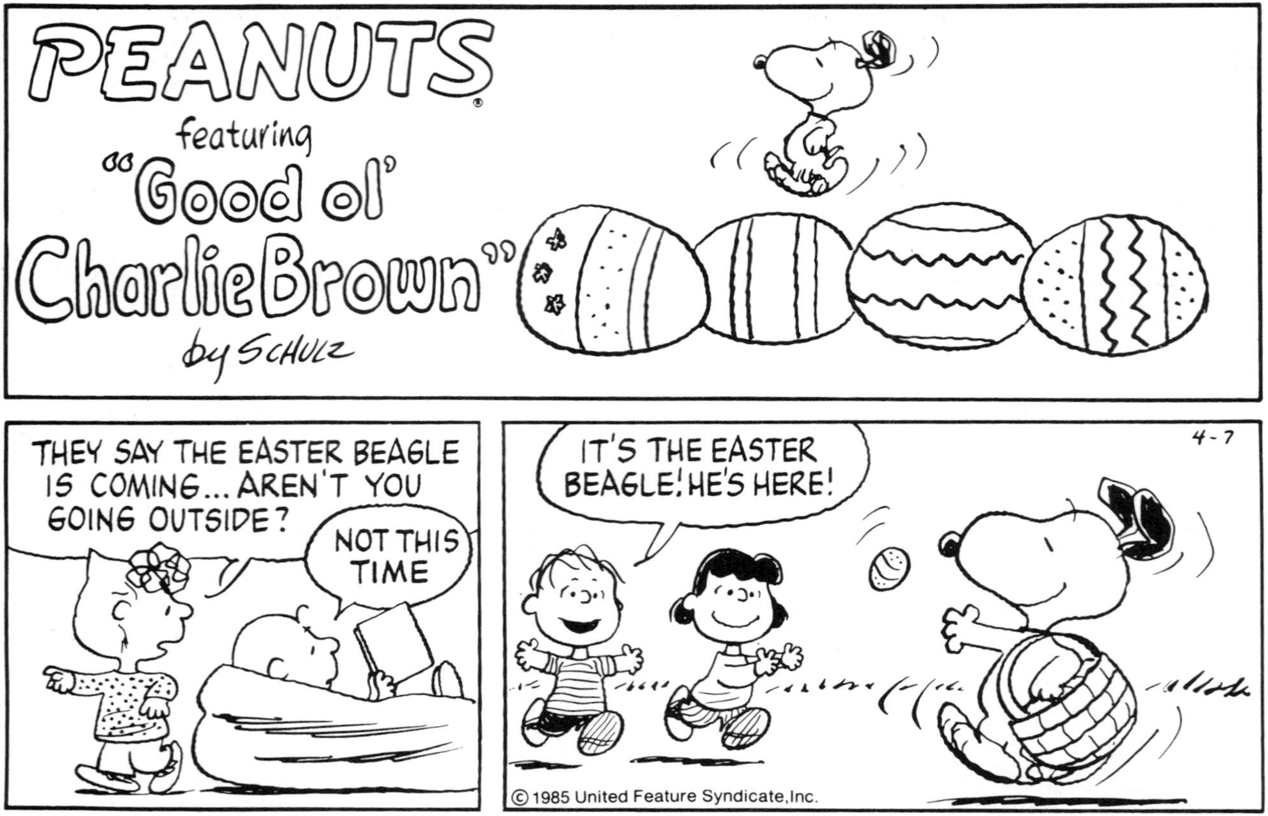
PEANUTS
featuring
"Good ol' Charlie Brown"
by SCHULZ
THEY SAY THE EASTER BEAGLE IS COMING... AREN'T YOU GOING OUTSIDE?
NOT THIS TIME
4-7
IT'S THE EASTER BEAGLE! HE'S HERE!
© 1985 United Feature Syndicate, Inc.

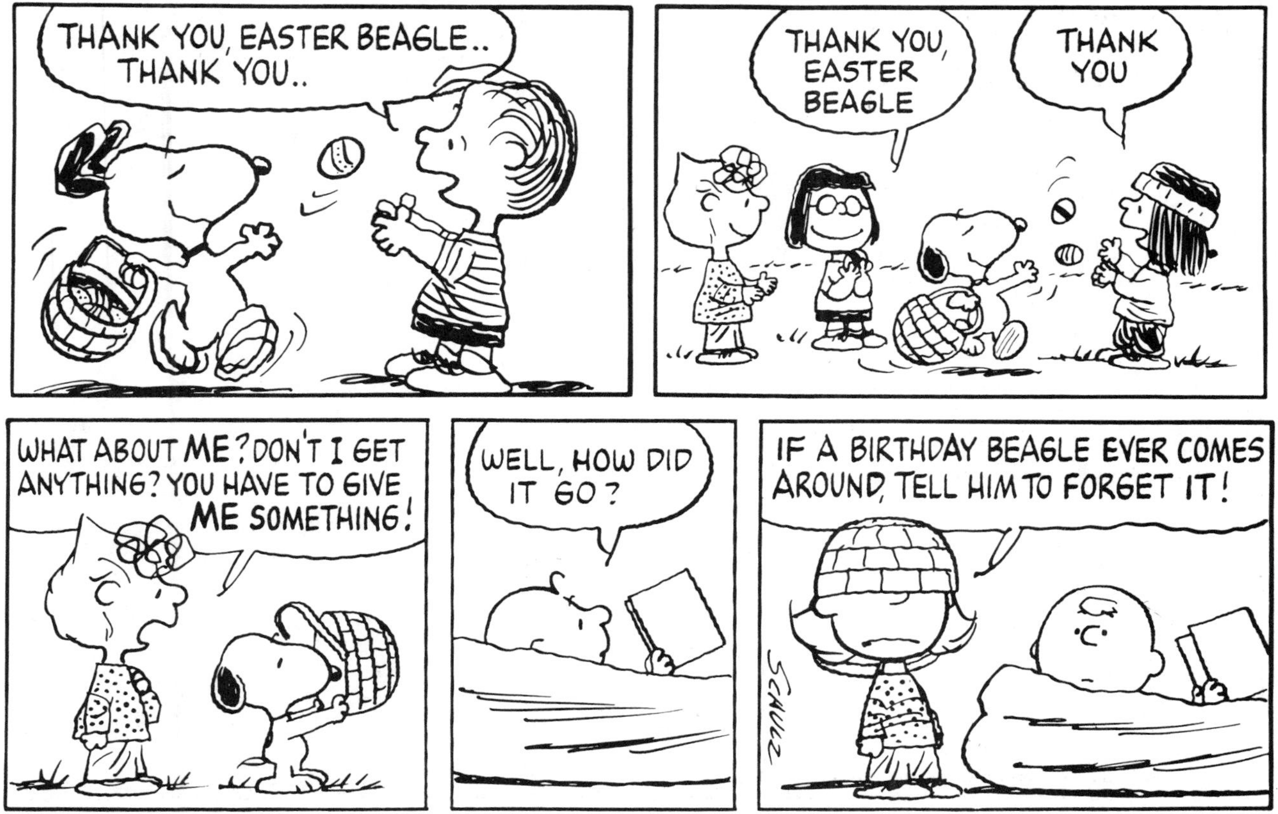
THANK YOU, EASTER BEAGLE.. THANK YOU..
THANK YOU, EASTER BEAGLE
THANK YOU
WHAT ABOUT ME? DON'T I GET ANYTHING? YOU HAVE TO GIVE ME SOMETHING!
WELL, HOW DID IT GO?
IF A BIRTHDAY BEAGLE EVER COMES AROUND, TELL HIM TO FORGET IT!
SCHULZ

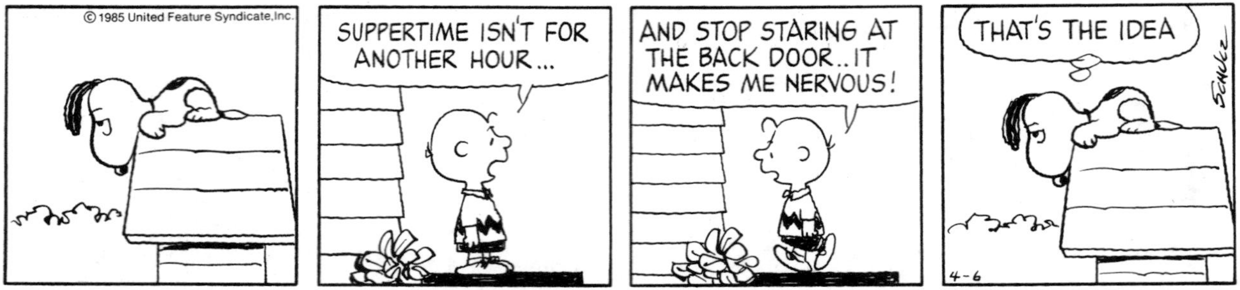
© 1985 United Feature Syndicate, Inc.
SUPPERTIME ISN'T FOR ANOTHER HOUR...
AND STOP STARING AT THE BACK DOOR.. IT MAKES ME NERVOUS!
THAT'S THE IDEA
SCHULZ
4-6

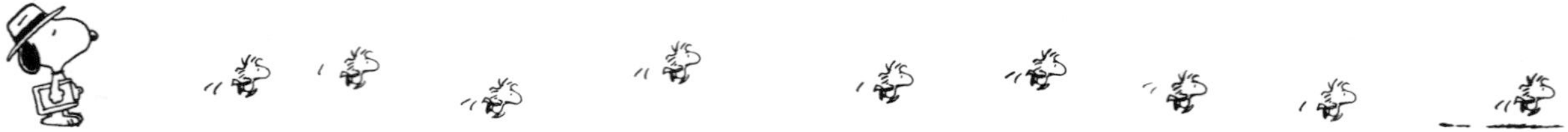

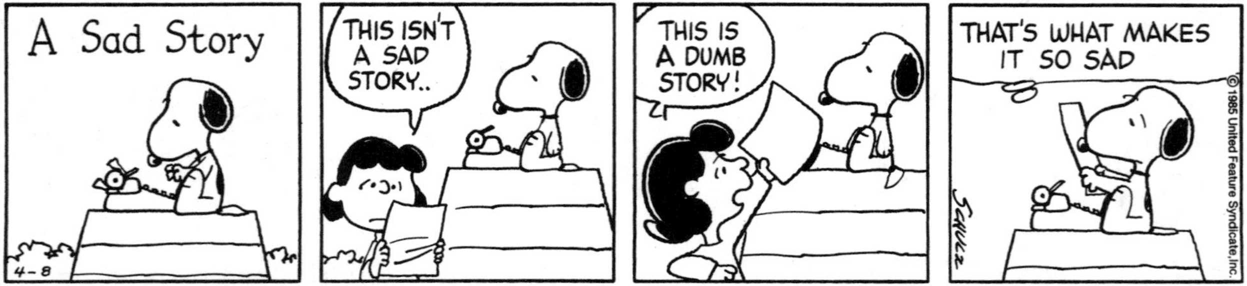
A Sad Story
4-8
THIS ISN'T A SAD STORY..
THIS IS A DUMB STORY!
SCHULZ
THAT'S WHAT MAKES IT SO SAD
© 1985 United Feature Syndicate, Inc.

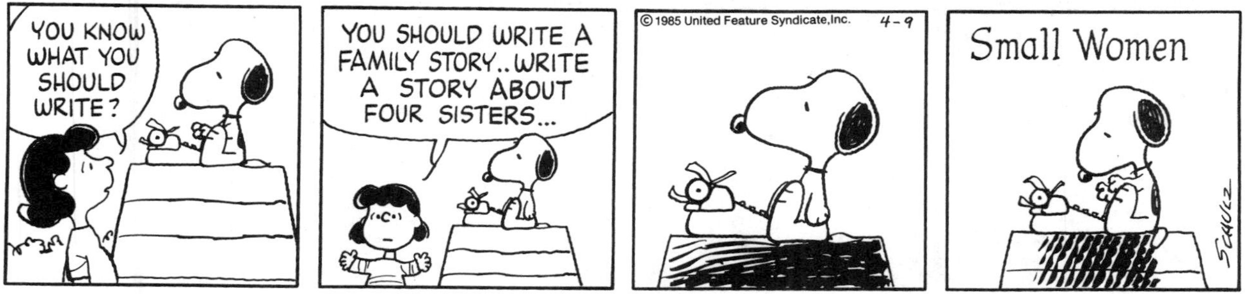
YOU KNOW WHAT YOU SHOULD WRITE?
YOU SHOULD WRITE A FAMILY STORY..WRITE A STORY ABOUT FOUR SISTERS...
© 1985 United Feature Syndicate,Inc. 4-9
Small Women
SCHULZ

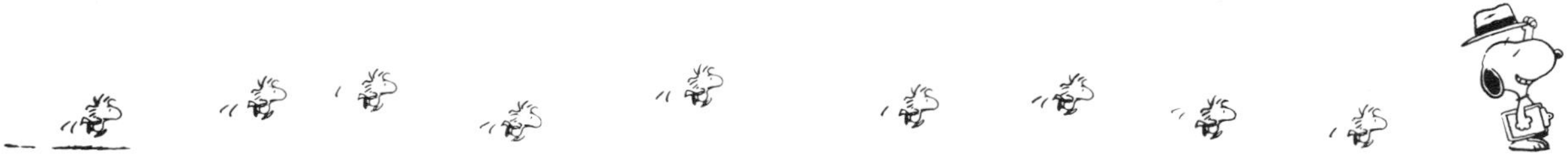

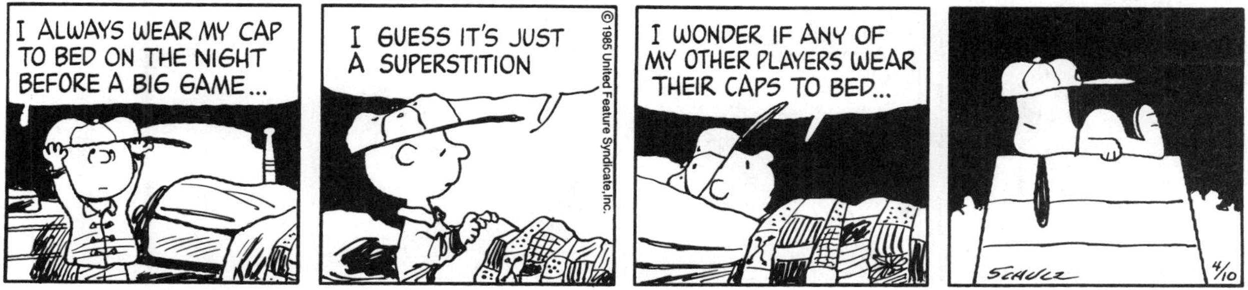
I ALWAYS WEAR MY CAP TO BED ON THE NIGHT BEFORE A BIG GAME...
I GUESS IT'S JUST A SUPERSTITION
© 1985 United Feature Syndicate,Inc.
I WONDER IF ANY OF MY OTHER PLAYERS WEAR THEIR CAPS TO BED...
SCHULZ 4/10

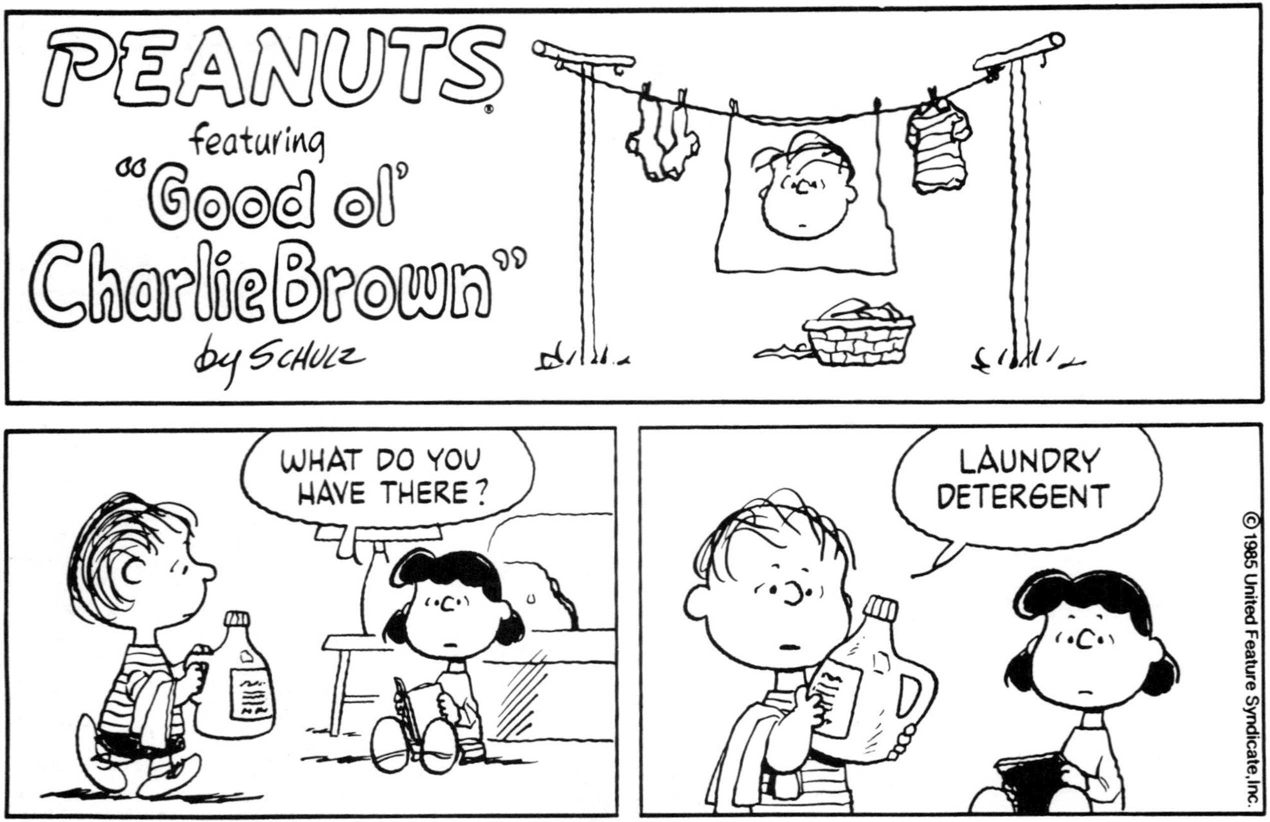
PEANUTS®
featuring
"Good ol' Charlie Brown"
by SCHULZ
WHAT DO YOU HAVE THERE?
LAUNDRY DETERGENT
© 1985 United Feature Syndicate, Inc.

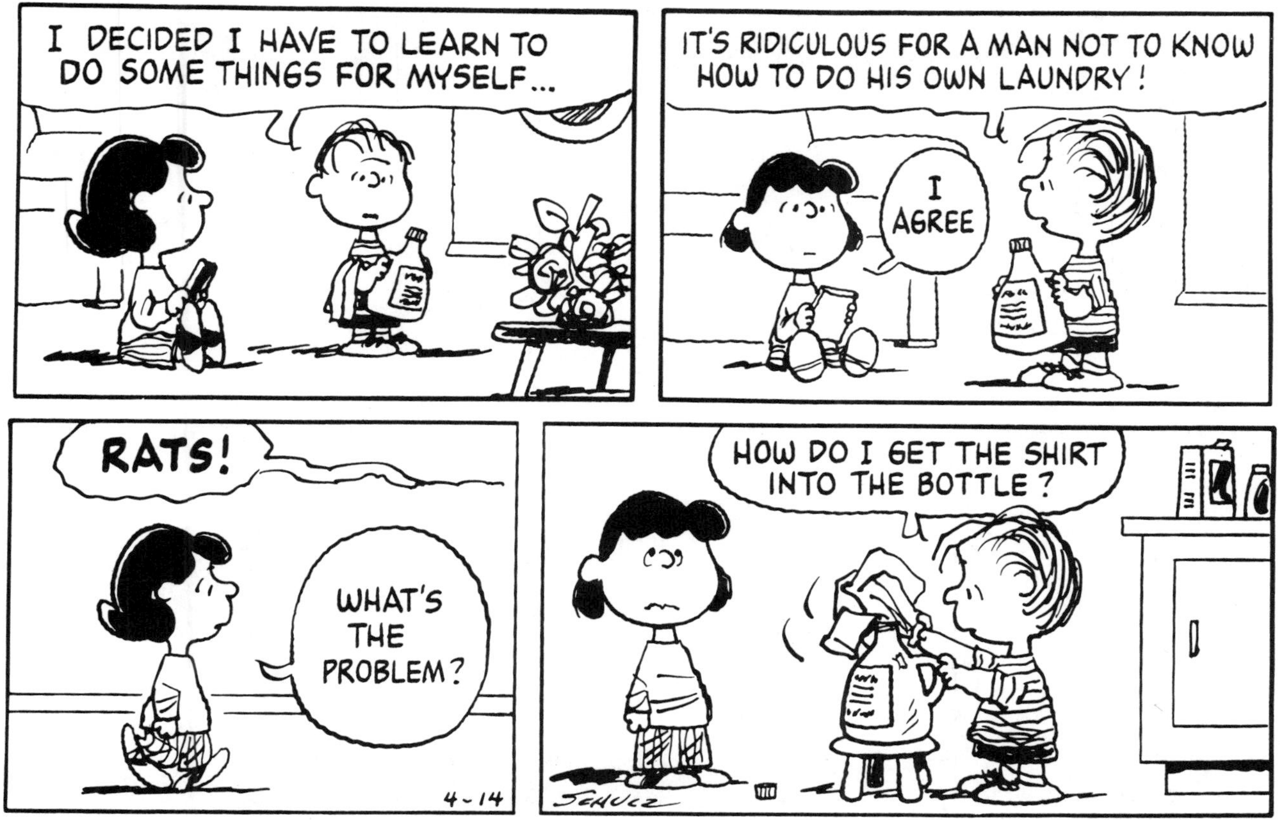
I DECIDED I HAVE TO LEARN TO DO SOME THINGS FOR MYSELF...
IT'S RIDICULOUS FOR A MAN NOT TO KNOW HOW TO DO HIS OWN LAUNDRY!
I AGREE
RATS!
WHAT'S THE PROBLEM?
4-14
HOW DO I GET THE SHIRT INTO THE BOTTLE?
SCHULZ

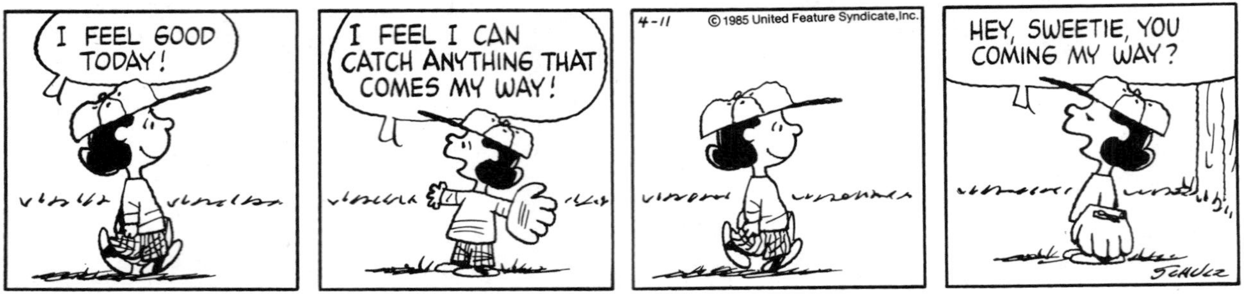
I FEEL GOOD TODAY!
I FEEL I CAN CATCH ANYTHING THAT COMES MY WAY!
4-11
© 1985 United Feature Syndicate, Inc.
HEY, SWEETIE, YOU COMING MY WAY?
SCHULZ

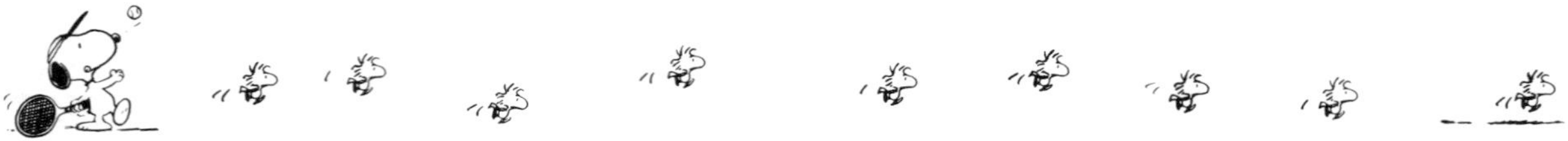

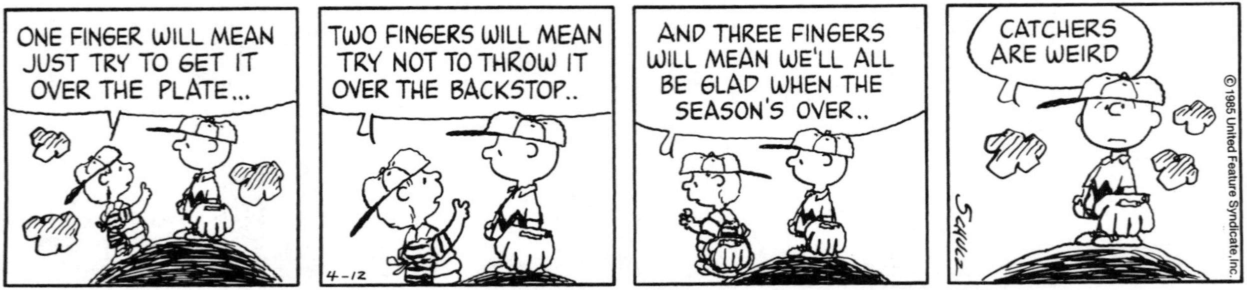
ONE FINGER WILL MEAN JUST TRY TO GET IT OVER THE PLATE...
TWO FINGERS WILL MEAN TRY NOT TO THROW IT OVER THE BACKSTOP..
4-12
AND THREE FINGERS WILL MEAN WE'LL ALL BE GLAD WHEN THE SEASON'S OVER..
SCHULZ
CATCHERS ARE WEIRD
© 1985 United Feature Syndicate, Inc.

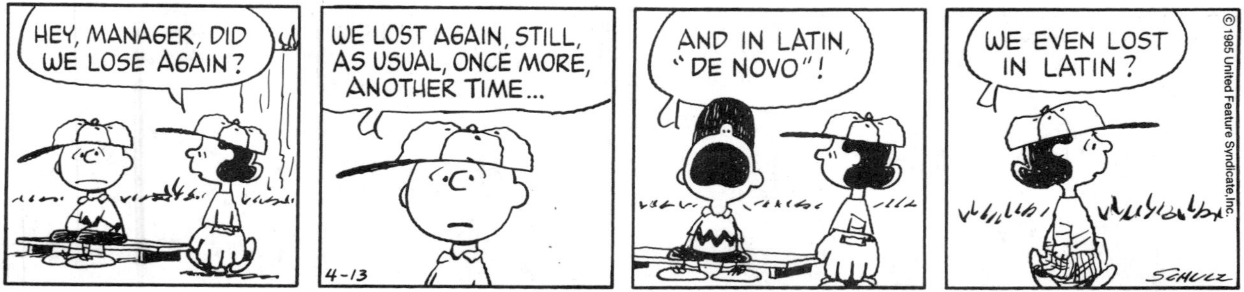
HEY, MANAGER, DID WE LOSE AGAIN?
WE LOST AGAIN, STILL, AS USUAL, ONCE MORE, ANOTHER TIME...
4-13
AND IN LATIN, "DE NOVO"!
WE EVEN LOST IN LATIN?
© 1985 United Feature Syndicate, Inc.
SCHULZ

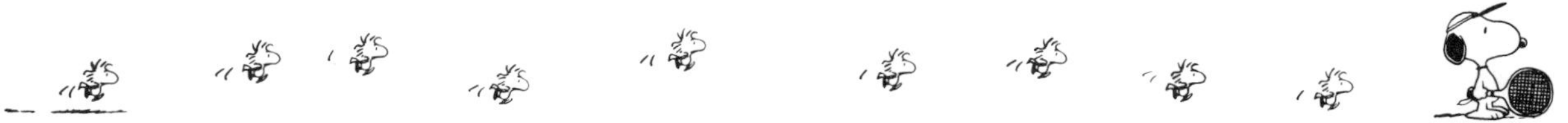

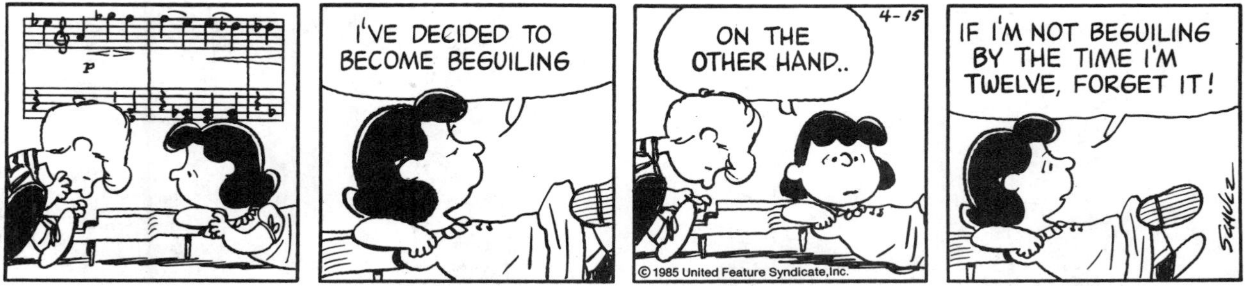
I'VE DECIDED TO BECOME BEGUILING
4-15
ON THE OTHER HAND..
© 1985 United Feature Syndicate, Inc.
IF I'M NOT BEGUILING BY THE TIME I'M TWELVE, FORGET IT!
SCHULZ

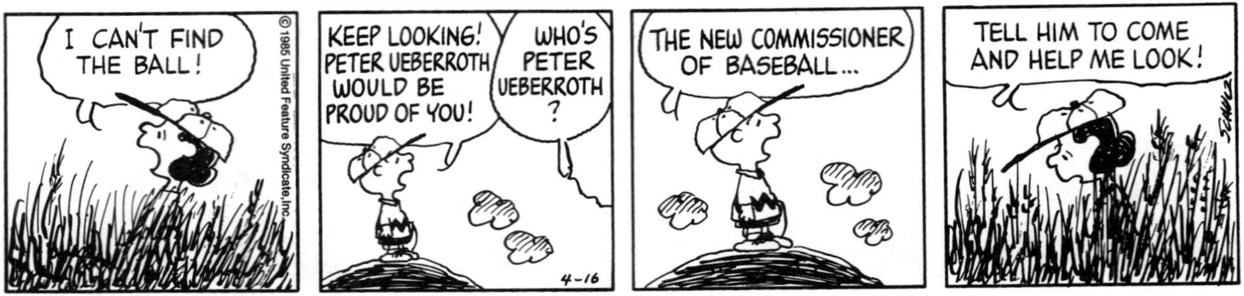
I CAN'T FIND THE BALL!
© 1985 United Feature Syndicate, Inc.
KEEP LOOKING! PETER UEBERROTH WOULD BE PROUD OF YOU!
WHO'S PETER UEBERROTH ?
4-16
THE NEW COMMISSIONER OF BASEBALL...
TELL HIM TO COME AND HELP ME LOOK!
SCHULZ

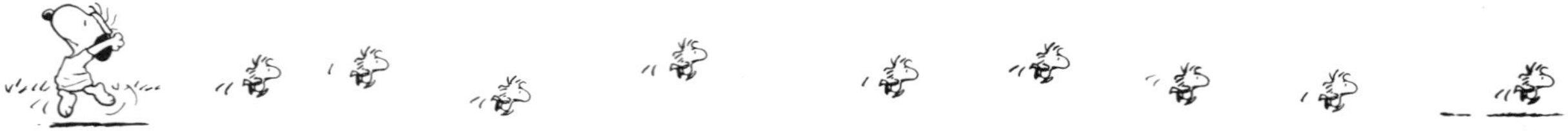

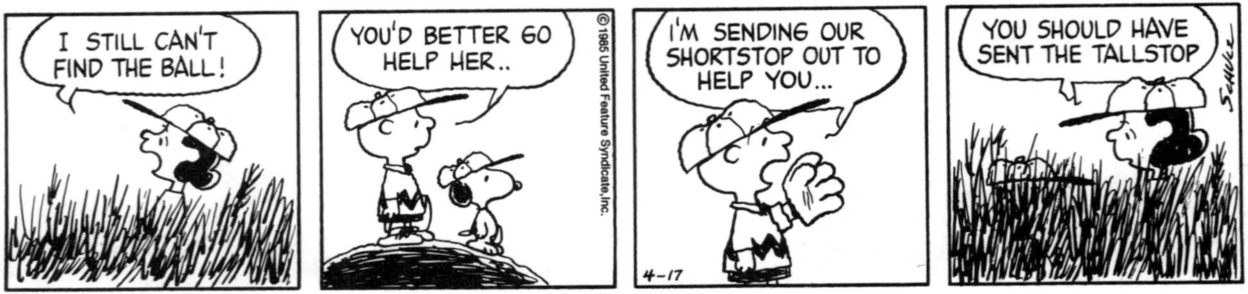
I STILL CAN'T FIND THE BALL!
YOU'D BETTER GO HELP HER..
© 1985 United Feature Syndicate, Inc.
I'M SENDING OUR SHORTSTOP OUT TO HELP YOU...
4-17
YOU SHOULD HAVE SENT THE TALLSTOP
SCHULZ

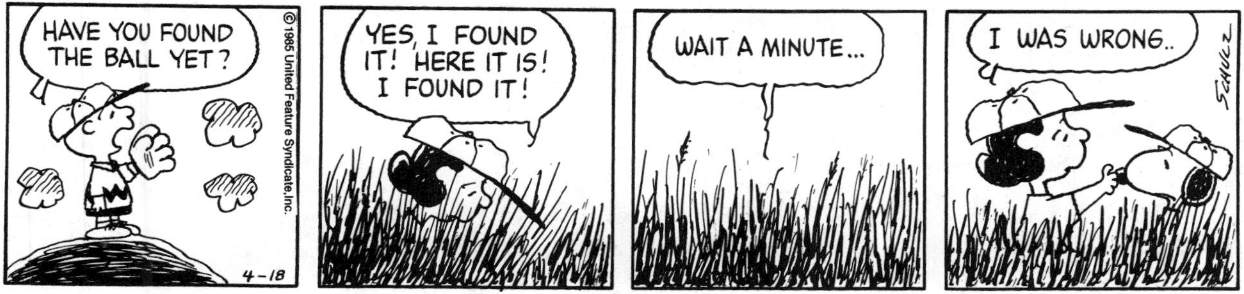
HAVE YOU FOUND THE BALL YET?
© 1985 United Feature Syndicate, Inc.
4-18
YES, I FOUND IT! HERE IT IS! I FOUND IT!
WAIT A MINUTE...
I WAS WRONG..
SCHULZ

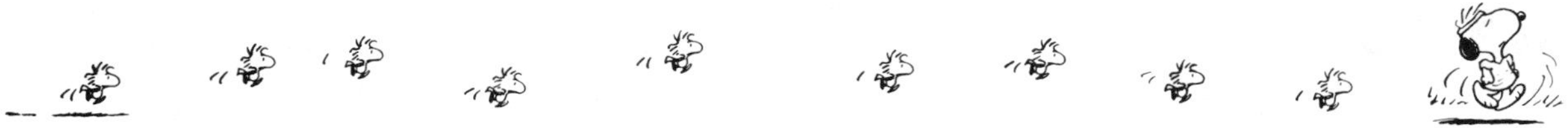

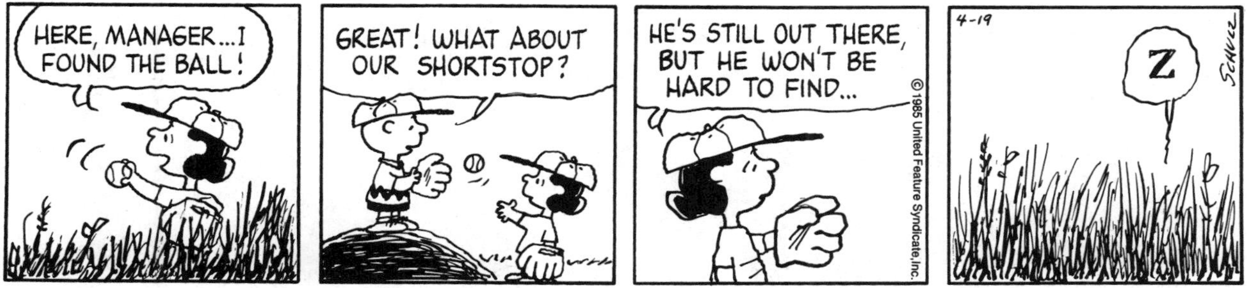
HERE, MANAGER...I FOUND THE BALL!
GREAT! WHAT ABOUT OUR SHORTSTOP?
HE'S STILL OUT THERE, BUT HE WON'T BE HARD TO FIND...
© 1985 United Feature Syndicate, Inc.
4-19
Z
SCHULZ

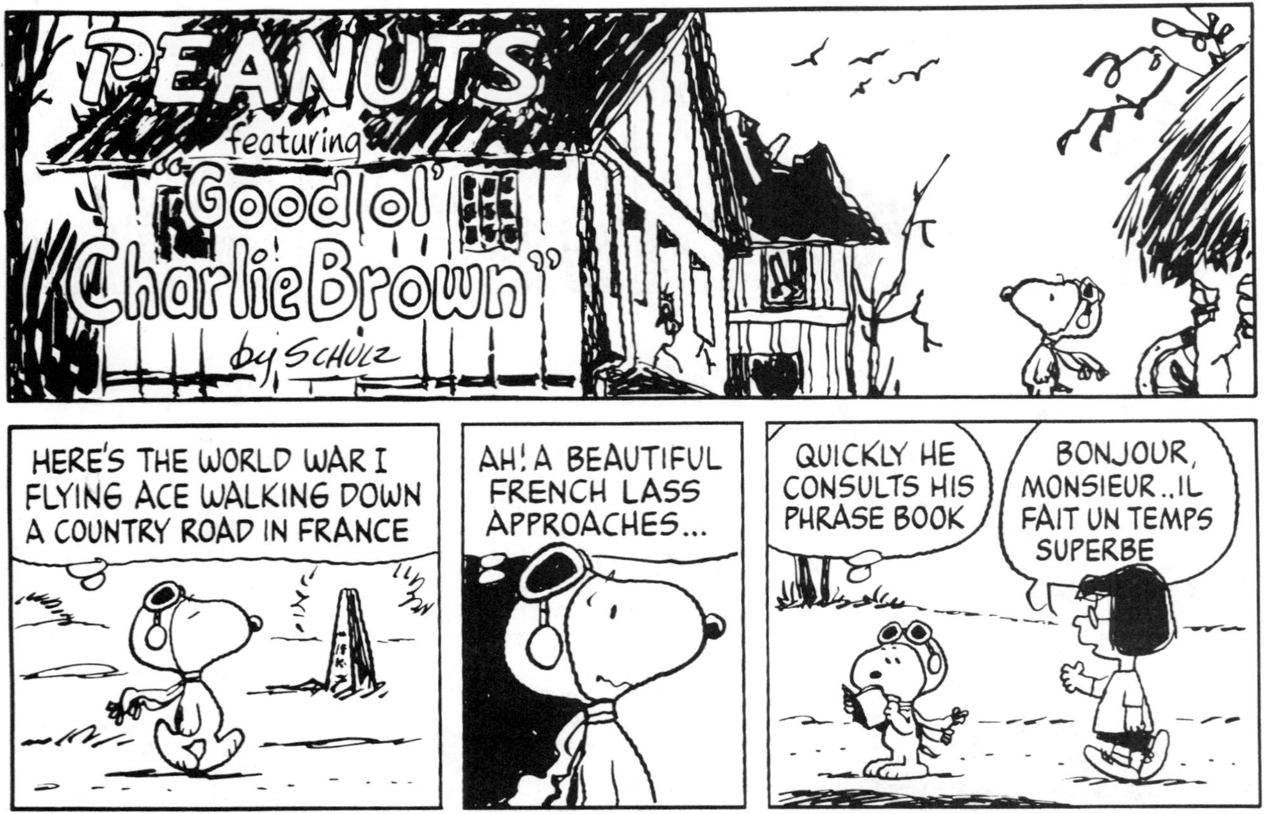
PEANUTS
featuring
"Good ol' Charlie Brown"
by SCHULZ
HERE'S THE WORLD WAR I FLYING ACE WALKING DOWN A COUNTRY ROAD IN FRANCE
AH! A BEAUTIFUL FRENCH LASS APPROACHES...
QUICKLY HE CONSULTS HIS PHRASE BOOK
BONJOUR, MONSIEUR..IL FAIT UN TEMPS SUPERBE

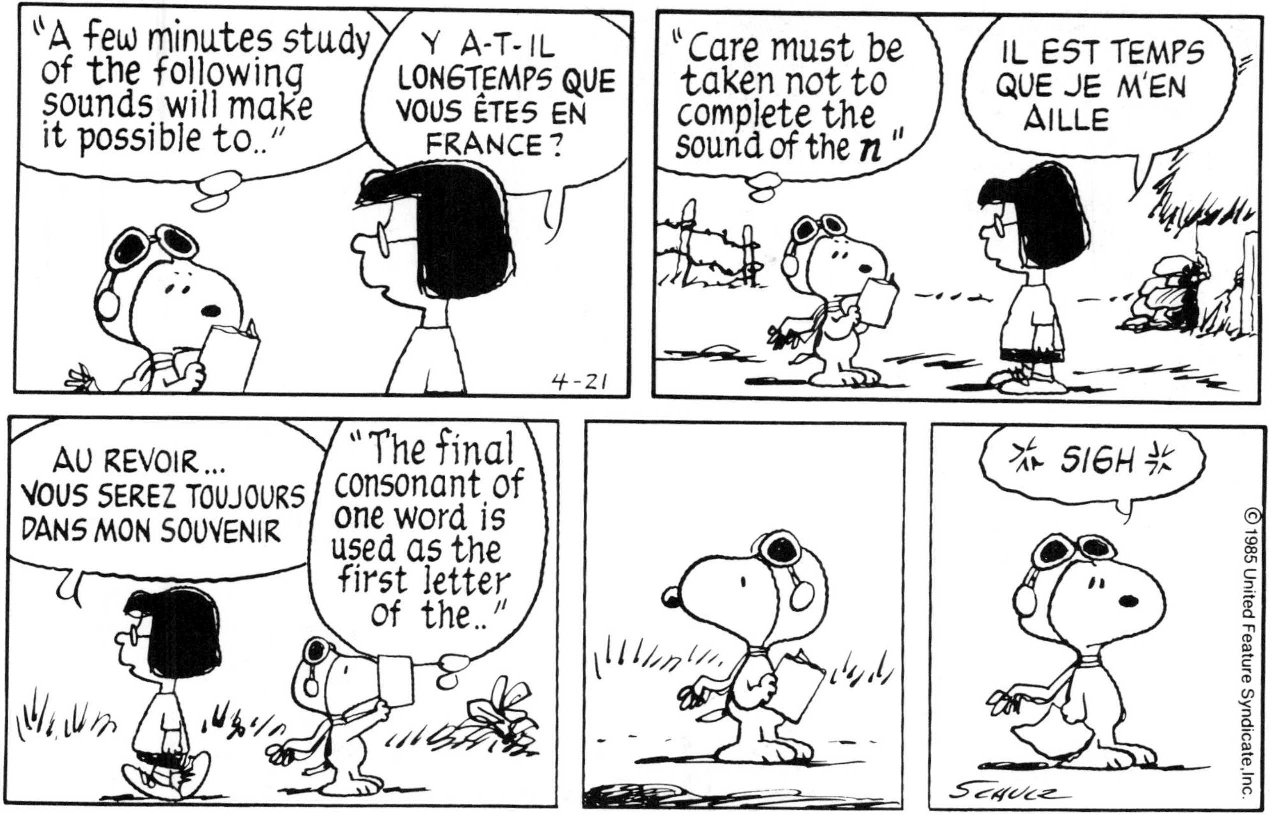
"A few minutes study of the following sounds will make it possible to.."
Y A-T-IL LONGTEMPS QUE VOUS ÊTES EN FRANCE?
4-21
"Care must be taken not to complete the sound of the n"
IL EST TEMPS QUE JE M'EN AILLE
AU REVOIR... VOUS SEREZ TOUJOURS DANS MON SOUVENIR
"The final consonant of one word is used as the first letter of the.."
SIGH
SCHULZ

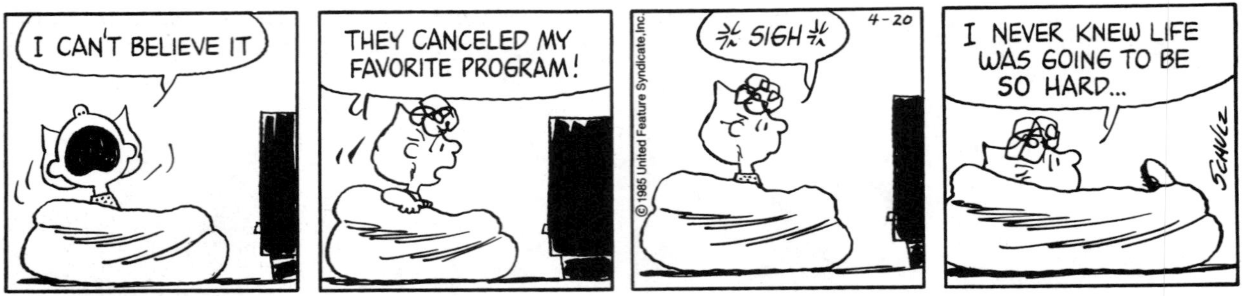
I CAN'T BELIEVE IT
THEY CANCELED MY FAVORITE PROGRAM!
© 1985 United Feature Syndicate, Inc.
SIGH
4-20
I NEVER KNEW LIFE WAS GOING TO BE SO HARD...
SCHULZ

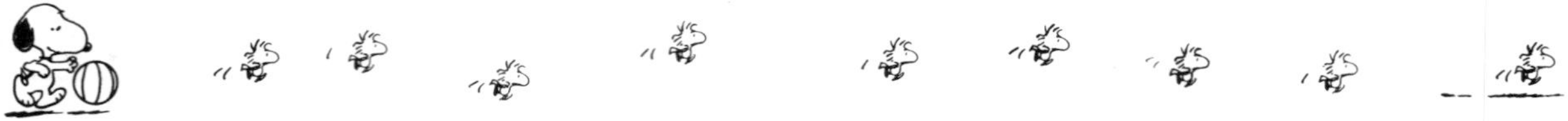

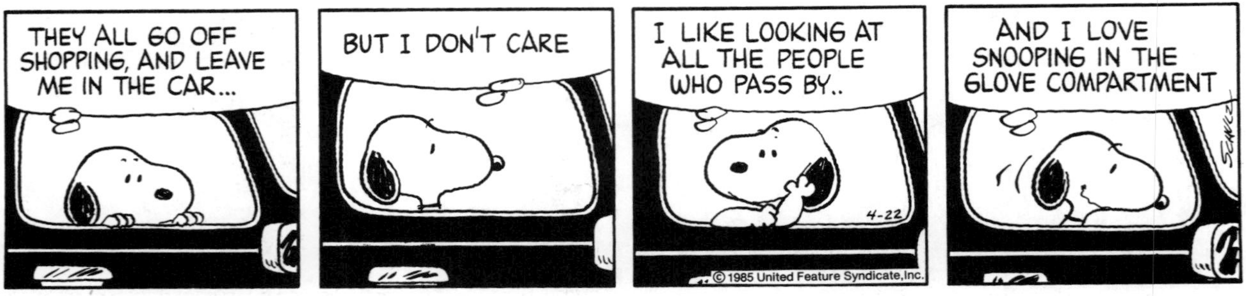
THEY ALL GO OFF SHOPPING, AND LEAVE ME IN THE CAR...
BUT I DON'T CARE
I LIKE LOOKING AT ALL THE PEOPLE WHO PASS BY..
4-22
© 1985 United Feature Syndicate, Inc.
AND I LOVE SNOOPING IN THE GLOVE COMPARTMENT
SCHULZ

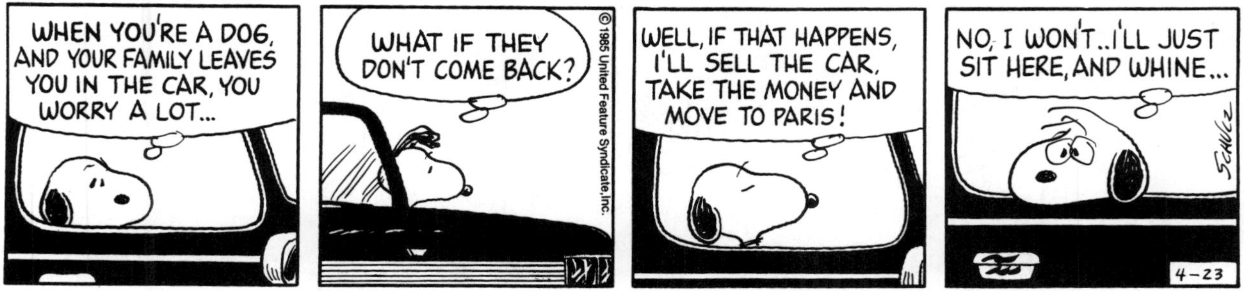
WHEN YOU'RE A DOG, AND YOUR FAMILY LEAVES YOU IN THE CAR, YOU WORRY A LOT...
WHAT IF THEY DON'T COME BACK?
© 1985 United Feature Syndicate, Inc.
WELL, IF THAT HAPPENS, I'LL SELL THE CAR, TAKE THE MONEY AND MOVE TO PARIS!
NO, I WON'T..I'LL JUST SIT HERE, AND WHINE...
SCHULZ
4-23

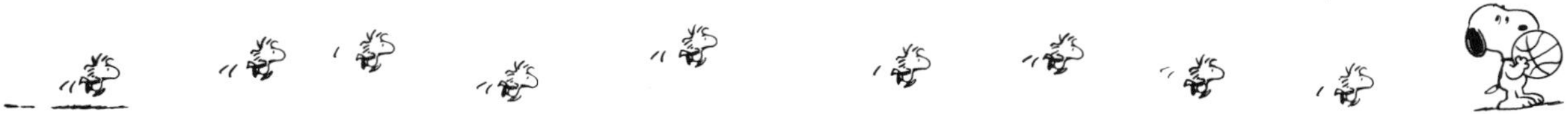

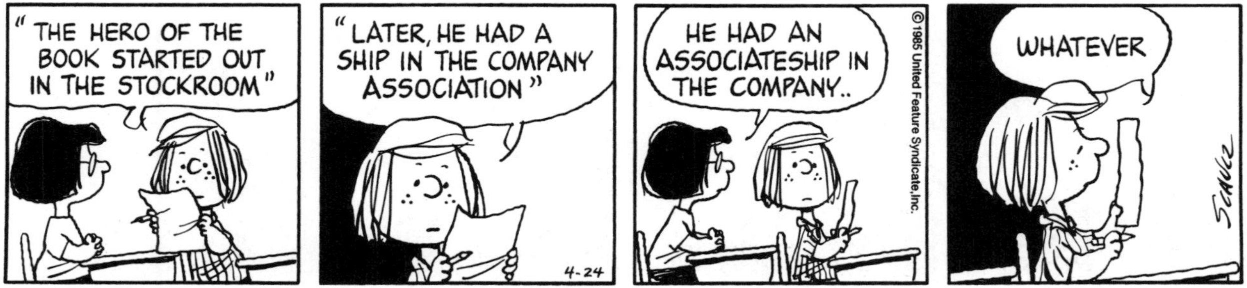
"THE HERO OF THE BOOK STARTED OUT IN THE STOCKROOM"
"LATER, HE HAD A SHIP IN THE COMPANY ASSOCIATION"
4-24
© 1985 United Feature Syndicate, Inc.
HE HAD AN ASSOCIATESHIP IN THE COMPANY..
WHATEVER
SCHULZ

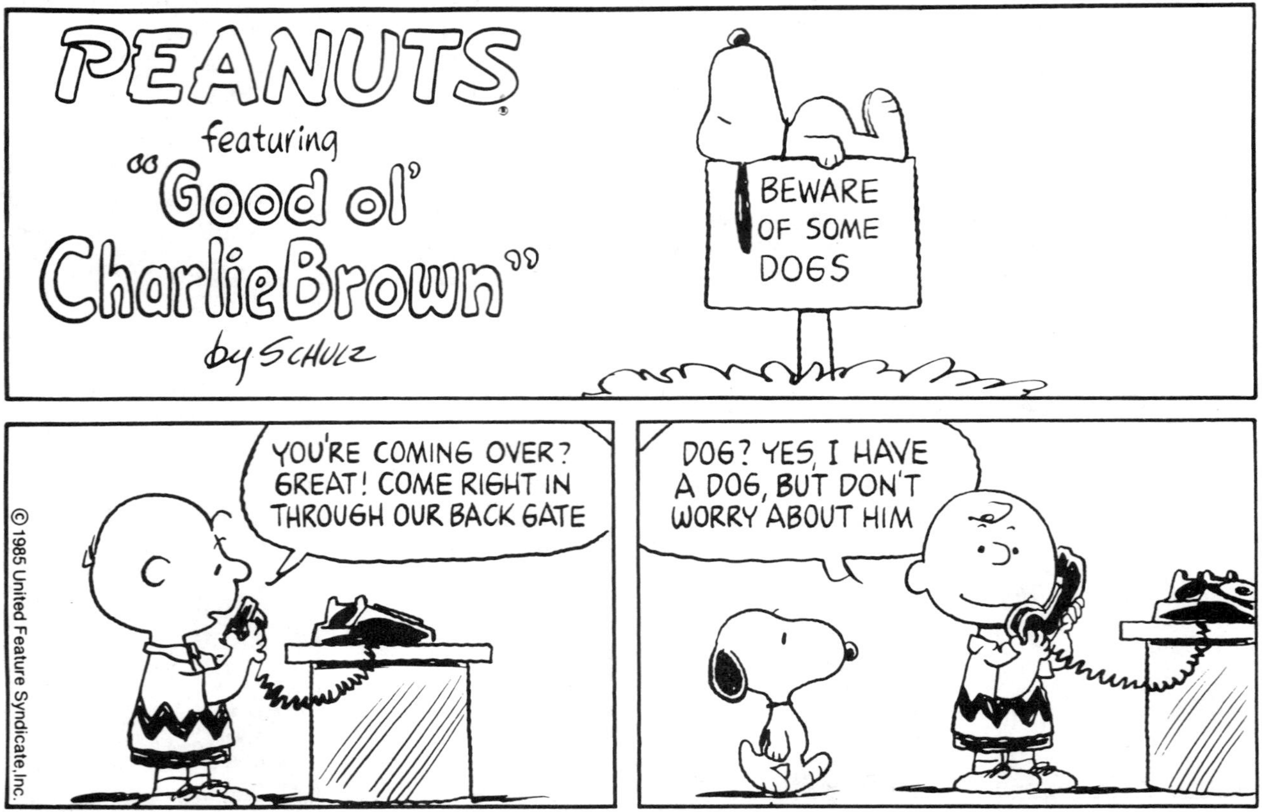
PEANUTS
featuring
"Good ol' Charlie Brown"
by SCHULZ
BEWARE OF SOME DOGS
YOU'RE COMING OVER? GREAT! COME RIGHT IN THROUGH OUR BACK GATE
DOG? YES, I HAVE A DOG, BUT DON'T WORRY ABOUT HIM

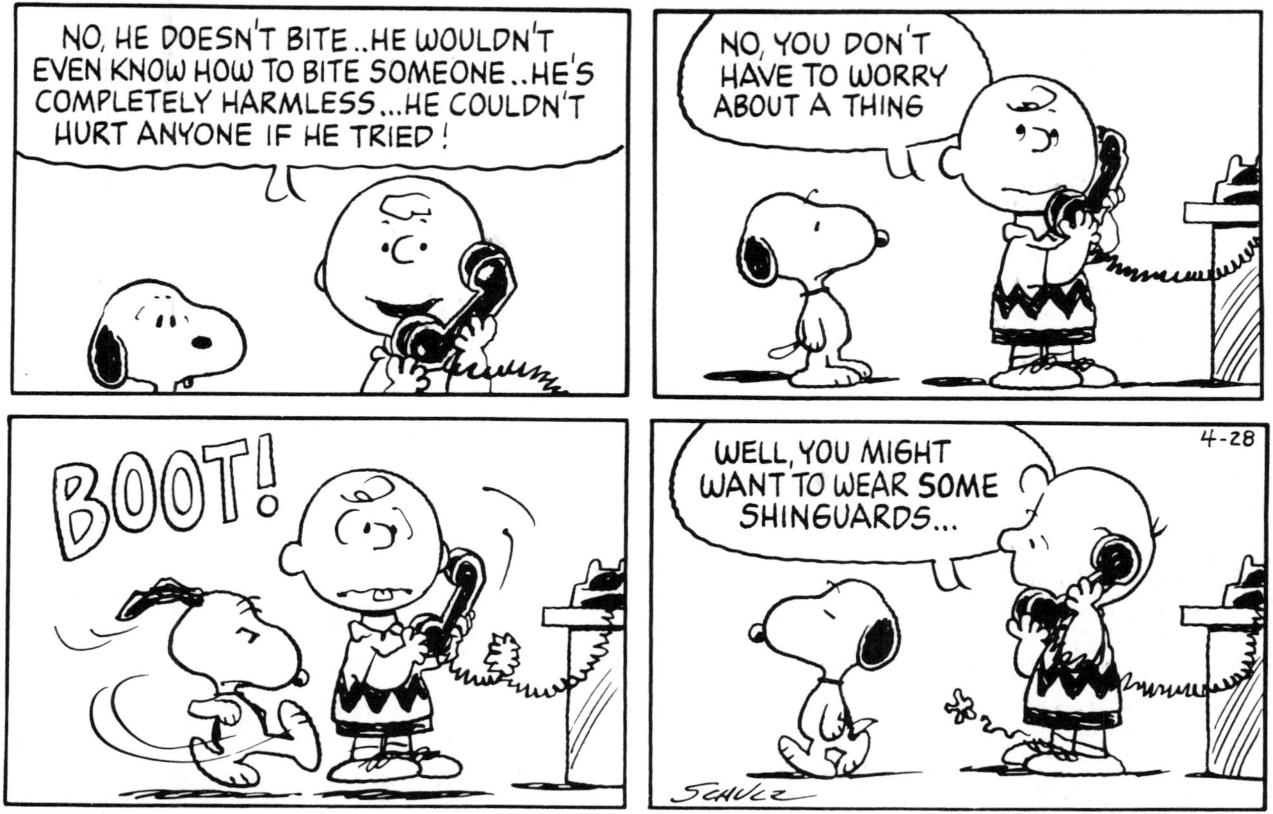
NO, HE DOESN'T BITE..HE WOULDN'T EVEN KNOW HOW TO BITE SOMEONE..HE'S COMPLETELY HARMLESS...HE COULDN'T HURT ANYONE IF HE TRIED!
NO, YOU DON'T HAVE TO WORRY ABOUT A THING
BOOT!
4-28
WELL, YOU MIGHT WANT TO WEAR SOME SHINGUARDS...
SCHULZ

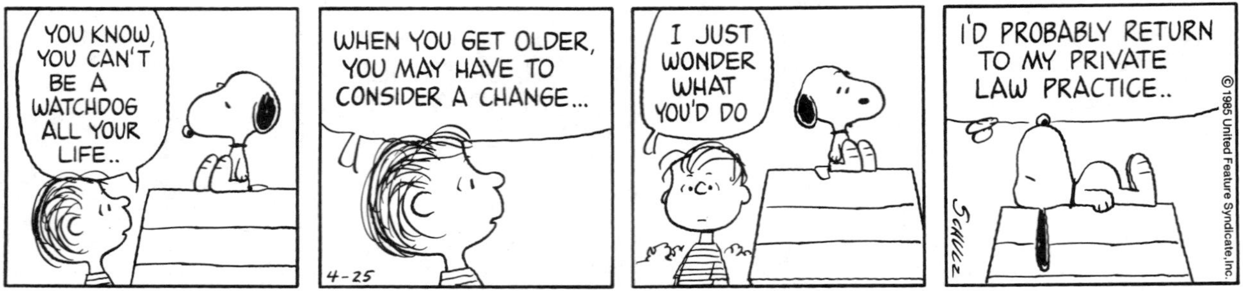
YOU KNOW, YOU CAN'T BE A WATCHDOG ALL YOUR LIFE..
WHEN YOU GET OLDER, YOU MAY HAVE TO CONSIDER A CHANGE...
4-25
I JUST WONDER WHAT YOU'D DO
I'D PROBABLY RETURN TO MY PRIVATE LAW PRACTICE..
SCHULZ
© 1985 United Feature Syndicate, Inc.

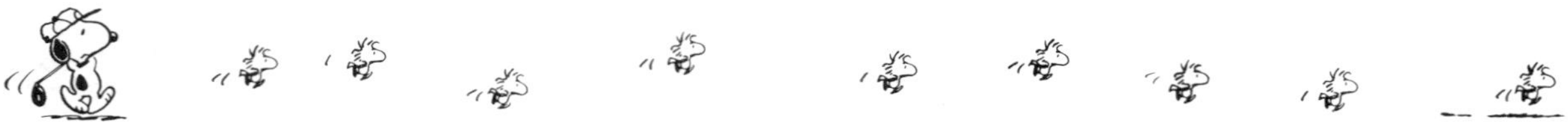

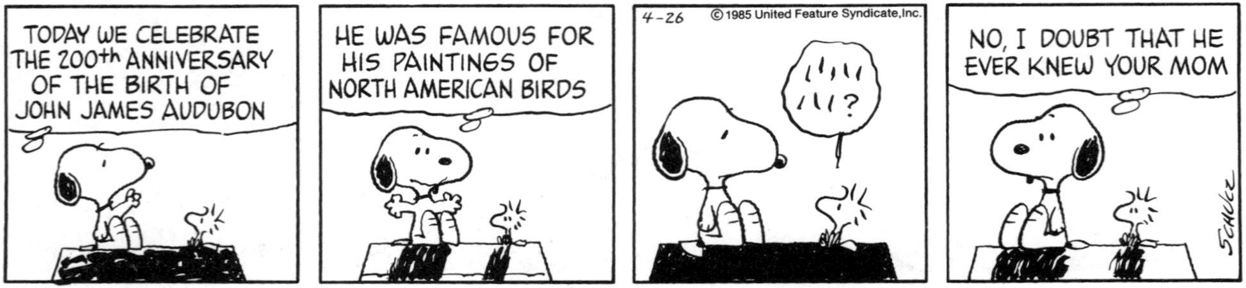
TODAY WE CELEBRATE THE 200th ANNIVERSARY OF THE BIRTH OF JOHN JAMES AUDUBON
HE WAS FAMOUS FOR HIS PAINTINGS OF NORTH AMERICAN BIRDS
4-26
© 1985 United Feature Syndicate, Inc.
?
NO, I DOUBT THAT HE EVER KNEW YOUR MOM
SCHULZ

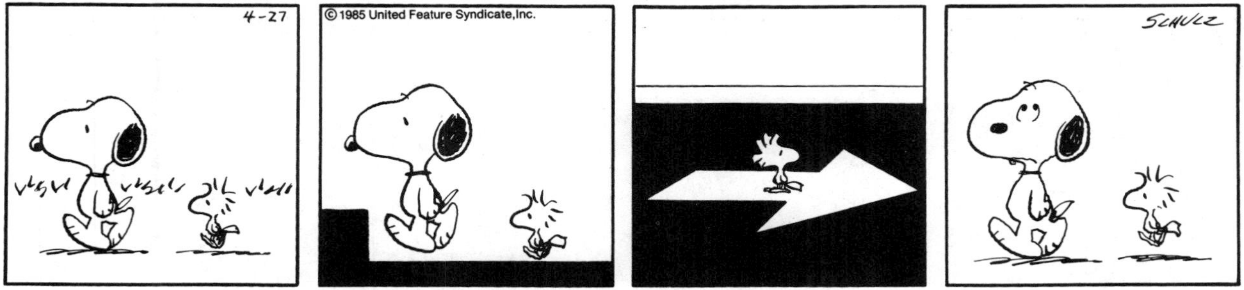
4-27
© 1985 United Feature Syndicate,Inc.
SCHULZ

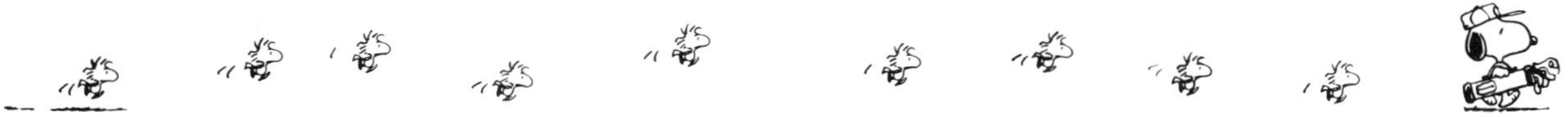

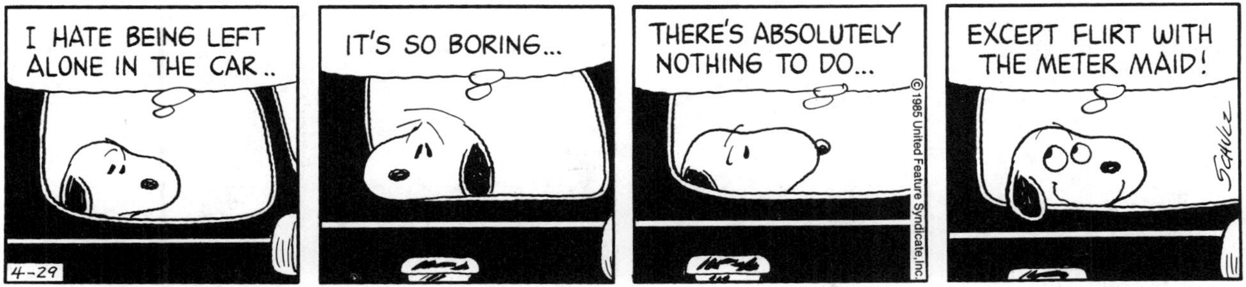
I HATE BEING LEFT ALONE IN THE CAR..
IT'S SO BORING...
THERE'S ABSOLUTELY NOTHING TO DO...
EXCEPT FLIRT WITH THE METER MAID!
4-29
© 1985 United Feature Syndicate,Inc.
SCHULZ

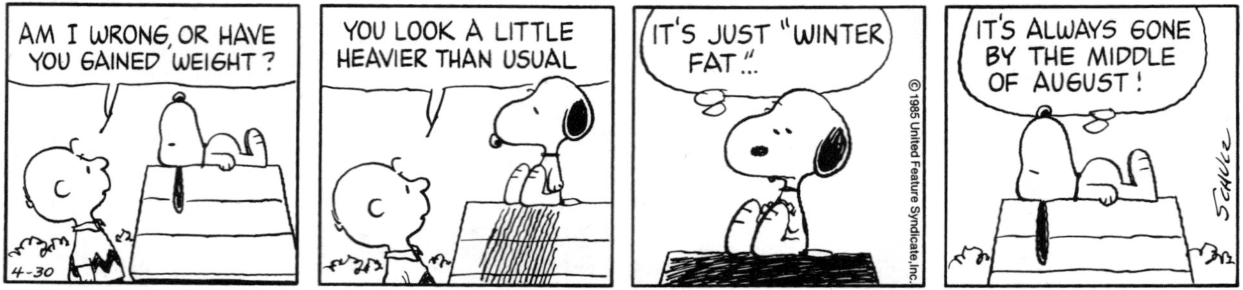
4-30
AM I WRONG, OR HAVE YOU GAINED WEIGHT ?
YOU LOOK A LITTLE HEAVIER THAN USUAL
IT'S JUST "WINTER FAT."
© 1985 United Feature Syndicate, Inc.
IT'S ALWAYS GONE BY THE MIDDLE OF AUGUST !
SCHULZ

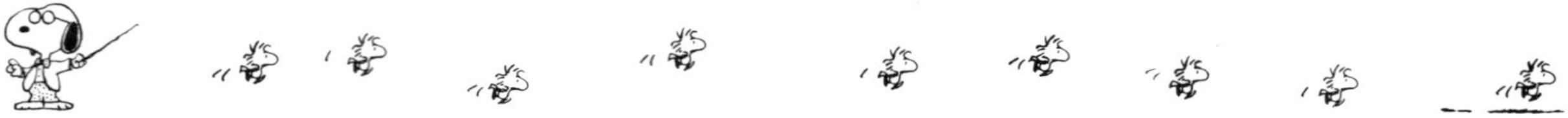

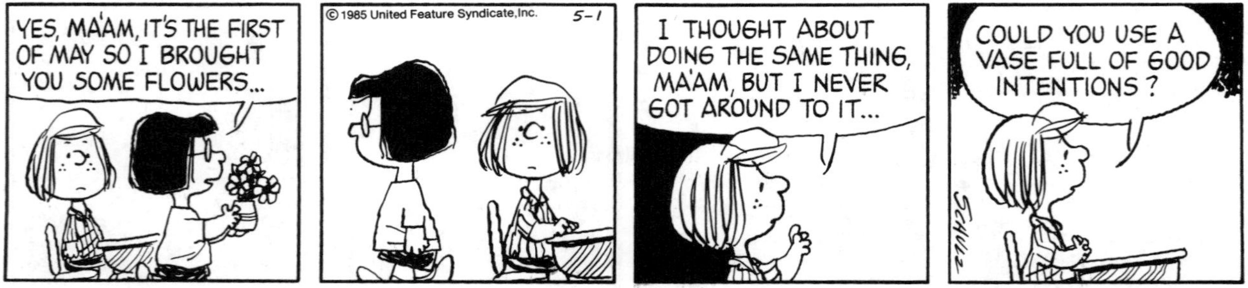
YES, MA'AM, IT'S THE FIRST OF MAY SO I BROUGHT YOU SOME FLOWERS...
© 1985 United Feature Syndicate, Inc.
5-1
I THOUGHT ABOUT DOING THE SAME THING, MA'AM, BUT I NEVER GOT AROUND TO IT...
COULD YOU USE A VASE FULL OF GOOD INTENTIONS ?
SCHULZ

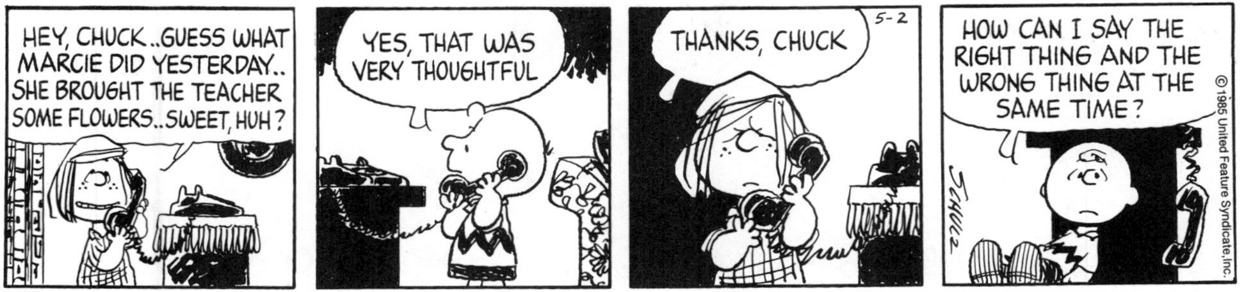
HEY, CHUCK..GUESS WHAT MARCIE DID YESTERDAY.. SHE BROUGHT THE TEACHER SOME FLOWERS..SWEET, HUH?
YES, THAT WAS VERY THOUGHTFUL
THANKS, CHUCK
5-2
HOW CAN I SAY THE RIGHT THING AND THE WRONG THING AT THE SAME TIME?
SCHULZ
© 1985 United Feature Syndicate, Inc.

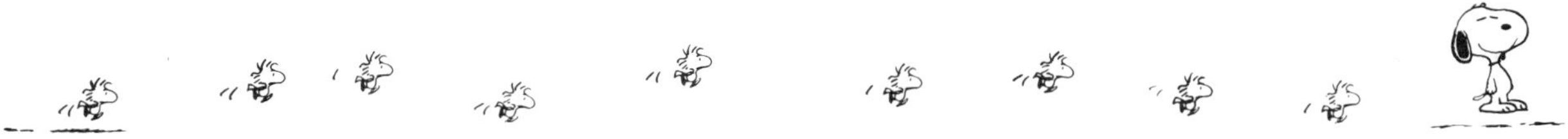

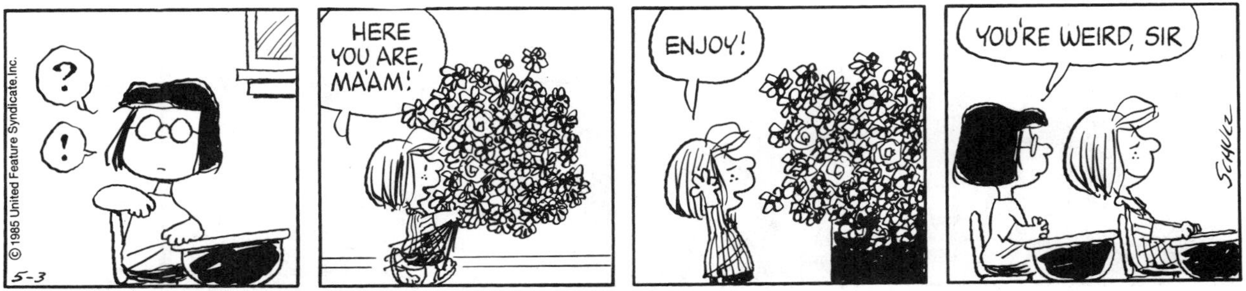
© 1985 United Feature Syndicate, Inc.
5-3
?
!
HERE YOU ARE, MA'AM!
ENJOY!
YOU'RE WEIRD, SIR
SCHULZ

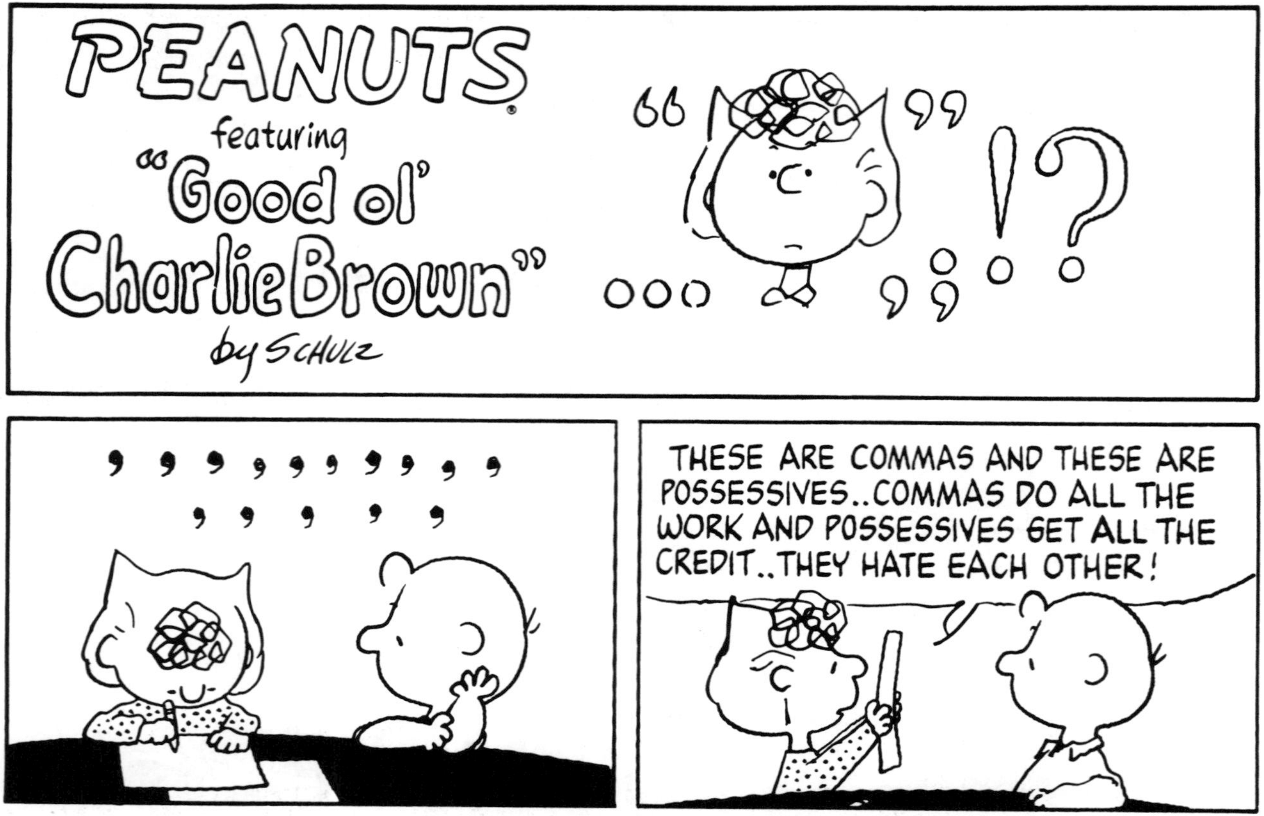
PEANUTS
featuring
"Good ol' Charlie Brown"
by SCHULZ
THESE ARE COMMAS AND THESE ARE POSSESSIVES..COMMAS DO ALL THE WORK AND POSSESSIVES GET ALL THE CREDIT..THEY HATE EACH OTHER!

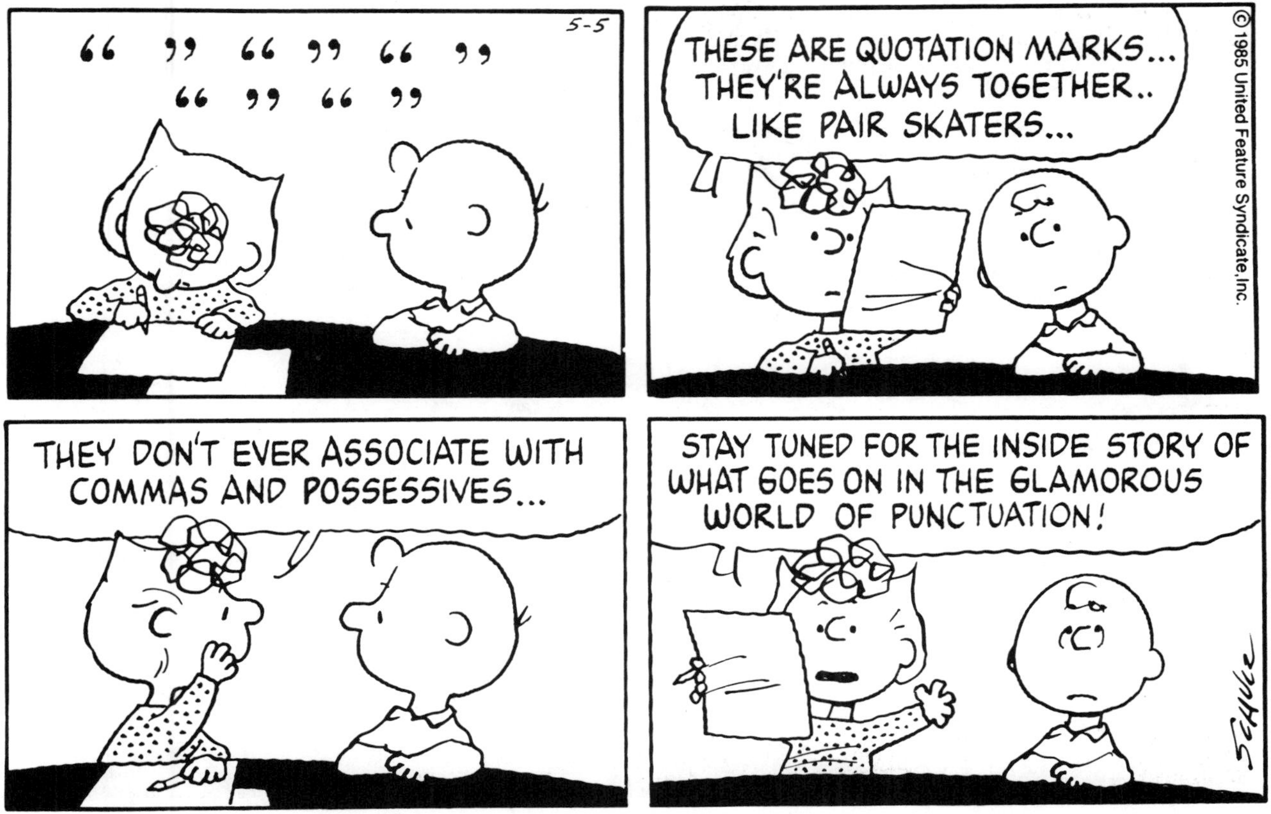
5-5
" " " " " "
" " " "
THESE ARE QUOTATION MARKS... THEY'RE ALWAYS TOGETHER.. LIKE PAIR SKATERS...
© 1985 United Feature Syndicate, Inc.
THEY DON'T EVER ASSOCIATE WITH COMMAS AND POSSESSIVES...
STAY TUNED FOR THE INSIDE STORY OF WHAT GOES ON IN THE GLAMOROUS WORLD OF PUNCTUATION!
SCHULZ

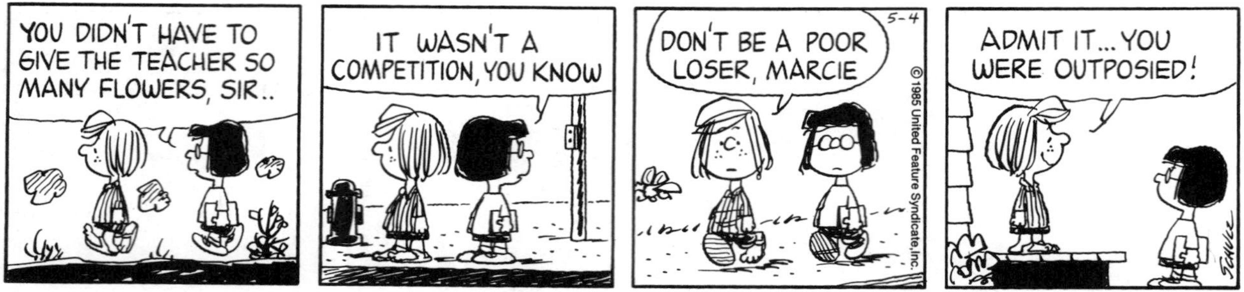

YOU DIDN'T HAVE TO GIVE THE TEACHER SO MANY FLOWERS, SIR..
IT WASN'T A COMPETITION, YOU KNOW
5-4
DON'T BE A POOR LOSER, MARCIE
ADMIT IT... YOU WERE OUTPOSIED!
SCHULZ

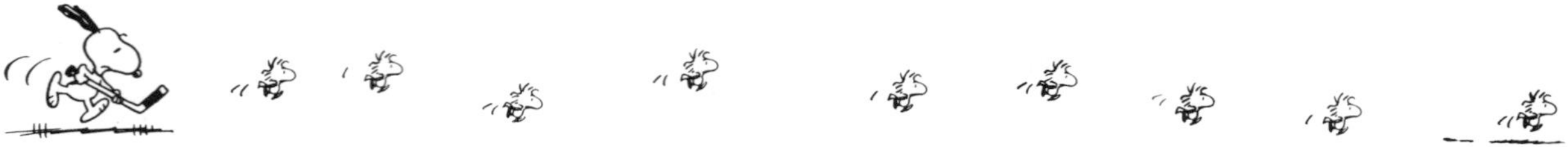

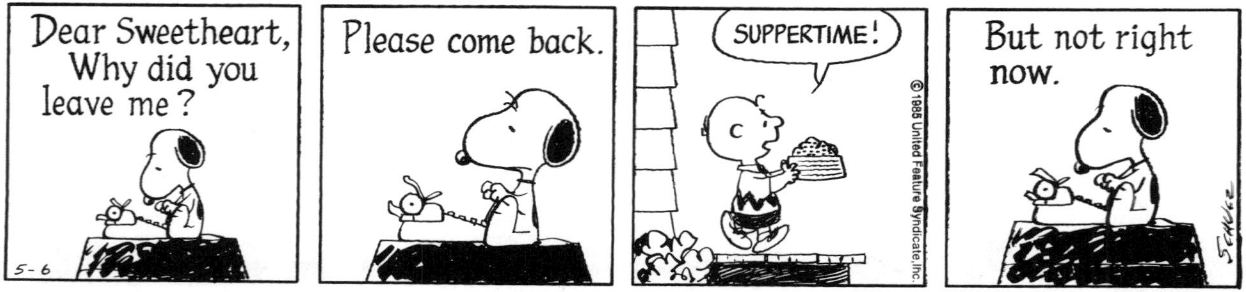

Dear Sweetheart, Why did you leave me?
5-6
Please come back.
SUPPERTIME!
But not right now.
SCHULZ

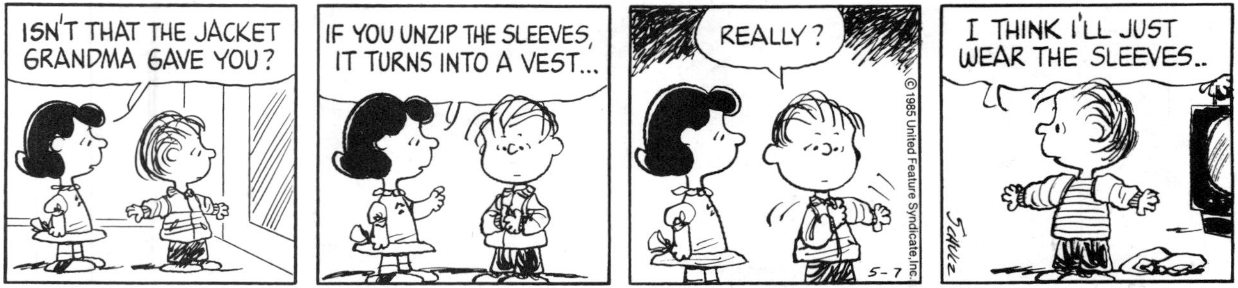
ISN'T THAT THE JACKET GRANDMA GAVE YOU?
IF YOU UNZIP THE SLEEVES, IT TURNS INTO A VEST...
REALLY?
© 1985 United Feature Syndicate,Inc.
5-7
I THINK I'LL JUST WEAR THE SLEEVES..
SCHULZ

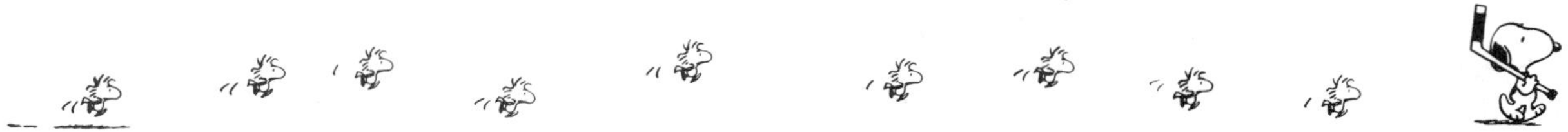

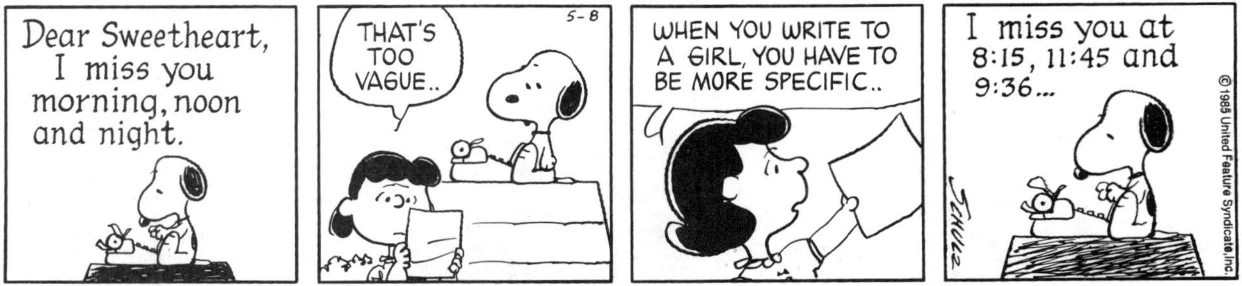
Dear Sweetheart, I miss you morning, noon and night.
5-8
THAT'S TOO VAGUE..
WHEN YOU WRITE TO A GIRL, YOU HAVE TO BE MORE SPECIFIC..
I miss you at 8:15, 11:45 and 9:36...
SCHULZ
© 1985 United Feature Syndicate,Inc.

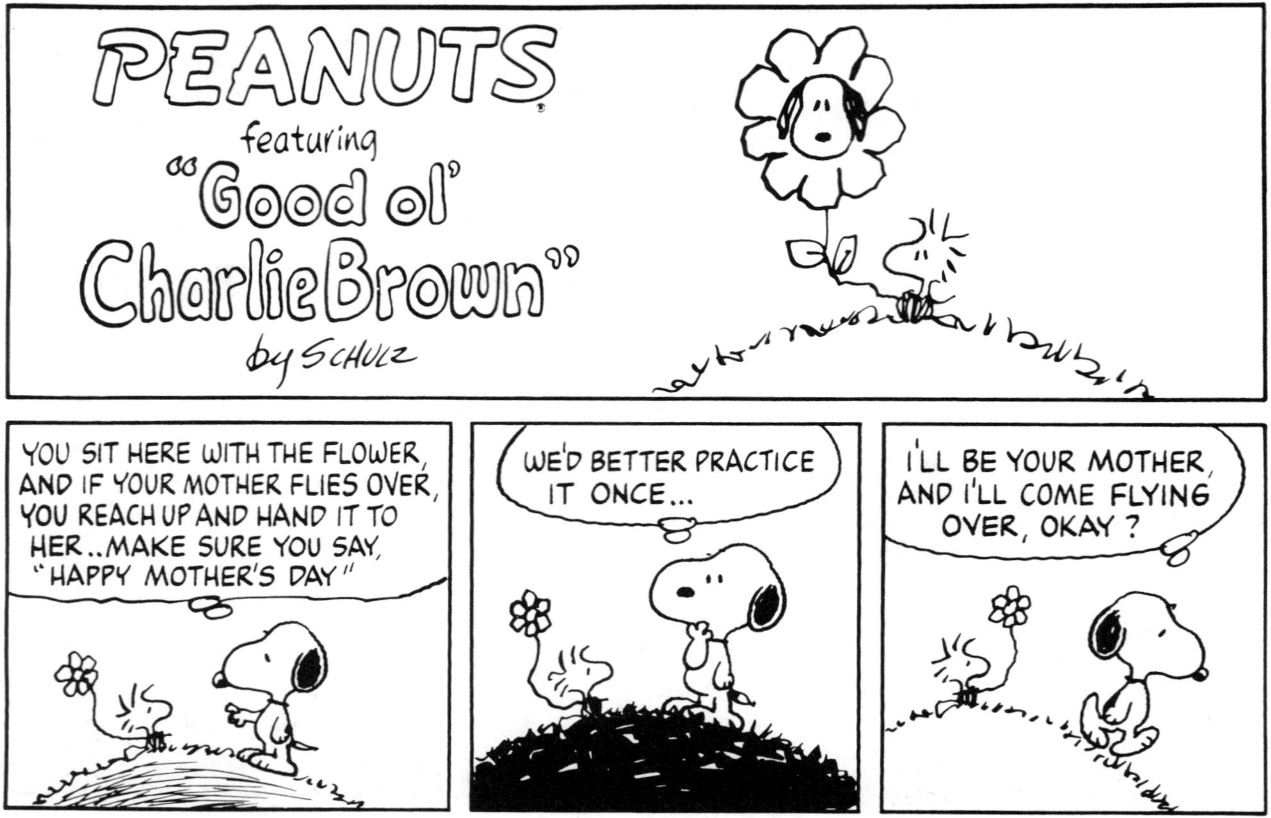
PEANUTS
featuring
"Good ol' Charlie Brown"
by SCHULZ
YOU SIT HERE WITH THE FLOWER, AND IF YOUR MOTHER FLIES OVER, YOU REACH UP AND HAND IT TO HER..MAKE SURE YOU SAY, "HAPPY MOTHER'S DAY"
WE'D BETTER PRACTICE IT ONCE...
I'LL BE YOUR MOTHER, AND I'LL COME FLYING OVER, OKAY ?

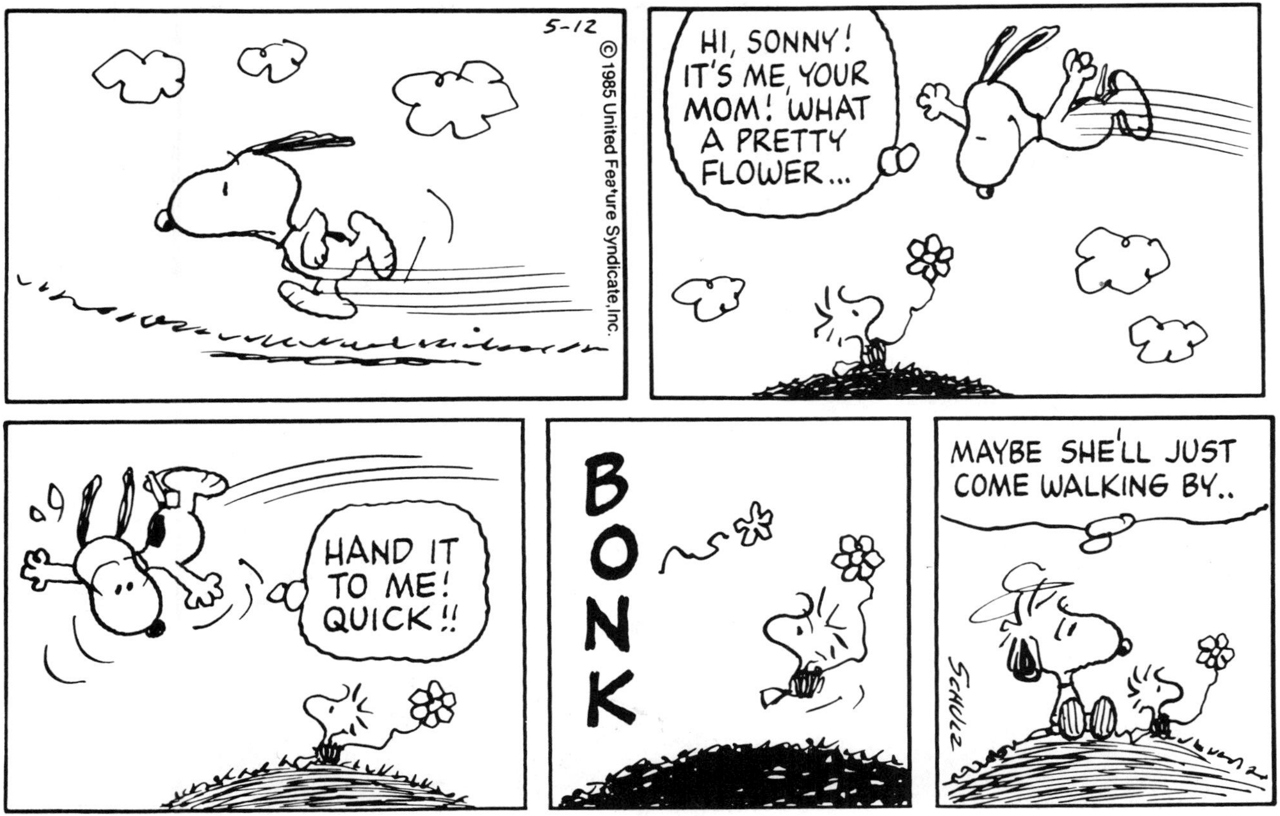

5-12
© 1985 United Feature Syndicate, Inc.
HI, SONNY! IT'S ME, YOUR MOM! WHAT A PRETTY FLOWER...
HAND IT TO ME! QUICK!!
BONK
MAYBE SHE'LL JUST COME WALKING BY..
SCHULZ

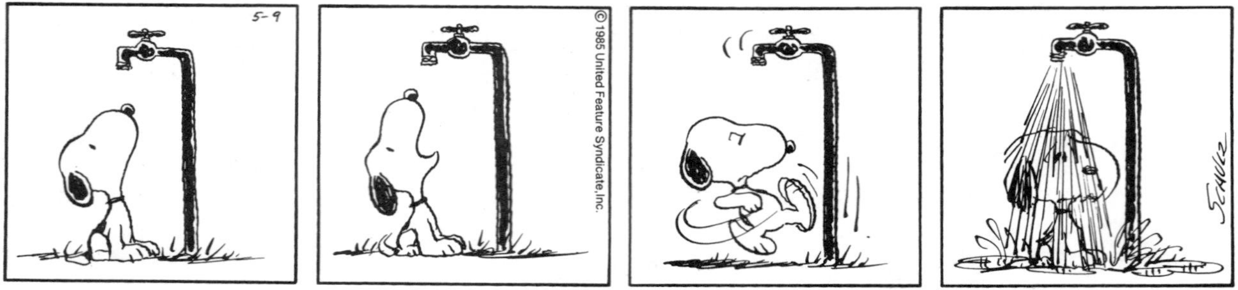

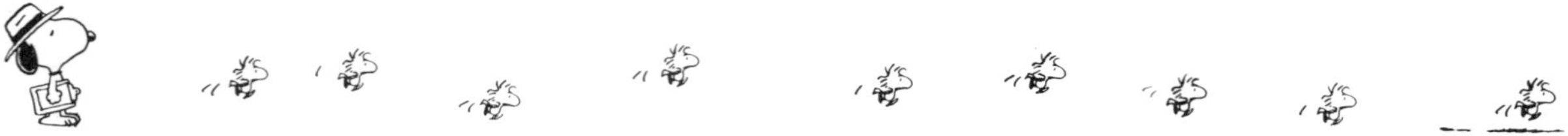

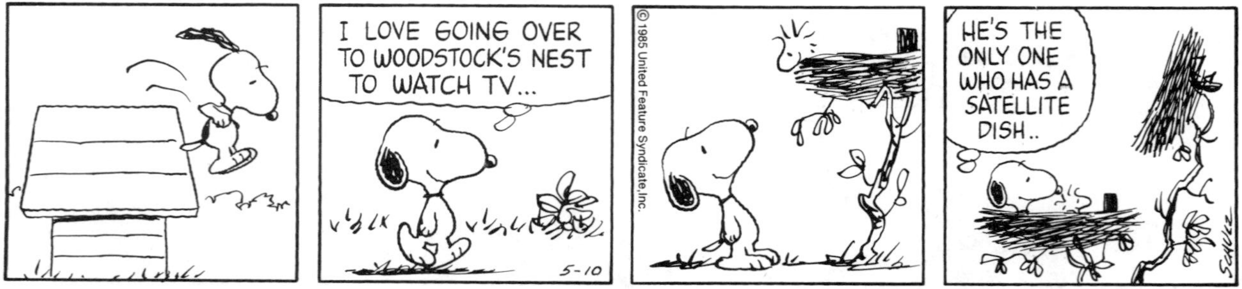
I LOVE GOING OVER TO WOODSTOCK'S NEST TO WATCH TV...
HE'S THE ONLY ONE WHO HAS A SATELLITE DISH..

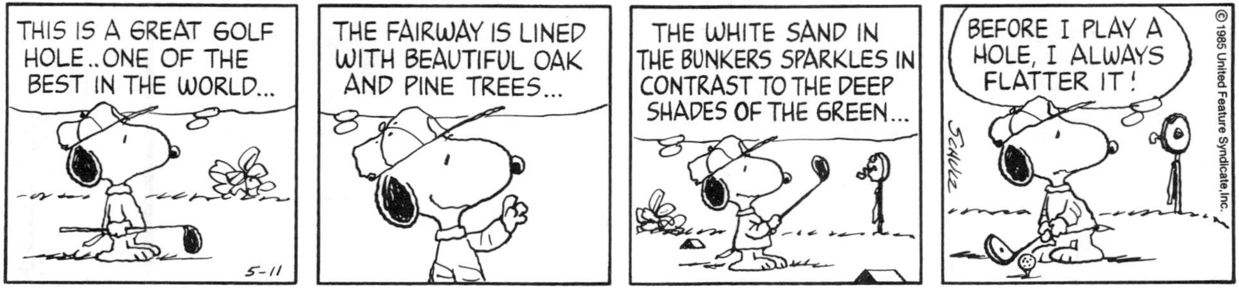
THIS IS A GREAT GOLF HOLE..ONE OF THE BEST IN THE WORLD...
THE FAIRWAY IS LINED WITH BEAUTIFUL OAK AND PINE TREES...
THE WHITE SAND IN THE BUNKERS SPARKLES IN CONTRAST TO THE DEEP SHADES OF THE GREEN...
BEFORE I PLAY A HOLE, I ALWAYS FLATTER IT!
© 1985 United Feature Syndicate, Inc.

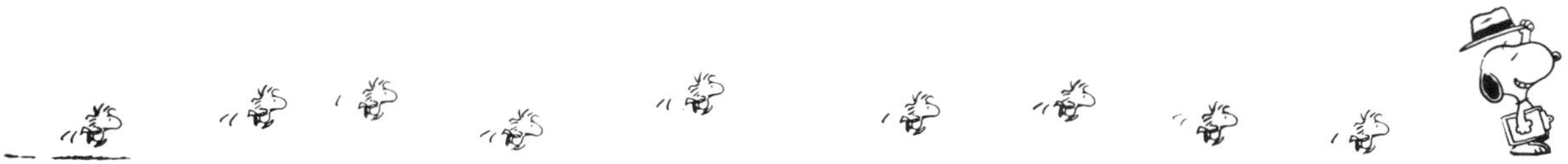

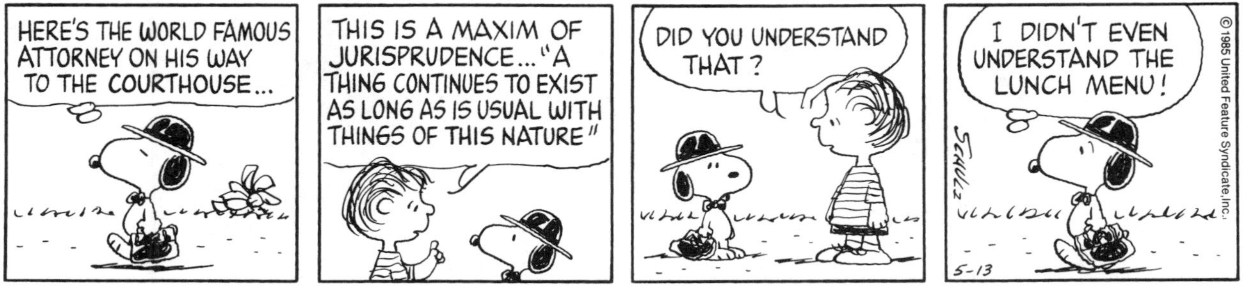
HERE'S THE WORLD FAMOUS ATTORNEY ON HIS WAY TO THE COURTHOUSE...
THIS IS A MAXIM OF JURISPRUDENCE..."A THING CONTINUES TO EXIST AS LONG AS IS USUAL WITH THINGS OF THIS NATURE"
DID YOU UNDERSTAND THAT?
I DIDN'T EVEN UNDERSTAND THE LUNCH MENU!
© 1985 United Feature Syndicate, Inc.

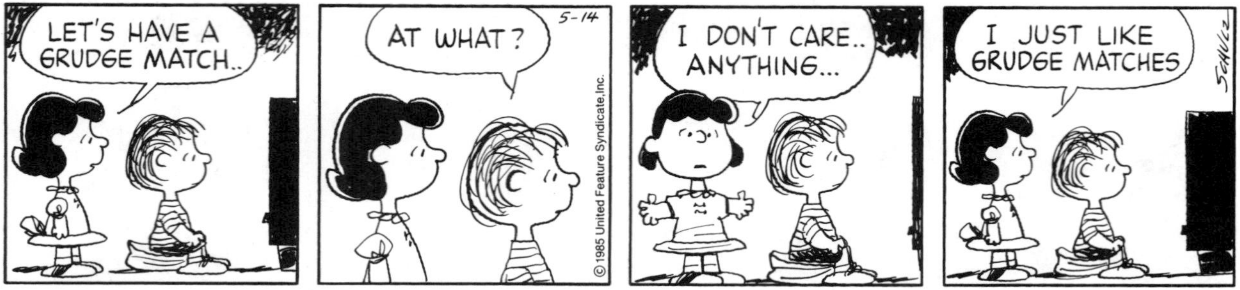
LET'S HAVE A GRUDGE MATCH..
AT WHAT?
5-14
© 1985 United Feature Syndicate, Inc.
I DON'T CARE.. ANYTHING...
I JUST LIKE GRUDGE MATCHES
SCHULZ

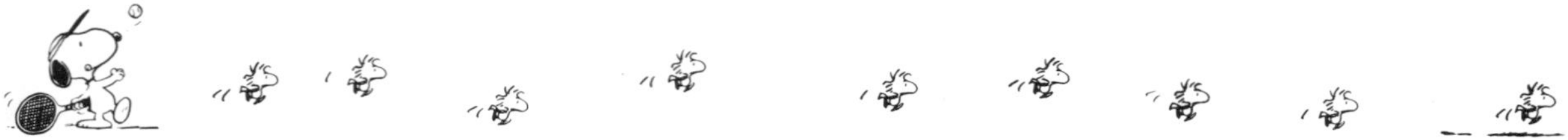

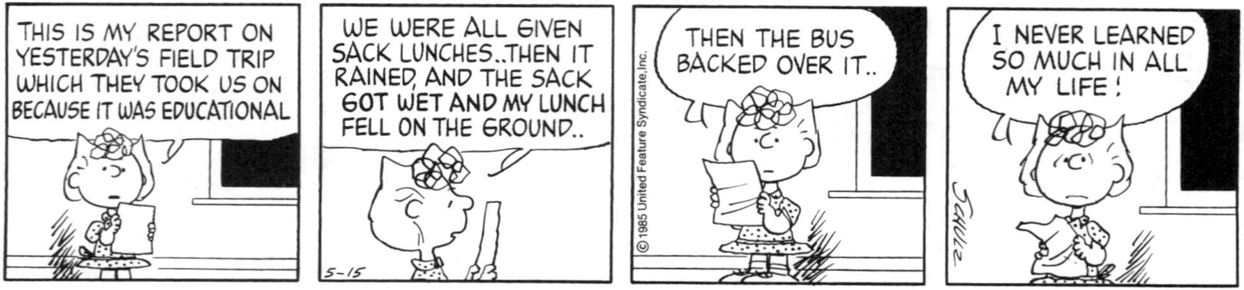
THIS IS MY REPORT ON YESTERDAY'S FIELD TRIP WHICH THEY TOOK US ON BECAUSE IT WAS EDUCATIONAL
WE WERE ALL GIVEN SACK LUNCHES..THEN IT RAINED, AND THE SACK GOT WET AND MY LUNCH FELL ON THE GROUND..
5-15
© 1985 United Feature Syndicate, Inc.
THEN THE BUS BACKED OVER IT..
SCHULZ
I NEVER LEARNED SO MUCH IN ALL MY LIFE!

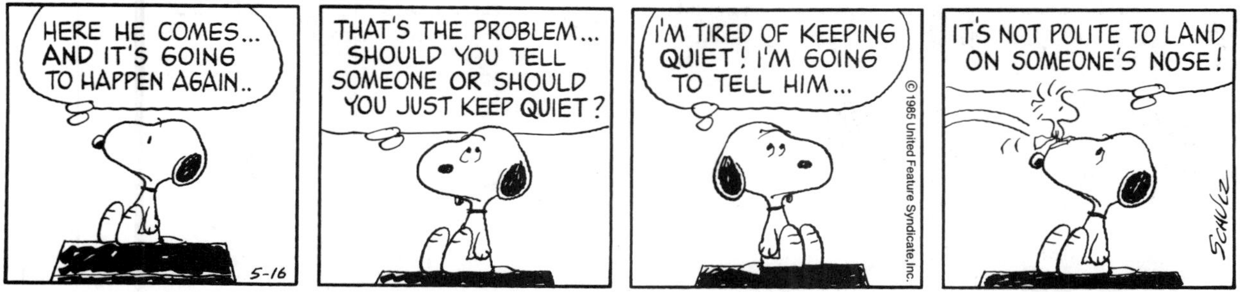
HERE HE COMES... AND IT'S GOING TO HAPPEN AGAIN..
5-16
THAT'S THE PROBLEM... SHOULD YOU TELL SOMEONE OR SHOULD YOU JUST KEEP QUIET?
I'M TIRED OF KEEPING QUIET! I'M GOING TO TELL HIM...
© 1985 United Feature Syndicate, Inc.
IT'S NOT POLITE TO LAND ON SOMEONE'S NOSE!
SCHULZ

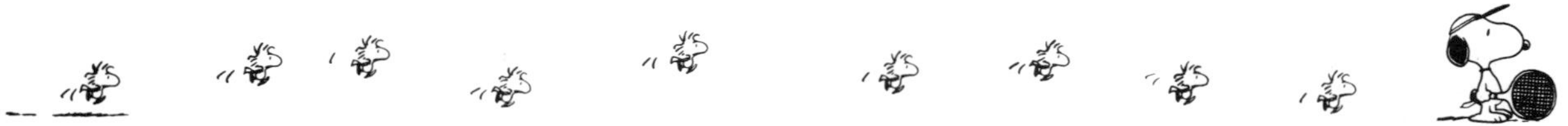

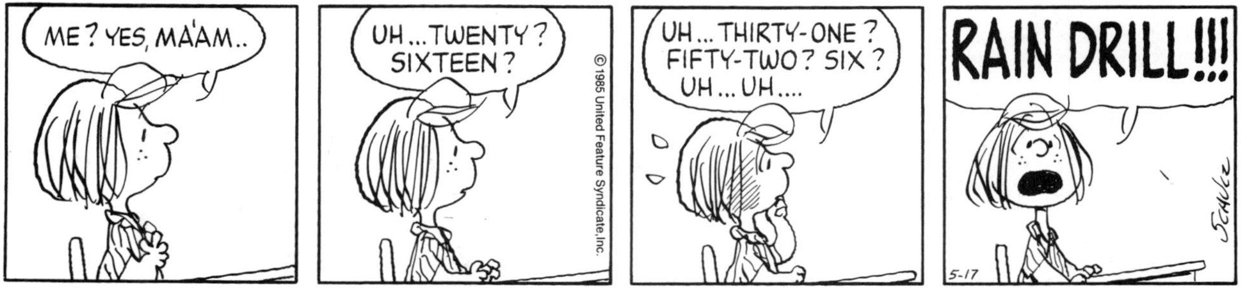
ME? YES, MA'AM..
UH...TWENTY? SIXTEEN?
© 1985 United Feature Syndicate, Inc.
UH...THIRTY-ONE? FIFTY-TWO? SIX? UH...UH....
RAIN DRILL!!!
SCHULZ
5-17

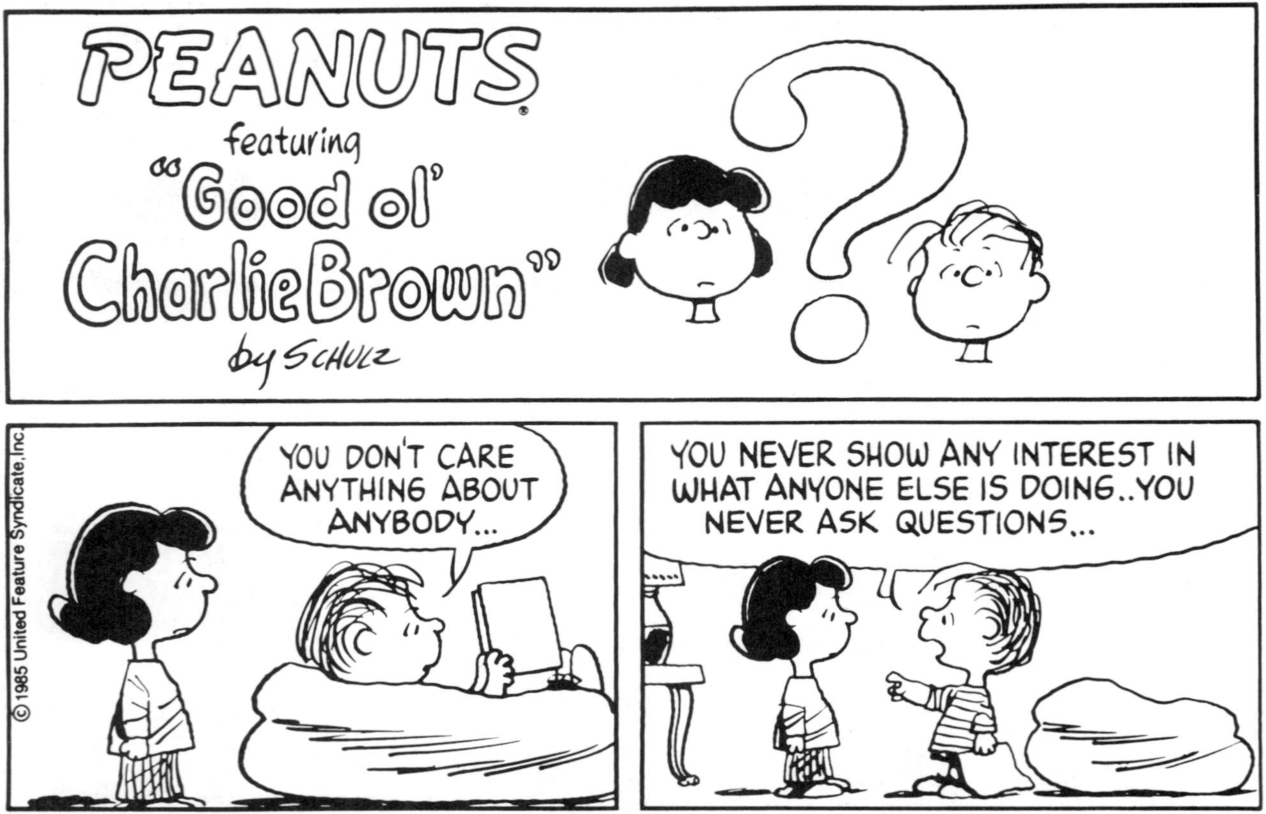

PEANUTS®
featuring
"Good ol' Charlie Brown"
by SCHULZ
© 1985 United Feature Syndicate, Inc.
YOU DON'T CARE ANYTHING ABOUT ANYBODY...
YOU NEVER SHOW ANY INTEREST IN WHAT ANYONE ELSE IS DOING..YOU NEVER ASK QUESTIONS...

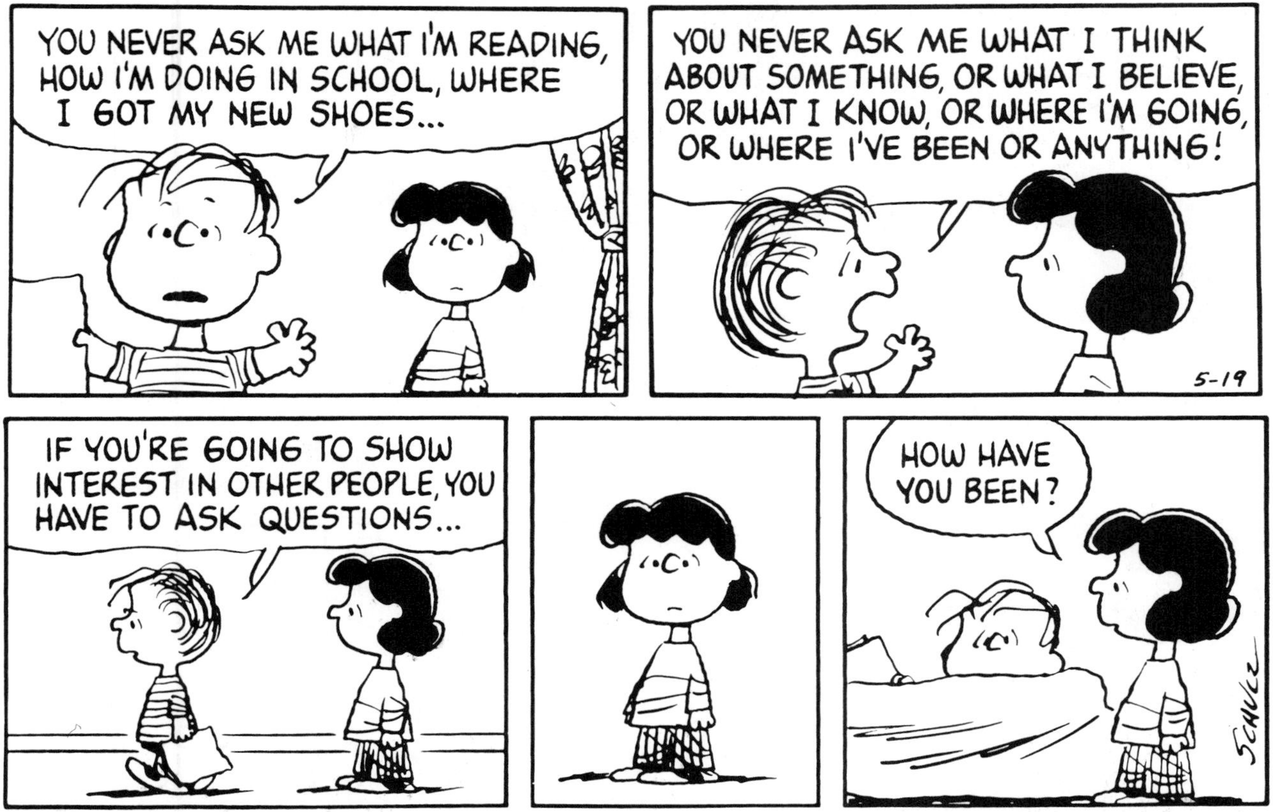
YOU NEVER ASK ME WHAT I'M READING, HOW I'M DOING IN SCHOOL, WHERE I GOT MY NEW SHOES...
YOU NEVER ASK ME WHAT I THINK ABOUT SOMETHING, OR WHAT I BELIEVE, OR WHAT I KNOW, OR WHERE I'M GOING, OR WHERE I'VE BEEN OR ANYTHING!
5-19
IF YOU'RE GOING TO SHOW INTEREST IN OTHER PEOPLE, YOU HAVE TO ASK QUESTIONS...
HOW HAVE YOU BEEN?
SCHULZ

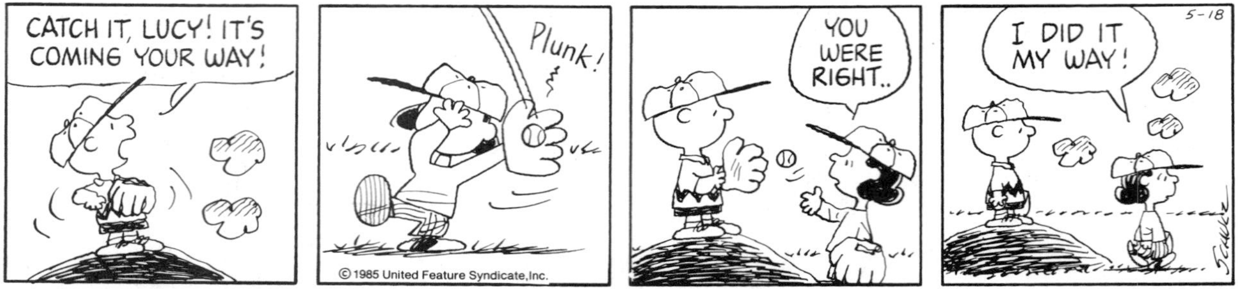
CATCH IT, LUCY! IT'S COMING YOUR WAY!
Plunk!
© 1985 United Feature Syndicate, Inc.
YOU WERE RIGHT..
5-18
I DID IT MY WAY!
SCHULZ

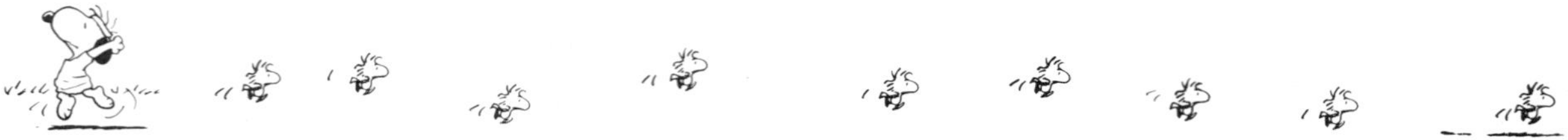

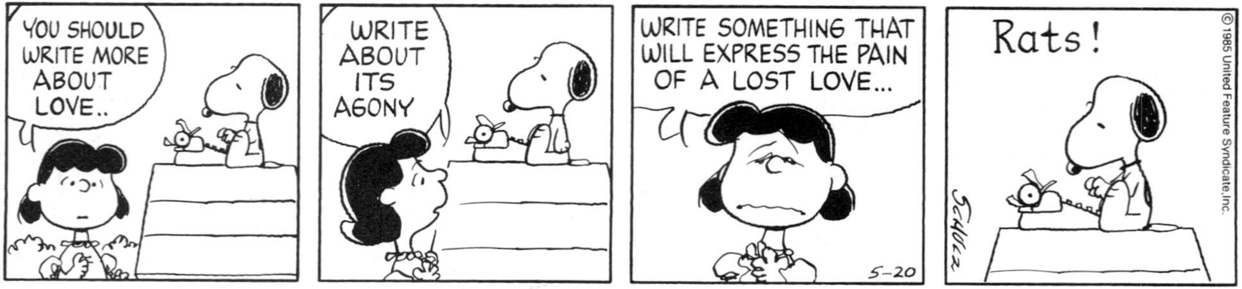
YOU SHOULD WRITE MORE ABOUT LOVE..
WRITE ABOUT ITS AGONY
WRITE SOMETHING THAT WILL EXPRESS THE PAIN OF A LOST LOVE...
5-20
Rats!
SCHULZ
© 1985 United Feature Syndicate, Inc.

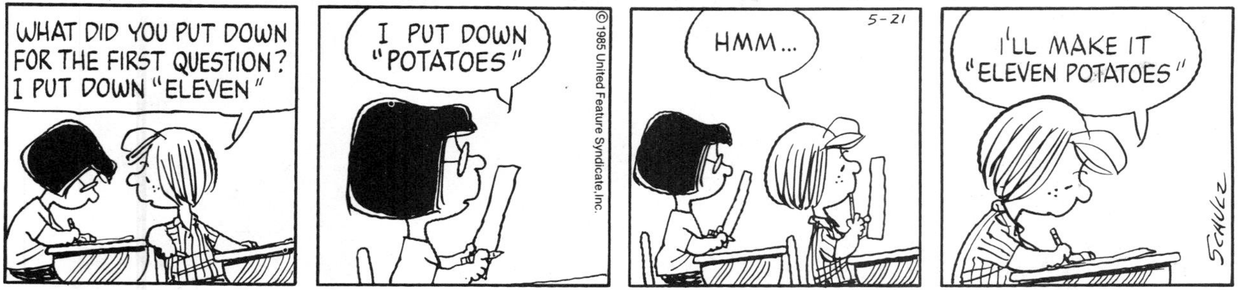
WHAT DID YOU PUT DOWN FOR THE FIRST QUESTION? I PUT DOWN "ELEVEN"
I PUT DOWN "POTATOES"
© 1985 United Feature Syndicate, Inc.
HMM...
5-21
I'LL MAKE IT "ELEVEN POTATOES"
SCHULZ

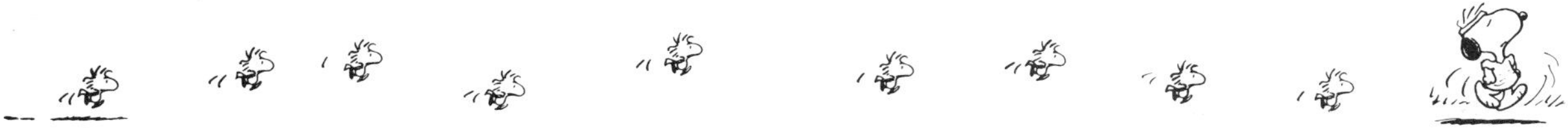

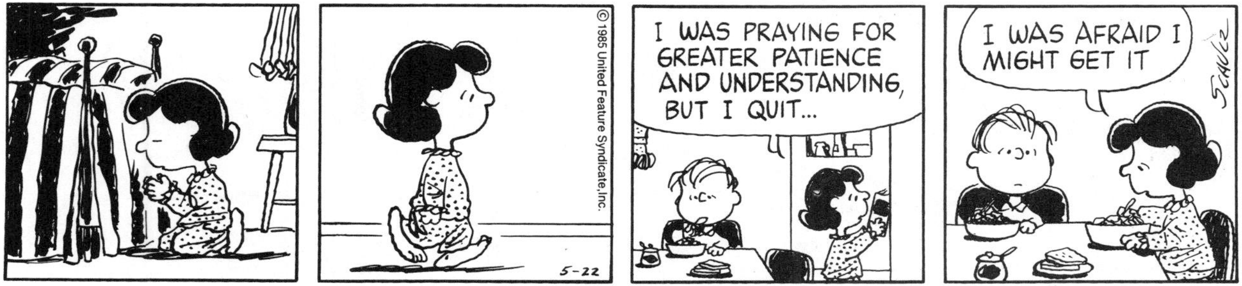
© 1985 United Feature Syndicate, Inc.
5-22
I WAS PRAYING FOR GREATER PATIENCE AND UNDERSTANDING, BUT I QUIT...
I WAS AFRAID I MIGHT GET IT
SCHULZ

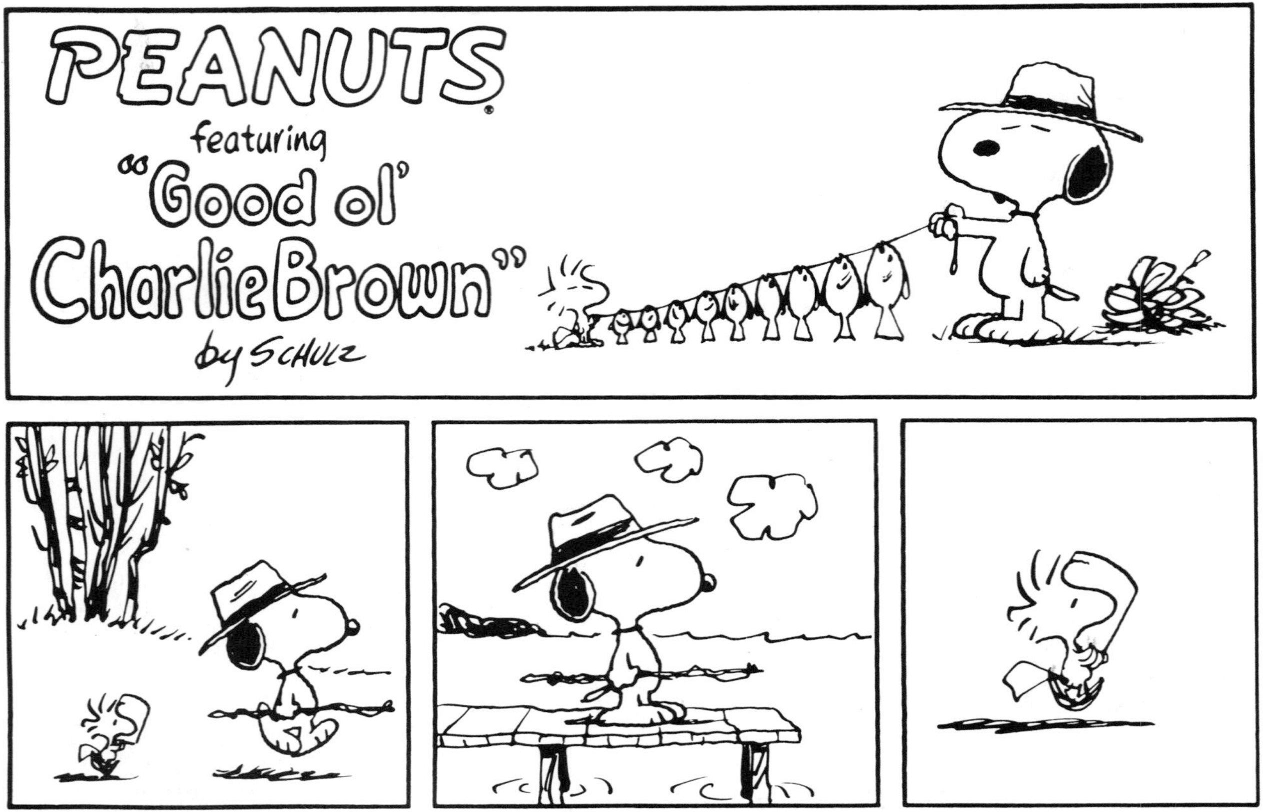
PEANUTS®
featuring
"Good ol' Charlie Brown"
by SCHULZ

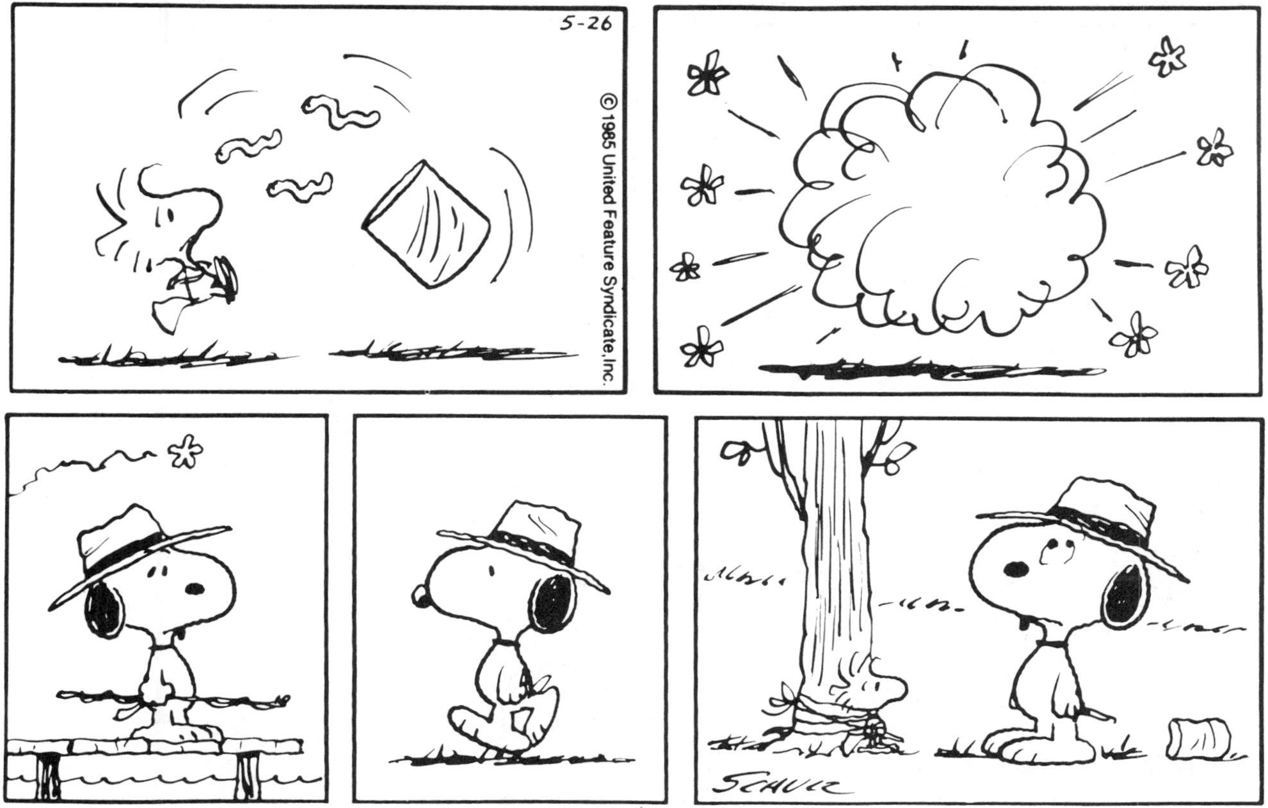
5-26
© 1985 United Feature Syndicate,Inc.
SCHULZ

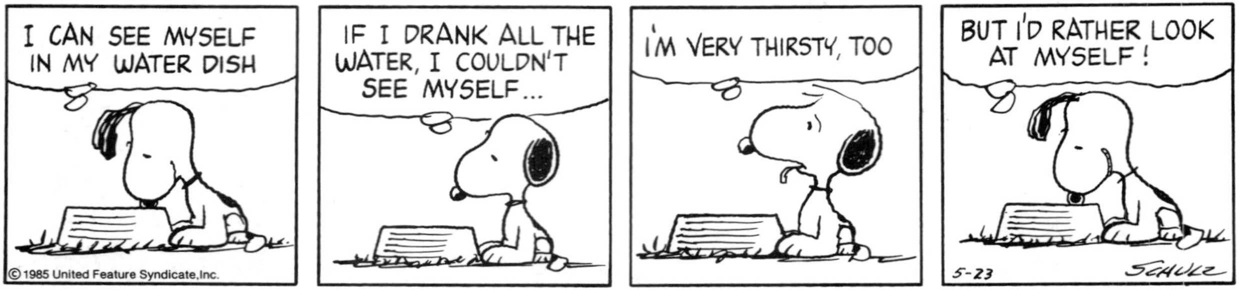
I CAN SEE MYSELF IN MY WATER DISH
©1985 United Feature Syndicate, Inc.
IF I DRANK ALL THE WATER, I COULDN'T SEE MYSELF...
I'M VERY THIRSTY, TOO
BUT I'D RATHER LOOK AT MYSELF!
5-23
SCHULZ

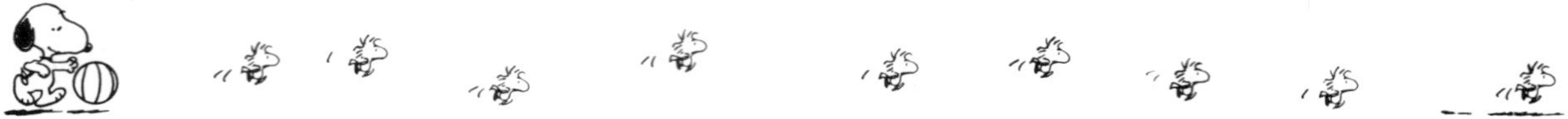

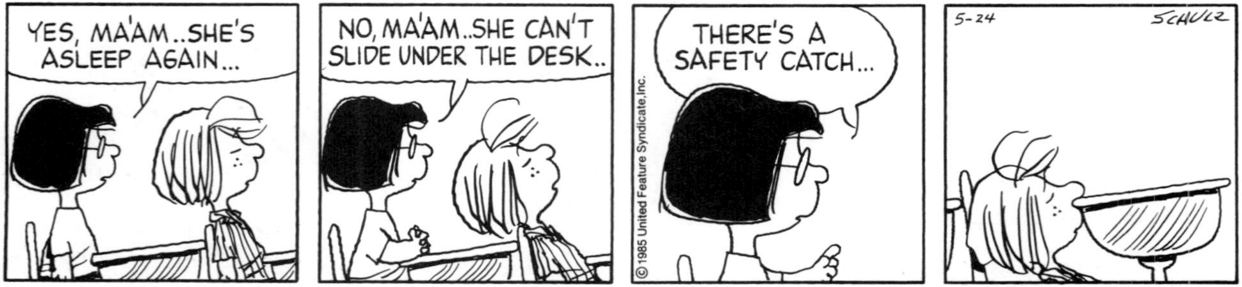
YES, MA'AM..SHE'S ASLEEP AGAIN...
NO, MA'AM..SHE CAN'T SLIDE UNDER THE DESK..
© 1985 United Feature Syndicate, Inc.
THERE'S A SAFETY CATCH...
5-24
SCHULZ

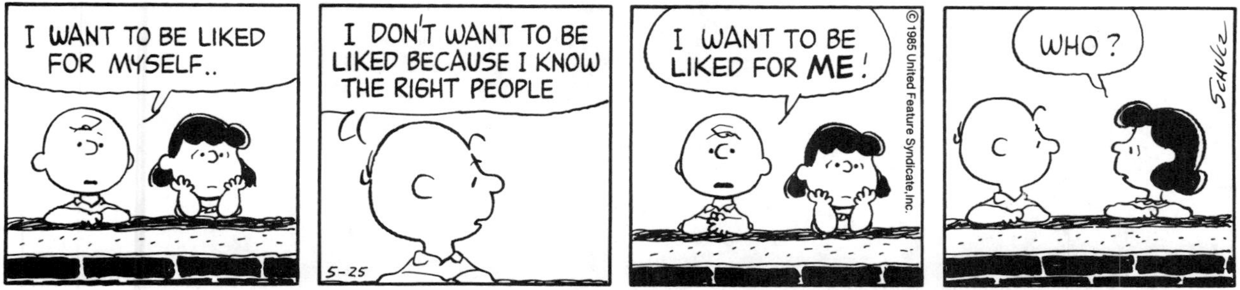
I WANT TO BE LIKED FOR MYSELF..
I DON'T WANT TO BE LIKED BECAUSE I KNOW THE RIGHT PEOPLE
5-25
I WANT TO BE LIKED FOR **ME**!
© 1985 United Feature Syndicate, Inc.
WHO?
SCHULZ

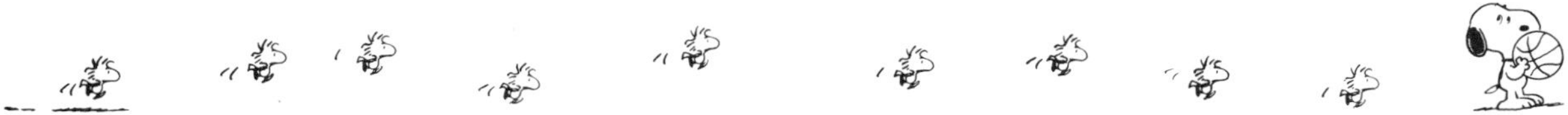

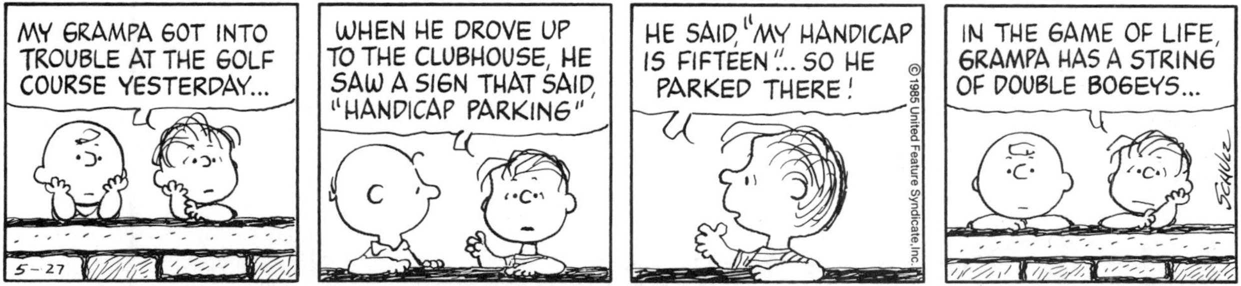
MY GRAMPA GOT INTO TROUBLE AT THE GOLF COURSE YESTERDAY...
5-27
WHEN HE DROVE UP TO THE CLUBHOUSE, HE SAW A SIGN THAT SAID, "HANDICAP PARKING"
HE SAID, "MY HANDICAP IS FIFTEEN"... SO HE PARKED THERE!
© 1985 United Feature Syndicate, Inc.
IN THE GAME OF LIFE, GRAMPA HAS A STRING OF DOUBLE BOGEYS...
SCHULZ

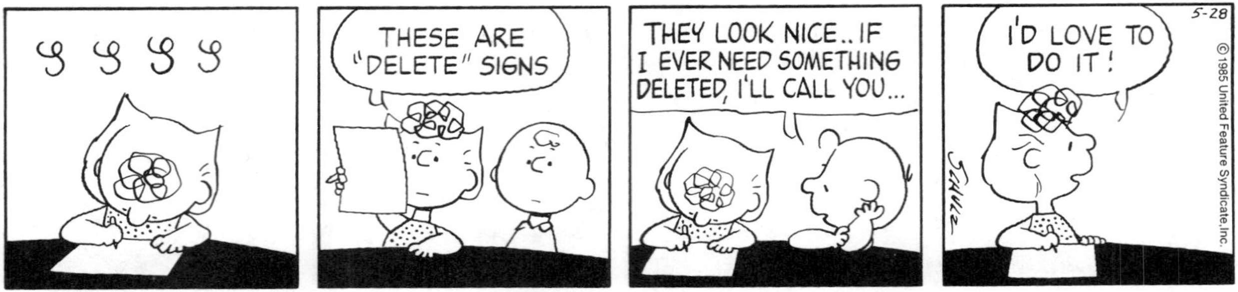
THESE ARE "DELETE" SIGNS
THEY LOOK NICE.. IF I EVER NEED SOMETHING DELETED, I'LL CALL YOU...
5-28
I'D LOVE TO DO IT!
SCHULZ
© 1985 United Feature Syndicate, Inc.

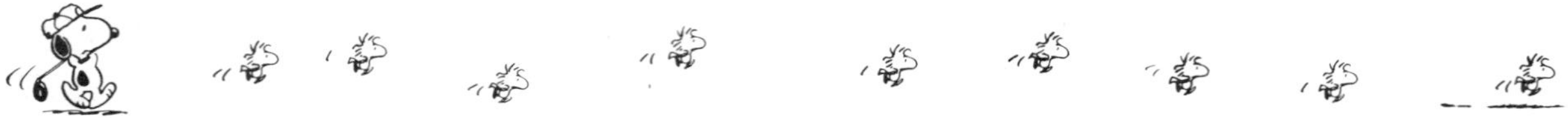

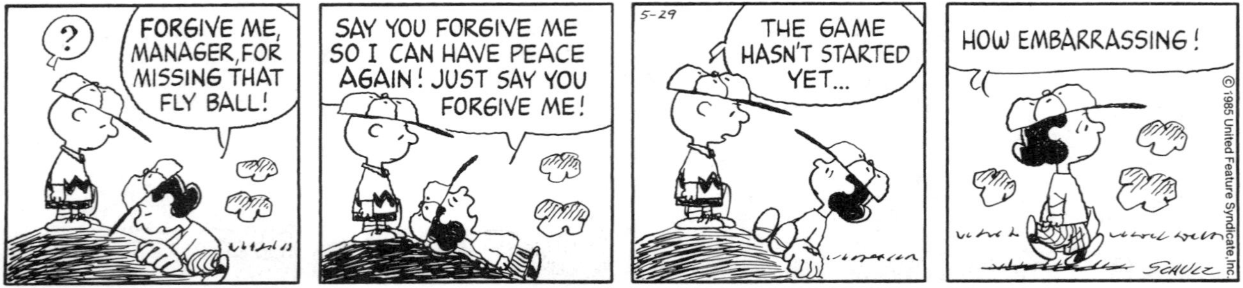
?
FORGIVE ME, MANAGER, FOR MISSING THAT FLY BALL!
SAY YOU FORGIVE ME SO I CAN HAVE PEACE AGAIN! JUST SAY YOU FORGIVE ME!
5-29
THE GAME HASN'T STARTED YET...
HOW EMBARRASSING!
SCHULZ
© 1985 United Feature Syndicate, Inc.

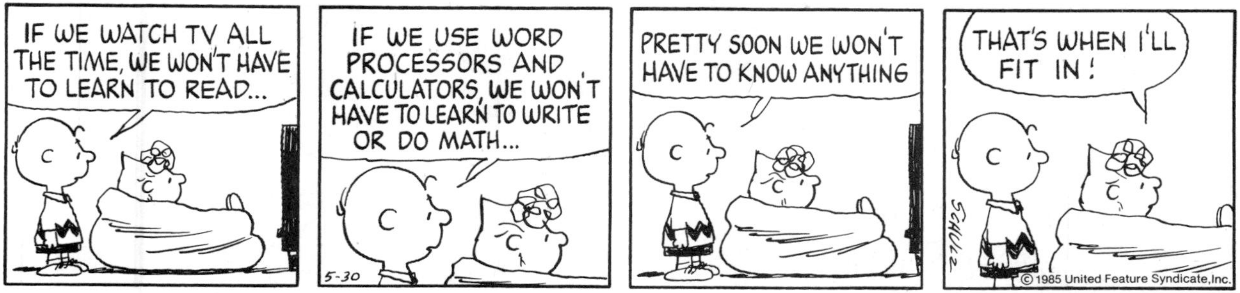
IF WE WATCH TV ALL THE TIME, WE WON'T HAVE TO LEARN TO READ...
IF WE USE WORD PROCESSORS AND CALCULATORS, WE WON'T HAVE TO LEARN TO WRITE OR DO MATH...
5-30
PRETTY SOON WE WON'T HAVE TO KNOW ANYTHING
THAT'S WHEN I'LL FIT IN!
SCHULZ
© 1985 United Feature Syndicate, Inc.

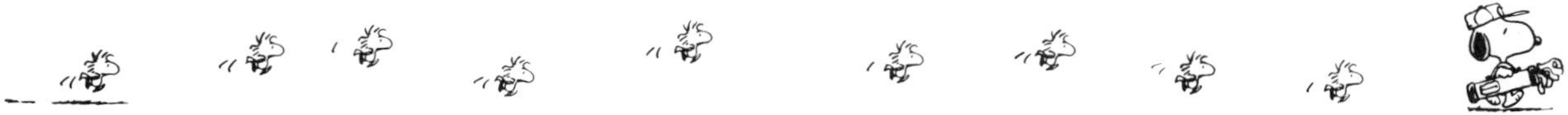

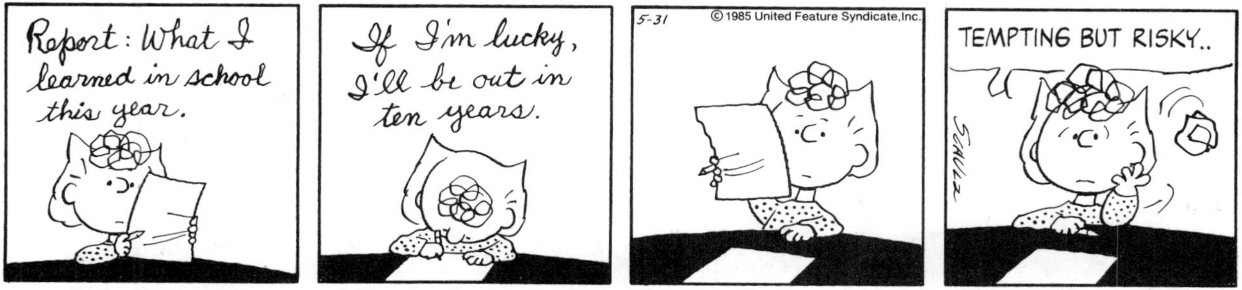
Report: What I learned in school this year.
If I'm lucky, I'll be out in ten years.
5-31
© 1985 United Feature Syndicate, Inc.
TEMPTING BUT RISKY..
SCHULZ

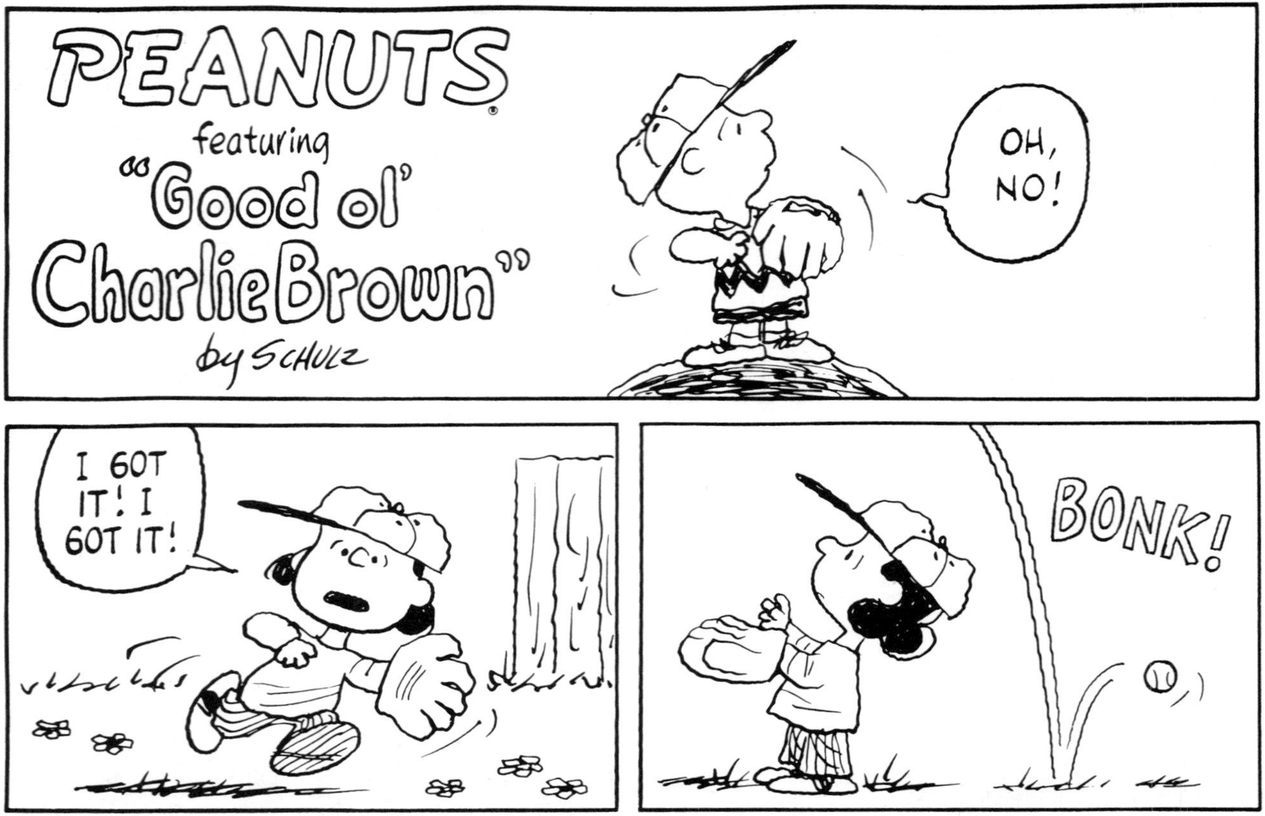
PEANUTS®
featuring
"Good ol' Charlie Brown"
by SCHULZ
OH, NO!
I GOT IT! I GOT IT!
BONK!

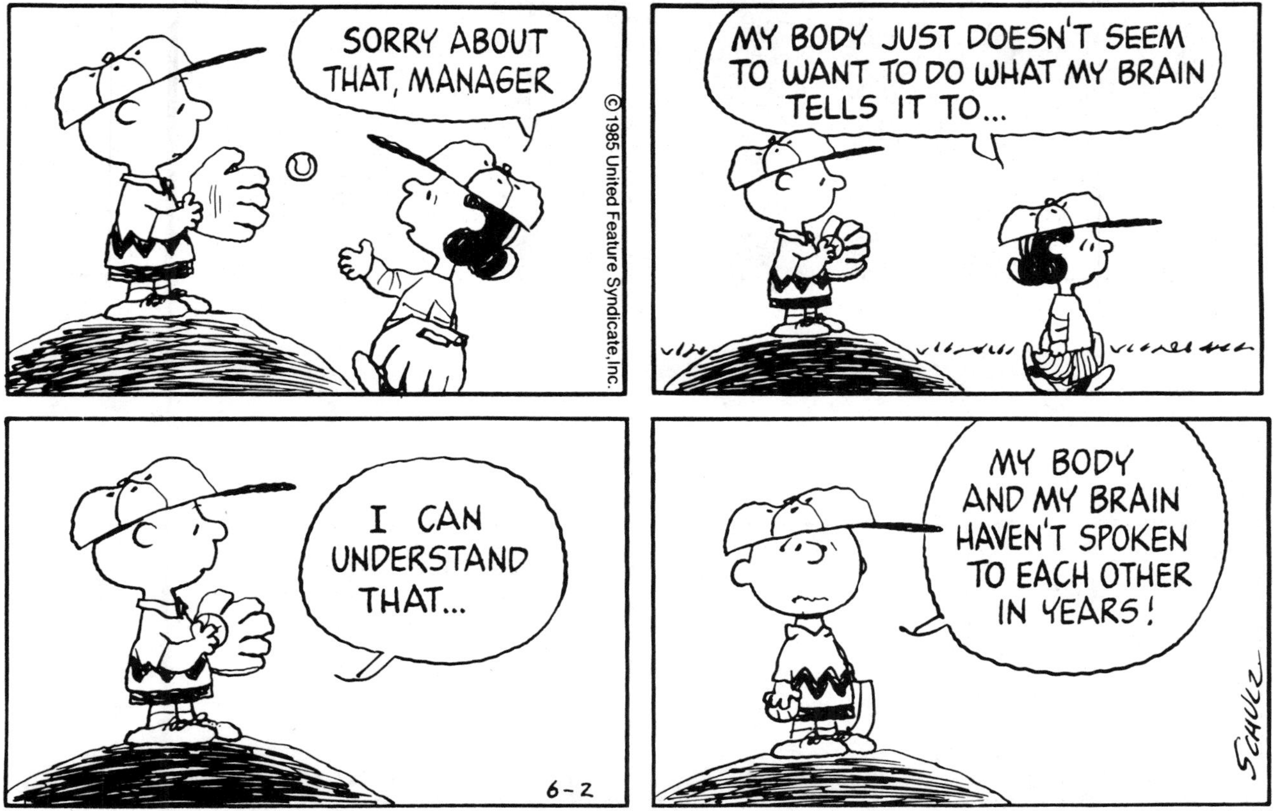
SORRY ABOUT THAT, MANAGER
© 1985 United Feature Syndicate, Inc.
MY BODY JUST DOESN'T SEEM TO WANT TO DO WHAT MY BRAIN TELLS IT TO...
I CAN UNDERSTAND THAT...
6-2
MY BODY AND MY BRAIN HAVEN'T SPOKEN TO EACH OTHER IN YEARS!
SCHULZ

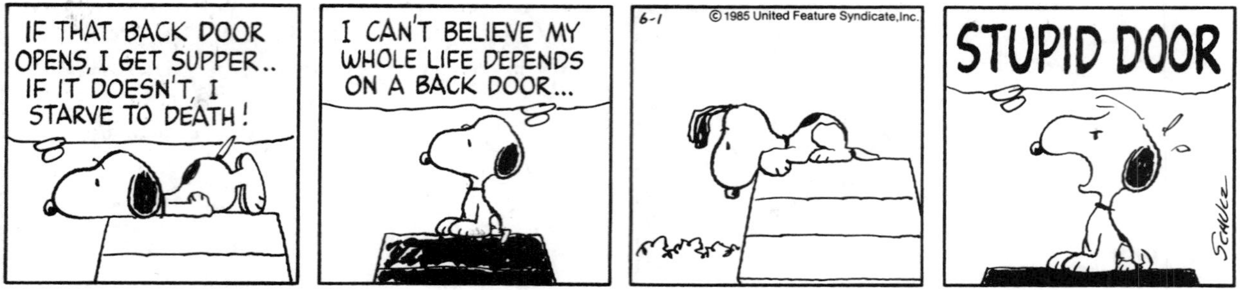
IF THAT BACK DOOR OPENS, I GET SUPPER.. IF IT DOESN'T, I STARVE TO DEATH!
I CAN'T BELIEVE MY WHOLE LIFE DEPENDS ON A BACK DOOR...
6-1
© 1985 United Feature Syndicate, Inc.
STUPID DOOR
SCHULZ

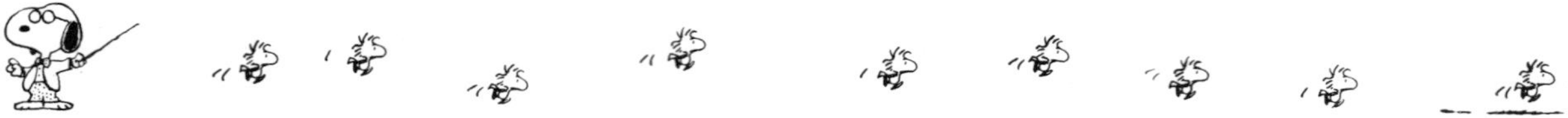

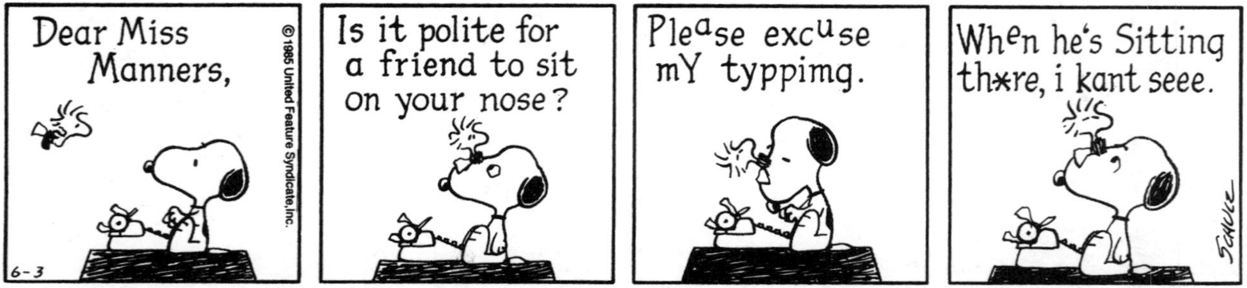
Dear Miss Manners,
© 1985 United Feature Syndicate, Inc.
6-3
Is it polite for a friend to sit on your nose?
Please excuse mY typpimg.
When he's Sitting th*re, i kant seee.
SCHULZ

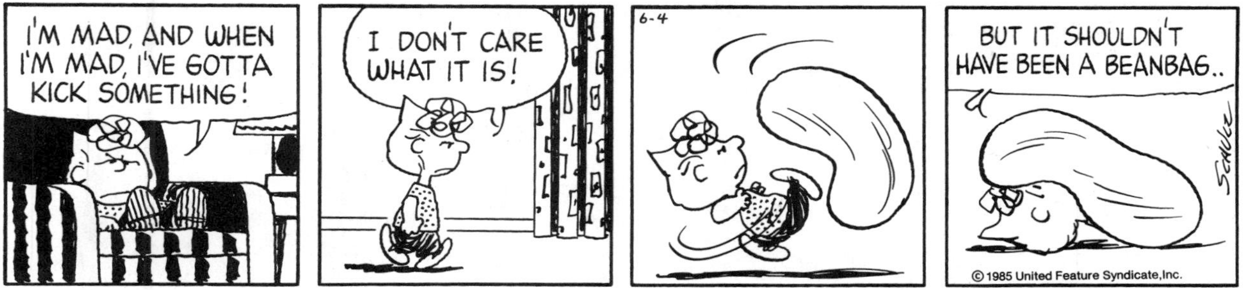
I'M MAD, AND WHEN I'M MAD, I'VE GOTTA KICK SOMETHING!
I DON'T CARE WHAT IT IS!
6-4
BUT IT SHOULDN'T HAVE BEEN A BEANBAG..
SCHULZ
© 1985 United Feature Syndicate, Inc.

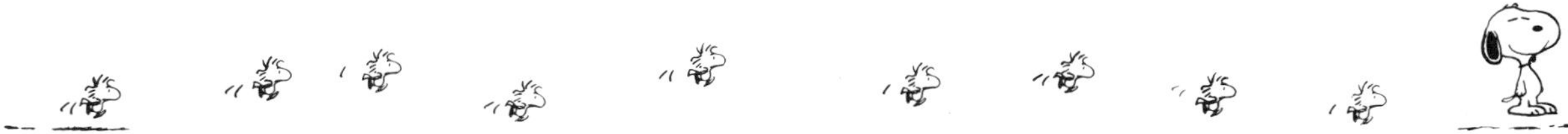

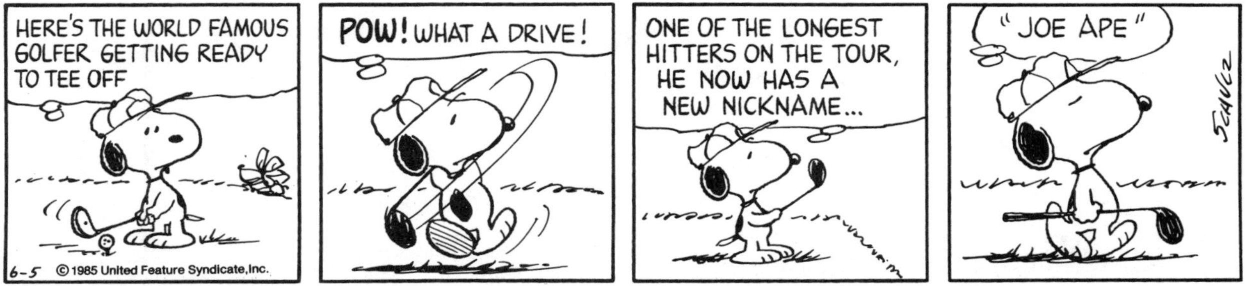
HERE'S THE WORLD FAMOUS GOLFER GETTING READY TO TEE OFF
6-5
© 1985 United Feature Syndicate, Inc.
POW! WHAT A DRIVE!
ONE OF THE LONGEST HITTERS ON THE TOUR, HE NOW HAS A NEW NICKNAME...
"JOE APE"
SCHULZ

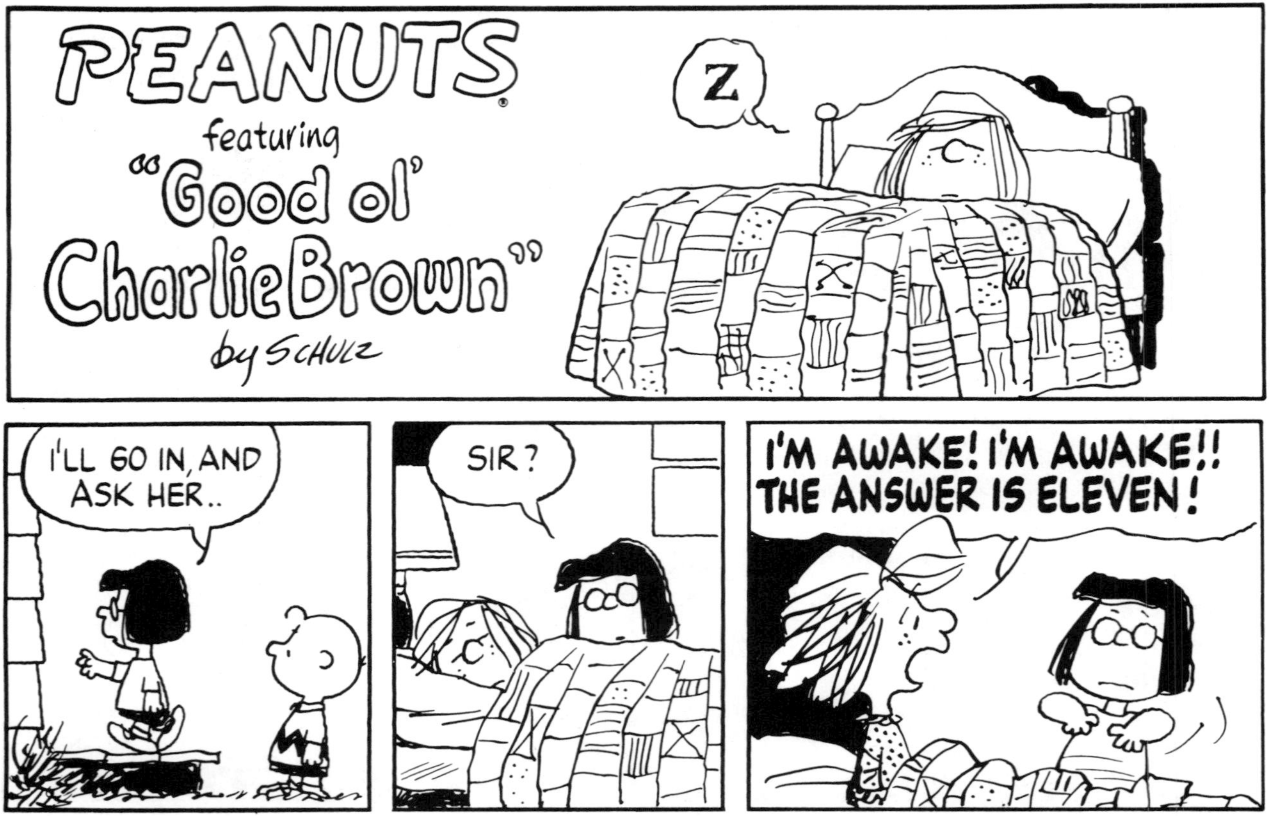
PEANUTS
featuring "Good ol' Charlie Brown"
by SCHULZ
Z
I'LL GO IN, AND ASK HER..
SIR?
I'M AWAKE! I'M AWAKE!! THE ANSWER IS ELEVEN!

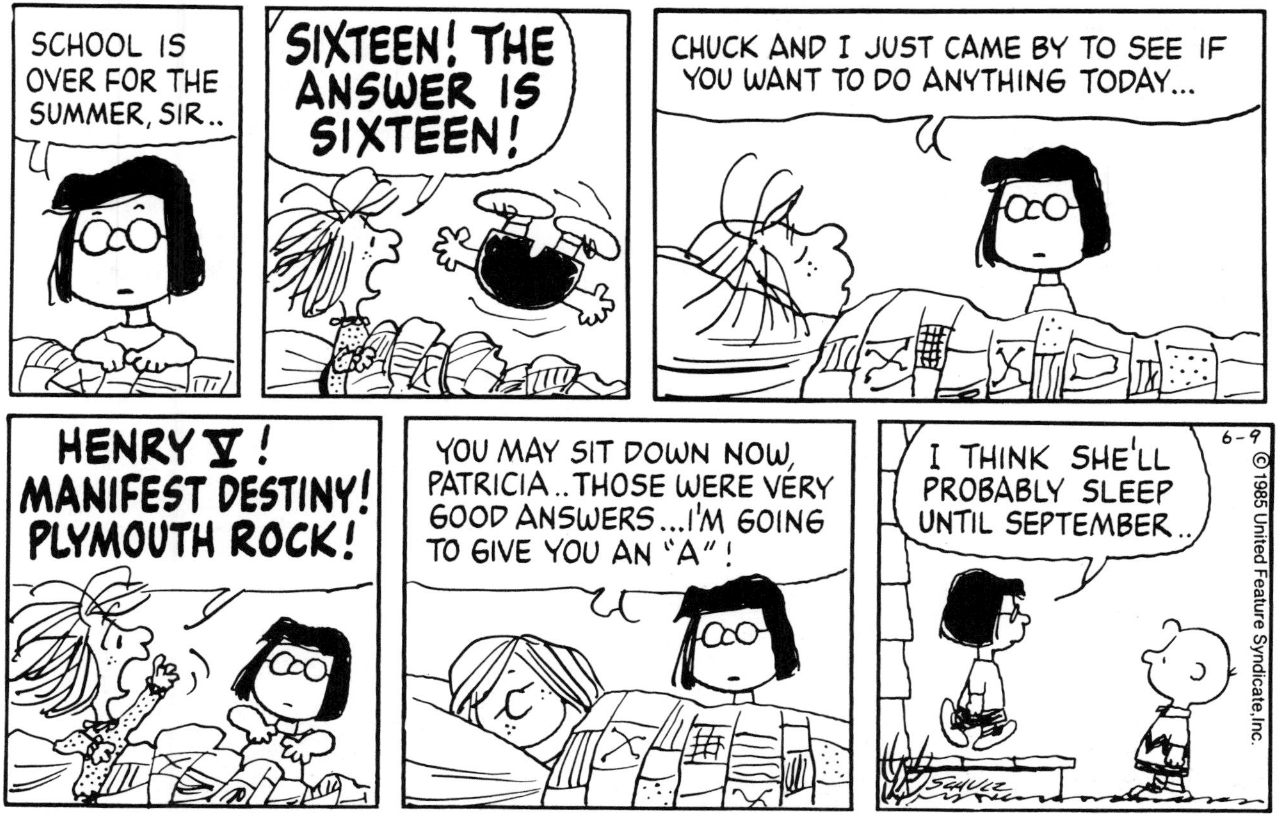
SCHOOL IS OVER FOR THE SUMMER, SIR..
SIXTEEN! THE ANSWER IS SIXTEEN!
CHUCK AND I JUST CAME BY TO SEE IF YOU WANT TO DO ANYTHING TODAY...
HENRY V! MANIFEST DESTINY! PLYMOUTH ROCK!
YOU MAY SIT DOWN NOW, PATRICIA.. THOSE WERE VERY GOOD ANSWERS... I'M GOING TO GIVE YOU AN "A"!
I THINK SHE'LL PROBABLY SLEEP UNTIL SEPTEMBER..
6-9
© 1985 United Feature Syndicate, Inc.
SCHULZ

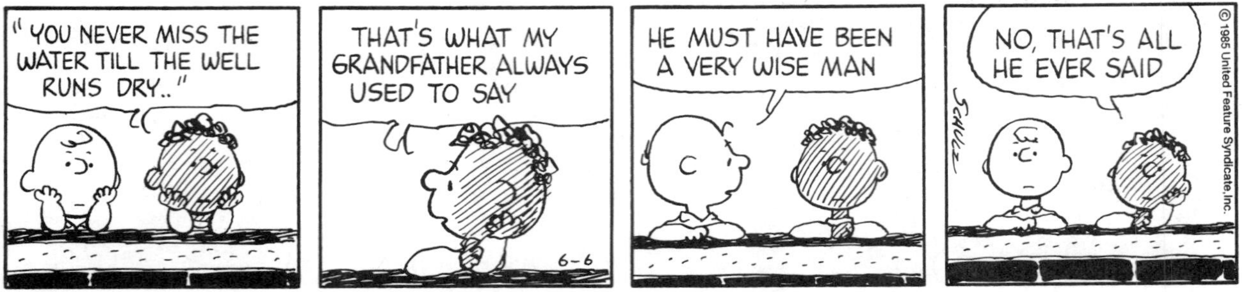
" YOU NEVER MISS THE WATER TILL THE WELL RUNS DRY.."
THAT'S WHAT MY GRANDFATHER ALWAYS USED TO SAY
6-6
HE MUST HAVE BEEN A VERY WISE MAN
NO, THAT'S ALL HE EVER SAID
SCHULZ
© 1985 United Feature Syndicate, Inc.

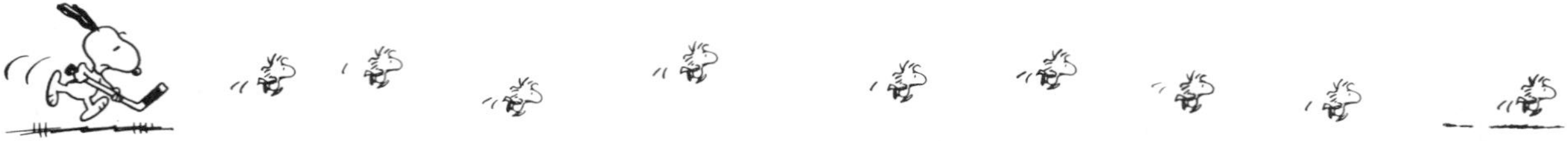

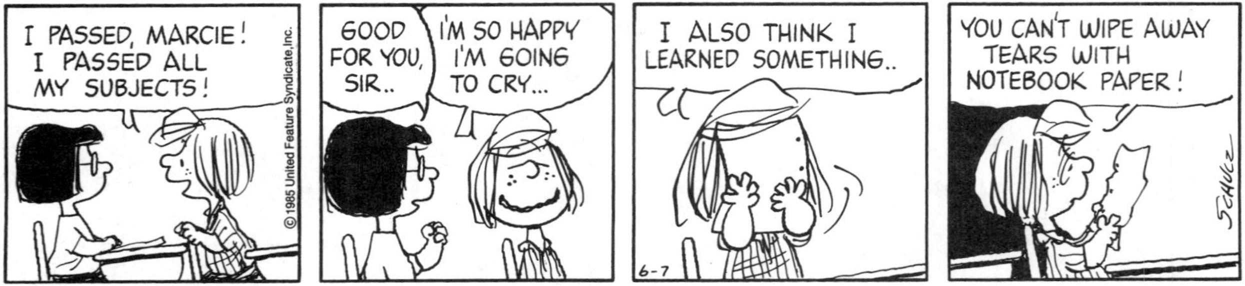
I PASSED, MARCIE! I PASSED ALL MY SUBJECTS!
© 1985 United Feature Syndicate, Inc.
GOOD FOR YOU, SIR..
I'M SO HAPPY I'M GOING TO CRY...
I ALSO THINK I LEARNED SOMETHING..
6-7
YOU CAN'T WIPE AWAY TEARS WITH NOTEBOOK PAPER!
SCHULZ

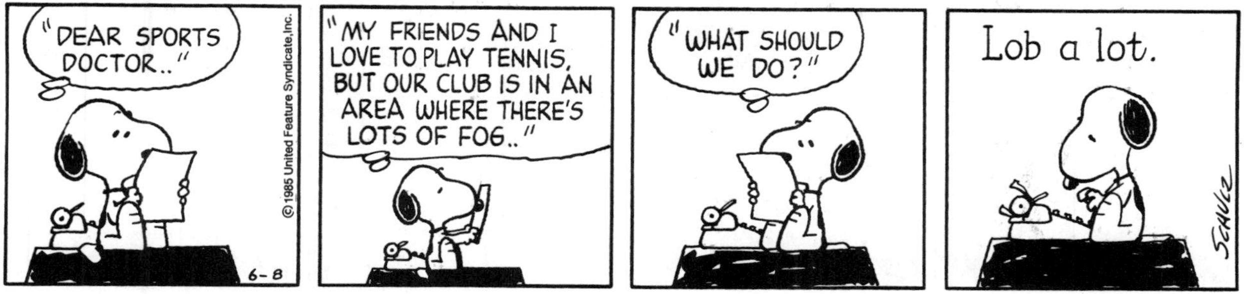
"DEAR SPORTS DOCTOR.."
© 1985 United Feature Syndicate,Inc.
6-8
"MY FRIENDS AND I LOVE TO PLAY TENNIS, BUT OUR CLUB IS IN AN AREA WHERE THERE'S LOTS OF FOG.."
"WHAT SHOULD WE DO?"
Lob a lot.
SCHULZ

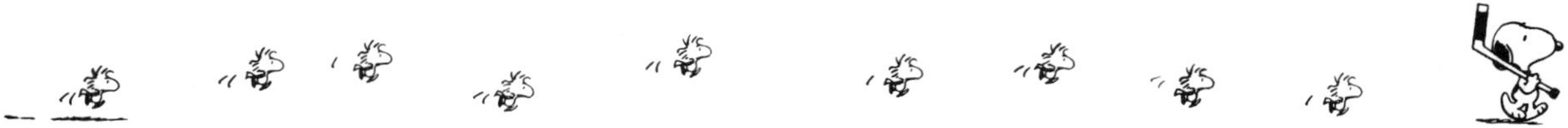

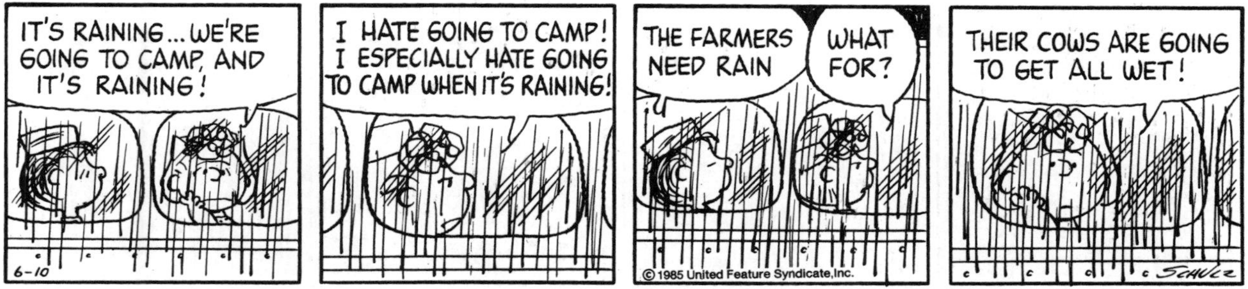
IT'S RAINING... WE'RE GOING TO CAMP, AND IT'S RAINING!
6-10
I HATE GOING TO CAMP! I ESPECIALLY HATE GOING TO CAMP WHEN IT'S RAINING!
THE FARMERS NEED RAIN
WHAT FOR?
© 1985 United Feature Syndicate,Inc.
THEIR COWS ARE GOING TO GET ALL WET!
SCHULZ

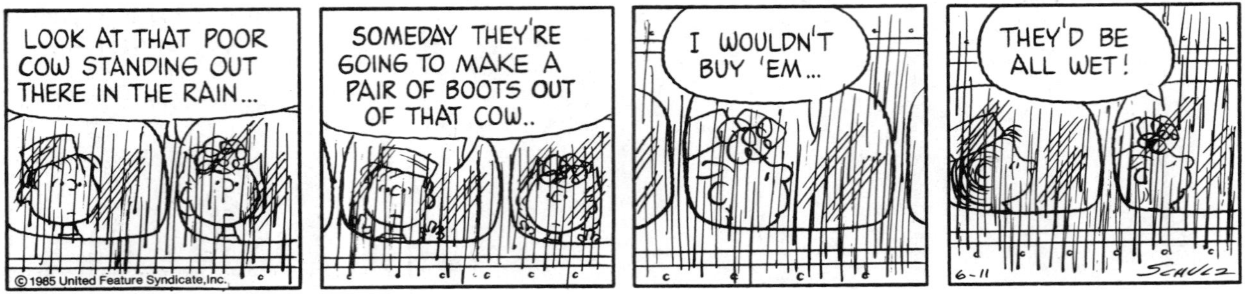
LOOK AT THAT POOR COW STANDING OUT THERE IN THE RAIN...
SOMEDAY THEY'RE GOING TO MAKE A PAIR OF BOOTS OUT OF THAT COW..
I WOULDN'T BUY 'EM...
THEY'D BE ALL WET!
© 1985 United Feature Syndicate, Inc.
6-11
SCHULZ

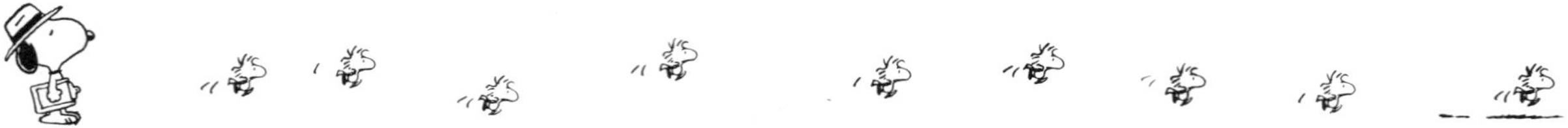

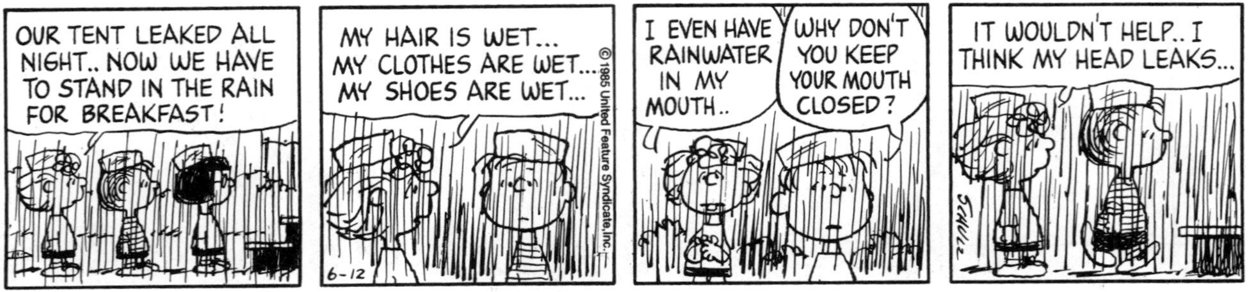
OUR TENT LEAKED ALL NIGHT.. NOW WE HAVE TO STAND IN THE RAIN FOR BREAKFAST!
MY HAIR IS WET... MY CLOTHES ARE WET... MY SHOES ARE WET...
© 1985 United Feature Syndicate, Inc.
6-12
I EVEN HAVE RAINWATER IN MY MOUTH..
WHY DON'T YOU KEEP YOUR MOUTH CLOSED?
IT WOULDN'T HELP.. I THINK MY HEAD LEAKS...
SCHULZ

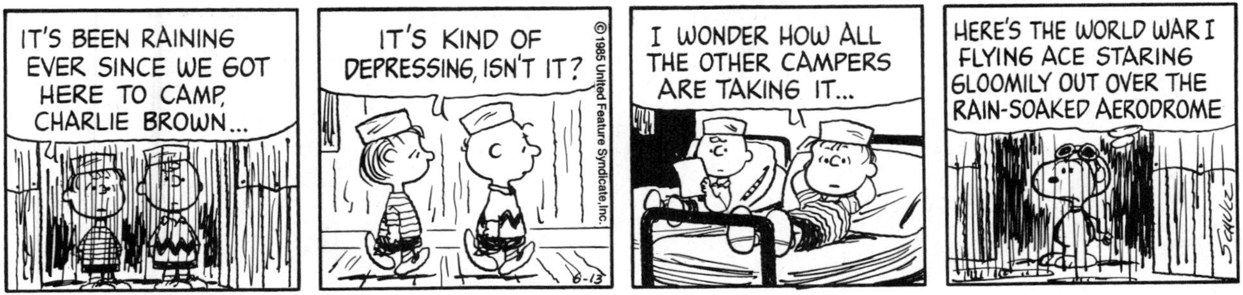
IT'S BEEN RAINING EVER SINCE WE GOT HERE TO CAMP, CHARLIE BROWN...
IT'S KIND OF DEPRESSING, ISN'T IT?
© 1985 United Feature Syndicate, Inc.
6-13
I WONDER HOW ALL THE OTHER CAMPERS ARE TAKING IT...
HERE'S THE WORLD WAR I FLYING ACE STARING GLOOMILY OUT OVER THE RAIN-SOAKED AERODROME
SCHULZ

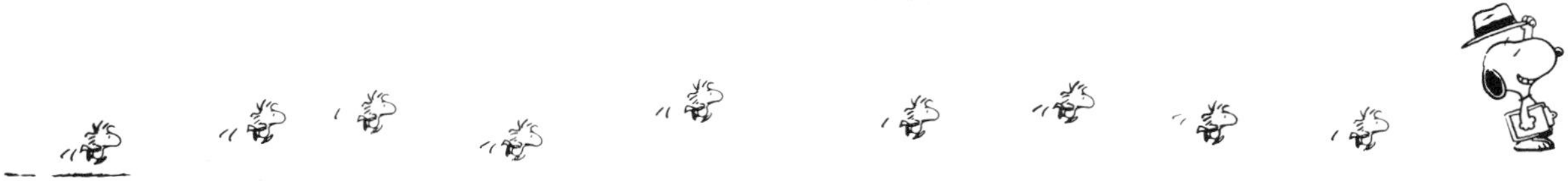

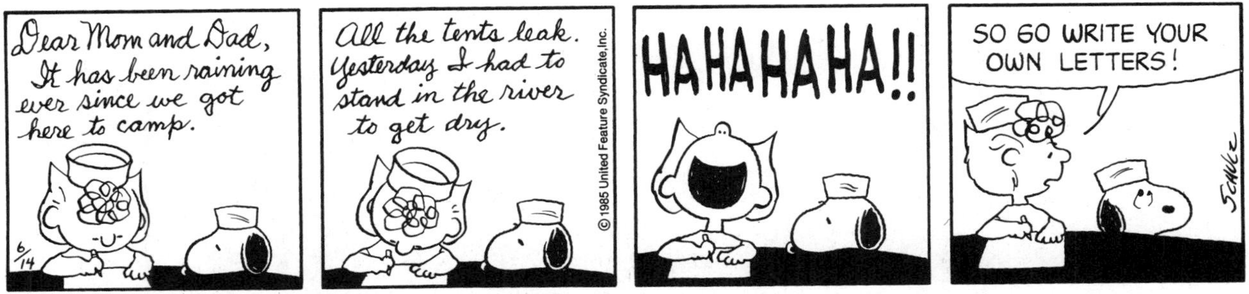
Dear Mom and Dad,
It has been raining ever since we got here to camp.
6/14
All the tents leak. Yesterday I had to stand in the river to get dry.
© 1985 United Feature Syndicate, Inc.
HAHAHAHA!!
SO GO WRITE YOUR OWN LETTERS!
SCHULZ

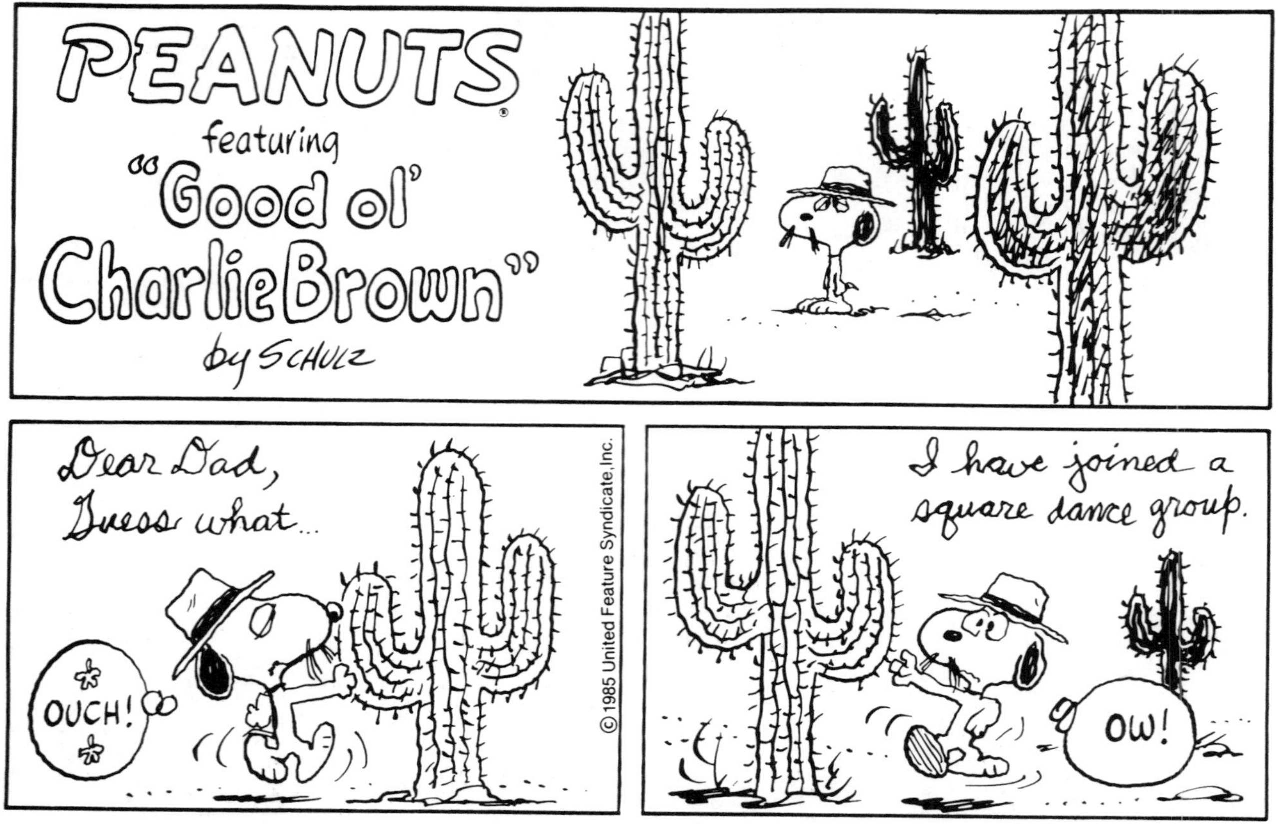
PEANUTS
featuring
"Good ol' Charlie Brown"
by SCHULZ
Dear Dad,
Guess what...
OUCH!
© 1985 United Feature Syndicate, Inc.
I have joined a square dance group.
OW!

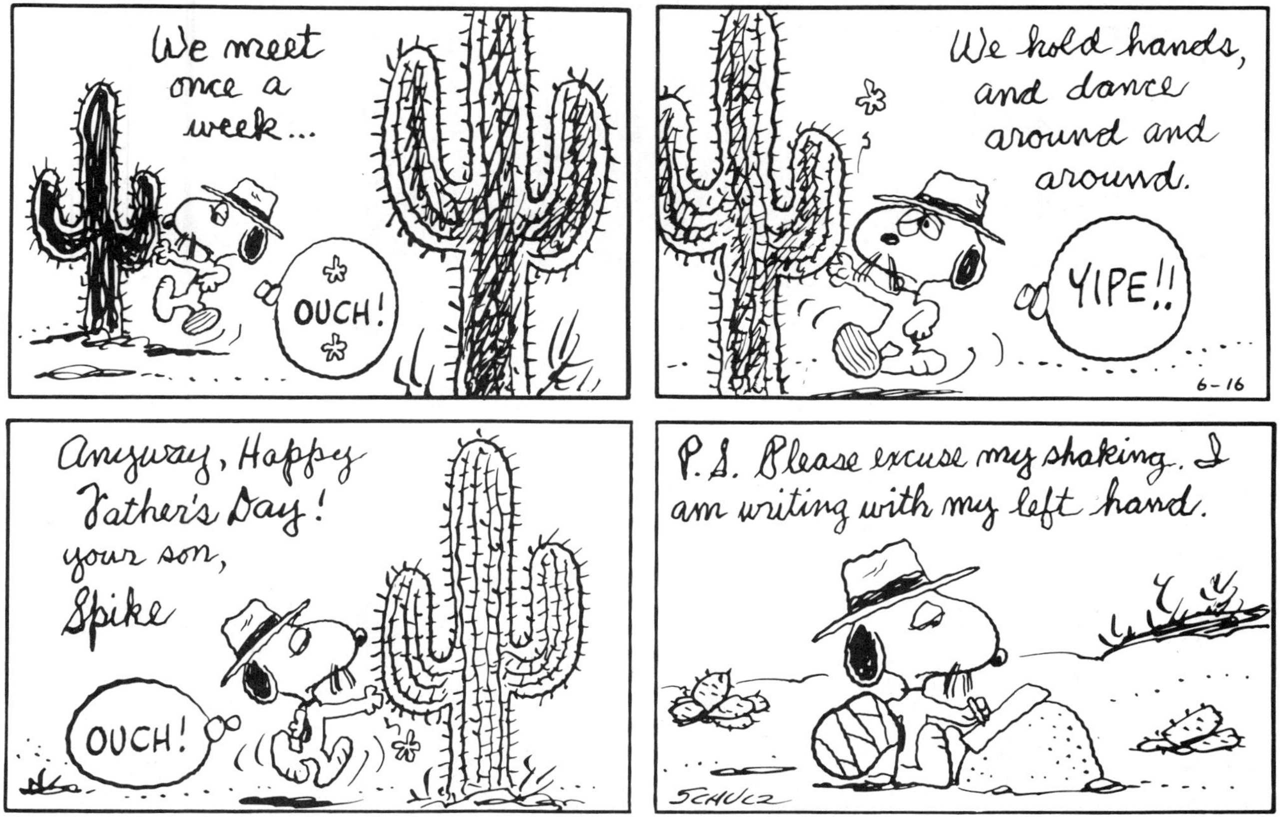
We meet once a week...
OUCH!
We hold hands, and dance around and around.
YIPE!!
6-16
Anyway, Happy Father's Day! your son, Spike
OUCH!
P.S. Please excuse my shaking. I am writing with my left hand.
SCHULZ

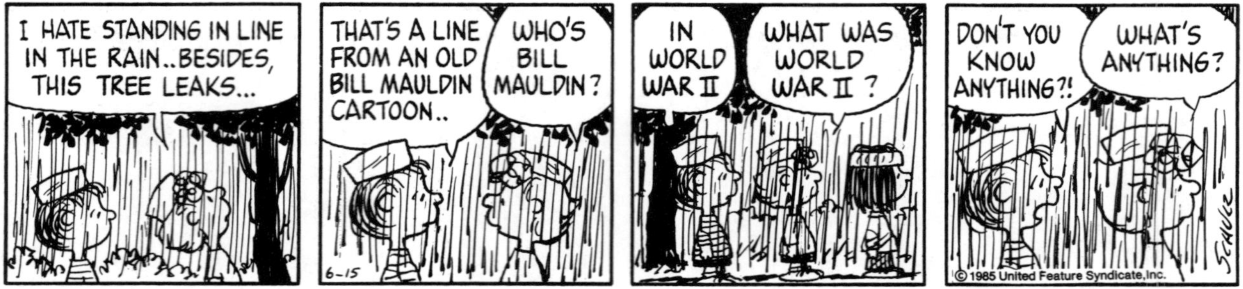
I HATE STANDING IN LINE IN THE RAIN..BESIDES, THIS TREE LEAKS...
THAT'S A LINE FROM AN OLD BILL MAULDIN CARTOON..
WHO'S BILL MAULDIN?
6-15
IN WORLD WAR II
WHAT WAS WORLD WAR II ?
DON'T YOU KNOW ANYTHING?!
WHAT'S ANYTHING?
SCHULZ
© 1985 United Feature Syndicate, Inc.

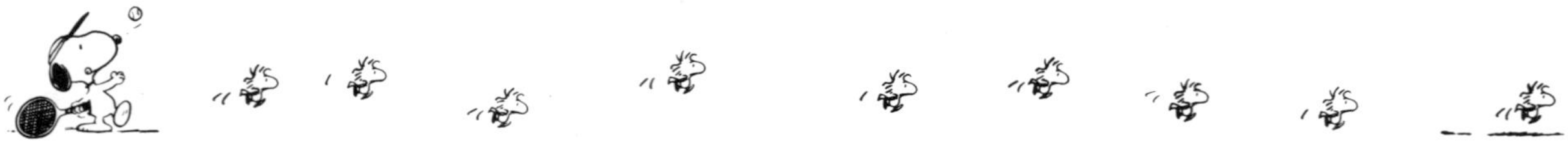

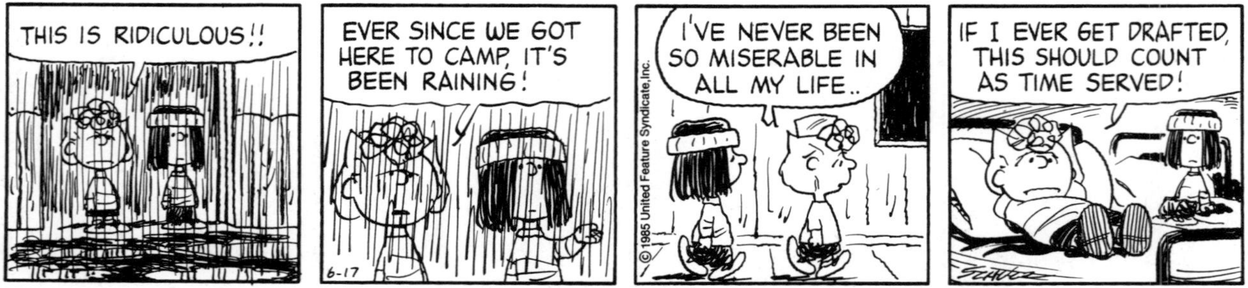
THIS IS RIDICULOUS!!
EVER SINCE WE GOT HERE TO CAMP, IT'S BEEN RAINING!
6-17
I'VE NEVER BEEN SO MISERABLE IN ALL MY LIFE..
© 1985 United Feature Syndicate, Inc.
IF I EVER GET DRAFTED, THIS SHOULD COUNT AS TIME SERVED!
SCHULZ

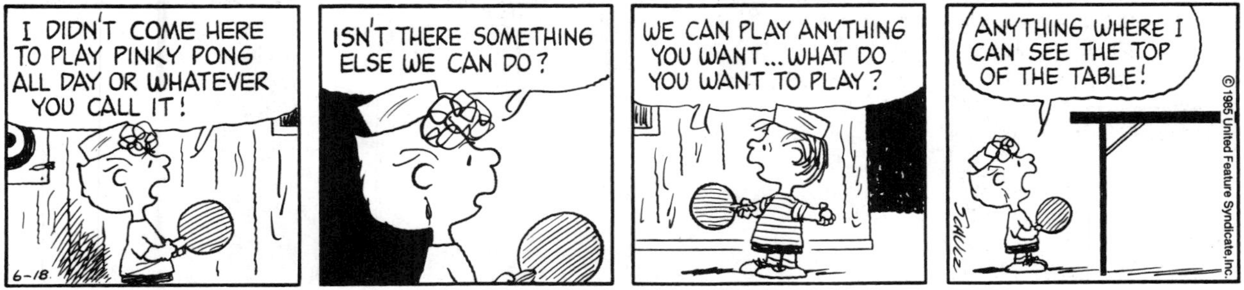
I DIDN'T COME HERE TO PLAY PINKY PONG ALL DAY OR WHATEVER YOU CALL IT!
6-18
ISN'T THERE SOMETHING ELSE WE CAN DO?
WE CAN PLAY ANYTHING YOU WANT... WHAT DO YOU WANT TO PLAY?
ANYTHING WHERE I CAN SEE THE TOP OF THE TABLE!
SCHULZ
© 1985 United Feature Syndicate, Inc.

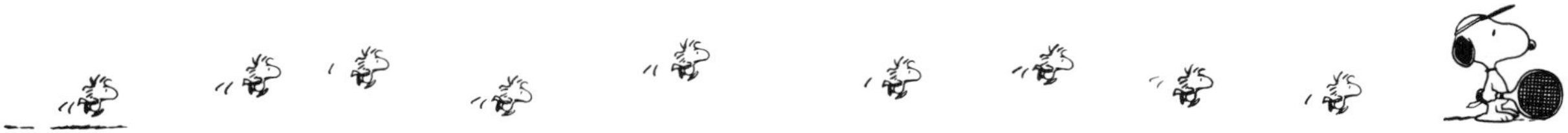

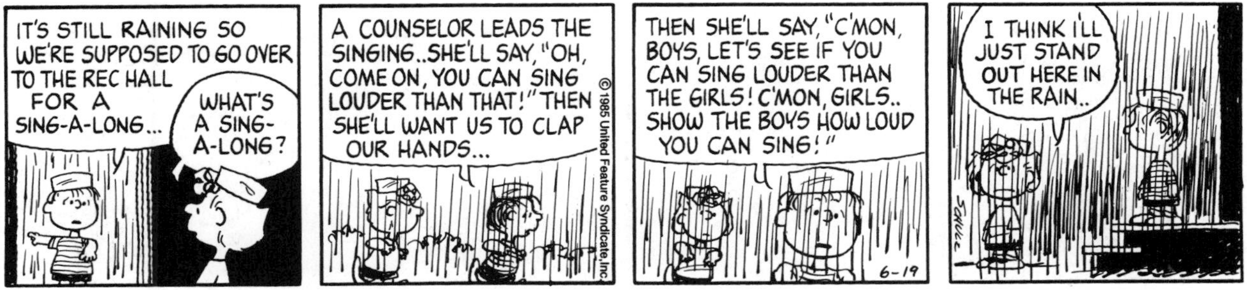
IT'S STILL RAINING SO WE'RE SUPPOSED TO GO OVER TO THE REC HALL FOR A SING-A-LONG...
WHAT'S A SING-A-LONG?
A COUNSELOR LEADS THE SINGING..SHE'LL SAY, "OH, COME ON, YOU CAN SING LOUDER THAN THAT!" THEN SHE'LL WANT US TO CLAP OUR HANDS...
© 1985 United Feature Syndicate, Inc.
THEN SHE'LL SAY, "C'MON, BOYS, LET'S SEE IF YOU CAN SING LOUDER THAN THE GIRLS! C'MON, GIRLS.. SHOW THE BOYS HOW LOUD YOU CAN SING!"
6-19
I THINK I'LL JUST STAND OUT HERE IN THE RAIN..
SCHULZ

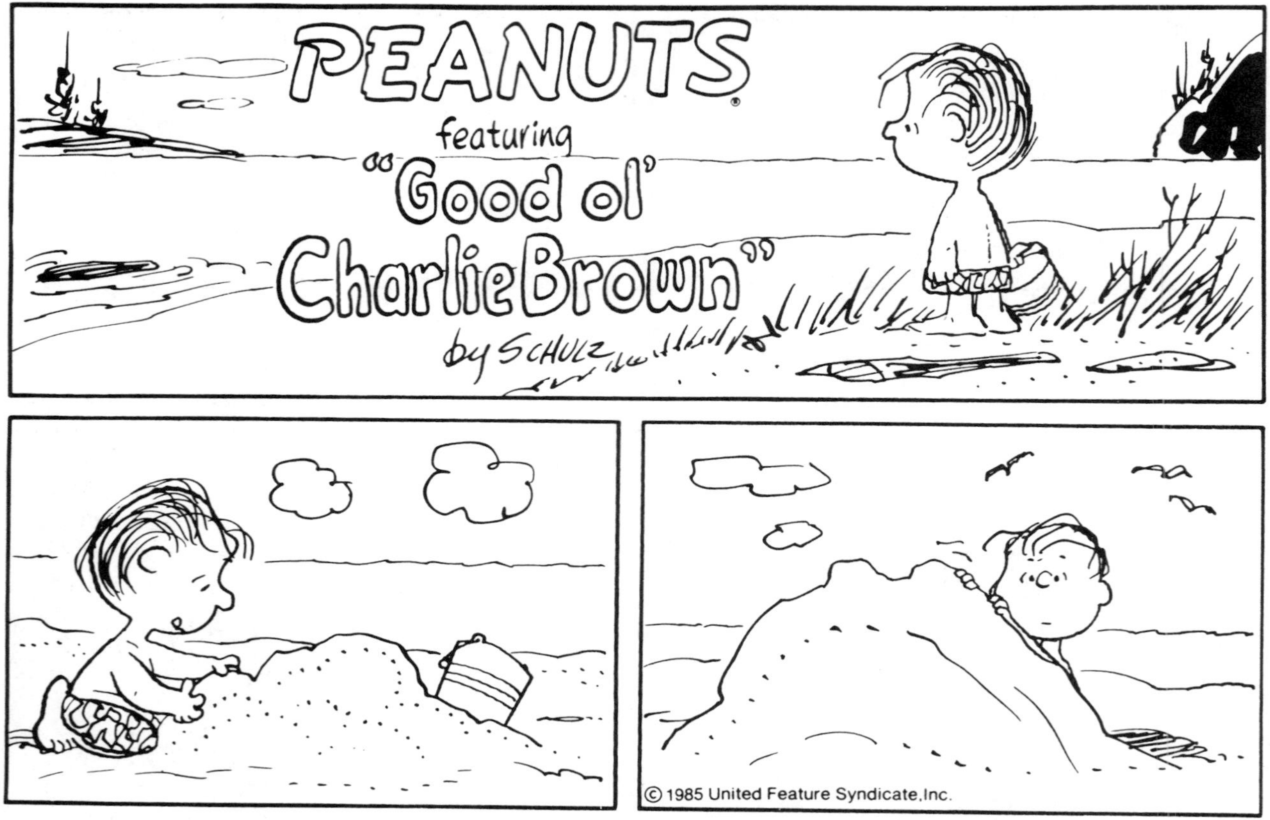
PEANUTS®
featuring
"Good ol' CharlieBrown"
by SCHULZ
© 1985 United Feature Syndicate,Inc.

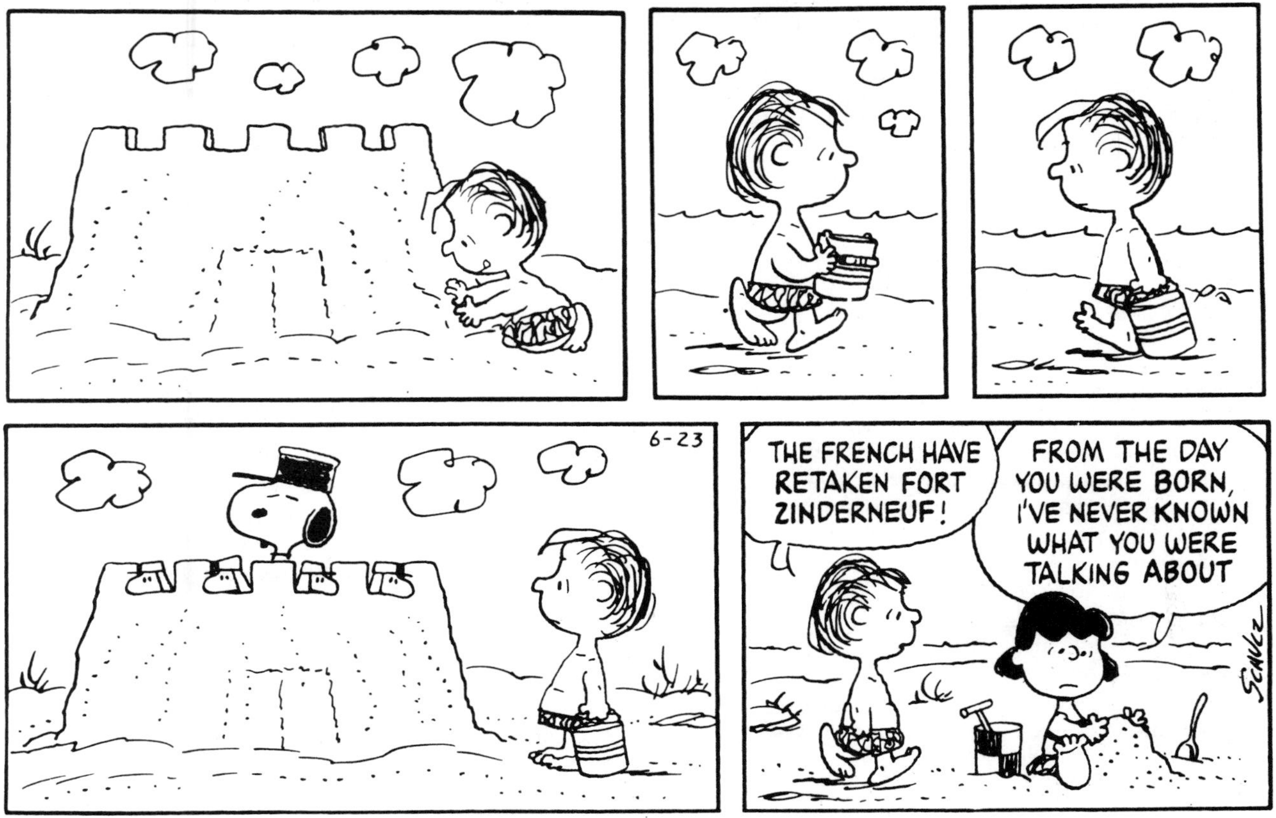
6-23
THE FRENCH HAVE RETAKEN FORT ZINDERNEUF!
FROM THE DAY YOU WERE BORN, I'VE NEVER KNOWN WHAT YOU WERE TALKING ABOUT
SCHULZ

ABOUT THE AUTHOR

It all began in Minneapolis in 1922 when Charles M. Schulz was born into a family that loved the comics. He soon acquired the nickname "Sparky" (a nickname he carries to this day) after the horse Sparkplug in the comic strip *Barney Google*. Encouraged by his parents, Sparky enrolled in a correspondence course in cartooning. After serving in the army during World War II, Schulz returned home to pursue his career in earnest.

In 1950, Schulz, after numerous "mailbox rejections," placed his strip with United Feature Syndicate. Initially carried in only seven newspapers, *Peanuts*® quickly amassed fans and acclaim. Over the years there came dozens of books, three full-length films, 27 television specials and countless awards, including National Cartoonists Society's Outstanding Cartoonist and Best Humor Strip of the Year, Yale's Humorist of the Year, Emmy and Peabody Awards.

It isn't hard to trace much of the essence of the *Peanuts* gang to Schulz's personal history. "When I was little, I was so convinced I had a very plain face that I was surprised anyone recognized me," Schulz says. So he gave Charlie Brown a face with few distinctive features, a barber father (like Schulz's own), and the name of a friend. Snoopy's attempts at writing the great American novel, which only lead to his collecting numerous rejection slips, recall Schulz's earliest efforts to find a home for *Peanuts*.

Schroeder's piano found its way into the strip because of a toy piano once owned by Schulz's oldest daughter. And again and again, Schulz calls on his avid love of sports to comment on the human condition, as he involves his characters in everything from ice hockey to baseball to kite flying.

Of Linus' security blanket, Schulz has this to say, "Of all the things in the strip, I think that I am most proud of Linus' security blanket. I may not have invented the term, but I like to think that I helped make it a part of our language."

After 36 years, *Peanuts* is still syndicated by United Feature Syndicate. The strip appears in over 2,050 newspapers worldwide and is seen by more than 100 million people each day. Transcending geographic boundaries, the strip is translated into 26 languages.

Sparky's continued singular devotion to his phenomenal creation is evidenced by the fact that to this day he writes and draws the strip without the aid of assistants, inkers, pencilers or ghosts.

Charles M. Schulz and his wife, Jeannie, reside in Santa Rosa, California.